The

BARON'S
HONOURABLE
DAUGHTER

The

BARON'S HONOURABLE DAUGHTER

A Novel

LYNN MORRIS

New York • Boston • Nashville

FaithWords
Hachette Book Group
237 Park Avenue
New York, NY 10017

www.faithwords.com

Printed in the United States of America

RRD-C

First Edition: May 2014
10 9 8 7 6 5 4 3 2 1

FaithWords is a division of Hachette Book Group, Inc.
The FaithWords name and logo are trademarks of Hachette Book Group, Inc.

The Hachette Speakers Bureau provides a wide range of authors for speaking events. To find out more, go to www.hachettespeakersbureau.com or call (866) 376-6591.

The publisher is not responsible for websites (or their content) that are not owned by the publisher.

Library of Congress Cataloging-in-Publication Data

Morris, Lynn, 1954–
  The baron's honourable daughter : a novel / Lynn Morris. — First edition.
     pages cm
  ISBN 978-1-4555-7559-6 (trade pbk.) — ISBN 978-1-4555-7560-2 (ebook)
  I. Title.
  PS3563.O874439B38 2014
  813'.54—dc23
                                    2013038710

In Memoriam

*For my mom, because I know in your heart
you always remembered.*

PART I

Chapter One

❧

CARRYING HER WATERCOLOR BOX, Valeria hurried down the arbored path. As was usual in summer, two gardeners were pruning the box trees that were trained to shelter the graveled walkway that wound around the west wing of the house. As she neared them, they glanced up and continued with their trimming. But when she reached them, they both looked startled, then snatched off their caps and bowed. Valeria was amused; she didn't wonder that they had mistaken her for a servant, as she was wearing one of her oldest drab muslins and a bib apron, with her hair tucked up into an unadorned wide-brimmed straw hat that shadowed her face.

Valeria was mistaken about this, for a more alert observer could never think she was a servant. At eighteen she was tall, with a gracefully erect posture and confident stride, although it was perhaps too decided for a fashionable young lady. She thought that her face was modeled too strongly, for she resembled her father rather than her mother. Her cheekbones were high and prominent, her jawline was pronounced, her mouth was wide and well shaped but not very full. What Valeria didn't realize, however, was that these distinctive facial characteristics inherited from Guy Segrave gave her an alluring and mysterious foreign look.

At least she did have a few marvelous features. Her hair was thick and luxuriant, a glossy chestnut brown, and had so much body it curled easily. Her wide-set dark eyes were framed by perfectly arched brows. In contrast, her skin was very white and creamy with no blemish.

"Good afternoon, Skelley, Tollar," she said pleasantly as she passed the gardeners.

"G'day, Miss Segrave," they replied.

As she drew away she heard Skelley, an older man, muttering darkly to young Tollar, "Keep yer eyes out sharp, boy, I'm not seein' wot I useter. Miss Segrave, she's apt to pop up here, there, and about anytimes..."

And so she was. On this diamond-bright August afternoon, she was going to the walled kitchen garden, normally the realm of only the gardeners and house staff. Since Valeria had first come to Bellegarde Hall as a child of eleven, she had loved the garden, and had played in it at every opportunity. As she grew older she had wandered farther afield, for the grounds and the park held many attractions for her: the Queen's parterre with its triple-tiered fountain, the intricate hedge maze with the gazebo at its center, the orchards, the Wilderness, even Maledon Wood, which was four miles away from the house. She often rode in the Wood, savoring the wild beauty and the solitude.

As she passed through the old arched gate, she frowned. She would much rather be painting the magnificent ruins of Roding Priory in the woods than the pastoral kitchen garden, which she had done many times. But watercolors weren't suited to the drama of such landscapes, and Valeria's stepfather, Lord Maledon, had flatly refused to let her try oil paints. "It's not a ladylike pursuit, oil painting," he had said. "Stick to your watercolors."

Valeria forgot her frustration as she came into the garden. The air was perfectly still, the only sounds the occasional distant mournful calls of the peacocks. In the height of summer the scents were heady: the rich loamy smell of warm earth, the tang of rosemary and sage and mint, the occasional whiff of lavender, in full bloom at the far end of the rows.

Slowly she walked along the graveled path by the orangery. Built of the same gray stone as the garden walls, it was glass-roofed and glass-fronted, and she could see the thick foliage of the orange, lemon, and citron trees, the brightly colored fruit pressing against the glass as if eager for the sunlight.

The beauty of the immaculately manicured kitchen garden far surpassed, she thought, that of the frigidly formal parterre and even the rose garden. Every possible shade of green glowed in the vegetable garden, the herb garden, the fruit shrubs, the espaliered apple and pear trees on the south wall. In particular the bushes bursting with white, red, purple, and black berries claimed her eye. A maid was bent over, picking the berries, unaware of Valeria's presence.

Crossing to the gardeners' worktable, she sat down on the rough oak bench. She had planned to try to paint the formal espaliered trees, with their glossy-leaved branches and young fruits arranged in intricate designs against the gray stone wall; above was the shaded secretive arbored path, and above that the west towers of Bellegarde Hall rose frowning against the peaceable blue sky. Valeria had thought it would be a picture of great contrast, and so it would have been, but it was a complex composition and would be extremely difficult to paint with watercolors. She was sure she could do it in oils, but it was foolish to contemplate that, so she studied the interior of the garden, and the girl, again.

Her spotless white apron and cap gleamed in the cheery summer sun, and the light yellow-green foliage of the currant and elderberry bushes showed up nicely against her dark-blue dress. As Valeria laid out her sketching pencils, paper, paints, and brushes, she realized that this girl must not be a housemaid, as she had first assumed, for their day uniforms were beige muslin with a small brown print.

Could this girl be a kitchen maid? Valeria didn't know the kitchen staff very well. Every day the entire house staff attended morning prayers, and Valeria must have seen this girl, but she had no recollection of her. No matter, she would make an intriguing central figure, with the colorful berry shrubs in the foreground and the tall lavender plants and rainbows of foxglove behind her.

Valeria began her sketch. The girl looked up, saw her, and immediately dropped her basket. Alarmed, she glanced around as if deciding where to run, then made an awkward curtsy to Valeria. Standing there, head down, she began to nervously finger her apron. Valeria had thought this might happen, for lower servants were supposed to remain out of sight of the family. Hastily she rose and went to the girl, who stood dumbly waiting.

"Good afternoon," Valeria said. "Please don't mind me. I'm just doing a watercolor study of the garden."

"Yes, miss," she whispered without looking up.

She was a slight girl, short and tiny. The long sleeves of her dress were shoved up above her elbows, and Valeria saw that her thin hands and forearms were a chafed red. *Scullery maid*, Valeria thought, and wondered if she had even ever heard the names of the scullery maids. "What is your name?" she asked.

The girl lifted her head and Valeria then saw that she couldn't have been more than thirteen years old, if that. "M-Mary Louise, ma'am. T'other scullery maid's name is Mary too, and so I'm called Mary Louise and she's called Mary Jane."

"I see. Well, Mary Louise, I wouldn't want to keep you from gathering the berries, I assume Mrs. Banyard is planning some delicious dessert for us tonight. Just go ahead as if I'm not here."

"Yes, miss," she said, dipping her head and curtsying again.

Valeria returned to her worktable and began again on her sketch. But it was proving to be difficult, for Mary Louise was so unnerved by her presence that she made a very poor study.

After retrieving the dropped basket, she stooped and picked a few berries, then glanced uneasily over at Valeria. When she realized that Valeria was sketching her, she dropped her basket again and hastily knelt to pick up the scattered crimson berries. Again she assumed her gathering, covertly looked up at Valeria, and snatched up a handful of leaves instead of fruit, which upset her. She stood up, staring down at the bunch of green in her hand as if unsure what to do with it. She saw Valeria watching her, threw down the leaves, dropped the basket, and curtsied again. Valeria sighed. This was not going well at all.

From the arbor, Valeria heard quick footsteps and voices and laughter. She looked up alertly. She recognized her stepfather's voice as he called, "Mavis, you vixen! Come back here, girl!"

A loud high-pitched giggle sounded. "Last night you were boasting that you could keep up with me, Maledon! Now we shall see!"

Lady Jex-Blake burst through the gate. Her long dark hair was falling down, swirling about her. She was holding both her skirt and her petticoat bunched up high, so that her shapely stockinged legs, up to her thighs, could be seen. One shoulder of her dress had fallen down, almost exposing her breasts. Still laughing, she looked behind, and Lord Maledon came hurrying in, grinning. With a mock shriek Lady Jex-Blake ran into the orangery. "Oh, I've got you now," he said hoarsely and followed her in. Their voices and laughter sounded a few more moments, and then there was silence.

Without realizing it Valeria jumped to her feet, standing bolt upright with her fists clenched at her sides. Glancing at Mary Louise, she saw that the girl stood transfixed, her dropped basket forgotten, her apron pressed up to her mouth, her eyes wide as she stared at the orangery. Valeria walked quickly to her and said grimly, "Come with me, hurry."

Valeria brushed by her but the girl seemed unable to move. Turning back to her, Valeria saw that her blue eyes were filled with shock. Lady Jex-Blake's cackle sounded from the orangery, and Mary Louise jumped as if she'd been scalded. Valeria moved close to her and took her hand. The girl looked up at her, and Valeria realized that she wasn't just horrified, she was actually terrified. Valeria whispered, "Mary Louise, please come with me. This way."

She led her to the small door at the bottom of the garden, rarely used. It opened out onto a swath of grass with steps leading up to the parterre. Still holding Mary Louise's hand, Valeria walked quickly up the steps and across the parterre, that coldly sterile garden of low-cut shrubbery with no flowers, and followed the knot-curved paths so as not to tread on the close-cut greenery. About halfway across she realized that she was taking long hard strides, unceremoniously hauling the girl by the hand, and the maid was out of breath. Valeria stopped and made herself calm down. "Everything will be all right, Mary Louise. I'll think of some explanation," she said evenly.

Mary Louise must indeed have been half out of her wits with fear, for instead of submissively answering, "Yes, ma'am," as she should have done, she asked in a frightened whisper, "But—however will you explain, miss? What shall I say?"

Valeria pressed her long fingers to her temples and closed her eyes. "I must think . . ." she murmured between clenched teeth.

How could her stepfather be so stupid? To behave in such a way, in his own house—in her mother's home? Lord Maledon had always been a rather severe man, but he had seemed to love his wife, and treated her with the utmost respect. Until about two years ago, Valeria reflected, when he had begun to change. Still, Valeria would never have imagined that he would brazenly carry on an affair with a woman here, at Bellegarde Hall, where his family lived.

And the disregard for the servants was appalling. Almost all of them were lifelong servants of the earls of Maledon; they were like a secondary family. Certainly they would gossip. Valeria wondered about the gardeners in the arbor. What had her stepfather done, just shoved them aside as he chased Lady Jex-Blake in their lascivious little game? Who else had seen them?

And how on earth was Valeria going to protect her mother? How could she possibly shield her from this?

Then Valeria realized that the only servant who would dare tell Lady Maledon was Craigie, her lady's maid. Craigie was in truth Regina Maledon's best friend, and for that matter was probably Valeria's best friend too, for she had been her nurse. Craigie would never tell her mother such a horrible thing. In fact, she would probably face down Lord Maledon himself if she had to, to protect her mistress.

Glancing at Mary Louise's wretchedly unhappy face, Valeria thought, *But what about all the other servants? They'll surely find out. Should I tell her to keep quiet about it?*

No. I will do everything in my power to protect my mother, but I won't try to protect him.

Drawing a deep breath, she said, "I know what I shall say, and it will satisfy, I'm sure. As for you, Mary Louise, I won't tell you what you can and cannot say. You must do what you think is right. Come along now, and don't be frightened." Valeria threaded her way out of the parterre and walked along the pathway around to the front of the house, with the maid flitting nervously behind her.

Again Mary Louise faltered, and she said with dread, "Oh, miss! I can't go through the Great Hall, I couldn't!"

"What?" Valeria said blankly, then realized that for a scullery maid to be upstairs—much less coming in through the front door—was a disciplinary matter and could even be grounds for dismissal. Again Valeria took the girl's small rough hand and pressed it reassuringly. "We must, you see. We don't want to go back around to the servant's loggia." That would mean circling back around by the kitchen garden. Still Mary Louise looked alarmed, so Valeria added, "You have nothing to worry about, Mary Louise. You've done nothing wrong, and I shall make that clear."

Gently and patiently Valeria led her around the west wing to the front entrance, two enormous oak doors that were, thankfully, unlocked during the day. Barely opening one of them, wincing when it groaned, the two girls slipped in and hurried through the echoing Great Hall to the dark passageway that led to the servants' staircase, unseen by anyone. Around and down they descended the spiral staircase with the iron railings, ornate for a servants' stairwell. Valeria could hear Mary Louise's audible sigh of relief when they reached the basement level. A long corridor led past the butler's rooms to the servants' workroom and the kitchen. No one was in sight, but they heard voices clearly coming from the servants' workroom.

"... *Lidy* Jex-Blake, she's a lidy if my little pinky is!" the cross nasal voice sounded. "Throwed a pillow at my head when I took in her tea and hot water this morning, and told me to get out! Then layin' abed past noon and then complaining that she had missed a hot breakfast!"

"The likes of her don't know that luncheon's properly a cold collation," another sarcastic female voice broke in, which Valeria recognized as belonging to Mrs. Banyard, the cook. "I'm fair amazed she don't call luncheon *dinner* and dinner *supper*. Then again, she's got right good at apin' her betters."

Valeria came in, with Mary Louise a small forlorn shape half-hiding behind her. The four housemaids, the two footmen, and the cook were seated at the servants' worktable, busy at various tasks. They looked up in surprise, then alarm, and then all of them jumped to their feet. The women curtsied and the footmen made deep bows.

"Hello," Valeria said calmly. "Please, sit down." All of them fidgeted and exchanged hesitant glances, and she realized that it was impossible for them to be seated in her presence. She went on, addressing the senior servant. "Excuse me for intruding, but I knew I must come down to explain, Mrs. Banyard, why Mary Louise won't be picking the currants and berries this afternoon."

The cook, a round red-faced woman with shrewd dark eyes and a sharp tongue, gave Mary Louise a baleful look. Hurriedly Valeria continued, "No, it is not at all her fault, it's entirely my own whim. I'm painting in the kitchen garden this afternoon, you see, and I wish to be alone. So I told Mary Louise that she may leave off her fruit-gathering, for today at least."

Mrs. Banyard's eyes narrowed. "Begging your pardon, Miss Segrave, but as you'll know I discussed the menu with her ladyship this morning, and she particular wanted currant ices for the dessert course."

"What about cherry ices?" Valeria brightly suggested. "I was in the orchard just yesterday, and the trees are simply glorious with ripe cherries!"

"Cherry ices," Mrs. Banyard said with ill humor. "Her ladyship finds currant ices more attractive, with the black currants and the red currants and the white currants making such a colorful display. She particular wanted currant ices for the dessert course, miss," she repeated, more slowly and with heavy emphasis.

"My mother loves cherry ices, I'm sure she will be fine with the change," Valeria answered. "I'll tell her myself, and explain to her."

"Very well, miss," the cook finally said begrudgingly.

She was still casting foreboding glances at Mary Louise, so Valeria said lightly, "I assured Mary Louise that she would suffer no consequences, Mrs. Banyard. You understand that this is all due to my wish to be left alone to paint."

"Oh, I understand that, Miss Segrave," the cook said with a sniff. "And I understand that the little goose has gone off and left the basket out there, and if it's not recovered it'll be stopped from her pay."

"No, it won't," Valeria said as pleasantly as she could manage. "I wanted to include the basket in my painting. If I think of it, I'll have it returned when I'm finished. In any event, Mary Louise certainly shouldn't have to pay for it. Good day."

Valeria turned on her heel and left in what even she recognized was a huff. The cook would never have presumed to speak so to her mother. But after all, Valeria was only the stepdaughter of the earl, and as such held a very tenuous position in the household. Mrs. Banyard had been with the Earl of Maledon for thirty-four years, coming to Bellegarde Hall as a scullery maid when she was ten years old. Valeria supposed that she had some excuse for feeling particularly proprietary about her position.

As Valeria ascended the spiral staircase back to the ground floor, she hoped fervently that she would find her mother alone. Besides Lady Jex-Blake, two other ladies had been invited by Lord Maledon, a Mrs. Purefoy and her sister, Miss Shadwell. Though they were not as coarse as Lady Jex-Blake, Valeria found them wearisome company, for they were shameless social climbers who simpered and fawned. If they were with her mother, Valeria decided she would ask if they could speak alone. She didn't want to go through this pitiful pantomime with strangers present. It was going to be hard enough to lie to her mother.

To her relief, Lady Maledon was alone in the drawing room.

In contrast to the grounds and park and woods, Valeria found Bellegarde Hall to be a formidable, cold house. The drawing room—always dim, with walnut paneling and coffered ceiling panels of carved oak that had darkened with age—was her least favorite room aside from the Great Hall. Dreary portraits of former earls and countesses lined three walls. One wall was completely covered by an enormous Tudor tapestry, now so faded that the design could hardly be distinguished. The furniture was upholstered with dull damask of blue and brown, with heavy gold trim. The room had four floor-to-ceiling sash windows, but the midnight-blue velvet draperies and swag valances seemed to absorb the light. The massive fireplace, dark and brooding even with the enormous bouquet of fresh flowers adorning it, seemed to overpower the room. The only warmth came from the full-length portrait of her mother, done by the distinguished portrait artist Sir Thomas Lawrence, hanging over the mantel. She was depicted in a blue satin dress, and her ethereal blonde curls and deep sapphire blue eyes seemed to glow.

The subject of the portrait now sat in an armchair by the window, staring out at the courtyard with its enormous statue of Perseus rescuing Andromeda, and the verdant park beyond. The summer sun glowed through the mullioned glass, lighting up the golden ringlets underneath her cap, and her perfect profile. Her needlework was in her lap, and she gently fanned herself with an exquisite mother-of-pearl fan, inset with garnets, with a tassel made of gold thread flecked with real gold. Valeria's throat constricted a little as she saw the fan; Lord Maledon had imported six fans from India for her mother, all of them studded with jewels, all of them likely very costly, when Regina had given birth to Lord Maledon's son, St. John. He hadn't always been the cruel, venal man he was now. In years past he had been gentle and courtly to her mother, seeming to delight in pleasing her. To Valeria he had always been distant, but he had never treated her unkindly. In fact he had given her some gifts that were extremely generous. When she had turned sixteen, he had given her one of the magnificent Maledon horses, a spirited stallion that she had named Tarquin. Indeed, Valeria's equestrian skill was the only thing that Lord Maledon seemed to admire about her, and the only warmly cordial conversations they had ever had were about the horses.

And he had once given every appearance of adoring his wife, who was sixteen years younger than he, and an acknowledged beauty.

She still is, Valeria thought. *She's thirty-five now, with no sign of gray hair or lines on her face. I wonder . . . will that change now . . . if Maledon keeps up with this awful behavior he's shown more and more the last two years?*

"Hello, Mamma. Where are our guests?" Valeria asked.

Regina turned to her with some surprise; she had been in a deep reverie, and apparently hadn't heard her daughter come in. "Oh, there you are, darling. The ladies decided to rest after luncheon. It seems the journey yesterday was quite tiring for them. The gentlemen are out touring the park with the gamekeeper. I believe they're assessing the shooting for the upcoming season."

One lady is certainly not resting, Valeria thought dourly. She studied her mother's countenance carefully. Regina's blue eyes held no hint of upset or worry, but Valeria thought she detected in her air a hint of distraction. Her mother was very difficult to read. "Please don't tell me they're going to stay that long," Valeria intoned, throwing herself into the armchair next to her mother and snatching off her hat.

With gentle disapproval Regina said, "Dearest, don't be rude. They are our guests, and I hope you'll do everything to make them feel comfortable."

"But they're not our guests. They're Lord Maledon's guests. Surely, Mamma, you see that they're nothing like our friends? Our real friends?"

"This is Lord Maledon's home, and his guests are our guests. Let us say no more about it," Regina said with a shortness uncharacteristic of her. "Where have you been? You seem flushed with exertion. You haven't been running again, have you?"

Valeria smiled a little. "No, I haven't been running. I've been out in the kitchen garden, I decided to paint it today. But I had a slight problem, and there's something I need to explain to you."

Regina gave a long-suffering sigh. "Go on."

Uncomfortably Valeria shifted in her chair. In her entire life, she had only lied to her mother one time, when she was six years old. She had said that Craigie had broken a nursery teapot, when actually she herself had broken it. Of course Regina had known the truth, and Valeria had never forgotten the shame that burned her when her mother kindly and lovingly explained to her about the sin of lying. From that time she had never considered even a slight dissimulation to her mother.

"I was painting the kitchen garden, you see, and one of the scullery maids was picking currants," Valeria said, speaking rapidly. "Actually I hoped to include her in my picture, but she grew so nervous as I was sketching her that she began to fidget, and it distracted me. So I took her down to the kitchen and explained to Mrs. Banyard that I wished to be alone in the garden to paint, and I asked that the girl do her berry-picking some other time."

Regina's sweet expression grew grave as Valeria spoke. "And what did Mrs. Banyard say?"

"She said that you and she had decided on currant ices for dessert this evening, but I said that cherry ices would do very well, and that I would explain the change in menu to you. That is all right, isn't it, Mamma? After all, cherry ices are just as delicious as currant ices."

"So they are, but that is hardly the point, Valeria," Regina said quietly. Slowly and gracefully fanning, she stared out the window again and spoke as if to herself. "It's really my fault, I suppose. You're eighteen now, and I should have been more strict in teaching you the particulars of running a household." Turning back to her daughter she asked, "Who was the maid in the garden?"

"Mary Louise."

Regina nodded. "Yes, the youngest scullery maid. Naturally she would feel unnerved at your presence, and especially by you staring at her and drawing her. But what you must understand, Valeria, is that for the maids to be able to go into the kitchen garden is truly a welcome diversion for them. In most houses the underservants never have an opportunity to even go out of doors, much less to go into a nice garden. Mrs. Banyard and Mrs. Lees have a detailed schedule of which maids may spend time in the garden at which times, and they are not necessarily assigned to perform garden chores, it is simply a leisure time for them. I'm assuming that Mary Louise was picking the currants because she enjoys such things. And now she has lost her scheduled garden time."

"I wasn't aware of all that," Valeria said lamely.

"As I admitted, it's my fault that you didn't know. Still, dearest, it was rather thoughtless of you to interfere with the servants as they go about their duties. They can hardly argue with you, even when you are wrong."

Even this gentle remonstrance was bitter to Valeria. She was sorry for Mary Louise, and sorry for herself. The injustice of it stung her, and at that moment she thought that she almost hated her stepfather. Sighing deeply, she said, "I am truly sorry, Mamma. From now on I will try to be more considerate of the servants."

Regina reached over and patted Valeria's hand. "I know you only did it through carelessness, not from selfishness. After our guests leave, I think I will start teaching you more thoroughly about managing the household."

"Yes, after our guests leave," Valeria said intently. "You do think they're staying for shooting?" Grouse season started on August twelfth; today was the seventh.

"Maledon hasn't told me so," Regina said cautiously, averting her eyes.

"Oh, how I hope not," Valeria breathed, and this time her mother didn't reprove her.

Picking up her needlework again, Regina did a stitch, then said lightly, "So, darling, after upsetting the entire household for the sake of your art, aren't you going to go paint the kitchen garden now?"

"Oh, yes, of course," Valeria said, rising and putting on her hat again. "If you'll excuse me, Mamma."

At the door she paused and looked back at her mother. Regina had again laid down her needlework, and was staring unseeing out the window at the bright visions outside.

Chapter Two

NATURALLY VALERIA HAD NO INTENTION of returning to the kitchen garden; angrily she thought of her watercolor cakes baking out in the August sun. After she left the drawing room she went upstairs to find Craigie. When they had guests, Craigie normally worked down in the servants' workroom, ironing, sewing, attending to Lady Maledon's wardrobe. But Valeria had noted that she wasn't there when she took Mary Louise down, so it was likely that Craigie was in her mother's sitting room and dressing room, which adjoined Lady Maledon's bedchamber.

Valeria was relieved to find her there. One of her mother's evening gowns, a satin of a deep emerald green, was hung on the dress form, and Craigie sat on the floor, sewing. The dress had a short train, and one of the bottom flounces of white lace had loosened. Craigie was a sturdily built, lively woman, a year older than Valeria's mother, though she didn't look it. She had bright red hair, sparkling blue eyes, and a sprinkling of freckles across her nose. She was pretty in an impish sort of way.

Valeria sat down on the floor beside her, ripped off her hat, and sighed dramatically. "Oh, Craigie, I must talk to you."

"Why? What's happened? And look at you, flinging yourself

about like a dairymaid. If you must sit on the floor, at least sit up straight and tuck your legs in proper," she said sternly.

"I can't think that it matters, no one will see me," Valeria mumbled, but she did straighten her back and primly pull her ankles to the side.

Regina Maledon had a long history with Elspeth Craigie Platt. Craigie was, in fact, much more of a friend and confidante to Regina than she was a servant. Craigie and Regina had faced some hard times together.

When Regina Carew, at sixteen years of age, married Baron Segrave of Ryals, Elspeth Craigie had been a housemaid at Ryalsmere, the family seat. A week after their marriage, Regina took Elspeth on as her lady's maid, and, as was proper, started calling her "Craigie." The two young girls grew very close. The next year, when Valeria was born, Craigie was as overjoyed as Regina and Lord Segrave. Craigie loved children, and had confided to Regina that she hoped to marry and have at least six of her own. It was only natural, and was Craigie's wish, that she serve both as Regina's lady's maid and as Valeria's nurse.

Two years later Craigie fell in love with the baron's head groom, Ewan Platt, a big, strapping, handsome man with tow-colored hair, blue eyes, and a ready smile. In most great houses, servants weren't allowed to marry. But Lord Segrave was a kind and understanding man, and he made special allowances for his servants, and allowed Craigie and Ewan to marry, even providing them with a cottage on the estate. Though Craigie's wish to start having children immediately didn't come true, she and Ewan were very happy. Ewan and Lord Segrave were on friendly terms, as Segrave was an avid horseman and Ewan Platt was a wizard with horses. Craigie had Regina, and she had Valeria.

Life at Ryalsmere was very good until 1798. On November first of that year, All Saints' Day, Guy, Lord Segrave, died at thirty-three years old. He and Ewan were out on the wild Northumberland moors, making visits to tenant farmers. It had snowed about two inches the night before, but the day was sunny and much warmer.

Later that night, his face streaming with tears, Ewan told Regina and Craigie, "He was looking back at me, talking of fixing up old Mr. Culver's cottage. Then, as fast as lightning strikin', Agrippa rears, screams, crashes down... by the time I got there I saw the adder a-slithering off, the devil! His lordship, he kept his seat, and... he... his head..." Then he had broken off into harsh sobs. As the horse had fallen onto his side, Guy's head had smashed against the same stone that the adder had been sunning on. He had died instantly.

At twenty-two years of age Regina, Lady Segrave, was a widow; and Valeria, at five years old, was fatherless.

As the years passed, through her own intuition, and from many things that Craigie had told her, Valeria had come to clearly see how important Craigie—and, for that matter, her husband Ewan—were to her mother. If it hadn't been for them, Regina might have slipped into a precarious decline after Valeria's father died. Her mother enjoyed fine physical health, but she was emotionally fragile. And, with customary sorrow, Valeria thought of how she had realized that Regina Segrave had loved her first husband utterly, to the very core of her soul.

And now? How had her mother come to marry such a man as Lord Maledon? Why?

"And so, are you going to tell me what's got you all in a to-do?" Craigie asked, interrupting Valeria's thoughts. "Or are you going to just sit there all sour and pruney-faced? Keep it up, it might get stuck that way, missie."

Her voice hard and angry, Valeria told Craigie all about the scene in the kitchen garden. As she spoke, Craigie stopped sewing and fixed her eyes on Valeria's face. Slowly her cheerful countenance grew cold, and her eyes narrowed.

" . . . and Mamma made me feel awful about Mary Louise. But it wasn't my fault!" Valeria finished bitterly.

"No, it wasn't," Craigie said tightly. Then, her voice softening, she said, "I know the unfairness of it galls you. But you did the right thing, the Christian thing, in protecting that poor little girl. And your mother."

"But for how long? If they keep on with this brazen behavior, my mother is sure to find out!" Valeria burst out with anguish.

"Aye, that's likely," Craigie said sadly. "But there's naught you nor I nor anyone can do about that."

Valeria wrapped her arms around her legs and rested her chin on her knees. Normally Craigie fussed when she did this, but now she seemed not to notice. Valeria said in a subdued voice, "That woman, Lady Jex-Blake. She looked wanton, like a cheap prostitute."

"And how would you be knowing what a cheap prostitute looks like?" Craigie snapped. "For all I have to agree with you. Wearing that low-cut gown during the day, with not a sign of a fichu or chemisette, she's no better than she ought to be."

"They're all of them just awful. Who *are* these people?" Valeria demanded.

Three days ago a message had been sent from London, from Lord Maledon, saying that he was bringing a party of five to Bellegarde Hall. They would arrive the next afternoon. It had been unforgivably rude for him to arrange such a large party without consulting with his wife; normally it took two or three weeks to make arrangements for five guests. Mrs. Banyard, the kitchen maids, and both footmen had been dispatched to scour the countryside for supplies. Then, to add insult to injury, the party had arrived at nine-thirty at night, when dinner had been ready since eight o'clock; and they were all, to one degree or another, drunk. Valeria had understood, when her stepfather made his careless introductions, that her mother had not been previously acquainted with any of the guests.

Valeria glanced at Craigie, who was mutinously silent. She knew that Craigie often struggled with how much to expose her to the seamier side of the world. "You can't protect me, Craigie. I have to deal with them, just as my mother does. It's ridiculous, really, that the servants should know more about our guests than I do."

"'S'true, we all know of them, mostly from that Thrale," she finally said with disdain. Robert Thrale was Lord Maledon's valet, a tall, dark man of twenty-five with a supercilious demeanor. Only the servants knew how insolent he had increasingly become in the last two years.

"Thrale," Valeria repeated, grimacing. "I'm glad I hardly ever see him."

"As am I, he's a bad 'un, no doubt about it," Craigie asserted, "and he'll tell anything and everything he hears about anybody, including his lordship. I'm of the mind that if Lord Maledon knew about his viper's tongue he'd send him packing."

"What? What does he say about my stepfather?" Valeria demanded.

Craigie frowned. "Personal private things that ought never to be said, and I'm not going to repeat them. That would make me just as bad as him. Why, I think the Lord might strike me down dead if I told private things about your mother!"

"Yes, yes, I see, Craigie," Valeria said thoughtfully. "You're right. But you can tell me about our guests, can't you? Surely you owe no such loyalty to them. It's just that I've never met people such as them; I don't know how to treat them."

"You'll treat them the way all fine ladies treat such people, as your mother does, with courtesy, for that's the only way you'll keep your dignity," Craigie said smartly. "Taking notice of their bad behavior is beneath you."

Valeria couldn't help but smile. "It was a little hard not to notice the behavior in the kitchen garden, Craigie."

Craigie wasn't amused. "Just so," she sniffed. "And that's why I don't feel the least guilty for telling you about these people.

"Lady Jex-Blake, as she is now, but when she were a housemaid for old doddering Sir Henry Jex-Blake she was plain Mavis Horner. Fool that he was, he married her when he were seventy-seven and she but twenty-five, and he obliged her by keeling over dead last year. No crape nor black bombazine for that one! Word is she were in London a month later, for the Season."

"And so my stepfather met her there, and I'm assuming the rest of them too. How nice for him to make such fine new acquaintances during the Season," Valeria said acidly. "If this is the crowd he's running with now, I'm glad that my mother and I weren't there!"

"And don't I just wish he'd left them there," Craigie muttered. "I see what Lady Jex-Blake is all about, and I'm thinking I know about the others too. Mrs. Purefoy and her sister Miss Shadwell, you know, are daughters of a gentleman, a respectable squire with a fair estate over in Surrey. Mrs. Purefoy married a Dr. Purefoy from there, and it's my understanding that she nags him all the day long to move to London and open a practice there for the Quality, like she would know what that were if it bit her on the nose. But there you are, her and her sister both are hangers-on, trying to climb up by hook or claw. I'm thinking their friends are going to get that tired of hearing about the Earl of Maledon."

"I thought that about them too. Their fawning manners embarrass me. Miss Shadwell actually asked me to call her 'Kit,' did you know?" Valeria said with delicate distaste. In a falsetto mocking voice she went on, "Oooh, my name is Katherine, but I do so dislike 'Kathy' or 'Kate,' but I simply adore 'Kit,' all my friends call me 'Kit,' and we are going to be good friends, aren't we, Miss Segrave?"

Craigie's bright smile showed itself again. "And what did you answer, may I ask?"

"I said, 'I find that it takes me many years before I consider a person a "good friend." ' That put paid to that nonsense quickly. As I said, it's a shame that she goes on and on, so coy and sickening-sweet, all of it such a pretense. If she would just be herself I might like her."

"I doubt it," Craigie said dryly. "She's a-carryin' on with that Mr. Mayhew, you know."

Valeria's eyes widened. "What? Here?"

"'S'far as I know, no one's seen them in what you might call a compromising position here."

" 'The Honourable' Henry Mayhew,' " Valeria said. "Mamma did tell me that he's the son of a viscount. That would be quite a catch for Miss Shadwell, even though he's a younger son. I thought she was very flirtatious to him, but with her it's so hard to tell, she makes love to everyone."

"How has he been with you, missie?" Craigie asked shrewdly.

"With me? He's treated me with the same bored disdain that he treats everyone, it seems, the silly fop. The only time I've seen him show any sign of life was at the card table, and he won a hand or two, I believe. His bleary eyes were quite sharp when they were gambling."

"Ah, but he lost too, didn't he? I heard that Lady Jex-Blake took all of the gentlemen last night."

Valeria was bemused; again the servants knew more about the family's activities than she did. Valeria, her mother, Mrs. Purefoy, and Miss Shadwell had been playing a sedate game of whist while Lady Jex-Blake had played all fours with the gentlemen. Valeria herself didn't know who had won and who had lost at the next table. "Did she? They were so loud and boisterous I finally just made myself ignore them."

"Oh, yes, your stepfather lost nineteen pound—nineteen pound! Though he laughed about it. Mr. Mayhew lost eight pound, and he can ill afford to lose it, for he's far overspent on his allowance and deep in debt, I hear. He's the fifth son, you know, and Lord Erdeswick's loath to keep bailing him out. Miss Shadwell might as well forget the likes of him, he'll be finding himself some stupid young girl, daughter of a merchant, I would imagine, with a hefty portion. And Colonel Bayliss is little better off, he's running his farm into the ground to finance his horses and carriages and town house and all his airs."

Valeria felt a deep shudder of revulsion at the mention of Colonel Bayliss's name. He was about the same age as her stepfather, in his early fifties, she supposed, a big bluff man with a barrel chest and thinning dark hair and small dark eyes. As he spoke to her, his gaze constantly crawled from her face down to her breasts in the most disagreeable manner imaginable. That had been bad enough, but then she had seen him do the same to her mother, and it had sickened Valeria so much that she could hardly eat.

"What is wrong with my stepfather?" she asked gutturally. "How can he subject my mother to this?"

Craigie's mouth tightened. "I think he's sick."

"You mean his dyspepsia? For two years now that's all he's complained about! Indigestion is no excuse for his horrible behavior!"

"That's not what I mean. I think something is really wrong with him, and it's affected his mind, like."

Alertly Valeria asked, "Has my mother said something to that effect?"

"No. But she wouldn't, even if that's what she thinks, not even to me."

Valeria grew quiet. She remembered when her mother had first married Lord Maledon. She was eleven, and all she could think of him was that he was so very *old*. She had come to understand that he wasn't, really; he had been forty-four when he married Regina. He was a tall, broad-shouldered man with a fine physique, thick salt-and-pepper hair, and a well-formed, strong face. In the last two years, however, he had aged much, and not well. He had developed a big belly while his legs and arms had grown thinner. His face was always red, and a tracery of crimson vein-lines had developed on his nose. Valeria thought this wasn't surprising, for he had begun to drink great quantities of port wine.

"I think he drinks too much," she said angrily, "and that's an even more pitiful excuse than dyspepsia. And he looks awful. How can my mother love him? Does she? Does my mother really love him, Craigie?"

Craigie's eyes softened to a velvety blue, and she reached out and patted Valeria's hand. "The things that I most admire about your mother are her code of honor, her loyalty, and her sense of duty. In those three things she's the strongest person I've ever had the blessing to know. Yes, she loves him. You and I may not be able to understand it, dear, but Lady Maledon loves her husband."

As Valeria walked the half mile across the park to the orchards later that day, she thought long and hard about what Craigie had said about her mother's loving Lord Maledon. She often thought about, wondered about, and dreamed about Love. She had a passionate nature, and she longed to fall in love with a handsome, strong, intelligent, witty man who, of course, adored her. This man was rather vague in her imaginings. Valeria had never conceived a crush on anyone, and so her dream lover was more of a thought than a vision. The few young men she had met had been, she thought, singularly unimpressive. Like the Honourable Henry Mayhew, with his affected heavy-lidded bored expression and dreary conversation.

And what about her mother and Lord Maledon? How could her mother love him? Or, more to the point, was her mother *in love* with him?

Is there a difference? she wondered. *Or is "falling in love" some sort of illusion?* Valeria honestly didn't know. The only thing she did know was that she couldn't possibly marry a man whom she merely esteemed and respected, if that was what her mother felt for Maledon, or at least had when she married him. Valeria knew she would have to love a man breathlessly, passionately, hopelessly before she could contemplate spending her life with him.

As if I should worry about it, she thought moodily. *My stepfather is never going to let me go to London, and the chances of meeting a man here are very slim. I'll probably end up a lonely spinster.*

Valeria was supposed to come out, and be presented at court, in the previous London Season, when she had turned seventeen. But her stepfather had told her mother and her that, due to King George's illness, no Drawing Rooms were being held by Queen Charlotte and it would do no good for them to go to London. He himself had gone because the beginning of the Season coincided with the opening of Parliament, and of course the Earl of Maledon sat in the House of Lords.

This year he hadn't even attempted to make any excuses, and Valeria hadn't asked him about her presentation at court, or going to London. By then she'd been loath to ask him for anything.

Valeria's bleak mood lightened when she reached the orchards. They covered several acres, with the walnut, plum, and cherry trees planted in neat long rows. The walnuts would not be ready for harvest until next month, but the plums and cherries were in season. Almost every tree had a ladder against it, with the regular gardeners, their children, and many of the children and young people from surrounding farms picking the ripe golden plums and the bunches of crimson cherries. Every man and boy doffed his cap as she passed, and the young girls made shaky little bobs on their ladders.

Valeria saw Tollar picking plums and whistling, and with a little chill of dread she wondered if he had still been in the arbor when

Lord Maledon and Lady Jex-Blake had come blithely running by. Of course he must have been, Valeria had passed him and Skelley only a few moments before. But as Tollar looked up, then doffed his cap to her, she saw no sign on his homely honest face, which made her feel a little better. "Have you seen my brother and Niall, by any chance, Tollar?" she called up to him.

"Yes, miss, they'm in the cherry orchard. I'm of a mind that there's a bit of a race on to see who can pick the mostest cherries," he answered cheerfully.

In truth, the servants weren't supposed to speak unless spoken to, and when asked a question, they weren't supposed to say a single word except to answer it. But in spite of the fact that Valeria barely knew the house servants, she knew all the gardeners because of her constant roaming about the grounds, gardens, and park, and because since she had arrived at Bellegarde Hall she had, over the course of the years, probably asked every one of them at least ten thousand questions. They were more at ease with her than were the house servants.

"Oh dear, poor Mr. Chalmers," she sighed. "He does have such a time keeping those two little rogues out of trouble."

"Don't we all, miss?" Tollar grinned.

Niall was Craigie's and Ewan Platt's son, not quite a year older than St. John. Like his mother and father, Niall held a special place in the family—at least with Regina and Valeria and St. John, if not with St. John's father the earl.

Craigie had finally gotten pregnant in 1804, after she and Ewan had been married for nine years. Regina had been rapturously happy for her. When she had gone into labor, Regina insisted that she be moved into one of the guest bedchambers and be attended by her own midwife and physician. It was fortunate that Craigie had such expert attendants, because the delivery had been a nightmare. After twenty long excruciating hours of labor, it was seen that the baby was in a breech presentation. At first the physician had thought that he might have to call in a surgeon to perform a cesarean section—an almost certain sentence of death for Craigie. Sepsis nearly always followed any abdominal surgery.

But the midwife, an old woman who had attended over three hundred births, had been able to shift the baby, and Niall was born a strong, strapping, healthy child. Unfortunately Craigie had been damaged internally, and would conceive no more. In the midst of her joy, Craigie mourned, and Regina mourned with her as deeply as any sister ever could have.

A year later, when St. John was born, it was inevitable that Craigie would be his nurse; indeed Valeria thought wryly that it would have been impossible for anyone to stop her. Certainly her stepfather hadn't been able to. He objected strenuously to the son of a coachman and lady's maid being brought up in the same nursery as his own son, but somehow—Valeria wasn't sure how—her mother had been able to persuade him. And again, when St. John turned five, Lord Maledon had engaged a tutor for him, a distant cousin named Gordon Chalmers, and there was Niall, in the schoolroom. Valeria smiled as she thought of how her stepfather had grumbled; yet he allowed it.

Ahead she heard the piping voice of her brother, six-year-old St. John. "I'm picking faster than you, Nee-All! My side of the tree will be finished before your side of the tree!"

"Oh, no you don't, Sayeent Jawn! I'm taller, I can pick higher!" Niall taunted back.

Valeria giggled as she heard them teasing each other about their names. The name St. John was pronounced *Sinjin*, and Niall was pronounced *Neel*. They had called each other by the correct pronunciations since they both were able to talk, but when they had learned the spellings, they had been greatly amused, and had teased each other ever since. Niall had much more ammunition than the son of the

Earl of Maledon, for St. John's full name was St. John Charles George Bellegarde, his courtesy title was Viscount Stamborne, and he was supposed to be addressed as Lord Stamborne. Niall carefully called him "my lord" and referred to him as "Lord Stamborne" in front of adults, particularly Lord Maledon; but when they were at leisure he made up creative nicknames. Sadly for St. John, there was not much he could do with plain "Niall Platt," but he still managed some puns about nails and flats and knees.

Valeria found the tree they had attacked, for on either side a ladder reached up into the thick foliage with hardly a sign of the boys buried in it, and their tutor, Mr. Chalmers, stood at the foot of one ladder, glowering. "My lord, get back down on that third step or I shall climb up there and haul you down bodily!" he shouted.

A vague "Yes, sir," was heard; branches shook and foliage rustled. Then St. John fell.

With a quickness and agility that Valeria could hardly credit to Mr. Chalmers, he stepped over and neatly caught St. John in his arms. But Mr. Chalmers was neither sturdy nor strong, and he crashed straight down onto his back, with St. John ending up sitting on his stomach.

Valeria rushed to her brother and slid to her knees. "St. John, are you hurt?" she cried.

He blinked. "Hullo, Veri. No, I'm not hurt."

"Are you sure?"

He stood up and stared down at his tutor. "Quite sure, thank you. Mr. Chalmers caught me."

Valeria looked down. Mr. Chalmers seemed to be in great distress. His blue eyes were stretched wide, and his mouth was gaping open. Valeria snatched off her hat and began fanning him with it. "Oh, Mr. Chalmers, please, do you—are you—" She was very frightened that he might be having apoplexy, or perhaps heart failure.

"I think I squashed the breath out of him," St. John observed.

"It happened to me once, when Niall hit me in the stomach with a cricket ball. I couldn't catch my breath for it seemed like forever."

Niall had hopped down and was standing over Mr. Chalmers. He muttered, "I didn't *mean* to."

Valeria had never been in the position of having the breath knocked out of her, and she thought Mr. Chalmers looked near death. The expression on his face was one of utter horror. Finally he gasped, and gulped in a deep breath. "Miss Segrave! I do beg your pardon!" he grunted painfully.

"What?" she said blankly.

He struggled, flopping a little and still gasping. Two gardeners who had come running up took his hands and helped him to rise. They started brushing him off, and he murmured in confusion, "No, really... thank you... no, that's fine... where is my hat?"

Valeria retrieved his straw hat and handed it to him. He put it on, then snatched it back off and made a shaky bow. "Miss Segrave, I do beg your pardon," he said again.

"Why should you beg my pardon, sir?" she rasped.

It's the way with adults who've witnessed a child doing a stupid, dangerous thing to get angry when they see the child is really all right. Valeria rounded on her brother. "St. John! Whatever were you thinking? You frightened me half to death, never mind squashing out poor Mr. Chalmers's air!"

"Sorry," he murmured. He bent his head, the crisp brown curls shining in the sun, and scuffed the grass with one toe. "I only wanted to pick some cherries that were up high." He looked back up at her, and Valeria could see real repentance in his unusual tawny brown eyes.

Sternly she said, "You must apologize to Mr. Chalmers."

St. John went to stand in front of his tutor and looked up at him appealingly. "I'm sorry I climbed too high, and fell down and squashed you, sir."

"That's all very well," he said kindly. "But next time, you will do as I say, and not climb up to the very top rung."

"So there will be a next time, sir?" St. John asked brightly.

"Yes, but not today. Getting squashed once a day is quite enough for me." He turned back to Valeria and made another bow, this time with elegance. "Miss Segrave, now that I have regained a semblance of my senses, I will say good afternoon in a more civilized manner."

"Good afternoon, Mr. Chalmers," she said, smiling. "Please don't worry, your manners are always without fault, even when you are—um—breathless. I came out, thinking I might do some cherry-picking myself, but I agree with you, I think we've had quite enough of that today. Why don't we return to the house, and have a cup of tea? I feel I need the fortification, and I'm certain that you must."

"But Veri, my bag is still up in the tree, and I'm sure I picked more than Niall," St. John said in a small voice.

"Before you toppled out of the tree like a dead crow?" Niall snickered.

"That's enough," Mr. Chalmers said sternly. "Miss Segrave has expressed a wish to return to the house and have a cup of tea. Gentlemen always accede to a lady's wishes."

Valeria came close to him and looked up expectantly. His fair smooth cheeks colored slightly, and he offered her his arm. He never made this gesture unless Valeria initiated it, she had found.

Valeria always made an effort to put him at ease, and she often wondered why it was necessary. Mr. Chalmers was masterful and authoritative with the boys, and was deferential but not unduly so to Lord and Lady Maledon. At first Valeria had thought that he was shy of her because she was the daughter of a peer, but since he had such an easy attitude with her mother and stepfather she knew that his diffidence with her couldn't be attributed to the awe that many commoners had for the nobility. Valeria really didn't know why she seemed to make him nervous, but she liked the tutor, so she did her best to overcome his reticence.

"May we run?" St. John asked, his eyes again bright.

"You may," Mr. Chalmers said, and both boys took off.

Valeria called, "St. John, tell Trueman we'll have tea in the glade by the weeping ash tree." Her brother turned and gave a cheerful wave.

Chapter Three

❧

*A*FTER A VERY PLEASANT TEA with Mr. Chalmers, St. John, and Niall, Valeria reluctantly returned to the house. Her conscience hurt her a bit for not being with her mother in the drawing room to entertain their guests; but she thought she had a good excuse for it, after the scene in the kitchen garden. It had taken her the last three hours to gain full control of her simmering anger with her stepfather and Lady Jex-Blake. Only now did she think she could face them with a semblance of equanimity.

As it happened, it wasn't necessary for her to face them just yet. Only Mrs. Purefoy and Miss Shadwell were in the drawing room with her mother. Valeria joined them, and she didn't ask where the others were. She didn't really care. Her mother was doing her needlework, and Valeria attempted to read, but the twitterings of Mrs. Purefoy and Miss Shadwell distracted her. They were busily writing letters. The earl had his stationery specially printed on the highest-quality parchment, with the heading "Bellegarde Hall" in gold block lettering, and the Maledon coat of arms as a watermark. The sealing wax was the signature slate blue of the Maledon livery, and the seal, which was also the coat of arms, was large and ostentatious.

"Such fine parchment, I declare I have never seen such quality,"

Miss Shadwell gushed. "I'm writing to my dear friend Miss Whicker, and you simply must allow me to read it to you, Lady Maledon, as I wish to convey my appreciation of your ladyship's exquisite hospitality." Then she proceeded to read: "'Bellegarde Hall is quite grand, and the gardens are quite the most beautiful I've ever seen. Lady Maledon is a quite wonderful hostess, so affable and welcoming...'"

Valeria tried to keep her expression neutral, but something of her weariness of the ladies' fawning must have shown, because by the very slightest sidelong glance Regina signaled a warning to her. Quickly Valeria assumed a look of polite interest.

The men came in at six thirty, talking loudly and smelling of horses and spirits. After greeting the ladies, they settled down to drinking Madeira—and Lord Maledon his port wine—and talking politics. As ladies were considered too delicate to interest themselves in the rough-and-tumble world of governance, the women took no part in the conversation.

Valeria did now wonder where Lady Jex-Blake was. It wasn't really unusual for guests to keep their own schedules, for Regina Maledon was a most obliging hostess. She took great pains to make all her guests feel comfortable, and made it clear that they were perfectly free to pass the time as they wished. *The ultimate betrayal,* Valeria thought bitterly. *My mother is so careful to make our guests feel at home... how does a woman like that dare hold her head up and look my mother in the eye? How can my stepfather?*

It was a vast relief to Valeria when the gong rang at seven o'clock, signaling them it was time to dress for dinner. They all went upstairs to their bedchambers.

Valeria's beautiful bedroom was another gift from her stepfather. All the other bedrooms at Bellegarde Hall had dark walnut wainscoting, dreary wallpaper, and old oak full tester beds with heavy velvet hangings. Lord Maledon had allowed Valeria and Regina to redecorate Valeria's bedroom in the French style. Regina had bought a full-size bed with headboard and footboard painted a cream color, with ornate carvings and a half tester canopy. The armoire, the dressing table, the chairs, and the side tables were all painted to match. For her linens and draperies Valeria chose a light green with pink trim. Regina had found a beautiful cream-colored damask wallpaper with a small green fleur-de-lis design. The carpet was the same soft ecru as the furnishings, with a green ivy design. The final touch, which delighted Valeria, was a recamier upholstered with the same green-and-pink damask as her bed hangings and comforter. Imported from France, it was almost as big as a bed, and luxuriously soft. As soon as she entered her bedroom, she threw herself onto it, laid her head back, and closed her eyes. She must, she *must* compose herself for the ordeal of dinner.

In just a few minutes Joan, the first housemaid, came to dress Valeria. She was the same age as Valeria, an attractive young woman, tall and strongly built, with handsome features and bright brown eyes. She was now wearing the evening livery of the maidservants, a dark-blue dress with a white lace-trimmed bib apron and cap. She was quite burdened down, for she carried a kettle of hot water, Valeria's freshly ironed clothes, and Valeria's watercolor box.

"My watercolors!" Valeria said, bounding up from the recamier to take it from Joan. "How wonderful, I thought my cakes must be leaching out completely in the . . ." Her voice trailed off and she said in a low voice, "Thank you, Joan. Did you retrieve it for me?"

"No, miss," she answered. "Miss Platt went to the kitchen garden herself to get it for you."

Valeria had to make a mental shift, as she always did, when she heard the servants refer to Craigie as "Miss Platt." The servants had rules for titles that were quite as rigid as the nobility's. Any lady's maid was referred to by her last name by the family, while the servants always called her "Miss," regardless of her marital status. The housekeeper and cook were always called "Mrs." by both the family and the other servants, whether they were married or not. The family called the butler by his surname, while the servants called him "Mr. Trueman," and the same rule applied to the valet. All the lower servants were called by their first names only.

Joan laid out Valeria's clothes on the bed, then poured out her hot water. It steamed gently, and she added some lavender to the bowl, stirred it with a silver spoon she had placed in the washstand for the purpose, then added some tepid water from the pitcher to make it lukewarm, which was how Valeria liked it in summertime.

Valeria turned her back to Joan so Joan could undo her buttons. "Did Mary Louise get into trouble?" she asked.

"Oh, yes, miss," Joan answered, her tone light and amused. "But then someone's always in trouble with Mrs. Banyard, she couldn't be happy unless she was grumbling."

"It wasn't over the basket, was it? Craigie returned the basket too, didn't she?"

"Yes, miss. Mrs. Banyard did go on about that basket until Miss Platt came in with it. Then Mrs. Banyard started telling Mary Louise that she was getting above herself, telling you she had two names." Joan imitated Mrs. Banyard's cross voice: "'And why would you be a-telling Miss that your name was Mary Louise?' And poor little Mary Louise said, ''Cause of t'other girl, Mary Jane, Mrs. Banyard, so Miss Segrave wouldn't confuse us.'" Again in Mrs. Banyard's growl, "'And why do you think Miss would care if we was all named Mary? Next time one of Them asks your name, you don't be a-tellin' what every servant on the place is called!'"

Both Joan and Valeria giggled. Now Valeria was undressed, and she went to wash with the refreshing spice-scented lavender water. "Poor Mary Louise," she said. "She is not having a very good day." Under her breath she said, "And she isn't the only one."

Joan gave her a compassionate look but said nothing. She went to Valeria's dressing table and began to dry and cut the stems of the flowers in the bouquet that would go in Valeria's hair.

When Valeria turned seventeen, she had officially "come out"; that is, she was no longer considered "in the schoolroom" and was able to join adult society. Now when there were guests at Belle-garde, she was able to have dinner with them. She also accompanied her mother when she made calls. But the most important sign was that she now wore her hair up, instead of down with the big girlish bows in the back. Her mother had also bought her a new wardrobe, of more mature styles. This meant that now Valeria needed more assistance to dress, and also to do her hair. Up until she came out, Craigie had helped her and had done her simple hairstyles. But a year ago Regina had directed that Joan attend Valeria.

At first Joan had been so proper and correct in her manner with Valeria that she said nothing except to answer questions. But slowly, over the past year, she and Valeria had begun to form a relationship that was closer to friendship than that of mistress and servant. Valeria was glad; she found Joan intelligent and amusing.

She finished washing, toweled dry, and began the ordeal of dress-ing for a formal dinner. Joan held up her chemise, a plain white knee-length shift. Valeria stopped to look more closely at it. On the neckline and the hem was a very small border of eyelet-embroidered lace. "Joan, what lovely white work! You added this to my chemise? Did you work it?"

"Yes, miss. Miss Platt is teaching me white work and tambour. That's my first attempt, I know it's not fine enough to trim a dress, but I thought it would do nicely for a chemise, them being so plain and all."

"I think it's perfectly wonderful," Valeria declared as she slipped the chemise over her head. "It looks quite as expert as does Craigie's. The next time you must trim one of my petticoats. Or really, you should trim your own petticoat!"

"Thank you, miss," Joan said with pleasure.

The fabric felt good against her skin. Commonly chemises were made of cotton, but Regina always ordered the finest of undergarments, so Valeria's chemises were made of the softest linen. To her gratification, Joan always ironed her chemises, which was rather superfluous since they were never seen, of course. But Valeria had found that it gave her an extra degree of comfort.

Next came Valeria's short stays, which were actually a very short corset that only came a couple of inches below her breasts. Valeria was grateful the style was for the high-waisted Empire dress, and women no longer had to wear long corsets that pinched in their waists. It took some shifting and pushing and pulling to get the tight stays right, but finally Joan laced them up firmly.

Over this went Valeria's petticoat. Some petticoats were made of two pieces, a bodice and a skirt, but Valeria had one-piece shifts that were tied tight just under her breasts, following the line of her dresses. For evening dress her petticoats were not embellished at the hem, as they were for afternoon dresses, promenade dresses, and carriage dresses. When one was engaged in the activities for which such dresses were worn, it might be necessary to lift the skirt so as not to get it dirty or muddy, and it was considered acceptable to lift the outer dress only, exposing the hem of the petticoat. But for evening dress this wouldn't be necessary, so her petticoat was plain linen.

Valeria sat at her dressing table, a fine long table with two drawers on each side and a triple mirror mounted on the top. Joan asked, "Now would you be wanting any jewelry or ribbons in your hair tonight, Miss Segrave?"

Valeria considered the dress laid out on her bed. Made of the finest cambric, so closely woven that it had a slightly glossy finish, it was high-waisted with a low-cut square neck and short puff sleeves. It was white, with a sky-blue stripe and a blue satin ribbon tied at the high waist. White Valenciennes lace trimmed the neckline, the sleeves, and the three flounces at the hem. It was a very pretty dress, but Valeria was always dissatisfied because young ladies were confined to pale pastels, and now, as it happened, white was the most popular color. Valeria's only resort was to add some color in her accessories, and sometimes she was very daring in her choices, her own small rebellion. "I think, instead of the blue forget-me-nots, I'll have some of those small orange rosebuds, and my coral jewelry," she decided.

Joan retrieved Valeria's jewelry chest from the armoire. She had a sizable collection of jewelry with which her mother had supplied her. After the French Revolution, in the spirit of republicanism it seemed, semiprecious stones had come into vogue, whereas before the nobility had worn only diamonds, emeralds, rubies, sapphires, and pearls. Valeria had no pieces of precious gemstones yet, though her mother had told her that when she went to London to be presented at court, Regina would see that she had some appropriate jewelry.

Joan's eyes sparkled. Valeria's accessorizing was always interesting and unique. She began taking down the tightly braided bun that Valeria wore during the day. "I think that would be lovely. And might I suggest that you wear the peach ribbon for a sash, and your peach-tinted slippers, instead of the blue?"

"Perfect!" Valeria said. "I shall be matched from head to toe."

Expertly Joan began to arrange Valeria's hair. After Valeria had worn a tightly braided bun all day, her hair had a deep wave, and Joan could make the most graceful loose chignon, right on the back of Valeria's head. Fashionable hairstyles were based on the classical Greek and Roman styles. Valeria's hair was so thick that the chignon precisely mirrored the extended bun on Greek statues. It was necessary for Joan to cleverly secure it with hairpins, but she had learned to do it so that they looked decorative instead of functional.

The prevailing fashion was for wispy tendrils of curls surrounding

the face and the back of the neck. Most women added to this classical simplicity by having flat curls frame the face, or wearing long
crisp ringlets in the back or over the shoulder. But Valeria disliked
wearing the rag-curls at night to effect tight curls and ringlets. Joan
had cleverly found a way to dress Valeria's heavy hair: she had con-
cocted a very light pomade, scented with meadowsweet. She would
moisten her fingertips with water, barely touch the pomade, then
take small baby-wisps of hair and rub them between her fingers,
making them curl sweetly. It gave a softening halo effect to Valeria's
rather strong features.

Although Joan had become adept at arranging Valeria's hair, it still
took a long time. Thoughtfully Valeria asked, "Joan, are you going
to be obliged to attend the ladies?"

Joan smiled mischievously. "No, miss, and that is due to her ladyship, and very grateful I am, too. Lady Jex-Blake, now she rang
when she finally woke up yesterday morning—or afternoon—and
demanded that Miss Platt attend her. Miss Platt did go to her then,
but when it came time to dress for dinner Sophie went to her. Then
Lady Jex-Blake goes sashaying out to find Mr. Trueman, and dressed
him down, she did, for sending her the second housemaid."

Valeria's eyes lit up. "Oh, how I wish I could have witnessed that!
How did Trueman bear up?"

"Oh, very well, as he always does. When she finished her little
tantrum, Mr. Trueman informed her that Miss Platt's duties took all
of her time, and before Lady Jex-Blake could even start in on me,
Mr. Trueman told her also that I was obliged to attend you, miss,
and that her ladyship had directed that Sophie dress her, and Amelia
and Laurie would do the other ladies."

"My mother seems to be rather too kind and gentle at times,"
Valeria said, "but she is very conscious of all of you, and takes your
welfare seriously."

"That she does, miss," Joan agreed heartily. "That's one reason why, since her ladyship came to Bellegarde, positions here are so much sought after. Neither her ladyship, nor you, miss, will ever lack for servants."

"Really? Just lately—in fact, just today—I've started wondering about the servants," Valeria said. "Do you get enough to eat?"

Joan looked incredulous. "Why, of course, miss! Whyever would you think such a thing?"

"It's just that Mary Louise is so very thin."

"Oh, yes, she's a scullery maid and they work harder, and longer than anyone, except the hall boy. I started out as a scullery maid, and I was that scrawny, skin stretched over bones, until I made housemaid. But there again, at Bellegarde, if you do your work well and keep yourself neat and clean and mind your manners, you'll likely rise in the household. That's not always true of the great houses. Now, miss, these orange roses do look right nice with your coral pins. I'm thinking, though, that we could add some little bits of this white yarrow, and maybe even one or two of the forget-me-nots?"

"As always, Joan, you have better ideas than I of how to show me off," Valeria said with a smile. "Why don't you make it three of the forget-me-nots?"

⁂

Valeria was perfectly dressed and coiffed when she went down to join the others at ten minutes to eight o'clock. The guests were gathered in the drawing room with her stepfather standing in the middle of the group, holding a cut glass tumbler full of port and talking loudly. "You should have seen Prinny's production at the fête! It was magnificent, I must admit, even for him."

Poor old King George III had finally gone irretrievably mad the previous year. Finally, after much political wrangling with the Whig-controlled Parliament, the Prince of Wales was named prince regent in February of 1811. With King George so very ill, the prince regent—indulgently called "Prinny"—could make no overt celebration of his rise to power, but he did decree that a grand party should be held June nineteenth, ostensibly in honor of the French royal family. Two thousand invitations were issued. Valeria wasn't surprised that her stepfather had been invited to the fête, for he was considered part of "Prinny's set." Certainly Lady Maledon would have been invited too, and Lord Maledon should have taken her with him, even if he didn't want her and Valeria in London. He hadn't, though, and Valeria was irritated that he'd talk about it now in front of them. She glanced at her mother, but her face was set in a polite smile.

Maledon went on, "Two thousand people, what a crush! The dining tables set up in the conservatory were two hundred feet long. At the prince's table were seated two hundred, and of all things, it had a fountain at the head of it, a stream flowing down it, with green moss and water-flowers, and it had fish swimming in it!"

Lady Jex-Blake, her dark eyes glittering, asked, "And so you were seated at the prince's table?"

"I was," he said loftily. "And a fine dinner it was too. Everything was served on silver, even the soup bowls. Never seen anything like it. Perhaps I might stock up on silver plates and bowls and mimic it."

Miss Shadwell trilled, "Oh, and the fountain and stream and fish too, my lord? Surely you must have that! Such grandeur, such exquisiteness!"

Valeria's mouth twisted; she was certain that *exquisiteness* was not a word. Her mother gave her a warning look.

Just then Trueman appeared at the arched doorway and announced sonorously, "My lady, dinner is served." He was a tall, barrel-chested man of forty-five, with a deep stentorian ringing voice. Valeria had never seen a single expression on his lantern-jawed face. He was the most impassive man she had ever known; he was so guarded that it seemed nothing at all could ever ruffle him, or impress him.

In Town, when guests for a formal dinner were carefully selected, it was imperative to follow a strict precedence in proceeding into the dining room. In the country, however, and with an informal party such as this, the rules were slightly more relaxed. It was customary for the host to lead, escorting the highest-ranking lady of the party, so Lord Maledon offered his arm to Lady Jex-Blake, who would be seated on his right. The others followed in a loose group, and selected their own seats. Colonel Bayliss quickly rounded the table to seat himself by Lady Jex-Blake; Mrs. Purefoy took her seat on Lord Maledon's left, and Mr. Mayhew took the chair next to her. Regina would be seated at the foot of the table, and so this left Valeria and Miss Shadwell to pick their seats. Hoping that she wouldn't be subjected to Colonel Bayliss's greedy gaze, and callously not caring that her guest Miss Shadwell might be, Valeria tried to take the seat next to Henry Mayhew. But Miss Shadwell deftly stepped in front of her, and with resignation Valeria went to take her place by Colonel Bayliss. The two footmen got all the ladies seated, then held the chairs for the men, and lastly Trueman seated Lord Maledon.

"I must say, Maledon, that this room is grand enough for silver and fountains and streams," Lady Jex-Blake commented. Valeria winced at her use of the familiar in addressing her stepfather, but her mother appeared not to notice.

The dining room was fine indeed. It was a long room with walnut wainscoting and deep-crimson wallpaper flocked in velvet with a highly stylized floral repeating design. The oak flooring was polished to a high sheen. The dining table was a long oval, covered with a gleaming white damask linen. The ornately carved William and Mary chairs had tall cushioned backs and plump seats, upholstered with Genoa velvet in a red-blue-and-black floral design. Over the table was an enormous crystal chandelier that cast a soft glow over the diners.

After all were seated, the two footmen began to serve the first course, a rich turtle soup. It was odd, Valeria mused as she surreptitiously watched them set the bowls in front of the diners with economical grace, that footmen's livery was now the exact style that only gentlemen wore in the previous century. The Maledon livery was slate blue and silver, and the footmen's long coats and waistcoats were heavily trimmed with silver cords and had large silver buttons. In the daytime they wore broadcloth knee breeches the same color as their coats, but in the evenings they wore white satin breeches, with white stockings and shoes with silver buckles. Their eighteenth-century attire was completed by powdered wigs, with a long queue.

The footmen were brothers; in fact, they were Joan's brothers. There were many Davieses in the parish, as they were an old family with a tendency toward having many children. They also tended to be uncommonly attractive people. Though they were often mistaken for twins with their similar handsome features and broad shoulders, Ned Davies was twenty-three and an inch taller than Royce, who was twenty and an even six feet tall. Both had dark hair hidden under their wigs, as well as that most important characteristic of footmen—muscular calves.

It was customary at formal dinner parties for the hostess to control the flow of conversation. During the first course, she opened a conversation with the person seated to her right, and the table followed. During the second course, she "turned the table," speaking to the person on her left, with the others following suit, and so on with each course. In this way no person was neglected by his or her partners.

But, Valeria disdainfully noted, apparently Lady Jex-Blake had not dined much in Polite Society. When Ned placed the bowl of soup in front of her, she looked up at him coquettishly and said in an over-loud voice, "Oh my, Lady Maledon, you do have such handsome footmen! You must be the envy of all of your acquaintance. I declare, I should very much like to steal them from you. What are their names, pray?"

Valeria saw that Ned and Royce looked startled, and their cheeks colored slightly. It was hard for her not to react herself to the crass mistakes in this little speech Lady Jex-Blake had made. First, she had called down the table to make herself heard to Lady Maledon; second, she had noticed the footmen, which was a grave breach of etiquette and offended and embarrassed them. Their pride was in serving quietly, without any intrusion whatsoever on the diners. Truly quality service was such that the food seemed to appear magically. It was understood that the lady of the house was never obliged to make any signal to the butler or footmen, or to take any notice of them at all.

But the most egregious error that Lady Jex-Blake had committed was asking Regina to name the footmen. This was unheard of, and Valeria observed, with a sort of vexed amusement, that one of Trueman's eyebrows shot up slightly, though he was as stony-faced as always. This was equivalent to anyone else's throwing his hands up in the air and shouting, and Valeria had to stifle a smile.

Unruffled, Lady Maledon politely answered, "Yes, they are very handsome young men. The footman serving you is named Ned Davies, and the other is his brother Royce. I would ask you not to steal them away from us, however, for they are very valuable members of our staff."

It was unusual for the lady of the house to call the footmen by their real names; it was crucial, in the status of the nobility, to have "matched pairs" of footmen, and so they were often renamed James and John or Will and Thomas. Lady Maledon had no use for such callousness—she also abhorred some women's insistence on simply calling their cook "Cook." Valeria was certain Lady Jex-Blake would comment on the names, but instead she said, "Very well," with a deep mock sigh. "But I'm sure I shall never be able to find such a fine matched pair. Mmm, this soup is delicious! Wherever were you able to find such good turtle this time of year, Maledon?"

By now the natural order of conversation was ruined, of course. Miss Shadwell was talking animatedly to Mr. Mayhew, but Lord Maledon was much taken up with Lady Jex-Blake, which stranded Mrs. Purefoy. But it wasn't such a bad thing, Valeria decided, because after a perfunctory greeting to her, Colonel Bayliss had turned to compete with Lord Maledon for Lady Jex-Blake's attention. At least his lecherous gaze wasn't crawling over her. Happily she started talking quietly to her mother.

"Mamma, you look absolutely stunning," she said. "I think that deep green suits you as no other color, but then again I think that with every dress that you wear. You're so fortunate, with that lily-and-rose complexion, that you can wear any shade and it flatters you."

"Thank you, my darling," she murmured. "I must admit that green is my very favorite. It might have something to do with the fact that of all jewelry, I most prefer emeralds, and I particularly love these." She gave a small secret smile to Valeria.

Valeria's father had given her the emerald necklace and earrings. Regina rarely mentioned her first husband, believing it was disloyal to Lord Maledon. She did tell Valeria things about Lord Segrave as her father; but she hardly ever referred to anything about him as a husband. Valeria returned her smile with a rapturous one of her own.

As the meal went on, Valeria and her mother spoke very little, for Regina was much distracted by the questions Lady Jex-Blake persisted in half-shouting down the table to her. Valeria had ample opportunity to observe all the guests, and her stepfather, and she learned much.

First of all she studied Lady Jex-Blake, as she was avidly curious about her. She presented odd contrasts, as her speech and dress were refined and tasteful, but her manners were crass. Valeria wondered how she had learned the refined diction of the upper class; she recalled that Craigie had told her that before marrying Sir Henry she had been his serving-maid. Always there was a clear distinction between the servants' accents and that of the gentry and nobility. How was it that Lady Jex-Blake had learned to modify her speech but obviously hadn't learned the simplest rules of etiquette? Valeria reflected that perhaps Mrs. Banyard was right, Lady Jex-Blake was very good at "apin' her betters."

It was with some envy that Valeria observed Lady Jex-Blake's dress. She was wearing a rich satin gown of a dark orange-red, the color of cinnamon, and it went very well with her rather sallow complexion. In spite of all Lady Jex-Blake's protestations, Sophie had done her hair very well. She had a braided bun, with three small braids descending in loops from the back, and small ringlets and curls all around her face and neck. A satin ribbon, the same color as her dress, made a bandeau high on her forehead and was intricately entwined in the braids. Diamond stars glittered in her dark hair, and she wore a heavy gold necklace with square-cut diamonds and small baguettes. Valeria reflected moodily that *she* would look very well in that color, and she wouldn't wear such oversized and ostentatious jewelry.

As they made their way through the first course, which was the soup and entrées of light meat dishes and fish and shellfish, Valeria was relieved to see that though Lady Jex-Blake was a crude woman, at least she was intelligent enough not to openly flirt with Lord Maledon, even if she used the over-familiar "Maledon" to address him. She smiled too much and laughed too loudly, but her attentions did seem to be divided evenly between him and Colonel Bayliss.

The footmen took away the soup bowls and began serving the meat and fish. Ned brought a silver platter heaped with veal fricandeau and unobtrusively bent over to offer it to Lord Maledon, while Royce began at the foot of the table, offering Regina curried lobster. They then served the guests. Next Ned brought around stewed mullet, and Royce brought fillets of salmon.

For perhaps the dozenth time Lady Jex-Blake called down to Regina. "I see that you are at the very forefront of fashion, Lady Maledon. In London it is all the rage to be served *à la russe* instead of *à la français*," she said with a supercilious air.

Her French accent was atrocious. She was correct, however; for many years among all but royalty, dinners had been served by the footmen's placing the dishes on the table, aligning them exactly along the sides. Whichever gentleman was sitting closest to the meat courses was expected to carve, which presented a difficulty to many men, for it was a skill that only experienced cooks were really good at. The diners helped themselves, usually from whatever dishes happened to be next to them, for it was considered boorish to call up and down the table to ask for dishes.

Service *à la russe* was when the food was placed on sideboards, the butler carved, and the footmen served each dish separately to the diners. It took longer, but it was decidedly more elegant and made for a more graceful table. Now, instead of great platters of meat and roasts in the center of the table, beautiful arrangements of flowers or fruit were set. Instead of each place setting's having a clutter of silver, different plates, and several different glasses, the footmen placed the correct dish, silver, and wineglass for each course.

As they were served the fish, Valeria again noticed something odd about Lady Jex-Blake, or rather she saw a peculiar furtive exchange between her and Mrs. Purefoy across from her. Mrs. Purefoy picked up the two fish forks and in a jerky movement held them up for a mere second, frowning. Lady Jex-Blake started, then set her dinner fork down and picked up the second fish fork. Apparently she hadn't known that instead of using a knife to cut up the fish, one used two forks to separate the soft flaky pieces. After this little exchange Valeria watched Mrs. Purefoy more closely, and saw that she did indeed signal Lady Jex-Blake each time to indicate the appropriate way to use the silver. It gave Valeria a perverse delight to see this further proof that Lady Jex-Blake was not only ill-mannered; she was ill-bred.

But all the while she was watching Lady Jex-Blake and her gaffes, Valeria closely observed her stepfather. By the time the dessert course was served, she was beginning to think that perhaps Craigie had been right. Her stepfather did not seem to be a healthy man.

He ate hardly anything at all, except the soup, and he ate two bowls of that. He took a small portion of each dish offered, but Valeria saw that he ate only a bite or two of the mullet, none of the lobster, none of the veal, and only a tiny bit of one of the meats of the second course, a roast rabbit. He didn't touch the vegetables, and used no sauce at all.

When giving formal dinners, her mother kept a sumptuous table, serving a different wine with each course. The footmen filled up the glasses of the diners, and it was up to them whether they wished to partake or not. Valeria never drank wine, for early on she had found that if she drank only one glass it gave her a headache, and if she drank two glasses her head swam. She drank either water or lemonade, which were also served.

Normally her stepfather heartily drank of the good wines served at his table, but on this night Valeria noted that he didn't touch a single drop of wine, yet he drank glass after glass of port. As the meal progressed, Lord Maledon's face grew redder, his voice louder, his conversation more reckless.

As Valeria was watching him, he laughed raucously at something Lady Jex-Blake had said. Then in a loud coarse tone, his words slurred, he said, "You are one wicked wench, Mavis! Oh, yes, a man must watch himself with you, get too close and he might get his eyes clawed out!"

Even Lady Jex-Blake had the grace to look embarrassed at this outburst, and the table grew silent. But Lord Maledon didn't seem to notice, as he began telling Colonel Bayliss about Lady Jex-Blake's superior horsemanship.

Valeria glanced at her mother. Regina gazed down as she delicately took a spoonful of cherry ice. When she looked up, only an expression of polite interest was on her face. But Valeria could now clearly see the sorrow in her eyes.

Chapter Four

༄

W HEN VALERIA HAD FIRST COME to Bellegarde Hall as a child, she had thought that it was an ancient, rather peculiar castle. Since then she had learned from Mr. Chalmers, who was interested in architecture, that Bellegarde was barely a hundred years old, and that the style, which had been short-lived, was called English Baroque. In 1710 one of the premier architects of the time, Sir John Vanbrugh, had designed it for the first Earl of Maledon.

A *corps de logis*, or central block, which held the principal state and living rooms, formed the center block of a three-sided court, with two flanking wings. The house was of grim gray stone, with an octagonal tower at each corner and square towers on the east and west sides that enclosed the great spiral staircases that went from the basement kitchen all the way up to the nursery floor. The towers were crowned by balustrades and pinnacles, which Vanbrugh had said gave the Hall his "castle air," so it was understandable that Valeria had seen the resemblance.

The east wing held the magnificent stables and the coach house on the ground floor, with quarters for the grooms, coachmen, and gardeners on the first floor above. The west wing held the office of the estate agent, and quarters for the house servants. Joan had told

Valeria that this was another reason that many young people were eager to go into service at Bellegarde Hall.

"We all of us have our own rooms, you see," she said, when she learned that Valeria had never been in the servants' wing. "Instead of being all crushed up into the attic cheek by jowl. And there's even a kitchen, so we can do hot water and morning tea for the upper servants instead of having to come back and forth from the Big House."

"What do you mean, hot water and tea for the upper servants?" Valeria asked curiously.

Joan seemed incredulous that Valeria didn't understand. "Why, the lower servants do hot washing-up water, and tea and toast, for the upper servants, miss. Ned wakes Mr. Trueman, I wake Mrs. Lees, Sophie wakes Mrs. Banyard, Royce wakes Mr. Thrale. Us maids clean their rooms too, and Wes does their boots and shoes and carries their coal and kindling."

"Who is Wes?"

"He's the hall boy."

"Good heavens," Valeria said. "I suppose I just thought that you all sprang up, in perfect livery and uniform, and set to work." Joan giggled.

Valeria finished dressing and went downstairs to morning prayers in the Great Hall. Though the interiors and decor in the rest of Bellegarde were reflective of the somber Jacobean early eighteenth century, the Great Hall was modeled after more ancient times. It was Elizabethan, with a high table and heavy ornate chairs. The great clerestory windows soaring above made it the lightest room in the house.

The servants were already gathered in orderly lines at one end of the table. Regina and St. John stood at the other end, and Valeria was surprised to see Mrs. Purefoy there, for none of the guests had come to morning prayers on the previous day. Quietly she took her place next to her.

Between them, Mr. Chalmers smiled and began.

"Today is the day of Saint Dominic. This was a man after my own heart, for he believed, and taught, so much of what I see as of vital importance to us as Christians today. First, he believed that each person could, and should, have a personal relationship to God, that we should know God Almighty as our Father, Jesus Christ as our own Savior and as 'that friend that sticketh closer than a brother,' and the Holy Ghost as our Indwelling Comforter.

"Saint Dominic also believed deeply in charity, every kind of charity. He taught that we must always be generous in giving to those less fortunate; but this is not always a matter of material gifts. Spiritual charity, which is love, should also be given freely to all, even to our enemies, for this is indeed the Love of Christ.

"He also stressed two very important aspects of a devout Christian's life: we should strive to learn, to educate ourselves, to understand the foundations of our beliefs and how they apply in our day-to-day lives; and, with this precious knowledge, we should be eager to share it. Dominic himself stayed up all night in an inn, talking to a man of the pagan sect of Albigenses. By dawn the man became a Christian. Saint Dominic regarded this as one of the greatest joys he ever experienced in his life.

"Now let us pray a prayer of Saint Dominic. I ask you to pray responsively."

May God the Father who made us bless us.
May God the Son send his healing among us.
May God the Holy Ghost move within us and give us eyes to see
    with, ears to hear with, and hands that Your work might be done.
May we walk and preach the word of God to all.
May the angel of peace watch over us and lead us at last by God's
    grace to the Kingdom.
Amen.

The servants filed silently back to the servants' passage. As Regina and St. John went toward the morning room, Mrs. Purefoy, following them, took Valeria's arm in a companionable manner. "What a sweet little homily that was," she said. "I was unaware that you had a family chaplain."

"Actually Mr. Chalmers is my brother's tutor," Valeria answered.

"Oh? But surely he wears clergyman's dress," Mrs. Purefoy observed.

"Yes, he is an ordained clergyman, educated at Cambridge. Unfortunately the benefice that he is promised is not yet vacant, and so he was gracious enough to accept the onerous responsibility of trying to educate my brother." What Valeria didn't tell this gossipy woman was that Mr. Chalmers had had to leave Cambridge early. His father was a gentleman, with a small estate near Bellegarde, but his bank had failed, and he had gone into bankruptcy. Mr. Chalmers had been forced to go to work to help out his parents. The Chalmerses were distant cousins of Lord Maledon's, and Regina had persuaded him to offer Mr. Chalmers the position of tutor at the exceptional wage of eighty pounds per annum.

The morning room was altogether a most cheerful room, and when no guests were at Bellegarde, the family took all their meals there. It was also the only room on the first floor that Lord Maledon had allowed Regina to redecorate and refurbish. From another dreary, dark parlor she had made it into a delightful breakfast room and sitting room. The earth-brown ceiling was painted a soft cool tan. The walnut paneling was painted cornflower blue, and the fireplace surround was painted white. Luminous botanical prints by Pierre-Joseph Redouté lined the walls. The draperies for the four large windows were a bright blue-and-yellow-striped damask. All the furniture was much more modern than the furnishings in the rest of the house; the sideboard and dining table and chairs were by Sheraton, and at the other end of the room the sitting area had comfortable sofas, settees, wing chairs, and side and tea tables by Hepplewhite.

Trueman stood by the heavy-laden sideboard, impassive as always. Regina, St. John, Valeria, and Mrs. Purefoy had all helped themselves and were already seated and eating when the others began to come in. Miss Shadwell, clinging to Mr. Mayhew's arm, was followed by Colonel Bayliss. Mr. Mayhew had a difficult time preparing his plate, as Miss Shadwell persisted in hanging on him and trilling on about his teaching her to play billiards. "Lady Jex-Blake learned so quickly, she assured me that I could learn quickly also, as she says—not that I believe it for an instant—but she says that I'm quite as dexterous as she—and she assures me that you are such an expert hand at the game..." On the previous evening, after more rowdy cards, the gentlemen had decided to play billiards. Lady Jex-Blake had insisted on accompanying them to the billiard room, which was particularly a male habitation, and declared that if they would teach her to play, she would soon beat all of them.

Finally Mr. Mayhew, Miss Shadwell, and Colonel Bayliss got their plates and seated themselves. When Miss Shadwell took a bite and her unending sentence paused, Colonel Bayliss said, "I've a mind for some coarse fishing this afternoon, Mayhew, what about it, eh? Maledon tells me the lake is full-stocked with carp, pike, and tench. I relish a good wrestle with a pike, they're cunning creatures. Good eating too, if you're careful of the bones."

Mr. Mayhew answered in his bored drawl, "Don't care much for coarse fishing myself."

"What about you, Lord Stamborne? Do you fish?" Colonel Bayliss asked.

St. John's eyes lit up. "Oh, yes, sir! And I do so like coarse fishing!"

"Then what about it, Lady Maledon? I'll take the boy fishing, and drag Mayhew along too. It'll do him good to match wits with a pike, wake him up."

Regina smiled. "That's very kind of you, Colonel. Now that St. John has heard you offer, I doubt I could say no even if I wished to. I do have a suggestion. Perhaps, ladies, we might have a picnic at the lake this afternoon, and watch the gentlemen in their struggles with the pike."

This was highly agreeable to Miss Shadwell and Mrs. Purefoy, and Valeria too. She had dreaded another endless afternoon in the drawing room watching Miss Shadwell and Mrs. Purefoy writing their letters. The ladies all began talking about the appropriate afternoon dresses and bonnets for a picnic.

Lady Jex-Blake came in, looking very heavy-eyed, for the billiard players had stayed up until after three o'clock in the morning. She greeted everyone, and took her seat by St. John, smiling down at him. Then she waited expectantly.

Although the footmen always served luncheon and dinner, they never served breakfast. The diners helped themselves from the sideboard. Trueman attended because he watched over the sideboard in case the dishes needed replenishing, replaced the silver warming-covers after the diners had helped themselves, and watched the warming candles to make sure they stayed lit.

Regina, perceiving the situation, was making very small indications by her expression to Trueman, when Mrs. Purefoy abruptly said, "Lady Jex-Blake, you really must try this kidney pie, I declare it is the most sumptuous I've ever had! Here, allow me to show you—" She jumped up out of her chair and went to the sideboard, staring intently at Lady Jex-Blake, who suddenly looked chagrined, but quickly recovered and went to prepare her plate.

Watching them, St. John looked greatly confused, and he opened his mouth, but quickly Regina said, "Lady Jex-Blake, we have decided to picnic at the lake this afternoon, for the gentlemen are going fishing. Would you care to join us?"

"A picnic? Hm. Maledon said I might go for a ride this afternoon, I long for some exercise," she answered.

"Of course you're welcome to ride," Regina said graciously. "It is a full two miles to the lake, so perhaps you might join us if you should decide to ride in the south park."

"I would like that very much, thank you," Lady Jex-Blake said.

They were all discussing how they were to be transported to the lake when Lord Maledon came in. His eyes were brighter than usual, and he looked excited. Valeria thought that he often seemed excitable, restless, even to the point of agitation, these days.

"Good news, good news!" he said, helping himself to dry toast at the sideboard. "Trueman, get me some ale, will you, can't stand tea for breakfast anymore." He sat down and announced, "Kincannon's sent us an invitation to join him up at his shooting box in the West Riding. I've heard he's got the best grouse and partridge south of Scotland. You know, I tried to get him to join us here but he said he had some affairs at home to attend to. He writes that he's all settled up, and is having a large party join him at Clayburn."

"Who is invited?" Lady Jex-Blake blurted out. "Who is included in the invitation?"

"All of you," Maledon said expansively. "He knew of the party, you see, and he's included all of my guests in the invitation."

"How thrilling! How kind, how obliging, how generous, for Lord Kincannon to include us!" Miss Shadwell said fulsomely. "After all, we only met him the one time, when you introduced us, Lord Maledon. How far, exactly, is it to his shooting box?"

"About two hundred miles," Colonel Bayliss said, frowning. "I was there last season. It's a devil of a journey. But worth it, eh? You're right about Clayburn, Maledon, it's the best shooting I ever saw. One day we killed over three thousand birds!"

Lady Jex-Blake said carelessly, "Well, Mrs. Purefoy, I for one think that traveling by post chaise to the West Riding would be the worst kind of nightmare. What about loaning us one of your carriages, Maledon? You can spare it, you have six."

"Seven," he said proudly. "Don't worry, I'll make the travel arrangements for us all, it's nothing. We'll leave tomorrow." He jumped out of his chair, then, as an afterthought, turned to speak to Regina. "By the way, my dear, Hylton sent us an invitation to Foxden Park for the opening of grouse. I'll decline it, of course, we couldn't possibly leave our guests stranded, could we?"

"Of course not, dear," Regina said softly. Again, only Valeria could see the trace of sadness in her mother's deep-blue eyes.

Valeria couldn't help but vent her anger to Joan as she was dressing for the picnic. "He's behaving as if he's some young bachelor rake, gadding about with his awful hangers-on!" she cried. "They all sat right there, so excited about going to Clayburn, making their plans, discussing it with such animation, right in front of my mother—who was not even invited!"

Soothingly Joan said, "I'm of the mind that her ladyship wouldn't wish to go anyway."

"She certainly wouldn't. I know of Lord Kincannon, he's been my stepfather's friend for a long time. I've never met him, but Lady Hylton told me that he's one of the worst libertines in England. He's extremely wealthy, and she said that he spends thousands of pounds on his rowdy parties. And there was my stepfather again, snubbing my mother, telling her that he'll decline *our* invitation to go to Foxden."

"Now Foxden is—?" Joan hinted.

"Foxden Park is Lord Hylton's shooting lodge. You did know that

Lady Hylton—the current baron's mother—is my godmother? And St. John's too. Yes, her family is connected with the Segraves. Lady Hylton adored my father, it seems, and she has always been a good friend to my mother and me." Valeria was silent as she recalled how Lady Hylton had been the only person able to persuade her mother to rejoin society—in fact, to rejoin the world—after Lord Segrave died.

The estate of the Baron Segrave naturally passed from father to son, but as Guy Segrave had had no male heir, Ryalsmere was inherited by his nephew, his younger brother's son. Guy's brother, Valeria's uncle, had died of typhoid fever in 1790, leaving one son, William. William was very unlike Valeria's father: he was a rather shy, bookish man who was completely dominated by his mother. When William inherited and became the twenty-fourth Baron Segrave, and his mother became Lady Segrave, they wanted to move into Ryalsmere immediately, and the new lady of Ryalsmere made it very clear that Regina and Valeria were not welcome.

In her grief Regina hadn't wanted to stay at Ryalsmere anyway, for the memories of her happiness with her husband there were simply too overwhelming. Regina's sole living relative was a younger brother, Matthew Carew, who had joined the navy at eight years old, and at the time had been twenty-two. Through Lord Segrave's influence, Matthew had gotten his step to lieutenant. He had a small dismal flat in the seedy navy town of Portsmouth. Regina bought a roomy, comfortable cottage in the nearby village of Haverhill, and she and Valeria and Matthew moved in. Valeria could hardly remember her uncle; he was at sea for a year or two at a time, so he had been in port only three times during their five years at Haverhill. He had been killed at Trafalgar.

Regina had seemed content, living quietly with Valeria, with Craigie and Platt their only servants. But after three years, Lady Hylton had insisted that Regina rejoin society and resume her life.

Although reluctant at first, finally, when Valeria was ten years old, Regina agreed to go to London for the Season, staying with Lady Hylton in her town house. There she met the widowed Earl of Maledon.

Lady Hylton had told Valeria once, long before her stepfather had started on his debauched downward spiral, "You know, Maledon was enchanted with your mother when she came to London with your father. His first wife was still alive then. Oh, he was very discreet, but I could plainly see that he was much attached to Regina. He never offered any impropriety, of course, for Regina would have been horrified and disgusted. But after the first Lady Maledon died, and Regina came out of mourning, he made it clear then that he was absolutely in love with her. He made your mother feel protected, cherished, secure. It was then, I think, that Regina came to see that though she might not be all aswoon with love, as she was with Lord Segrave, she could still find comfort and companionship with a husband."

Valeria begrudgingly thought that she understood, a little at least, why her mother had married Maledon. But what she could not understand was her mother's loyalty to him now.

Sighing, she murmured, "Oh, how I wish we could go to Foxden! My mother loves to spend time with Lady Hylton, and I, too, miss her. I just wish I could *do something*. Sometimes here at Bellegarde I feel as if I am literally stifled with boredom."

Joan finished tying Valeria's stays and held up her petticoat to slip on. "Maybe her ladyship would like to go to Foxden after *they've* left," she intoned.

Valeria brightened. "You know, she very well might. Lady Hylton always includes St. John in her invitations, and Mamma really doesn't like to go anywhere without him."

"But what about her son, the baron? Do his invitations include you and his lordship too?"

"Hm, I don't really know. But he and Lady Hylton are close, I believe. I would imagine that he goes along with her wishes."

"You don't know the baron?" Joan asked with surprise.

"Lady Hylton's husband I knew, but he died two years ago. Their eldest son that inherited, Alastair, I only saw once, when my mother married Lord Maledon. I was eleven at the time, and he was about twenty, I believe. I remember thinking that he was very handsome but he took no notice of me whatsoever. I decided that he must not care for children, and that he was an old, mean man," she said lightly.

"I doubt you'd find that so now," Joan said with amusement. "So, is it to be the yellow, or the white?"

"The white," Valeria decided. "Since now I know our guests are leaving so soon I have determined that at least until tomorrow I shall be very modest in my dress and very demure in my manner."

"That'll put one in Lady Jex-Blake's eye," Joan said with relish.

Valeria did look fresh and virginal in her picnic dress. It was a sturdy jaconet muslin with a checkerboard white-on-white weave. The sleeves were long, with four puffs tied with pink satin ribbon. Around the hem was a delicate pink floral embroidery that her mother had done. Valeria trimmed all her own bonnets, an art that she particularly enjoyed. This was a deep-brimmed chip straw that she had trimmed with pink satin ribbon, pink-and-white satin rosettes with pearl centers that she had made herself, white lace, and dried baby's breath. She wore kid gloves and soft leather half boots of the same buff shade.

Ewan was waiting for them outside with the open landau, and Regina, Valeria, Miss Shadwell, and Mrs. Purefoy rode down to the lake, enjoying the errant breezes on the warm August air. Now that Valeria knew that they would be gone the next day, she looked at the two ladies with a slightly more charitable eye. Miss Shadwell was silly, ignorant, and flirtatious, but Valeria thought that she really wasn't immoral in her conduct; she now doubted that "Kit" and

Mr. Mayhew were truly "carrying on" in the physical sense. As for Mrs. Purefoy, Valeria thought that she was actually rather dim, and had very little judgment. Apparently she really couldn't see the perfidy in her friend Lady Jex-Blake's behavior; her enchantment with titles, no matter how insignificant, appeared to be the sole guide informing her perceptions.

At the lake there was a pleasant scene. Colonel Bayliss was standing between St. John and Niall, for as always St. John had insisted that his friend join him. The colonel was showing them how to bait. Mr. Mayhew sat on the bank a little ways off, placidly watching his motionless cork float.

The footmen, Ned and Royce, had already brought down the cart with all the food and supplies. Invitingly laid out on a pallet underneath a spreading oak tree were several platters with silver covers, big baskets of all kinds of fruit, a silver coffee service and tea service, bottles of wine and punch and lemonade, crystal tumblers, and plates of Meissen china. Splendid in their livery, Ned and Royce stood by, unmoving and expressionless as statues.

As they drove up, St. John turned around and grinned. Holding his hand up high, he shouted, "Look, Mamma! Look, Veri! We have maggots, and they're perfectly *huge*! Did you know that we have maggots? Colonel Bayliss says they are the very best bait for pike."

"Ah, the joys of having a six-year-old," Regina said to the ladies. "I never thought a person could get excited about maggots. But then again, I'm not really surprised."

"I noticed that Lord Stamborne calls you 'Veri,'" Miss Shadwell said to Valeria. "That's a lovely nickname. I'm surprised he didn't call you 'Val,' which I think is also a lovely nickname, like my nickname, 'Kit.' I think that Lord Stamborne may call me 'Kit.'"

To Valeria's surprise, her mother demurred gently. "I'm sorry, Miss Shadwell, but I insist that my son call all adults by their proper names. Except for his own sister, of course."

"Oh! I'm so sorry, I meant no offense, Lady Maledon, of course it's only proper that children address adults respectfully—not that I think anyone who calls me 'Kit' is being disrespectful—the style of address between friends is more relaxed, isn't it, and I do so dislike 'Katherine' or 'Kate' or even 'Kitty'..." Here Miss Shadwell went on with her paragraph-length sentences that lasted until the other ladies were seated on the pallet. Then she abruptly cut off her rambling and practically ran to join Mr. Mayhew.

"Ned, Royce, you may serve now," Regina said. "Valeria, Mrs. Purefoy, would you care for tea?" Ned and Royce knelt down on the edge of the pallet and removed the covers from the serving platters. There was ham, cold roast beef, three kinds of pies, a cucumber-and-celery salad, several kinds of cheeses, and fresh-baked bread. With their usual grace the footmen served up the ladies' choices, then peeled the pears and apples and plums for them.

"Oh, dear, the peacocks have found us," Regina said regretfully. Two male peacocks, their magnificent tails fully displayed, strutted out of the glade and headed straight for the pallet. They were something of a nuisance, as they were aggressive in begging for food.

"It's all right, Mamma, I'll feed them," Valeria said lightly. "As long as they get their fair share—"

At this point confusion ensued, as Mrs. Purefoy was apparently deathly frightened of peacocks. With a screech she gathered up her skirts, ran to the cart, and clambered up onto the driver's seat. "Oh, dear," Regina said again, rising to her feet. "Ned, try to drive them away. I'll go to Mrs. Purefoy."

"Yes, my lady." Ned sighed. It was almost impossible to drive peacocks away from food.

Laughing, Valeria came to his rescue. "Come, let's get some of the grapes and we can lure them back into the glade, at least."

"And then they can follow us right back," Ned grumbled under his breath.

"Well, perhaps Mrs. Purefoy will have to picnic in the cart," Valeria said with satisfaction.

They got the peacocks to turn around by taking a step, then offering each of them a grape, which they greedily snatched. Slowly they made their way back toward the wood. When they were about halfway across the clearing, Lady Jex-Blake and Lord Maledon suddenly came thundering out of the wood on horseback, nearly running down Ned, Valeria, and peacocks all. Lady Jex-Blake's horse came so close to Valeria that she could feel its steamy breath as he reared and screamed.

Then with horror Valeria saw that Lady Jex-Blake was riding her own horse, Tarquin. She stood motionless, staring with huge dark eyes and dead-white face at the horse. He was foaming, chomping hard at the bit, his eyes rolling and showing the whites. His front hooves crashed to the ground a bare foot from Valeria. She watched as Lady Jex-Blake yanked hard on the reins to pull him to a stop; but still her left foot, underneath her skirt, was pounding Tarquin's side so that he kept prancing, dancing, restlessly half-rearing. Lady Jex-Blake's face was a picture of fierce, savage joy. She was making a display, and she was making sure that Valeria saw her. They stared at each other for long moments.

Valeria was barely conscious that the peacocks, frightened by the rampaging horses, had fled into the woods. Lord Maledon rode on up to the cart, where the grooms were waiting to take his horse. After an intense face-off, Lady Jex-Blake turned and spurred Tarquin to a dangerous gallop for the short distance to the cart. Numbly Valeria returned to the group.

Lord Maledon helped Lady Jex-Blake down. It was then that Valeria saw the blood streaming down her horse's side. Lady Jex-Blake was wearing a sharp spur. Clenching her fists, Valeria ran to the two of them. "That's my horse!" she cried accusingly to Lady Jex-Blake. "How dare you use the spur on my horse! He's never known the touch of a spur in his life, he's never required one, he has such spirit—"

"Be silent!" Lord Maledon roared, his face growing dangerously crimson. "Who do you think you are, you little chit? Speaking in that manner to my guests! I'll have you know that my guests can ride any of my horses in any manner they wish, and you've nothing at all to say about it, now or ever!"

"But, sir, Tarquin is my horse!" Valeria argued vehemently. "I know him, I know best—"

Maledon stepped forward and slapped Valeria across the face, hard.

Though stunned, she didn't cry out; nor did she weep. Instead she turned her face back and glared fixedly at him, her eyes glittering with hatred. Maledon took an uncertain step back.

Without a word Valeria mounted Tarquin; she barely touched his side, and the horse galloped off at full speed. She didn't look back.

Chapter Five

❧

THE DEEP BRIM OF HER BONNET blocked Valeria's view in her headlong ride. Heedlessly she tore it off. Tarquin ran as fast as he ever
had, and she bent low over his neck and gripped the reins so hard
her fingers ached; her right leg, clenched on the sidesaddle leaping
horn, burned with pain. Still Valeria thought she would just ride on
and on, away from Bellegarde Hall, away from her stepfather and
Lady Jex-Blake. She wished mightily that she could, but of course it
was impossible.

They reached the courtyard still at full gallop, but Tarquin knew
he was at his own stable now, so he came to a sliding stop, reared,
and then stood, his skin quivering. Two grooms came running out
of the stables to assist her, but heedlessly Valeria jumped down and
threw her arms around the horse's neck. It was soaked with sweat
and foam. "Oh, Tarquin, Tarquin, I'm sorry, I'm so sorry..." she
murmured over and over again. After long moments she felt him
ease up somewhat, and he reached his head around to nose her side
affectionately.

One of the grooms had taken Tarquin's reins, the other stood
close. Both of them were staring at her with shocked expressions.
Valeria realized then that her hair was falling down in wild abandon.
Her white afternoon dress, a round gown with a narrow bottom,

was ripped up one side seam. Tarquin's blood was smeared along the hem. "Where is Timothy?" she asked tightly. "I want Timothy."

"Yes, miss," they gulped, and one of them ran back into the stables.

Timothy Buckley, the youngest groom, had attended Tarquin's birth, and Valeria had fallen in love with the beautiful black colt with the diamond blaze on his forehead as soon as he was born. She and Timothy had become good friends, as he had, at her insistence, taught her everything about taking care of Tarquin.

He came running out, struggling into his coat, for the Bellegarde grooms wore livery, a brown coat and waistcoat, tight buff pantaloons, and top boots. He was a slight but sturdily built young man of eighteen with ash-brown hair and plain features, including friendly brown eyes. He skidded to a stop and grabbed Tarquin's reins from the other groom, who slipped away. Timothy looked aghast as he took in Tarquin's agitation, the blood on his side, and Valeria's state.

"Oh, Timothy, look what she's done," Valeria muttered in a strangled voice. "How could anyone be so cruel?" She grabbed the horse's bridle and pressed a kiss to his nose, again murmuring endearments to him.

"I'm so sorry, miss," Timothy said quietly. "I thought she needn't be riding Tarquin; but his lordship was telling her that you were the better rider. Her ladyship didn't take it kindly, like, and insisted that she'd show him."

Valeria gritted her teeth, and several extremely unkind epithets came into her mind, but of course she would never say them out loud. With one last stroke of Tarquin's nose she murmured, "You'll take good care of him, I know, Timothy. I couldn't bear to leave him if it weren't for you."

"Yes, miss, thank you, miss. And just so's you'll know, as Tarquin is *your* horse and all, I believe I'm seeing he's got a stone bruise on his off hind. I'm thinking he mustn't be rode for a day or two," he said with grim determination.

"No, he surely mustn't," Valeria agreed gratefully. "Thank you."

She hurried into the house and to the sanctuary of her bedroom, seeing no one in the Great Hall or on the stairs. Slamming the door closed behind her, she went to her dressing table and sat down, staring at herself in the mirror.

Her eyes widened, and she touched her left cheek, only now aware that it was stinging painfully. The crimson print of a long-fingered hand showed on it as clearly as if it had been painted on. She thought of how very white her face was, as pale as the moon, except for that handprint; and her eyes were stretched wide and seemed a flat lifeless black. Her throat was constricted so tightly that it hurt, but not because she wanted to weep. She didn't feel in the least like crying. She felt anger, but it was not sharp and vengeful now. It was a low dull throb in her chest.

Her head felt as if it were stuffed with cotton wool, and she had difficulty in comprehending what she had just been through. Never in her life had she been subjected to such a terrible scene, she had never even imagined that people could behave in such a manner. With sudden dread she tried to marshal her thoughts—had St. John seen? *Oh, please, merciful Lord, not that...*

Resting her forehead on her hand, she closed her eyes and forced herself to replay the scene. Her mother standing at the cart, comforting Mrs. Purefoy because of the peacocks; the landau pulled up behind it, and Ewan Platt and the grooms standing there, ready to take the riders' horses; her stepfather and Lady Jex-Blake on this side of the landau as she came to confront them; beyond, Colonel Bayliss, St. John, and Niall at the lakeside...on the far side of the oak where the picnic pallet was spread. No, they could not have witnessed the ugly spectacle. Valeria felt a measure of relief.

It was short-lived as she thought of her mother, however. No matter how awful she herself felt, she knew that her mother must have been even more sickened than she. And Valeria had escaped, but her mother couldn't. This wasn't because she would worry about the etiquette of leaving her guests; she knew that her mother would have hurried to her if it hadn't been for St. John. Dully Valeria wondered about the aftermath, and how everyone had reacted. Then she realized that they would act as all well-bred Englishmen acted, as if nothing bad or shameful or embarrassing ever happened in polite company.

After a few painful moments, she was sure that they had all gone about their picnic, and her mother would have to stay there and play-act along with them, for St. John's sake.

The door opened, and Craigie came in, carrying a tray. She set it on a side table in front of the open window, then came to Valeria and, without a word, put two fingers under her chin and lifted her face. Valeria stared up at her with some bewilderment; she still wasn't thinking clearly. Craigie's eyes narrowed to sparking blue slits, and she grimaced.

"What happened?" she asked tightly.

Valeria bowed her head and said numbly, "I can't speak of it. Ask Platt when he returns."

"Come over here, my love, I've brought tea," Craigie said with sudden gentleness. She took Valeria's arm and led her to the side table, sat her down, then pulled up a chair and sat next to her. Pouring out a lightly steaming cup of tea, she said, "Drink this, it'll help."

"Green tea, yes," Valeria murmured. "Thank you."

Craigie sat in silence as Valeria sipped the tea. After a while Valeria said vaguely, "I lost my bonnet. In the glade, down by the lake."

"Don't worry about that, my love, Platt will find it."

"It was very expensive, I believe. And I've torn my dress . . . and . . . and there's blood on it."

"So I see."

Another long silence. Valeria reflected that Craigie was one of the most comforting people in the world to be with. She was silent and economical in her movements, and she had a stillness about her when she was listening that was very peaceful.

Valeria finished her cup of tea, staring unseeing out the window. Carefully she set the teacup down, then slumped her shoulders tiredly. "I—I feel—soiled. I need a bath, a very hot bath."

Craigie patted her shoulder and rose, whispering, "Poor little mite."

"I don't want to be a poor little mite," Valeria cried in a strangled voice. "I want to be strong, like my father!"

Craigie said quietly, "You are exactly like your father, Valeria." Then she quietly left the room.

In a few moments she and Joan returned, each carrying a trifold screen. They set them up to screen Valeria from the far end of the room, for manservants had to carry in the heavy copper tub and the water. Valeria poured herself another cup of tea and tried to prepare herself for what was going to be a terrible ordeal—attending dinner. She tried to imagine how she would conduct herself.

She heard them bring in the tub, and immediately she heard water splashing into it, bucket after bucket. A delicious smell permeated the room, and Valeria sniffed appreciatively. Craigie used different herbal bath preparations for different times. This time it was lavender, chamomile, and rosemary: a soothing bath. Wearily Valeria thought that it would make her sleepy, and wondered if she had time for a short nap before dinner. She had no idea of the time; she couldn't think how much had passed since she'd left the picnic. It troubled her.

Craigie came around the screen and said in a businesslike manner, "Let's get you undressed, and take your hair down. I've brought some new hair-wash that her ladyship ordered special from London and just came in today. It's rose-and-lilac-scented, and by all accounts it's good for both fair and dark hair, to give it a special shine."

As she had done when she was a child, Valeria stood limp and yielding as Craigie undressed her down to her chemise. More buckets of water splashed, and the sweet scent in the room grew stronger. Joan came around the screen and curtsied. "May I do anything else, Miss Platt?"

"No, I'm just going to brush out her hair and then we'll have our bath," Craigie answered briskly as she sat Valeria down again at the dressing table. Valeria grew more alert. "What time is it, Craigie?"

"It's going on five o'clock, miss."

Valeria said, "Craigie, when my mother returns she is going to need you. I'm sure she'll need a bath too, and most likely she'll be suffering from headache. Joan can attend me."

"Are you sure, miss?" Craigie asked doubtfully.

"I'm sure," Valeria asserted in the most purposeful tone she had used since she had come home.

Craigie left, and Joan came to take down Valeria's hair and brushed it out until it was smooth, with not a single tangle. She adjusted the screens, so that they were now in front of the door.

Gratefully Valeria sank into the hot bath. Pinching her nose, she fully immersed herself for so long that Joan must have begun to worry, but finally she came up spluttering and already feeling cleaner and better. Taking the bath brush, she rubbed herself so vigorously that her skin began to turn red, but it felt delightful. "My back, please," she murmured, then wrapped her arms around her knees and leaned forward. With satisfaction she realized that Joan had observed her and knew her wishes, as she scrubbed Valeria's back hard. Then she washed Valeria's hair, rubbing her head vigorously to work the hair-wash into a foamy lather. Lastly she poured two buckets of warm water over Valeria's head for clean rinsing.

Valeria got out and began toweling herself down. Joan moved

the screens again, then went out and instructed the maids to empty the tub and have the manservants return to take it away. She returned and finished drying off Valeria. Wrapping her wet hair in a large soft flannel she said, "Now, miss, if you'll just lie down I think you'll feel even better after a massage. I believe we'll have the lilac-scented cream, as it'll blend nicely with that wonderful hair-wash." It amused Valeria that Joan was turning out to be just as motherly and bossy as Craigie. Then it struck her that she had relaxed enough to feel such a light emotion as amusement.

Joan had strong hands, and the massage she gave Valeria was expert. Valeria felt the last bit of tension draining away from her body, and she almost dozed off. But with determination she said, "That will do, Joan, I'm getting too sleepy. We need to start drying my hair, or I'll be going down to dinner with it still dripping."

Joan dressed her in her softest chemise and a light dressing robe, and again Valeria took her seat by the window, so that the late afternoon sun blazed in on her head. Joan fetched several smaller flannels and began partitioning sections of Valeria's hair and drying them.

The bath and the screens were soon cleared away, and almost immediately afterward Regina came into the room. She was hurrying, for she hadn't even taken off her bonnet.

"Valeria, my darling... please excuse us, Joan." The maid curtsied and left.

Regina untied the ribbons on her bonnet and took it off, then sat down, her eyes never leaving Valeria's face. "I'm all right, Mamma," Valeria said evenly.

Regina nodded and swallowed hard. Valeria saw tears start in her eyes. Reaching over, she grabbed her mother's hand and said, "Please, Mamma, please don't weep. It would only make me feel worse."

"Then I won't," Regina said, wiping her eyes. "Of all things, I don't wish to make you feel worse. Oh, Valeria, I'm so sorry."

"It wasn't your fault," Valeria said gutturally. "You're not responsible for what he does, Mamma, never think that."

"But I am," she said quietly. "He is my husband. I must share his burdens. I know that he will never apologize to you, Valeria, and so I must beg for your forgiveness for him."

"No, I can't! I won't! How can you even say such a thing? You—you should never have to be—subjected to—exposed to—" Valeria's voice, along with her sudden rage, faded away. Finally she went on, "Mamma, how can you stand it?"

"Because I promised that I would." She rose and went to Valeria's secretary and returned with Valeria's prayer book. Opening it, she turned to a page that she evidently knew very well. Softly she said, "This was my promise: *I, Regina Carew, take thee, St. John Edward Charles Bellegarde, to be my wedded husband, to have and to hold from this day forward, for better for worse, for richer for poorer, in sickness and in health, to love, cherish, and to obey, till death us do part, according to God's holy ordinance; and thereto I give thee my troth.*"

She looked back up at Valeria, and in her face Valeria now saw no sorrow, no sadness, only compassion. "Oh, Mamma," she sighed, "I shall never be as good as you."

"Nonsense, my love. You're so young, too young to understand, really, and I would give my life if you weren't forced into the position where you need to fathom such hard things," Regina said regretfully. "But we are here, and we must learn to live with the trials that we have. And so again, Valeria, I beg your pardon for your stepfather, and ask that you forgive him. No—don't say it, I know very well what you're feeling. And it's useless for me to tell you that you must have charity, and to insist that you must forgive even your enemies. Only the Lord can give you this kind of love, and the ability to forgive. If you will ask Him, you will find charity, and love, and forgiveness."

Valeria was reminded of Mr. Chalmers's homily at morning

prayers. *Charity . . . love . . . forgiveness . . . it's all very well for Mr. Chalmers, and my mother. They are truly virtuous, pious people, always kind, with no hint of pride. But I'm not like that! I feel—such anger, such bitterness, I can't even think how to begin to be such a devout Christian!*

Still, Valeria felt a strong sense of responsibility to her mother, and she determined that at least she could make Regina proud of her right now. "I will try, Mamma," she said humbly. "Anyway, I promise you that I will behave with all decorum and grace at dinner tonight."

"You're not going to be able to come to dinner tonight," Regina said matter-of-factly. "You have a headache, and you are excused."

"But—I really don't—"

"Yes, you do," Regina said with a small smile. "You see, I learned a very hard lesson today, dearest. I know that for so long you've struggled to protect me, and I have appreciated it more than you can know. But I was wrong to let you struggle alone. I am the one who must protect you and St. John."

"But how can you? You can't, I know that you can't, any more than I could protect you," Valeria said passionately.

With more determination than Valeria had ever seen in her gentle mother, Regina said, "With God's grace, I will find a way. I promise you, Valeria, that somehow I will find a way to protect you and St. John, so that we may never have a day such as this, ever again."

※

Just before dinner, Regina brought Valeria a sleeping draught. She had never had one before, and doubted that it would be effective. After the sedative effect of her bath and massage had worn off, she had become disturbed and upset again. She tried to read a novel called *Forest of Montalbano*, but she found the prose overheated and melodramatic, and couldn't lose herself in it. In her mind she replayed the events of the afternoon over and over again. She thought she would never be able to sleep.

But she did, soundly and dreamlessly. When Joan brought her toast and tea at eight o'clock, she awakened feeling much better emotionally, though she was sluggish. "Mm, I can't seem to come all the way awake," she said, yawning hugely as Joan set her breakfast tray in front of her.

"It's from that sleeping draught, miss," Joan said, pouring out the tea. "You'll feel better after you get up and have a proper breakfast. That is, if you would be going down to breakfast, miss?"

"I certainly am," Valeria answered sturdily. "I want to look particularly well this morning, so I will wear the lemon sarcenet. And you'll take care with my hair."

"Very good, miss."

Valeria went down to morning prayers and greeted her mother and St. John with a smile. Regina looked pale but composed, and St. John was his usual rowdy self. It seemed to Valeria that Mr. Chalmers regarded her, as he spoke of Christ's forgiveness of sin, with a special empathy that held no pity, for which she was grateful.

Valeria retained her gracious composure all through breakfast. She even greeted Lady Jex-Blake cordially. Her stepfather didn't come down, and Valeria was glad, but she was determined to say a pleasant good-bye to him.

As the Bellegarde servants were so efficient, the company was ready to depart by eleven o'clock. Lord Maledon finally came down as they were all gathered in the Great Hall, saying their farewells. He didn't meet Valeria's eye as he shook his son's hand, then gave Regina a chaste peck on the cheek. Purposefully Valeria went to him and said politely, "Farewell, sir. I hope you have a pleasant journey and that the shooting is good."

He looked surprised, and Valeria thought she could sense some shame in him, although his ruddy face betrayed little of it. "Goodbye, Valeria. Take care of your mother and brother."

It was the first time that Lord Maledon had ever referred to St. John as Valeria's brother.

After they left, Valeria felt a strange lassitude. She and her mother spent the afternoon picking flowers and arranging bouquets, and they said little to each other.

At three o'clock Regina asked Trueman for tea, and asked that he tell St. John and Mr. Chalmers to join them.

Elegantly pouring for all of them, Regina said, "Since our guests and Lord Maledon have left, I've directed that we shall go back to our old routine. We're going to have dinner at six o'clock, so that you can join us, St. John, and Mr. Chalmers, of course you must round out my table."

It was an old joke, that the addition of the tutor at table would make two men to the two women. He smiled happily. "Thank you, my lady, I would be honored."

"Huzzah!" St. John exulted. "I'm so glad all of those strange people are gone."

Valeria expected Regina to scold St. John, but she was wrong. With a sweet smile Regina said, "I must admit that I'm glad those strange people are gone too, St. John."

"You are?" he asked in amazement. "Even my father?"

"Your father enjoys shooting so very much," Regina answered lightly. "So I'm glad that he was invited to Lord Kincannon's shooting box, for Clayburn is reputed to have some of the most plentiful birds in the country. Your father will enjoy the season, I know."

St. John seemed satisfied at this, and began asking questions of Mr. Chalmers about the different shooting seasons.

Valeria often wondered about St. John. Like his marital bond, Lord Maledon's relationship with his son had deteriorated. Maledon had been wildly happy to have an heir. He had been married before, for eighteen years, to a woman eight years older than he. They had had no children, and the first Lady Maledon had died in 1803, tragically in childbirth; the baby girl had lived for only a few hours. When St. John was born, it seemed that Lord Maledon couldn't be around the baby enough, and as he grew into a precocious toddler, Maledon was as proud of him as if he were a prodigy. That had all changed in the last two years. He barely took any notice of St. John at all anymore. Valeria doubted that St. John could remember when he was only three or four years old, and Lord Maledon adored him.

But, Valeria reflected as she watched her brother, how animated he was, how bright and cheerful, and she thought that she had little to worry about. He seemed to be a confident, well-adjusted little boy.

In the days following, the household regained the homey, relaxed atmosphere that had become routine over the last couple of years, as Lord Maledon had been at home less and less. Although Valeria was still angry with her stepfather and Lady Jex-Blake, particularly when she rode Tarquin, slowly she came to a better understanding of the disastrous scene at the lake. Painfully she faced the fact that she herself had acted wrongly, for she never should have confronted her stepfather with such heated rage. She tried hard to be repentant for her own behavior, but she simply couldn't do it, and soon gave up the futile exercise.

But one thing she would not even attempt to do. She would never forgive Lady Jex-Blake . . . nor the Earl of Maledon.

Chapter Six

✣

As they were finishing breakfast Regina said to Valeria, "I have an appointment to meet with Mr. Wheeler this morning. I'd like for you to join me."

"Of course," Valeria said. "Is this part of my new program for learning more about managing the house?"

"It is," Regina said. "And after our meeting with Mr. Wheeler, I think you should attend when I meet with Trueman and Mrs. Lees and Mrs. Banyard. I really didn't comprehend how little you know about managing servants, dearest. You must learn, for after you're married, managing the household will be your most important responsibility."

"I don't ever want to get married," Valeria said vehemently, then regretted it when she saw the pained look on her mother's face. The earl and his party had been gone for four days now, but Regina still looked pale and strained.

In a low voice she said, "I promise you, darling, that one day you'll understand that marriage can be the most wonderful thing in this world."

"Oh, I suppose," Valeria said lightly, "it's just that I don't want to wear those awful caps." Generally married women were expected to wear lace caps at all times, except when they were in formal dress.

"Valeria, you really can be outrageous," Regina said, now smiling a little. "I expect that if you don't want to wear them, then you won't, and you'll shock all of us dowagers terribly." They rose and Regina said to Trueman, "We'll meet with Mr. Wheeler now."

Regina and Valeria went to the other end of the morning room and seated themselves on the sofa. In a few moments Trueman returned and said, "Mr. Wheeler, my lady."

George Wheeler was a sturdy, capable, somber man of about forty, with thinning dark hair and rawboned features. He was the earl's largest tenant farmer, and he also managed the Maledon estate. He had never had a formal meeting with Regina, for he dealt only with Lord Maledon. He looked mystified as he bowed and greeted her and Valeria.

"Please sit down, Mr. Wheeler," Regina said, indicating a nearby chair. "Thank you for agreeing to meet with me and my daughter."

"Of course, my lady," he said hesitantly. "How may I assist you today?"

"I believe the harvest is going well?" she asked.

"Oh, yes, my lady. The hay's in, and I'm expecting to have all the corn in the first week in September." *Corn* was the farmer's all-purpose word for wheat, rye, and barley.

"Very good," Regina said with satisfaction. "So am I right to assume that we might have the Barley Mow Fair the second week of September?"

For a hundred years the earls of Maledon had sponsored a harvest fair. It was a three-day event, with the locals supplying the booths with their goods and crafts. The entertainment was as elaborate as that of Bartholomew Fair in London, with fire-eaters, sword-swallowers, jugglers, gypsies with trained bears, even wire-walkers. The villagers, farmers, and servants looked forward to the fair throughout the year.

Mr. Wheeler looked troubled. "I'm sorry to say, my lady, that his lordship left me no instructions concerning the fair this year. I did ask him about it, and he said he would attend to it before he left. But I'm afraid it must have slipped his lordship's mind, for he said naught of it to me."

"I see," Regina said quietly. "I'm certain, however, that it is the earl's wish to sponsor the fair this year. It's such a long-held family tradition."

"Ye-yes, my lady. It's just that—it's quite an expense," Mr. Wheeler said hesitantly.

"I'm sure it is. Tell me, does the estate have the funds to finance the fair?"

Carefully he replied, "You would have to consult with his lordship's solicitors for an exact accounting of the estate funds on hand, my lady."

"But it has been a profitable harvest this year?"

"Oh, yes, my lady."

"Then I am authorizing you to expend the necessary funds for the fair," Regina said firmly. "Let us consult the calendar, here. We will have the fair on September twelfth, thirteenth, and fourteenth. Will that give you enough time to make the arrangements, Mr. Wheeler?"

"Yes, my lady. That will give me ample time."

"Very well. Also, Mr. Wheeler, we will have the Earl's Procession to the Black Star'd Horse on this, the last Friday in August. Please also make the appropriate arrangements with Mr. and Mrs. Davies."

Mr. Wheeler's eyebrows shot up. "His lordship will be back by then?"

"No, he will still be in Yorkshire," Regina said evenly. "But I and my son and daughter will make the announcement."

"Yes, my lady," he said, and a furtive look of admiration came into his dark shrewd eyes. "I'll be glad to attend to it."

"Then that will be all, Mr. Wheeler."

"Yes, my lady." With another deep bow he left.

Valeria said, "I'm so glad you thought about it, Mamma, since apparently Lord Maledon didn't. Everyone would be so disappointed if we didn't have the fair. And you handled that wonderfully. At first I thought he was just going to say no to you! That would have been insolent."

"Not really," Regina said mildly. "He is, after all, employed by Lord Maledon, not me. I'm afraid I put him in a rather uncomfortable position, but it had to be done."

"But Mamma, you're the Countess of Maledon," Valeria argued. "You have as much right to the Maledon estate as Lord Maledon does."

"That's not true, Valeria. When I married Lord Maledon, what was mine became his, but what is his is not mine. That's simply the way of it, dearest. It's the law."

Valeria wrinkled her nose and twisted her mouth with disgust. "Then it's a stupid law."

"If you keep doing that," Regina said with a smile, "your face may get stuck that way."

Trueman returned, with Mrs. Lees and Mrs. Banyard. "Are you ready to instruct us, my lady?" he asked.

"Yes, thank you." Regina didn't ask them to sit down; the house servants never sat in the presence of the family. "First I would like to compliment you, Mrs. Banyard, on the greengage vol-au-vent last night. It was delicious. I believe this was your first attempt?"

"Yes, m'lady, it was. Thank you, m'lady," she said, her eyes brightening.

"I shall be adding it to our menus when we have guests, for it will surely be a success. I went over the menus you gave me yesterday, Mrs. Banyard, and found them satisfactory. Did you have any questions or requests for me?"

"Just one, m'lady. The last saddle of mutton we received is much too tough. I was wondering if your ladyship might want to exchange the mutton on the menu for venison instead?"

"That will be fine. And if the mutton is indeed so tough as to be inedible, don't inflict it on the servants either. I suppose you could feed it to the pigs."

Trueman said, "My lady, the mutton will do perfectly well for the servants' hall if it is stewed properly. Mrs. Banyard was just acting on the knowledge that your ladyship doesn't care for stewed mutton."

Valeria noted with interest that Mrs. Banyard gave Trueman an intensely resentful stare. Regina said calmly, "I understand, thank you, Trueman. Mrs. Banyard, please use your own judgment about the mutton. Is there anything else concerning the kitchen?"

"No, m'lady, thank you," Mrs. Banyard said quickly. "Everything is just fine in my kitchen."

Regina said, "Mrs. Lees, I saw that the housemaids' aprons appear to be getting slightly thin. I would like for you to order each of them two new ones."

"Yes, my lady," Mrs. Lees said. She was a buxom, motherly woman of forty-five, with graying hair and a kind homely face. "I'm afraid I must report that I broke one of the tops of the Meissen serving dishes last night. Of course I will pay for the replacement."

Trueman said in a deep baritone, "Mrs. Lees, that is not precisely what happened, is it? My lady, Joan broke the piece. It is she who should pay for it."

"Mr. Trueman, in fact Joan was handing the top to me as she was checking in the china after dinner. What *precisely* happened was that we were both holding it when it slipped," Mrs. Lees said spiritedly.

"It really is of little consequence, it is easily replaced," Regina said. "And you all know that I don't require anyone to pay for breakage if it's a simple accident. Mrs. Lees, order the replacement and include it in your expense accounting for the month."

Stiffly Trueman said, "My lady, I must protest, in all conscience.

I have found that Joan has become unaccountably irresponsible in the past few weeks. Just today, after I inspected the billiard room, I found that there was a cigar ash on the carpet, underneath the draperies. It really is unforgivable. And last night she appeared to be in such a hurry to finish her duties that it was only through her carelessness that the china was broken."

Valeria said with some heat, "Joan's responsibilities have been doubled, you might say, as she has been attending me. And she's done a marvelous job, too."

"If you'll pardon me, miss, that is not an excuse. If she is unable to attend you and also perform her duties as first housemaid then she is not fit for either position," Trueman intoned.

Mrs. Lees said, "Mr. Trueman, all of my girls perform their duties well. It was simply an accident that the china was broken. And one cigar ash on the carpet is also just a mistake, that I have already addressed with the maids. That room was an unholy mess, I tell—oh, I beg your pardon, my lady."

Slight amusement flickered in Regina's eyes. "It's quite all right, Mrs. Lees, it might do me good to be reminded exactly how hardworking all of you are. Trueman, I am perfectly satisfied with all of the servants. So, is there anything else? No? Then I'm very glad to tell you now. The Barley Mow Fair will be held next month, on the twelfth through the fourteenth. You will schedule time off for all of the servants. On the first day, as is traditional, as many of the servants as can be spared will be allowed to attend. Mrs. Banyard, on that day you will only be responsible for breakfast, and we will have a simple cold repast for both luncheon and dinner. Mrs. Lees, Trueman, we will not require attendance that day, so you are both welcome to plan on going to the fair."

Mrs. Lees's face lit up with pleasure, but Trueman looked as if he had been handed a death sentence. "I will not be attending, my lady, so I will be happy to serve the family that day."

Regina nodded. "Very well. Also, I want to tell you that the Earl's Procession will take place on the last Friday of this month. Perhaps some of the servants may wish to take a half day, to join the celebration."

"That has never been done before, my lady," Trueman said stiffly. "His lordship never indicated that the servants should take time off for the Earl's Procession."

"It is my wish," Regina said in a velvet-over-iron voice. "That will be all, thank you."

After the servants had left, Valeria said, "Heavens, I never thought I'd see the stone-faced Trueman in such a huff!"

"You must understand, dearest, that Trueman is a very strict disciplinarian, and exceedingly mindful of the servants' place. I think that the first Lady Maledon's attitude toward the servants was very different from my own. It seems that she left all things concerning the servants up to Trueman. In many ways he believes that I interfere with his status."

"But she is not here, and you are," Valeria said. "You run this household, not him. I think that he's simply trying to regain some of his power, with all this fuss and bother about broken china and a cigar ash on the floor."

"Actually, I can see his point, and you should too, Valeria. In most houses the servants are required to pay for the things they break, and they accept it as one of the terms of their employment. And there should not be a cigar ash left on the floor, it means that the maids didn't sweep thoroughly."

"But Mamma, should you really have to attend to such minor things? Do they actually report to you every time someone spills a cup of sugar, or if a speck of dust is on a chair?"

"Of course they aren't required to, but it does give Trueman such satisfaction that I allow him to do it," Regina said lightly. "You see, darling, men can be so fragile that we must allow them their little triumphs now and then."

"Men," Valeria grumbled. "If they'd just do as they're told the world would be a much better place."

Regina laughed.

⁂

The first Earl of Maledon had had a favorite retainer, his manservant, a man named Edward Davies. When Davies retired, the earl set him up in his own public house in the village of Abbott's Roding. To show his gratitude, Davies named the tavern after the horses in the Maledon stables, a fine bloodline of mostly black horses with distinctive white markings on their foreheads. The Black Star'd Horse had been enlarged through the years, and now it was a tavern, an eatery, and a coaching inn. It was still owned by one branch of the Davies family.

In that year of 1712, the earl decided to sponsor a grand harvest fair for the parish. He and his countess and children dressed in their best finery, took their best carriage, and went to The Black Star'd Horse to make the announcement. They dined with the publican and his family. Then, since the parish had been alerted, the earl made a speech to the crowd gathered, and announced that in a fortnight they would have three days' holiday to attend the fair. The announcement itself had become a holiday of a sort, because it came at the end of the long harvest. Most of the parish gathered in Abbott's Roding to witness the Earl's Procession.

Now, a hundred years later, the scene was much the same in the charming village. The old half-timbered pub faced out onto the village green, which was overspread by an ancient gnarled yew tree. The public house was full, and about a hundred people were picnicking on the green. For the occasion the earl had provided bowls of punch, and fruit from the Bellegarde orchards. Two tables had been set up beneath the yew tree, and on one were four great silver bowls of Captain Radcliffe's punch, regent's punch, and the more sedate lemon and orange punches. The other table was riotous with grapes, pears, cherries, apples, oranges, currants, and plums.

The villagers expected pageantry in this time-honored tradition, and the Countess of Maledon provided it for them. Leading the procession was Valeria, riding Tarquin, the perfect black star'd horse. She and her mother had very carefully chosen what they would wear. Though they saw everyone at church, this was the only time that many of the villagers and farmers would ever see the nobility in their full finery.

Valeria told Regina and Craigie, "All of the clothes young ladies wear nowadays are so boring! Just white and bland pastels. I'd love to wear something different, something daring."

"If you mean you're thinking on showing your bosom at high noon, I'd say not," Craigie said, frowning, then asked Regina, "But my lady, what about that Turkey red velvet of yours? It's so striking, and you've hardly worn it."

"Oh, could I?" Valeria said excitedly. "I don't care if it's too early for velvet, and of course I know it would never do in London. But for the Procession, it would be perfect."

And so Valeria was wearing the simple but queenly dress, of the color known as Turkey red, though it wasn't actually a deep crimson. It was more of a rust red that complimented Valeria's white skin amazingly. It was high-waisted, but instead of being a round gown it had tight gathers from the sides around the back, giving her room to ride sidesaddle. With the medium-length train it draped gracefully. The sleeves were long and close-fitting, with three layers of lace for cuffs. As it was an evening gown, the squared neck was low-cut, so she wore a fine lace tucker trimmed with pearls. Instead of kid gloves she wore lace knit mittens. Her bonnet was trimmed with fresh flowers: white and yellow and red roses, French marigolds, and Persian buttercups, with sprigs of mint leaves for greenery.

Behind her, Regina and St. John rode in the town coach in great state. Ewan drove, dressed in his full coachman's livery. He wore a gray suit with a slate-blue waistcoat, buff breeches, top boots, a greatcoat with three short capes at the shoulders, and a gray top hat. His impassive expression hid the fact that he was sweltering in the August sun.

The Maledon town coach, usually used only in London, had been polished and shined to perfection. The midnight-blue lacquer shone like glass, and the brass fittings gleamed. On the doors was the Maledon coat of arms, worked in pewter and gold. Standing on the footboard behind were Ned and Royce, dressed in their full formal livery, resplendent in blue and silver, their perfect powdered queues topped by tricorn hats trimmed with swansdown.

This year Regina had added an innovation to the Procession. Following the coach were two of the Bellegarde farm carts. They were decorated with flowers and greenery, and in them were more baskets filled with fruits. Craigie, Niall, Mrs. Banyard, Mrs. Lees, Joan, and Sophie rode in the first, with six more servants riding in the second.

As they came into the village, the people lined the street leading to the front entrance of the pub. The glass windows of the town coach were lowered, and Regina and St. John cheerfully waved. This was the single time that the commoners were permitted to call out to the nobility, and there were many friendly greetings. "Hallo, m'lady, m'lor'—Good day to you, m'lady—Miss Segrave, Miss Segrave, ain't you a pretty sight on this fine day!"

When they reached The Black Star'd Horse, the carriage stopped perfectly in front of the open door. Royce ran ahead to lift Valeria down and hold Tarquin. Ned opened the carriage door and lowered the steps. Regina alighted, splendid and glowing in moss-green satin, with diamonds in her hair. St. John managed to look very dignified in a black coat with silver buttons, gray satin waistcoat, gray satin knee breeches, white stockings, and black pumps with bows.

The crowd around them grew silent, then all the men removed their hats and bowed deeply, and the women curtsied. Mr. Davies, the publican, stepped forward and bowed. In a sonorous, ceremonial voice he said, "My lady, my lord, Miss Segrave. You do my house great honor. Welcome to the Black Star'd Horse."

Chapter Seven

❦

LETITIA, LADY HYLTON, FINISHED READING the letter and stared at the fire, deep in thought. A few raindrops spit at the window. She rose to look out at the park and the lake below. The sky was heavy and low; thunder rumbled in the distance.

She was not a tall woman, but she carried herself so proudly that she seemed taller than she was. At forty-eight she had pure white hair that was still thick and curly. She had never been a beauty, but because of her wit and vivacity, the brightness of her blue eyes, and her mobile expression, she was still considered a handsome woman.

She was thinking about the letter from her friend Regina Maledon. The letter had been very light in tone, relating Valeria's activities, St. John's antics, small homey things about Bellegarde. But the final paragraph worried Letitia.

I do so regret that we were unable to join you at Foxden. It is such a comfortable place, and each time we've been there I've felt so relaxed and, I must admit, a vast relief to have an interval away from the strain and cares of Bellegarde. I miss you, Letitia. Especially lately I've longed for the comfort of your counsel and the benefit of your wisdom. I hope that we can come visit you upon your return to Hylton Hall.

Letitia had known Regina for twenty years, and it was the first time she had ever heard even a hint of a complaint from her. For Regina to admit that Bellegarde was placing strain and cares on her was comparable to a long dire lament from anyone else. Letitia thought that the last two sentences sounded wistful, and it pained her.

A faint commotion sounded from the back of the house. The shooting party was returning early, and they were laughing and talking rather loudly in the gun room. In a few minutes Letitia's son came in, followed by the butler, Fleming, who had a particularly distressed look on his face. "But my lord, your Hessians have been cleaned and polished, it won't take a moment for me to fetch them," he pleaded.

Lord Hylton pulled a fat wing chair up close to the fireplace, sat down, and propped his muddy boots on the fender. "I doubt that my mother will have vapors because I'm tracking mud into the sitting room. I'll go up and change shortly, but first I'd like a strong hot cup of tea, it's a raw day out." Defeated, Fleming left.

Letitia resumed her seat on the settee across from him and said, "Those boots really are a disgrace, Alastair. Fleming's much more upset about you being mussed than he is about you tracking in."

"I'm not mussed, I'm disheveled and muddy. Come to think of it, I hope Fleming doesn't have the vapors."

He was not at all disheveled, though his boots were spattered with mud. His fine mane of blond hair was styled in fashionable waves and curls that took much effort to look so artless. Alastair's face looked like a Greek statue, with a broad forehead, a high-bridged ruler-straight nose, a firm mouth, and clear eyes of an unusual gray-blue. He was a couple of inches over six feet tall, with long legs, and a well-proportioned body that was muscular but not bulky. His buckskin breeches were perfectly fitted and spotless, as were his green striped waistcoat and plain chocolate-brown coat. His intricate cravat was flawless.

Alastair continued, "Fleming really should learn to loosen his stiff upper lip here at Foxden. I grow weary with grandeur sometimes. I like sitting by the fire in muddy boots."

Foxden Park was a rustic hunting lodge dating from the early eighteenth century. It was well furnished and comfortable but it wasn't a grand manor. When the Hyltons were in attendance here they never dressed formally, and rarely had guests, only close family friends such as the Maledons. This season, since Lord Maledon had decided to stay at nearby Clayburn House, and Regina had felt that she couldn't come to Foxden, only the family were here: Letitia, Alastair, his sister Elyse, and Elyse's husband Lord Lydgate.

The latter two came in then, followed by Fleming with a tea tray. Elyse was twenty-two, with glossy ash-brown hair, dark sparkling eyes, and a sprightly prettiness. Her lively manner was in complete contrast to that of her husband, Reginald, who was inevitably called Reggie. He might have been called an average, rather nondescript man but for an endearingly amiable expression and manner, much like a friendly dog's. Letitia was amused to see that he was in his stocking feet.

"Please note, Alastair, that Reggie's much more considerate of the servants than are you," she said. "He didn't go stamping through the house in muddy boots."

"Mine were in much worse shape than Alastair's," Reggie said mournfully. "Stepped right into a great puddle. I say, Alastair, how about giving up your chair? My feet are cold."

"Pull up your own chair," Alastair retorted. "I was just expressing my supreme happiness at being in this one."

Reggie pulled another chair up close to the fire and Elyse joined her mother on the settee. Elyse said, "Alastair, your great feet practically take up the entire fender. Move over and make room for Reggie. Fleming, please go fetch some comfortable warm slippers for my husband."

"Yes, ma'am," he said, and scurried off.

As Letitia was pouring for them she asked, "How was the shooting?"

"Not bad, until the storm started coming in," Alastair answered. "It's peculiar how the birds can sense such things, they became very difficult to flush before we realized it was going to rain. Still, we managed to bag around three dozen."

"I even got one today, Mamma," Elyse said enthusiastically.

"I still don't think it was the one you were aiming for. That poor bird was halfway across the moor when your wild shot downed it," Alastair said.

"I most certainly was aiming for that exact one!" Elyse said indignantly. "Just because it was a long shot doesn't mean I wasn't aiming."

"Yes, you do aim," Alastair admitted. "You aim everywhere. If Reggie isn't more careful to stand farther behind you he's likely to end up shot in the posterior region."

"Oh, do be quiet. Brothers are so annoying," Elyse said. "Mamma, why couldn't you have had all girls instead?" Elyse was the only girl, with three brothers. Philip Hylton was in the Coldstream Guards, and the youngest, Robert, was at Cambridge.

"I did try," Letitia said dryly, "but I'm afraid your father insisted on sons. Did you see Kincannon's party today?"

"We did, in fact we lunched with them. Kincannon sets a fine spread even out in the field," Alastair said with narrow amusement. "No hunk of cheese and bottle for him. There were more servants than there were sportsmen."

"And sportswomen," Elyse added slyly.

"Some of them were indeed *sporting*, you might say," Reggie chortled. "I'll say one thing about Kincannon, his parties are always the most interesting mix of guests."

"A motley collection of rabble, I'd call it," Letitia sniffed. "I know one of those guests is his current mistress, that actress person."

With a slightly mischievous air Alastair said, "Her name is Maura Ruskin, as you well know, since you've seen her on the stage several times. She really is an accomplished actress."

"Speaking of rabble," Letitia said heavily, "did you see Maledon?"

"No, he and some of the others were on the south downs for the pheasant." Alastair frowned. "Kincannon said he's not doing much shooting, he mostly stays at the house with the ladies and drinks up all the port."

"I've had a letter from Regina today," Letitia said tightly, "and I can tell she's deeply distressed. Though she has the highest sense of honor and the strongest principles of anyone I've ever known, she's still fragile. Her sensibilities are so delicate, she's like a hothouse orchid, the merest careless touch can wilt her. I cannot fathom what Maledon is thinking, to treat her in such a manner!"

"And poor Valeria," Elyse said with some distress. "Mamma, I sat by Mrs. Purefoy at lunch, and she told me the most dreadful thing. Apparently Lord Maledon and Valeria had words, and he slapped her."

"What!" Letitia said with outrage. "He struck her? Mrs. Purefoy witnessed this?"

"Yes, along with Lady Jex-Blake and several servants. And I'm afraid Lady Maledon saw it too."

"My poor, poor Regina," Letitia moaned. "Did St. John see?"

"Apparently not," Elyse answered.

"Thank the merciful Lord for that. Oh, I could strangle Maledon myself! You're his nearest relation, Alastair, why don't you try and talk to him?"

"I'm his sixth—or fifth—cousin, I forget which, that hardly makes us close kinsmen. And I have no intention of talking to him about his personal affairs, it's none of my business. Aside from that, it would make no difference now, the damage has already been done," he said rather coldly.

Letitia considered him with some concern. Alastair was a dutiful son who met all his obligations conscientiously. He was good to his family, his servants, and his tenants. But there was some deep core of reserve in him, a certain stringent self-containment that kept him from forming attachments. Ladies pursued him relentlessly, for the Hylton family was wealthy, and aside from that he was a very handsome man. But he had never shown the slightest inclination toward marriage, for it seemed he cared nothing for any of the eligible women he'd met. *No one has touched his heart,* she thought with a hint of sadness. *It seems so difficult for him to love. I know that he cares for his family and close friends, but he keeps himself so strictly guarded.*

"Well, then, if you won't talk to him," Letitia said sarcastically, "I suppose I'll have to reconsider my plan to strangle him."

A knock on the door in the middle of the night is always ominous. But loud insistent banging and shouting at three a.m., with the cold wind howling across the moors like evil banshees, can fill even the stoutest heart with dread.

Alastair threw on his banyan and reached the door even before Fleming. When he opened it the wind flung it out of his hand to crash backward, and raked him with icy fingers. "Kincannon, come in, man, you look shattered!"

Lord Kincannon was two years younger than Alastair, only twenty-five years of age. He was handsome in a rather feminine sort of way, with a sleepy, indolent manner. But now he looked pale, his eyes wide and staring. He stalked into the sitting room and hunched over the last embers of the dying fire. "I'm—I'm freezing," he said shakily. "I need a brandy, Hylton."

By now everyone in the household had run downstairs: Letitia,

Elyse, and Reggie hurried in while Fleming and the other servants huddled at the doorway.

Alastair ordered, "Fleming, bring us some brandy. Ellen, fetch coal and stoke up this fire." Everyone took a seat and waited in silence until Fleming returned with the brandy and the maid stoked up the fire. Kincannon tossed a tumblerful of brandy back, then held out the glass for another. Collapsing into a chair, he mumbled, "That's better. I've had quite a shock."

"What's occurred?" Alastair demanded.

Kincannon looked up at him with a helpless expression. "I'm—afraid—there's been—not an accident, really—but it's—I can't explain—I don't know—"

"Get hold of yourself, Kincannon," Alastair said brusquely. "Just say it."

Kincannon took another long drink of brandy, then blurted out, "Maledon is dead."

A long shocked silence was heavy in the room. Grimly Alastair said, "You said it wasn't an accident. How did he die?"

"I don't know. I mean, he—apparently—" Kincannon swallowed hard. "Colonel Bayliss says that he suffered some sort of acute hemorrhage."

"What does that mean?" Letitia demanded. "How did this come about, how did you find him, now, in the middle of the night?"

With acute discomfort Kincannon explained, "It—I'm afraid it was Lady Jex-Blake who—who—discovered him, or—anyway, she ran up to the servants' quarters and started banging on one of the maids' doors. She was hysterical. The maid answered the door, and saw that Lady Jex-Blake was—that she had blood on her nightdress, and even—even—in her hair, and was screaming that she needed a hot bath immediately. Then the maid got hysterical, and by this time the whole house was awake, and all the women were terrified and suffering from the hysterics.

"Except for one lady, who managed to calm down Lady Jex-Blake enough to understand what had happened, that it was not Lady Jex-Blake who was—injured, it was Lord Maledon. When we went to see about him, he was already deceased."

Alastair asked, "What have you done? What arrangements have you made?"

Helplessly Kincannon said, "This only happened an hour or so ago. As you may imagine, the house is in an uproar. Colonel Bayliss is trying to calm the servants and organize them. Miss Ruskin has kept a cool head throughout, she and the housekeeper are attending the ladies. I knew, Lady Hylton, that Lady Maledon is your close friend. I've only met her two or three times. And Hylton, you are a relation of Maledon's, are you not? I just thought it would be best if I came to ask your advice on how to proceed."

Impatiently Alastair said, "You'll have to send for a doctor and the coroner, Kincannon. There must be an inquest, which I hope will be a mere formality, done quickly, hopefully tomorrow. Arrangements will have to be made to take him back to Bellegarde."

Kincannon ran a trembling hand over his forehead. "What a cursed tangle! Everyone is packing up to leave, and we don't have enough carriages, there's already a scramble among the ladies . . . that reminds me, two of Maledon's carriages are at Clayburn. At least there were two of them when I left, although Lady Jex-Blake was already demanding that she leave now, tonight, in one of them."

Letitia's eyes narrowed to glittering blue slits. "You must have taken leave of your senses, Kincannon, if you think that I'm going to allow that woman anywhere near what are now *Lady Maledon's* carriages." She turned to Alastair. "He's hopeless, Alastair, we shall have to attend to this. I'll make arrangements for a funeral wagon to take Maledon back to Bellegarde, and Elyse, Lydgate, and I will accompany him in one of the Maledon carriages. Regina wrote me that Miss Shadwell and Mrs. Purefoy were respectable ladies, I'm sure she wouldn't mind them taking the other carriage back to Surrey. You'll just have to figure out how to dispose of your other guests as best you can, Kincannon."

"But—Lady Maledon—notifying her—?" he asked uncertainly.

"This is hardly the kind of thing to send by express," Alastair rasped. "I'll leave at first light for Bellegarde. If I travel hard, I should be able to make it in four days, before Lord Maledon's body arrives."

It was a bleak dawn when Alastair left Foxden Park. The West Riding of Yorkshire was an unforgiving landscape of harsh moors and barren downs. He loved the country for shooting; at times he even enjoyed the stark solitary beauty of the countryside. But it offered him little comfort now, on his bitter errand.

Any man would dread telling a woman that she had just become a widow. But Alastair was especially apprehensive about delivering such a message to Lady Maledon. He actually didn't know her personally very well; most of what he knew of her was from his mother. Alastair had lived separately from his parents for many years now, as he had gone to Eton at the age of eight, and then to Cambridge. At twenty-one, when he graduated, he had taken a flat of his own in London, at St. James's. He and the friends he'd made at school moved in different circles from his mother and father. When his father had died two years earlier, and Alastair had inherited, he had spent more time at Hylton Hall than since he was a small child, and subsequently had grown closer to his mother. Still, he had a social life very separate from hers.

He had learned much, however, about Regina Maledon, because his mother had a particular affection for her friend, and spoke of her often. The few times Alastair had met Lady Maledon in London during the Season had confirmed his impression of her. She evidenced a particularly sweet nature and warmth that were clear to see. But Alastair had also perceived something in Lady Maledon that he thought perhaps his mother didn't, and couldn't, comprehend completely. He had had much experience with women, though he had never been in love with any of them, and he thought he understood them very well. In Lady Maledon he had seen a certain trait that he recognized: a sort of very feminine dependence on men. She had, he thought, identified herself completely with her husband, and her life had revolved around his. Such a trait in a wife was going to make his task that much more difficult.

Aside from Regina Maledon's fragility, Alastair was uneasy because he knew that he was not the type of man to be of much comfort at such a difficult time. It was not that he was completely devoid of sympathy; it was simply that he had never learned how to be manfully supportive of dependent women. He had had little patience with the women in his life who evidenced a need for him; in fact he had shunned several young women he had courted when he was younger because of what he regarded as their tendency to cling too closely to him. Even when his father had died, his mother and sister were such self-sufficient women that he hadn't been obliged to nurture them in any way. It worried him to try to conceive of how he might be any help to Regina Maledon now.

As for the children, he felt even more at a loss. He had never met St. John, and couldn't recall how old he was now. As for Valeria, he had a vague memory of an awkward, gangly little girl with a mass of dark hair and great tragic eyes. He couldn't remember how long ago he'd seen her, or where.

Alastair did feel a deep regret for Lord Maledon's untimely death. He had known Maledon all his life, and had especially seen much of him in the last two years, as they both sat in the House of Lords, and both of them were members of two of the exclusive London men's clubs, White's and Boodle's. Alastair had seen Maledon's slow decline, both physical and social, in the last couple of years. It had seemed that Maledon was half-drunk during the day and fully drunk at social events at night. It had been common knowledge a couple of years ago when Maledon had gone through a series of mistresses, and then ultimately settled on Lady Jex-Blake. This was not at all uncommon in fashionable society, whose leader was the hedonistic Prince of Wales, now prince regent. In the epicurean atmosphere of the times, it was understood that in the upper classes, most men did take mistresses; in fact, after a wife had given her husband an heir, it was barely remarked upon if she herself had love affairs. Still, Alastair had disapproved of Lord Maledon's affair with Lady Jex-Blake, first because she was a coarse, ignorant woman, and second because of Maledon's flagrantly reckless behavior. Although it was socially acceptable to be promiscuous, it was expected that well-bred men be discreet. Lord Maledon and Lady Jex-Blake had created embarrassment in more than one London drawing room and assembly. Polite Society had begun to shun him.

And now he had died far from his home, with people who cared nothing at all for him. It saddened Alastair.

But the thought of Lady Maledon saddened him even more.

Chapter Eight

❧

$\mathcal{T}$ HE BARLEY MOW FAIR WAS the most exciting event in the little village of Abbott's Roding; in fact it was usually attended by everyone in the parish. The first day was by long tradition for the servants and tenant farmers only, so the upper classes did not attend. The Bellegarde servants had returned with such glowing reports of how wonderful the fair was this year that St. John was almost beside himself on the second day, waking up at dawn and insisting that Valeria be awakened too, to get ready. "It takes you forever to put on a dress," he told her when he came bouncing into her bedroom at seven a.m.

Callie, the fourth housemaid, was engaged in building the fire in Valeria's bedroom. She flinched when St. John came in, and cast a distressed look at Valeria. She always did her duty in strict silence, for the lower housemaids were never to awaken the family before their attendants brought up their tea and toast at eight o'clock. In fact, she was not supposed to even be seen by the family.

"It's all right, Callie, you didn't awaken me, this little scoundrel did," Valeria reassured her. As Valeria had not asked her a direct question, Callie made no answer. It was an embarrassment to a lower servant to be addressed by the family, as that meant her presence was an intrusion. So she hurriedly stirred the growing fire, grabbed her bucket of kindling, curtsied, and fled.

Valeria demanded, "Whatever are you doing here, St. John? Where is Mr. Chalmers?"

"He has the day off, remember? He went to see his parents. Even if he was here, it's too early for him," he said gleefully.

"It's too early for anyone," Valeria grumbled. "Get along with you now and go bother someone else. But not Mamma."

"I'm going to find Niall." He ran to the door and looked back at her suspiciously. "You're not going back to sleep, are you?"

Valeria yawned. "I doubt if I could, thank you very much. Send Joan to me, will you?"

Soon Joan came with tea and toast. "His lordship says to tell you, miss, that he and Niall are having breakfast in the kitchen, and he begs that you will not take all morning to put on your dress," she said with amusement.

Valeria found that she too was very much looking forward to the fair. As she dressed it occurred to her that it was rather pathetic that a country fair could be such a great adventure to her. Was her life really that dull? How she longed to go to London for the Season! To go to parties, to balls, the theatre! She was very unlike other young ladies her age, for their main goal in going into society was specifically to find a husband. Valeria still was so disgusted with her stepfather that she thought she would never be able to trust a man enough to marry. *As if there's a danger of anyone asking me to marry him*, she thought dryly. *One would be obliged to make the acquaintance of a man first. I doubt that Mamma will ever want to go to London while my stepfather is there.*

"I'll wear the white with the rose embroidery and my spencer with the matching parasol," she decided. "No bonnet today. I think I'd like the topaz comb and earrings. I hope St. John will manage to restrain himself long enough for you to do my hair."

"I'll try and keep his lordship and Niall from coming to kidnap you," Joan said, "which those two will try to do if they think of it. When Mr. Chalmers isn't here they do carry on wild."

"It amazes me that Mr. Chalmers is so shy, yet he keeps those two ruffians under such good management," Valeria observed.

"He's not really shy, ma'am," Joan said. "I think it's just that he's reserved, you might say, with some people, Now, miss, I don't think the matching slippers will do for the fair. What about your buff kid half boots, and the gloves?"

"Yes, that will do very well."

By eight thirty—record time, though Valeria doubted that St. John would agree—she was dressed and ready to go. Her dress was a simple white jaconet with a lace stand-up collar worked with a rose ribbon, and rose-colored embroidery trimming the hem. The spencer, a tight-fitting short jacket, was of the same dark-pink shade as the dress trim. It had gold Maltese buttons with gold braid frogs, and was tied at the throat with gold tassels. She had a delicate Chinese parasol of exactly the same shade of deep rose, with gold tassels. Joan had arranged her hair with a wealth of disordered curls, and secured the braided bun at the back with an ornate gold-and-topaz comb; the stone, which was called sherry topaz, was a rich beige color with a hint of rose in its depths. This was one of Valeria's favorite ensembles, and she was cheered when she saw how well she looked. The color gave a pink cast to her fair complexion. She had once despaired of ever having any womanly form, for since childhood she had been thin and angular, with long legs and arms. But when she turned sixteen she had begun to fill out, and now she had soft curves with a wasp waist. She was still somewhat dissatisfied, as she was more slender than the current notion of perfect English beauties—short small women with plumply rounded figures—but at least she wasn't skin and bones and awkward anymore.

She went to her mother's room and found that Regina was still in bed, drinking tea and reading *Ackermann's Repository*. Craigie was laying out Regina's morning dress. Valeria came to sit on Regina's bed. "Oh, is that the newest, Mamma? I didn't know it had arrived."

"That's because I hid it from you," Regina replied with a smile. "That's how selfish I am. We can look at it together tonight. You're up and about very early."

"My brother woke me up practically before dawn. He and Niall have probably taken off by themselves to run all the way to the fair by now."

"Platt's got them two in hand," Craigie said sturdily. "They'll be out in the stables, I'm sure."

Valeria said, "Mamma, are you sure you don't mind if we all desert you? I shouldn't mind staying at home with you, at all."

"Nonsense, you go and have a good time, dearest," Regina said. "Craigie's here, and of course you know that Trueman would never lower himself to appear at a fair. And Mrs. Lees is staying here today, she'll be attending tomorrow, so I'm very well looked after."

Valeria gave her a kiss and said, "I must admit, I'm looking forward to it myself. It should be such fun. We'll be back this afternoon, Mamma."

The fair was set up on a field that was part of Bellegarde park, adjoining the village. Ewan drove Valeria, St. John, and Niall in the town coach. As they neared the fair, Valeria could hardly keep the boys from jumping out of the moving carriage.

Even as they drove up, a wire-walker was suspended twenty feet above the crowd, holding a slender pole and mincing his way along a thin stretched-out wire. All around were booths, stalls, exhibitions, and all kinds of entertainment. Ewan stopped the coach and a groom took the horse's heads. Opening the door and lowering the step, he laid a single finger on St. John's chest and said sternly, "My lord, where are your manners gone to? Always ladies first."

"Yes, sir," St. John said, stepping back to allow Valeria to alight. Then he and Niall burst out of the carriage as if they had been propelled. Their faces shone with excitement. Looking at each other, they said in unison, "Wire-walker," and took off at a dead run.

Valeria called, "St. John, wait!"

Ewan said comfortably, "They'll come to no harm here, miss. I'll just go hitch up under the trees, and then I'll come find you."

"Thank you, Platt," Valeria said with relief. At a more sedate pace she followed St. John and Niall. The crowd parted obediently for them, the men snatching off their hats and the women curtsying. Valeria barely noticed; it was the way of life.

The wire-walker stopped, his pole teetered up and down, and one foot slipped. Men gasped and some women screamed. St. John breathed, "He's going to fall!"

Niall, a more worldly-wise little boy, snorted, "Not hardly. He's just putting on."

Indeed the wire-walker did recover and make his way safely to the platform.

The next few hours were spent sampling all the delights of the fair. There was an illusionist who performed mystical wonders; a sword-swallower; knife-throwers; fire dancers; acrobats; tumblers; and posture-men who mimicked the expressions and gestures of the crowd to perfection. A bear wearing a green jacket with a green feather stuck behind his ear danced, with a chattering monkey on his back that passed the hat to the crowd after the dance. Valeria's favorite entertainment was three small white dogs that could count. Their trainer would ask, "What is two plus two?" and one of the dogs would bark four times, and so on.

The crowd was very merry, and Valeria saw several acquaintances. Dr. Thaxton and his wife greeted her happily and joined them in watching the sword-swallower's performance. Reverend Emmery, his wife, and their three daughters, who were Valeria's good friends, watched the knife-throwing exhibition together. She saw Ned and Royce escorting two pretty young ladies, and several of the other servants. In the crowds she kept losing St. John and Niall, as they were tearing about at top speed, but Platt easily kept up with them.

By noon Valeria was very hungry, as she had eaten only two slices of buttered toast for breakfast. There were several food stalls, and one of them was selling hot shepherd's pies. On one side of the booth had been set up tables and benches. "I'm famished," she said to Platt. "I think I'll sit here and have a bite, if you'll keep an eye on those two." Platt obligingly fetched her a pie and a cup of tea, then herded St. John and Niall over to watch the puppet show, which was Punch and Judy.

She ate about half of the pie, which was delicious, and sipped her tea contentedly. The puppet booth was nearby, so she could hear Punch's wild gleeful cackle and see his wife Judy when she began beating him for not watching The Baby, whom he had dropped several times. Naturally Punch fought back, and soundly beat his wife with his slapstick.

It's amazing that we find this sort of thing so amusing, Valeria mused. *It's quite violent. I suppose, since the puppets look nothing like real people, it's just a form of farce, and harmless . . .*

Still Valeria couldn't help but think that in truth it was anything but funny to really be struck. Every day, usually several times a day, she thought of her stepfather, with burning resentment. She had tried to pray and ask the Lord to show her how to forgive Maledon, but it seemed impossible to her. She knew that this was her own failure, not the Lord's, but somehow she couldn't find a way to lessen her simmering anger.

At morning prayers they had recited the Great Litany, and now a line and response from it came to her clearly.

From all blindness of heart; from pride, vainglory, and hypocrisy; from
  envy, hatred, and malice, and all uncharitableness,
Good Lord, deliver us.

She thought it ironic that just now The Devil came in to kill Punch, and a life-and-death fight ensued. Of course Punch would beat The Devil to death. *If only it were that easy, but is it the devil, or is it my own uncharitable heart?*

Suddenly a horse and rider came thundering right onto the fairground, scattering the crowd. Startled, Valeria stood up, seeing that it was a Maledon horse, a great black stallion named Achilles.

And then she recognized the rider, though she hadn't seen him for seven years. Valeria forgot that she had thought him old, and mean, for all she could think was that Alastair, Lord Hylton, was the most handsome man she had ever seen. He was tall and broad-shouldered, his face like a classical statue's set in marble, his seat on the horse perfect, his control of the horse magnificent. He dismounted, and stared right at her with heated recognition. His gaze was of such intensity that it almost overcame Valeria; she felt hot and cold at the same time. He started toward her, and she waited.

By stationing horses and fresh coachmen from Hylton Hall along the way, Alastair had managed to make it to Bellegarde Hall by Friday at about noon. He felt travel-grimed and weary, but he had no intention of delaying his errand to stop and clean up. When the carriage stopped at the front door of the Hall he jumped out and ran up the steps to bang on the door with the great lion's-head knocker.

Trueman answered and stared at him with a moment's loss of composure. Then he bowed deeply and said, "Lord Hylton, please come in, sir."

Alastair handed him his hat and greatcoat and said brusquely, "I must see Lady Maledon immediately."

"Yes, my lord," Trueman said. "I shall be happy to tell her ladyship that you are here. If your lordship will just come into the drawing room?"

"No, no. I would much prefer to go to her." He frowned. "Is she alone?"

"Yes, my lord."

"The children?"

"They are at the harvest fair, my lord."

"I see." Alastair bowed his head in thought. "I have some most distressing news for Lady Maledon, I'm afraid, and she should not be alone when she receives it. Is her lady's maid a close companion to her?"

Though Trueman was clearly more than a little curious, he would never put himself forward to ask any questions, so he answered evenly, "Yes, sir, Miss Platt is very close to her ladyship, and would be a comfort to her, I'm sure."

"Then bring her to me. I'll wait here." Alastair paced in the Grand Hall until the two returned. Craigie stood, waiting expectantly, and Trueman asked, "Would you like for me to take my leave, my lord?"

"No, I might as well tell you, since I have to let—what is your name?"

"Craigie, my lord."

"Since I have to let you know, Craigie, before we speak to Lady Maledon. I'm afraid a tragedy has occurred. Lord Maledon has died." Alastair spoke with a neutral voice; he had not been able to conceive any other way to deliver such dreadful news.

Craigie evidenced no shock, though her mouth tightened. Alastair noted that all color drained from the butler's impassive face.

Alastair continued, "Craigie, do you know where your mistress is just now?"

"Yes, my lord. She's having tea and reading out in the garden," she answered steadily.

"Then we must go to her." They went down the long hallway to the south side of the house. Behind them Trueman stood staring into space, unmoving.

Alastair thought that Regina Maledon presented an ethereal, almost angelic picture. She was seated at a linen-covered table holding a silver tea service, dressed in pale blue with a white shawl. The table was in a grove of larch trees, and a shaft of sunlight filtering through the deep verdant shade lit her head, which was bent over a book. She looked up, and Alastair was again struck by her glowing beauty; he had forgotten what an exquisite woman she was.

Her eyes widened, and then she closed them for a moment, as if in pain. She rose and came to meet them. "Lord Hylton," she said in a whisper.

He bowed, and spoke in a much gentler tone than before. "Lady Maledon, I'm afraid that I am the bearer of very bad tidings. Lord Maledon fell ill, gravely ill, and last Monday night he passed away."

She stared at him, her eyes uncomprehending. He stared back at her helplessly. With one slender white hand she made a curiously awkward, fumbling gesture. Craigie reached out to her. At that moment her eyes rolled up and she crumpled.

Alastair picked her up and held her securely in his arms. "Take me to her bedchamber," he ordered Craigie.

Without a word they returned to the house and upstairs to Regina's bedroom. With infinite tenderness Alastair laid her on the bed. Her face was as white as the linens beneath her, and her breathing was very shallow.

"How may I be of assistance?" he asked Craigie in a guttural voice.

"Tell Trueman to send Mrs. Lees," she answered tightly, "and then, my lord, if you will be so good as to go to the fair and bring Miss Segrave and his lordship home. Most all of the servants are at the fair, you see."

"I'll take care of it," he assured her.

He found Trueman, now pacing in an aimless sort of way, still in the Great Hall. "Are you quite all right, Trueman?" he asked.

Trueman was so shocked at this solicitation that he gathered his scattered wits. "Yes, my lord, I'm quite well, I beg your lordship's pardon," he answered stiffly.

"Craigie asked if you would find Mrs. Lees and send her to Lady Maledon's bedchamber to help her, as her ladyship is ill." Without waiting for the butler's reply Alastair went out to the stables. He saw that two grooms were assisting his coachman with his horses and carriage. "We need to saddle up a couple of horses. I need to ride to the fair and find Miss Segrave and Lord Stamborne, and I'll need one of you to accompany me." It gave Alastair a small chill to realize that now St. John was actually Lord Maledon. In some odd way this made the tragedy of Maledon's death more real to him than anything else.

Alastair chose a great fiery stallion and began to saddle him, while a young fresh-faced groom saddled a chestnut gelding in the next stall. Thoughtfully Alastair asked, "How old is Lord—Lord Stamborne now?"

"His lordship is six years, my lord."

"And Miss Segrave?"

The groom gave him an odd look. "Miss turned eighteen a few month ago."

"Eighteen?" Alastair was surprised. He had that waif-faced child still in mind.

When they were saddled Alastair said, "Lead on. And we're in a hurry."

The groom, who was Timothy, had already heard the news from Lord Hylton's coachman, and he took out across the park at a dead gallop, followed closely by Alastair. When they reached the fairground Timothy stopped and began to dismount to search, but Lord Hylton flashed by him and galloped right into the crowd, pulling the horse to a rearing stop right in the middle of the grounds.

As if he were being directed, Alastair immediately saw Valeria, and knew her. He was confused and startled for long moments. She had the same wealth of lush dark hair, the same wide dark liquid eyes, the graceful raven's-wing eyebrows on a smooth white brow. But this was no coltish child; she was a tall, willowy vision, alluring and mysterious. She looked directly into his eyes, and he saw the glimmer of recognition. He was relieved, because it made him somewhat less uncomfortable, and also because he thought that introductions at this time would be ludicrous.

He dismounted; she watched him, her gaze direct and unwavering, as he came to her. She curtsied gracefully. "Good afternoon, Lord Hylton," she said in an attractive, throaty voice.

"I'm so glad that you recognize me, Miss Segrave," he said, bowing. "It makes my task a little easier. I know it's unorthodox, but would you mind sitting down with me, please?" He didn't want to take the risk of another lady's fainting dead away at the news, but then he somehow knew that Valeria Segrave would do no such thing. The contrast between her and her mother was apparent, and it had nothing to do with their looks. Alastair could see strength, even fortitude, in Valeria's countenance. He was reminded of Lord Segrave in the vigor of his prime.

Without a word Valeria sat down on the bench and watched him. He sat close to her but didn't touch her. "I've been to Bellegarde and have spoken to your mother. I have very bad news for you and Lord Stamborne."

He hesitated. Her unfathomable expression didn't change. "Please continue," she said quietly.

"Lord Maledon fell very ill, and he died Monday night."

As had her mother, Valeria stared at him for long moments, but there was complete comprehension in her eyes. Then her face darkened with pain, and she said what was, to Alastair, a very odd thing. It was the first line of the Great Litany.

In a ragged voice she whispered, "O God the Father of heaven: have mercy on us miserable sinners..."

PART II

Chapter Nine

❧

$\mathcal{V}$ALERIA'S FIRST SENSATION AT THE NEWS of her stepfather's death was sickening remorse. Her stepfather had died without her forgiveness. She knew very well that this would have had no effect on the state of his soul, but that she had withheld it was a stain upon hers. To forgive him now, simply because she was sorry that he had died, would be no act of Christian charity. It was too late. Bitterly she thought that regret must be one of the cruelest results of sin.

But she realized that she would have to sort out her own troubled heart later. Just now she must be mindful only of her mother and her brother.

Lord Hylton was watching her with a sort of detached curiosity, she thought. With an effort she sat up perfectly straight and regained her composure. "How did my mother receive this?" she asked.

He grimaced. "Not well at all, I'm afraid, Miss Segrave. She went into a deep swoon. Her lady's maid is attending her."

Valeria nodded. "Craigie can help her." She looked around, trying to gather her thoughts. It occurred to her how very strange the scene felt. She was surrounded by people smiling and laughing, the antics of the performers, the high endless cackle of Punch, the catcalls and cheers from the puppet show audience. For a moment she felt that she and Lord Hylton were not really there, they were alone in some dark place where tragedy filled the air rather than laughter.

She saw Timothy holding his and Lord Hylton's horses, and the sight of his dismay as the young groom glanced at her helped her to focus. "Before I tell my brother, please relate to me the circumstances of my stepfather's death," she said.

Lord Hylton seemed to be groping for words, so Valeria went on evenly, "I know I'm young and that men think young women are so dainty and excitable that they shouldn't be exposed to anything unsavory. But I assure you, sir, that I already know how my stepfather was living, and I won't be overcome with shock to hear how he died."

After a moment Alastair said, "Yes, I can see that, Miss Segrave." He went on to relate to her the events of the night of Lord Maledon's death. He told her in a clinical manner that Lady Jex-Blake had discovered the body, leaving out the details of the lurid scene. "I was obliged to leave before we got word of the doctor's report, so my knowledge of the exact cause of death is incomplete."

"I see. Do I understand that you and Lady Hylton made the decisions, and the arrangements, and not Lord Kincannon?"

"I am a kinsman. I felt it was my duty, and my mother is so close to your mother that she felt it was incumbent upon her to offer her help in Lady Maledon's stead."

"This is a great comfort to me and my family," Valeria said sincerely. "What arrangements have been made? Where is my stepfather now?"

"An inquest was necessary, of course, but my mother and Kincannon were sure they could expedite that. Lord Maledon is returning here in a funeral wagon, and my mother and my sister and brother-in-law are accompanying the body. It is my hope that they will be here sometime tomorrow, but I can't be sure of it. We didn't want to post any communications to Bellegarde, for fear that I might be delayed, and it would have been disastrous for the news to reach your mother in such a manner. Also, my mother wouldn't have tried to leave messages at the coaching inns along the way, because I traveled faster than the post."

Valeria's eyes widened. "You—you said that Lord Maledon died on Monday? And you traveled that great distance in three and a half days? That must have been a very difficult journey, sir. I cannot adequately express my appreciation for your thoughtfulness."

"As I said, it is my duty," he said formally.

Valeria was slightly taken aback. Lord Hylton had an air of assurance and authority, which was reassuring. But he couldn't be said to have a comforting presence. His manner and expression were dispassionate. The direct gaze of his unusual gray-blue eyes was cool and distant. His reserve was somewhat chilly.

With dignity she responded, "Still, I thank you for your efforts, sir. I must give Timothy some instructions, then. If you would be so kind, I'll ask that you speak to our coachman, Platt. I'll take St. John to the carriage and tell him there."

"I'm happy to be of any service, Miss Segrave."

They went to speak to the groom. Valeria asked, "Do you know what's occurred, Timothy?"

"Yes, miss, his lordship's coachman told us that the earl has died."

"Yes. I'd like for you to find Dr. Thaxton and ask him if he can attend Lady Maledon as soon as possible. Then find Reverend Emmery and ask him if he can come to Bellegarde to conduct our evening prayers. I saw both families here earlier today, but if you cannot find them here at the fair, go on into the village to give them the messages."

"Yes, ma'am," he replied, and led the two horses to the nearby grove of trees to hitch them.

Valeria said, "Lord Hylton, my brother is over there, at the puppet show, with his friend Niall, who is Platt's son. I'll tell my brother to come with me to the carriage. Meanwhile, please tell Platt about

Lord Maledon, and tell him I'd like for Ned and Royce to accompany us back to Bellegarde."

Valeria found it odd that the time since she'd first seen Lord Hylton ride up had been so short that the puppet show was still going on. Again she had that peculiar feeling of time and place being somehow out of joint. She went to St. John, who was seated on the ground with a crowd of noisy children in front of the brightly colored booth. Reaching down, she took his hand and said, "St. John, I need you to come with me, please."

"But, Veri, Punch is only now—" His bright expression faded when he saw her face and he nodded and rose, still holding her hand.

"Niall, come along," she said, and the boy followed them to where Ewan was standing behind the crowd of children. "Platt, this is Lord Hylton, he needs to speak to you. St. John and I will be in the carriage, waiting."

Ewan said without expression, "Yes, miss."

Valeria and St. John walked to the carriage in silence. With a feeling of bittersweet poignancy Valeria watched as St. John opened the carriage door, pulled down the steps, and then stood back for her to get in. He sat across from her and stared at her, his expression a mixture of dread and suspense. Valeria took his hand again. "St. John, I'm so sorry, but I have very bad news. Your father fell ill while he was in Yorkshire, and it was quite sudden. On Monday night he passed away."

His fawn-brown eyes darkened, and he dropped his head. Almost inaudibly he said, "My father is dead?"

"Yes, dearest, he is."

"Does our mother know?"

"Yes, that gentleman with me was Lord Hylton. He traveled down from Yorkshire, and he first went to Bellegarde to speak to Mamma, and then came here to let us know."

He nodded slightly. "We should go home now, to Mamma."

The desolation in his child's voice deeply wounded Valeria, but she knew that she must now, of all times, disguise her distress. She must, she *must* be strong for her mother and St. John.

In only a few moments Ewan and Niall returned with Lord Hylton, and Ned and Royce followed them. Ewan began un-hitching the traces while Ned and Royce took their usual station on the footboard. It struck Valeria how incongruous they looked, standing at the rear of the fine carriage in their everyday clothing of breeches and top boots and brown coats, instead of their grand livery.

Lord Hylton came to the door of the carriage, and Valeria real-ized she must perform introductions. "Lord Hylton, may I present my brother St. John, Lord Stam—" She stopped abruptly with an unpleasant shock.

Though he was grave, Alastair now spoke with an ease that sur-prised Valeria. Bowing slightly, he said, "I am a kinsman of yours, sir. I am Alastair, Lord Hylton. I'm glad to finally have the pleasure of making your acquaintance, Cousin, though I am deeply sorry it is under such tragic circumstances."

"Thank you, sir," St. John said woodenly. "I'm St. John." He hadn't seemed to notice Valeria's sudden discomfort.

"And you may call me Alastair." He turned to Valeria and said softly, "Miss Segrave, you seem to have everything well in hand. Is it your wish that I return to Bellegarde? I know this is an extremely difficult time for your family, and I would be most happy to stay at the inn in the village so as not to impose upon you and your mother."

Valeria considered this. Though she was reluctant to ask favors from him, in a way his detachment was a sort of relief to her, es-pecially since he seemed to have no expectation that she should be grief-stricken. Also, though she felt confident that she could take care of her brother and her mother, and even take charge of the household, she was very unsure of all the things that must be done in the aftermath of the earl's death. Finally she answered, "Sir, it would be a very great service to me and my mother if you would consent to stay at Bellegarde for now. I know I will need your assistance, and advice. While my mother is unwell, it will necessarily fall to me to deal with matters, many of which I'm sure I am not qualified to manage."

"Somehow I doubt that," he said gravely. "But I will help you in any way that I can, Miss Segrave. It will be my honor."

⸎

Craigie told Valeria and St. John, "You mother is ill and weak, but she insisted she wanted to see you as soon as you arrived."

They went into Regina's bedchamber. All the heavy velvet draperies were closed, and the room was as dark as midnight of the new moon. A single candle burned in a far corner. Regina was lying in bed with her golden hair spread about her on the pillow. A cloth lay over her eyes. When Valeria and St. John reached her bedside she removed it and looked up at them with tortured red-rimmed eyes. Weakly she whispered, "Oh, my darlings, I'm so very sorry I'm not feeling well . . . I'll try to get up later, to take care of you . . ."

"No, Mamma," Valeria said gently but firmly. "You must rest. I am quite well, and St. John is being very strong. Craigie and Platt and Niall and I will take care of him, you know. And Lord Hylton is here, he has consented to stay until Lady Hylton arrives. All will be well."

"Thank the gracious Lord for His loving-kindness," Regina murmured. "St. John, I promise you that I will be fine by tomorrow, my love."

"Yes, Mamma," he said obediently. "Veri is sending Dr. Thaxton to you, and you know he always makes you feel better. Don't worry about me, just get well."

Fresh tears welled up in Regina's eyes, and her face twisted with pain. Valeria soaked the cloth in the basin of cool water at the bedside and tenderly replaced it over Regina's eyes. "Rest now, and don't worry yourself about us, Mamma."

They slipped out of the room and Craigie returned to attend Regina. Valeria said, "St. John, why don't we go to my bedchamber and talk?"

"All right, Veri," he said in a subdued voice.

They sat down close together on Valeria's recamier. "St. John, I know how hard this is for you," she said quietly. "You know, my own father died when I was even younger than you are now. I remember very well how sad I was, and how lost I felt."

He looked down and picked at his trousers. In a small voice he asked, "You loved your father a lot, didn't you, Veri?"

"Yes, I did."

He nodded. "I wish...I wish...I feel bad, because I...p'raps I should be crying, shouldn't I?"

Suddenly Valeria knew exactly what was most troubling to St. John. It wasn't because he loved Maledon so much that he was devastated; it was because he didn't feel a terrible sense of loss for the father he'd barely known. She put her arms around his shoulders and pulled him close. As St. John had gotten older, he had, as boys do, come to disdain hugs and kisses, but now he clung to her and buried his face in her shoulder. "St. John, your father loved you so very much. When you were born, he said it was the happiest day of his life, and that you were the very best thing that had ever happened to him. And you loved him, St. John. Don't think any of this is your fault, or that you failed your father in some way. You're a good son, and he was proud of you."

And finally St. John cried.

After a time his tears dried up and he seemed to feel better. "Veri, since Mr. Chalmers isn't here, could I please stay with you?" he pleaded.

Valeria chided herself for not having thought to send for St. John's tutor. She knew that Gordon Chalmers was a sort of anchor of security for St. John, much as Craigie had been for her when she was a child. "Of course you may," she answered. "I'm afraid there is much dull business to be attended to, however, and you may find it tiresome. I believe I'll send for Mr. Chalmers, and later you and he and Niall can join me for supper."

St. John brightened somewhat. "That would be jolly. No, I don't mean jolly, of course..."

"It's all right, St. John. I know what you meant. Now, we'd better go on downstairs and attend to poor Lord Hylton, who's probably wondering what to do with himself."

"And will you tell him what to do with himself, Veri?" St. John asked with innocent childish curiosity.

"I rather doubt that anyone tells Lord Hylton what to do," she said dryly.

They went downstairs and found Alastair in the morning room, as the drawing room was not opened and aired. Trueman stood by the sideboard that held the spiritous liquors, and since Lord Hylton hadn't wished to have a drink, Trueman seemed at a loss for what to do.

Valeria said briskly, "Trueman, assemble the servants here, I need to speak to them."

"But, miss, many of them are still at the fair," he said hesitantly.

"Then bring whoever is here," Valeria said shortly. Still the butler looked slightly confused. It raised Valeria's ire when Trueman seemed to look to Lord Hylton for instruction, but she hid her resentment and continued calmly, "Trueman, I know that we've all sustained a great shock, and I know that the house is in confusion because of that, and the fair. But just now I need to speak to the servants who are here, and then when the others return, you and Mrs. Lees may explain to them."

"Yes, miss," he finally said, and left.

Alastair commented, "What a proper butler he is, to be sure. I always think that such men have icy water rather than blood in their veins."

Valeria sighed. "Yes, and he's been with the earls of Maledon since he was ten years old. He started out as a hall boy, and by the time he was twenty-eight he was the butler. In some ways I think this will be almost as hard on the longtime servants such as Trueman as it will be on the family."

St. John asked Alastair, "Sir, you said you were my cousin, and so you must be my father's cousin too. Were you friends with him?"

Alastair considered the question for long moments before answering carefully, "I knew your father well, I should say, because our two families have been close for a long time, and also because we sat in the House of Lords together, and had many meetings. But your father was somewhat older than I, and so we had different people for friends."

St. John seemed satisfied at this, and Valeria appreciated the discreet wisdom Alastair showed in answering the thorny question.

Trueman returned with Mrs. Lees, Mrs. Banyard, Ned, Royce, and Joan. The other servants were still at the fair. They all curtsied and bowed respectfully.

Valeria said, "I assume you all know by now that Lord Maledon has died. It is particularly difficult, because the house is all at a standstill since many of the servants are not in attendance. But my mother and I understand this, and we know that everyone will do their very best to set things aright in these difficult coming days.

"Lord Hylton has kindly consented to stay here at Bellegarde to assist us. He has had a long, difficult journey here from the north country, and his man didn't travel with him. Ned, you will attend Lord Hylton and act as his valet. I assume, Lord Hylton, that this is agreeable to you?"

"Yes, Miss Segrave, I'm grateful for your consideration." To Ned he said, "Collect my trunk from my carriage, and also see to my coachman's accommodations."

"Yes, my lord," Ned said, and hurried out.

Valeria said, "Royce, do you know the Chalmers farm?"

The handsome young footman replied sturdily, "Yes, miss, just southwest of the village."

"I want you to take a message to Mr. Chalmers as to what has occurred, and ask him to return to Bellegarde as soon as possible. I'm sure it will relieve my mother's mind to know that he is here. You may go."

Next Valeria turned to the cook, who looked bewildered, as if she were in shock. "Mrs. Banyard, I know that tonight we were expecting only a simple cold collation for supper, and that is still perfectly acceptable. However, we are hoping that tomorrow—" She glanced cautiously at St. John. He looked subdued, but not stricken. She continued, "Tomorrow we hope that Lord Maledon will arrive, accompanied by Lady Hylton and Lord and Lady Lydgate. I intend to ask them to stay here at Bellegarde for a few days. I realize this will put a strain on you, to make arrangements for guests just now, but do what you can to assure that we have foodstuffs and supplies. In the morning you may submit menus for two days only, and we will go on from there."

"Ye-yes, miss," she said.

"Mrs. Lees, guest rooms must be aired and ready, and also I know you will assist Mrs. Banyard and the kitchen staff."

"Yes, Miss Segrave," Mrs. Lees said. "Don't worry, miss, we'll have everything readied and well in hand by tomorrow."

"Thank you. That will be all, Mrs. Lees, Mrs. Banyard. Joan, I shall need to speak to you later about some other arrangements that must be made, but for now just help Mrs. Lees."

"Yes, ma'am," she said. The three ladies left, leaving only Trueman.

Now Valeria fell into a brown study, her brow furrowed. After long moments she glanced at Alastair uncertainly. Smoothly he said, "It's very difficult to think of all of the things that must be done at times like this, so may I assist you with some advice, Miss Segrave?"

Gratefully she replied, "Yes, thank you, sir."

"Messages must be sent to the solicitor, the bank, and to Lord Maledon's London physician."

Valeria nodded. "Truman, I believe all of the papers and records are in the earl's study?"

Reluctantly Trueman replied, "Yes, miss. They are in a locked drawer in his desk."

"And you have the key, I presume?"

"Yes, miss."

"Well then," Valeria said evenly, "please come with me to unlock the drawer so that I can make these arrangements."

A very faint look of stubbornness came over Trueman's face. "I beg your pardon, Miss Segrave, but I'm not certain that would be perfectly proper."

Valeria frowned darkly. "And why not, may I ask? These things must be done, and immediately."

"Oh, yes, I'm aware of that, miss," he said with a supercilious air that made Valeria want to shout at him. "But this situation has put me—and, if I may be so bold, you, miss—in what might be called a delicate situation. It seems to me that it is her ladyship who must attend to these matters."

"But Lady Maledon is indisposed, and quite unable to attend to them right now," Valeria said with a steely note in her voice. "I am perfectly capable of representing her."

"But you do not, you cannot, represent the earl, ma'am," Trueman said with a stony face.

"But Trueman," St. John said in a small voice, and the adults were startled, for they had all but forgotten the forlorn figure huddled in the corner of a sofa. "I am the Earl of Maledon now, am I not?"

Trueman's eyes widened. He was speechless at first, and then he managed to answer, "Yes, my lord, that is true."

"Then I want Veri to help me," he said sadly. "For I don't know what to do, and my mamma is ill, and Veri is clever and knows things. I think you should let her have the papers."

Trueman, after long moments, bowed deeply. "Yes, my lord. Miss Segrave, I will show you where the records are kept."

Valeria gave St. John a small smile. "Thank you, my lord."

He managed to smile back, and said their little private pun. "Very welcome, Veri."

Trueman said, "Miss Segrave, the earl's study is not aired. With your permission, first I'll open it up and have a fire built so that you will be more comfortable."

"Very well. Right now I think we'd all like some tea."

Valeria rose from her chair and went to stare out the window. Naturally Alastair couldn't remain seated while a lady was standing, so he stood up. St. John looked quizzically at him, and Alastair winked and motioned for him to stand. Comprehension, and amusement, came over his face, and he jumped up.

Valeria turned around and regarded them with surprise. "Where are you going?"

St. John said, "Gentlemen don't sit while a lady is standing."

Valeria looked disconcerted. "Oh, yes. Of course. Please, Lord Hylton, do keep to your chair, it's really quite all right. St. John, sit down, silly." She started pacing.

St. John sat back down, but Alastair said, "Miss Segrave, it's impossible for me to lounge in a chair while a lady is standing up. It's simply not done."

"But I must think," she argued.

"Can you not think while sitting down?"

"Of course I can think while sitting down," she retorted, and with great precision sat on the edge of a chair, then gestured sarcastically toward Alastair's chair. "Don't ladies ever stand up in your presence, my lord?"

"Of course, in company, ladies rise and walk about the room as they wish. But when a gentleman is engaged in conversation with one lady, and she suddenly hops up and starts prowling around the room like a caged tiger, then the gentleman must stand too."

"I did not hop, and I was not prowling," Valeria retorted. She saw the amusement on St. John's face, and her temper subsided. "Well, perhaps I was prowling, but I most certainly did not hop, and don't you dare tell Craigie, St. John."

"I won't," he promised. "But I must tell Niall, for you were funny, Veri."

Trueman returned and said, "Tea will be up in a few minutes, Miss Segrave, and the study will be warmed soon."

Valeria nodded. "Thank you, Trueman. Now, here is what must be done. Send one of the maids to the village, to Mrs. Barnard's shop, and instruct her to make at least forty black armbands. We'll also need a quantity of black ribbon for trim.

"I intend to send Joan and Royce to London. Joan will go to our dressmaker and order mourning clothes for me and my mother. Royce will take the messages to the persons we spoke of before. Have them prepare to leave quickly, as soon as I get the information and write the letters."

"Miss Segrave, again, if I may advise you," Alastair said quietly, "it is a strict protocol that His Majesty, or in this case the prince regent, be advised immediately when a peer of the realm dies. A letter of notice should be sent to his chamberlain at St. James's."

"I was unaware," Valeria said thoughtfully. "I assume there is a certain form to be followed in this notice?"

"Yes, there is. If you wish, as a kinsman of the earl, it would be perfectly proper for me to write it."

"Thank you, Lord Hylton, that would be of immense help." Valeria again addressed Trueman. "I hope that Joan and Royce may leave in an hour. They will need money. Where are the household funds?"

Trueman's mouth tightened. "I beg your pardon, miss, do you mean to just hand cash over to two lower servants?"

Valeria tried to keep the irritation out of her tone, but she wasn't quite successful. "That is exactly what I mean to do, and I think that the reasons for it are perfectly obvious. I must insist that you stop questioning every order that I give, Trueman."

"Yes, miss," he said stiffly, his mouth curling slightly. "The safe-box with the household moneys is also in his lordship's study."

Valeria continued, "Then I shall need access to it. That will be all for now."

Trueman went out into the hall but immediately returned and announced, "Mr. Chalmers, Miss Segrave."

The tutor came into the drawing room and bowed deeply. Valeria received him graciously and performed the necessary introductions. St. John said, "I'm sorry you lost your holiday, Mr. Chalmers."

"I was thinking of that, my lord, and I suggest that we might continue my holiday together. And with Niall, of course. Perhaps we might visit the stables, and have a riding lesson?" he said kindly.

Hesitantly St. John asked, "Could we, Veri? Would it be all right, do you think?"

"I think that is a very good idea, and yes, St. John, it is all right," she said, smiling. "Thank you, Mr. Chalmers."

"Yes, yes, of course, Miss Segrave, anything I can do for—to help," he stammered.

"Your presence here is a very welcome help, Mr. Chalmers," she said warmly. "Especially now I'm glad, not only for St. John, but for my mother and myself too."

He blushed so furiously that his entire thin face turned scarlet. He seemed unable to speak, but fortunately for him St. John, oblivious, came to his rescue. "May we go now, Mr. Chalmers? Tea's coming, I don't suppose you would have to wait and have tea, would you?"

"No, I don't suppose so," he answered in a calmer fashion. "Miss Segrave, my lord," he said, and he and St. John took their leave. While they were walking out St. John reached up and took his hand.

Alastair noted how flustered Chalmers became when he spoke to Valeria, a telltale sign that wasn't evident when he addressed St. John or himself. Curiously he watched Valeria to observe if she, as so many beautiful young women would, deliberately tried to charm the smitten young man. To his surprise he thought that she hadn't the slightest notion of her effect on Chalmers. Her manner of address to the tutor seemed no different from her normal mode of conversing. This seeming lack of vanity on Valeria's part intrigued Alastair.

In fact, all of this long extraordinary day Alastair found himself surprised, bemused, and perplexed by Valeria Segrave. He had never met a woman quite like her. In his experience he had found fashionable young ladies frivolous and shallow, thinking only of dresses and balls and catching a husband. He had never seen a young woman so forceful, so confident, so capable of managing such a complex, disordered, even sordid affair as Lord Maledon's death was.

He watched as she marshaled and organized the entire household. Trueman, it seemed, was at last put in his proper place, and gave Valeria the keys to the earl's desk. Together Alastair and Valeria wrote the messages to be sent to London. Valeria instructed Joan about the dressmaker, giving her several patterns for mourning clothes from *Ackermann's Repository* and *La Belle Assemblée*. Moneys were handed out to the footman and maid, and they left for London in good order.

Alastair stayed with Valeria while she met with the steward, Mr. Wheeler, and found out about the earl's hatchment, which was promptly recovered from the gun room and placed on the door. She instructed the gardeners to make mourning wreaths for the south entrance and the windows on the lower floor. It amazed Alastair that she had the presence of mind to think of all of these details.

By nine o'clock that night, Alastair found that he was exhausted. He and Valeria were alone, now in the drawing room. The night was cool and damp, and he watched her as she sat, straight and erect, in a chair near the fire. She was still wearing her short-sleeved white dress, and she pulled her shawl closer about her shoulders. Alastair was sitting across from her, watching the firelight play on her face. Quietly he said, "Miss Segrave, I must tell you that I have great admiration for the way you've managed this extremely distressing situation so well."

"Do you?" she said blankly. "It seems to me that I've been scurrying about like a mouse in a maze."

The thought came into Alastair's mind that there was nothing at all mousy about Valeria, but he merely said, "Not at all. You've been organized, efficient, and, I might add, very effective, especially with the servants." Valeria had encountered the same passive resistance from the steward, George Wheeler, that she had experienced with Trueman. The agent was more courteous, but he was obviously reluctant to discuss any part of the Maledon estate with Valeria.

Impatiently she said, "It is so difficult, so needlessly difficult! I suppose it's because they are so accustomed to an earl's rank, and I'm only the daughter of a mere baron!"

Alastair's mouth twitched as she looked up at him, aghast. "Oh, dear! I—you're—I didn't mean—"

"It is true, I'm a mere baron," he said carelessly. "But I don't think that's the problem here. You do see that the servants and employees are confused, and with some reason."

She sighed. "Yes, I know, and I suppose it is understandable. I am only the late earl's stepdaughter, of no blood relation. But until my mother is well enough to manage, I can see no alternative other than that I must take charge."

"As I've said, you do that very well," Alastair said.

She eyed him with dry amusement. "What you mean is that I'm a bossy female."

He replied, "No, what I mean is that you are intelligent and steady."

"Intelligent and steady," Valeria repeated. "Hmm. That makes me sound like an aged governess."

"Miss Segrave," Alastair said dryly, "I assure you, there is nothing whatsoever about you that would ever remind anyone of a governess."

Chapter Ten

🌿

THE FOURTH EARL OF MALEDON returned home for the last time on September fourteenth, 1811. It was an incongruously cheerful day, with a high golden sun set in a cloudless pale-blue sky. The funeral wagon, a black low cart completely enclosed in glass, stopped in the courtyard of Bellegarde Hall precisely between the looming statue of Perseus and Andromeda and the entrance to the Great Hall.

Valeria, Alastair, and St. John came out to meet the carriage accompanying Lord Maledon's hearse. Lady Hylton alighted and without a word went to kiss and embrace Valeria. Valeria clung to her, and suddenly felt overwhelming relief. Her godmother was a decisive, commanding woman and Valeria knew that Lady Hylton would shoulder much of the terrible burden she had felt.

St. John bowed, and Lady Hylton looked pleased. "Child, how much you have grown since last I saw you! Come here. Though I know very well you'll hate it I shall kiss you anyway."

"I won't hate it, Lady Hylton," he said shyly, and submitted to her embrace willingly.

Valeria had met Alastair's sister, Lady Lydgate, several times since her mother married Lord Maledon, and she had met Lord Lydgate twice. She curtsied, and Elyse quickly embraced her and said,

"None of that, silly. We're practically sisters. Godsisters, anyway. You must call me Elyse, Valeria."

As Valeria had known she would, Lady Hylton immediately took charge. "Let's go inside. I've already instructed the coachmen."

Trueman was waiting for them at the door. Lady Hylton said, "Trueman, I don't wish to sit in that dreary drawing room, take us to the morning room."

The footmen took hats, coats, bonnets, and walking sticks, and Trueman conducted them all into the morning room. Lady Hylton collapsed into an overstuffed wing chair. Valeria saw that she looked weary, the faint age lines on her face seeming more prominent. But her blue eyes were still as sharp and shrewd as ever.

"Will you take some refreshment, ma'am?" Valeria asked. "We've kept the kettle on for tea all day, anticipating that you'd be fatigued when you arrived."

"I don't want tea, I want a glass of sherry," Lady Hylton responded. "And Trueman, our meals on the road have been so haphazard, I simply can't wait for dinner. Have Mrs. Banyard prepare us a light luncheon."

The footmen served, and after taking a sip of sherry, Lady Hylton resumed the inevitable required ladylike position, sitting up straight on the edge of the seat without her back touching the chair. "Tell me about Regina first," she demanded.

Valeria said, "She took the news very ill indeed, ma'am. She had to take to her bed immediately. Dr. Thaxton has been attending her, and he says that she's very weak, and that she's having a great deal of trouble taking nourishment. She did come down for luncheon, but ate little. She's resting now."

Lady Hylton said, "I feared it would be so. I'll see her as soon as she's awake. Alastair, tell me everything that has been done, who has been notified, what news."

"Yesterday messages were sent to London, and late last night we received express messages from Maledon's solicitor, banker, and physician that they are on the way; in fact, I would imagine that they may have already arrived," Alastair answered. "Also Lord Yarmouth sent to tell us that he will arrive tomorrow." Lord Yarmouth was the prince regent's vice chamberlain.

"Excellent. This has been such a hurried, chaotic affair that I can scarcely believe how you've managed. I saw that the hatchment has been placed, the funeral wreaths, the armbands," Lady Hylton said.

"I cannot take credit for such excellent management, ma'am," Alastair said. "Miss Segrave has done everything, I have scarcely been allowed to be of use at all."

"Is that so? Well done, Valeria," Lady Hylton said approvingly.

"Thank you, ma'am," she said with pleasure.

Lady Hylton's sharp gaze rested on St. John, who sat on the sofa close to Valeria. He was attentive, but listless. In a gentler tone she said, "St. John, I know this is very hard for you, so I want to tell you a few things. First, your mother will be all right, you know. You mustn't worry about her, we'll take very good care of her and in a day or two she'll be herself again."

He nodded. "She told me today that she's already feeling better than yesterday. She said she's sure she'll be able to come down to dinner, and that I might have dinner with you tonight."

"Good. Now, about your father. We're going to help your mother—and your sister—take care of everything, so you needn't worry about that either."

He sighed, too deeply for a small boy. "Thank you, ma'am."

In a crisper tone Lady Hylton continued, "Just now we're going to be discussing plans that I'm sure you'll find boring. Of course, St. John, you may stay with us. But I think that you'd much rather be out and about with your friend Niall, causing all sorts of trouble for Mr. Chalmers. So if you wish, you may be excused."

He looked up at Valeria. "Would it be all right, Veri? Should I stay?"

"No, dearest, there is no need," she answered kindly. "We can talk later."

Eagerly now he jumped up, made a courtly bow, and ran out. Lady Hylton watched him thoughtfully. "He seems to be holding up very well. I have to admit that I'm most pleasantly surprised. I'm proud of both you and St. John, Valeria."

Alastair said, "You must tell us about the doctor's report, and the inquest, Mother." He saw his brother-in-law casting doubtful glances at Valeria, and continued evenly, "From what little I heard from Kincannon that night I'm sure this will be very hard to hear, Miss Segrave. I'm not certain that it's necessary that you be privy to all the details."

Stiffly Valeria said, "Again, Lord Hylton, I feel that I am in the position of representing my mother. Until she's better I must assume all of her responsibilities."

"Quite right," Lady Hylton said. "Obviously Valeria is more capable than is Regina just now. And somehow I doubt that Valeria is going to have the vapors, even though the news is grim. The doctor's report basically said that Maledon must have been suffering from some disease of the blood, but he had no way of ascertaining what the disease might have been. Apparently Maledon died from severe hemorrhage, the onset of which was sudden and acute. The coroner agreed with his finding, as sketchy as it was, and ruled it 'death from natural causes.' And his comment to me was that it was ironic, because it seemed most unnatural to him."

This was met with a grim silence that lasted long moments; then Lady Hylton continued, "And there is more bad news, Valeria. It's impossible that Maledon lie in state. This is partly because his body was already so adversely affected by disease, and partly because he was such a long distance from here when he died. It's my decided opinion that the funeral should be held as soon as possible."

Valeria said with distress, "Oh, my poor mother will take this so hard. This—this entire thing is like some awful nightmare to her already."

In a hard voice Lady Hylton said, "It certainly is, and it is all Maledon's fault. Don't look at me like that, Reggie, I'm not such a fool as to think I'll be cursed for speaking ill of the dead. I have every intention of making Lady Maledon understand that all of this happened the way it did only as a result of decisions that Lord Maledon made, and no one on this earth could have helped him, only Almighty God."

Valeria hoped with all her heart that her mother would come to see these hard truths. She knew that if anyone could help Regina to see them, Lady Hylton could. "Oh, Lady Hylton, I'm so glad you've come," she said quietly.

"As am I, Valeria," she said. "Now, we must talk about making arrangements for the funeral . . ."

Valeria listened with only half her mind, for she was much distracted by Lord Hylton's direct gaze. He seemed to study her often, and she was having difficulty understanding why. His manner and air were so distant and severe that she thought he must be continually finding fault with her. He had seemed irritated before, when he had remarked that he had been of little use here. Could her determination not to rely on him have offended him? Did he feel that only a man should be in charge? It did seem that when she had spoken so warmly of how glad she was that Lady Hylton had arrived, his eyes had held some sort of reproof.

He's a complete stranger to me, she thought crossly. *What did he expect? That I would just assume that since he's a man, he would know better than I how to conduct my family's private affairs? I think not!*

Valeria made herself pay strict attention to what Lady Hylton was saying. She determined that she would take no further note of Lord Hylton's assessing gaze.

But this, she found to her dismay, was impossible to do.

Without asking questions, Regina acceded to Lady Hylton's insistence that Maledon's funeral be held the very next day. Lord Lydgate and Lord Hylton went to the rectory and made all the arrangements with Reverend Emmery, and alerted the men who had come to the village to attend the funeral.

It was a cool clear autumn morning. The funeral wagon holding Maledon's casket, now filled with white lilies, waited in the courtyard. Ewan, dressed all in black, parked the coach behind it, the Maledon coat of arms on the doors now bearing a single black silk ribbon across. At nine o'clock the toll began; the solemn church bell sounded faint at Bellegarde, but the fifty-one knells, one for each year of the Earl of Maledon's life, could still be heard.

St. John looked very small and vulnerable as he walked across the courtyard with Lord Hylton and Lord Lydgate. Behind them Regina, Valeria, Lady Hylton, and Lady Lydgate followed. Regina placed a single red rose, the last in the garden, atop the pile of white lilies. She bowed her head and her lips moved, but no one could hear her soft whispers.

The two men and the small boy climbed into the coach. The women returned to stand on the steps and watch them drive away.

Valeria had always thought it odd, even somewhat silly, that it was thought that women were too emotionally fragile to attend funerals. But now, seeing her mother's desolate face, she was glad.

Chapter Eleven

❧

TRUEMAN ANNOUNCED IN HIS FUNEREAL baritone, "Mr. Cecil Broadbill."

Cecil Broadbill, Esquire, of Broadbill and Bent, Solicitors, came into the drawing room and made a deep bow. He was a tall man, with long thin legs, and Valeria thought he looked like a stork. He was, however, exquisitely dressed in the current understated mode. He wore a black tailcoat perfectly cut, a discreet gray-and-blue-striped waistcoat with the fob and watch chain appended in exactly the correct arc, and black pegged trousers. His rather wispy brown hair was fashionably styled in careless curls and waves, and when he bowed a large round bald spot shone. His eyes were close-set and he had a slight hook in his nose, which gave him a sort of predatory look.

Regina made the introductions in a weak voice. "Mr. Broadbill, this is my son St. John and my daughter Miss Segrave. This is Lord Hylton and Lady Hylton, and this is Lord Lydgate and Lady Lydgate."

Valeria was worried about her mother. Though she had attended every meal, she ate scantily and was still so weak that she had been obliged to retire afterward. Such listless introductions were utterly uncharacteristic of Regina. Normally even to tradesmen she worded introductions more graciously. And Valeria thought it was telling that she had introduced St. John by his given name, when she should have introduced him by his title. Her mother seemed so distracted by grief that she was barely able to function.

Broadbill acknowledged the introductions with fawning deference and then launched into pompous, wordy condolences. When eventually he fell silent Regina nodded wearily and said, "Thank you, sir. Shall we retire to the earl's study?"

"Certainly, my lady," he said, and made a vague gesture to offer Regina his arm. She appeared not to see it. When she rose she clasped Alastair's arm tightly and leaned on him. Valeria noted that Broadbill looked utterly nonplussed as Alastair and Lady Hylton accompanied them down the hall to the study.

The study was also the library, a somber room with glass-fronted bookcases lining every wall. At one end was an old refectory table with several comfortable armchairs grouped around it. At the other end was a massive mahogany desk. Broadbill sat behind the desk. In five side chairs precisely lined up in front of it, Lady Hylton sat by Regina, then St. John, then Valeria, and Lord Hylton sat by her. Valeria reflected how odd it was that the solicitor seemed to be holding court, and the distinguished personages in front of him seemed to be merely his attendees. He was conscious of it too, she thought. Although he cast a few nervous glances at Lord Hylton as he opened his leather portfolio, as he took long moments to shuffle papers fussily he assumed a pompous air.

"We have here the last will and testament of the Earl of Maledon," he pronounced as if he were reading Scripture. "With your permission, my lady, I will read it aloud." Without waiting for her permission, he picked up a single sheet of paper and read:

"'In the name of God, amen,

"'I, Edward Charles Robert Bellegarde, Earl of Maledon, Viscount Stamborne of Essex, Baron Bellegarde of Roding, in the

County of Essex, on this the twenty-fifth day of May in the Year of Our Lord 1805,

" 'Being *compos mentis* and of sound memory, do make and ordain this to be my last will and testament.

" 'As touching such of worldly Estate wherewith it has pleased God to bless me in this life, I give demise and dispose of the same in the following Manner and Form.

" 'Item: I give and bequeath to my wife Regina Bellegarde, Lady Maledon, the sum of ten thousand pounds.

" 'Item: All and Singular of the residue of my estate I give and bequeath to my son St. John Charles George Bellegarde.

" 'I constitute, make and ordain that Cecil Broadbill, Esquire, of Broadbill and Bent, Solicitors, London, be the Executor of this my last Will and Testament.' "

Broadbill laid the paper down, looked up, steepled his fingers precisely. "The rest is the signature, the seal, the witness, and the executor's acknowledgment."

A long heavy silence greeted this. Valeria glanced at her mother and saw that she looked stunned, as if she had received a blow; beside her Lady Hylton looked as grim as death. Valeria looked up at Alastair, and though he kept his customary aloof expression, she saw that his eyes had narrowed to cold slits as he regarded the solicitor. Broadbill fidgeted for a moment, then said deprecatingly, "It is a simple document, but legally complete. We'll be happy to answer any questions you may have, your ladyship, but it really is very clear."

Valeria waited for her mother to say something, but Regina seemed unable to speak, so Valeria said, "Well, I do have questions, Mr. Broadbill, several of them. First of all, what about my annuity from my father? I know that I receive two thousand pounds per annum from the Segrave estate."

"Just so, Miss Segrave," he said in a condescending voice, and steepled his fingers again. "We're sure you are also aware that your stepfather was the sole trustee of your annuity, and therefore had the funds at his disposal to manage them as his lordship believed would be in your best interest. Of course there is an accounting for the annuity, and we will be happy to present that at the time I have the final summing up of all of the earl's assets and liabilities up to the time of his death. You do understand that it will take some time before we're able to present a complete and comprehensive final report."

"What are you talking of, sir?" Valeria demanded. "My annuity has nothing to do with Lord Maledon's assets and liabilities. It's *my* money."

He pursed his lips. "There are several very delicate legal points here, Miss Segrave, of which we fear you are not quite cognizant. Again, we must ask that you wait until the final accounting has been completed. In the last year, his lordship's account was active, in the sense that many transactions were made, and we are at this time still gathering information concerning the outstanding debts, the balance of certain investments, and tabulating the incomes and outlays of the harvest, which has only just ended. It would be remiss of us to make any pronouncement concerning any single aspect of his lordship's estate before complete and final tabulations are made."

Angrily Valeria said, "I will not wait! I demand that you tell me this instant, sir: where is my money?"

Abruptly Regina's shoulders sagged and she pressed her hands to her forehead. "What have I done...what am I to do..." She moaned softly.

In a stricken whisper St. John breathed, "Oh, Mamma..."

Valeria took a deep breath. "I beg your pardon, Mamma. Please don't distress yourself, we will sort all of this out later." She turned back to the solicitor, who looked very wary. Coldly Valeria said, "At least, Mr. Broadbill, tell us of how my mother's settlement is to be paid. Does the estate have such moneys on hand?"

"Er...ah..." he muttered uneasily, then cleared his throat. "Miss Segrave, we're afraid that you still don't quite comprehend your position in these proceedings. There is a concept in law called *legal standing*. Such concept addresses the exact rights, under the law, of parties in legal proceedings. In the case of a testator's last will and testament, the only parties who have legal standing, in the most exact sense of the term—"

Rudely Valeria interrupted, "I know what legal standing is, sir, and you are saying that I don't have it. Very well. Would you prefer that I turn to my mother and tell her what to ask you, including the exact wording, so that she may then parrot it to you? Is such patent absurdity really necessary?"

"Miss Segrave, we have very clear responsibilities under the law," he said heavily. "As the late earl's solicitor, and the executor of his lordship's will, it behooves us to give vital and private information only to persons with legal standing. That would, in truth, be his lordship"—he nodded politely to St. John, who almost, but not quite, made a face at him—"and since he is a minor child, we must defer to her ladyship, and only her ladyship, regarding his estate."

He turned to look straight at Regina. "My lady, it appears that we may make a suggestion at this time. His lordship's death was sudden, and must have been a grievous shock to you. It is clear that your ladyship is quite overcome with grief, and under the circumstances it must be almost impossible for you to cope with handling the complexities of the Bellegarde financial affairs. Broadbill and Bent could set up a trusteeship for Lord Maledon. It would, in truth, be little different from what has been our position for the last fifty years. The earls of Maledon have always entrusted us completely with all responsibilities pertaining to the accounting of the estate. In general, the earls direct us in broad terms, understanding that we will faithfully manage the small details. In this way your ladyship would be relieved of much of the onerous responsibilities of administration."

Regina looked utterly bewildered. "I—I don't know, I—"

"No, Mamma!" Valeria cried. "You can't! You mustn't!"

Mr. Broadbill's sparse eyebrows drew together. "Really, Miss Segrave, we must protest. Our highest concern is to help her ladyship in any way that we can."

Valeria almost shouted, "But you're not helping! Everything you've said has been the awfullest bunch of legal flapdoodle I've ever heard! And who is *we*? Is there a Mr. Bent, or are you using the majestic plural?"

Lady Hylton said in an ominous tone, "Valeria, that will be quite enough."

Valeria clamped her mouth shut.

Lady Hylton rose and said, "Mr. Broadbent—bill—or whatever, we are going to retire to discuss these matters. You will wait here. Give me those papers."

Broadbill shot out of the chair as if he had been catapulted, groped for a few seconds, then handed his portfolio to Lady Hylton. Valeria noted with rather mean triumph that his hands shook.

Lady Hylton sailed imperiously down the hall to the morning room, where Trueman and the two footmen were in attendance. "You may go. We'll ring when we need you." Impassively they filed out.

Lady Hylton seated herself on a sofa and patted the seat next to her. "Come here, my dear, and sit next to me," she said to Regina. "You look as if you're about to fade away again. Will you take some sherry?"

"No, thank you, I'm very well," she answered faintly.

Lady Hylton said decisively, "I think not. Alastair?" He poured a small glass of sherry for Regina, who did sip it gratefully. Alastair stooped and stirred the fire, then took an elegantly negligible stance, leaning on the mantel. He looked at Valeria, and she thought she saw amusement in his eyes. It irritated her in the extreme.

Lady Hylton looked at the three papers in Broadbill's portfolio. "Just the will," she muttered impatiently. "I suppose it was too much to hope for that he would bring some sort of statement of financial condition."

"What if there is not ten thousand pounds for me to place in the funds?" Regina said fearfully. "And even if there is, however am I to manage on five percent interest? That's—that's only five hundred pounds per annum. I can't possibly maintain Bellegarde on five hundred pounds a year!"

"Mamma, you are not thinking clearly," Valeria said, trying to hide her impatience. "That ten thousand pounds is yours, for you alone. Bellegarde is a profitable estate that generates its own income, although I have no idea how much that might be."

"I really don't know either," Regina said in a distracted manner.

Alastair said, "I do, actually. Bellegarde is worth about twelve thousand pounds a year. In addition to that, Maledon told me that he has investments in some funds, some bank securities, and other things such as the India Company. I have no idea of the principal in these investments, but he said that they had been giving a fairly steady rate of return of around six percent per annum."

"How do you know all of this?" Valeria asked abruptly.

"We belong to the same clubs, we frequent the same coffeehouses, we meet often in London, Miss Segrave," he answered coolly. "Men of business often discuss these kinds of things. I can assure you that I have not been meddling in your private family affairs."

After an awkward moment Valeria said begrudgingly, "I almost wish that you had. Then you might know where my settlement from my father is. Apparently this is a deeply complicated mystery that only Broadbill and Bent can decipher."

"Hmph!" Lady Hylton grunted. "That man can spout some of the most meaningless, useless legal drivel I've ever heard. I wouldn't trust him with a Brummagem farthing."

"But surely you can't think he's dishonest," Regina said rather timidly. "Broadbill and Bent have been the Maledon solicitors for many years. I can't believe Maledon would have tolerated any fraud or thievery."

"I don't trust him," Lady Hylton repeated forcefully. "He was extremely evasive, Regina, and he was bullying you. And he tried to bully Valeria too, but that is obviously not a very easy thing to do."

"Nevertheless, he didn't answer me," Valeria said. "Tiresome man."

"I think that in a way he did," Alastair said. "It seemed to me that he was saying that your annuity, Miss Segrave, is included in the Maledon estate."

Valeria blinked several times. "But—you mean that my stepfather just took it?"

Alastair shrugged slightly. "That's only my impression. Just now we can't really know for certain."

Regina sighed deeply, a soft and helpless sound. "Oh, Letitia, you did try so hard to persuade me, and I simply wouldn't listen to you. At the time it seemed unconscionable, for me to insist upon making cold and calculated financial arrangements. He was going to be my husband, and I trusted him. What have I done?" She bent her head and began to weep.

St. John ran to kneel by his mother. "Mamma, please don't cry! If I have any money, you can have it, and Veri can too!"

She leaned over to hug him. "Oh, my darling, it's not that simple, and it's not just that, it's—it's—"

"Actually it is just that simple, Regina," Lady Hylton said gently. "Please calm yourself, my dear."

"Yes, I must, I will try," she said, releasing St. John and patting him on the shoulder. "I'm so sorry, I just—it just seems that I cannot make myself think straight. This has all been so very—" She made a helpless fluttering gesture with one hand, and dabbed at her eyes. The tears still ran freely.

Watching her mother, Valeria was filled with dismay. She had never seen her so visibly upset. Regina had always had such a delicate reticence, she never showed the slightest high emotion. Always, even under such difficult and wrenching circumstances as when she had seen Maledon the last time, with the company he had brought to Bellegarde, Regina had behaved with the calmest composure and graciousness. Her mother must have been suffering indeed, to keep breaking down in this way, in public, as it were.

"Mamma," she said softly, "why don't you go and rest? It's plain that you're still very weak and fatigued."

"But—but Mr. Broadbill—" Regina said.

"We will take care of him," Valeria said solidly. "Apparently he has nothing meaningful to say right now, anyway, since he hasn't finished his *tabulating*. Go take a nap before dinner, you'll feel so much better."

"I agree, Regina, if you don't rest you're just going to collapse again," Lady Hylton said, rising to ring the bell. "And St. John, unless you have an overwhelming desire to hear more about annuities and legal precedents and tabulations, I think you may be excused. Lydgate said you two had made some plans for this afternoon."

"He did say he'd take me and Niall for a ride in the phaeton," St. John said. "And I really don't care about tabulations."

"Then you may go," Lady Hylton said.

He went to the door and then turned and said, "But—I s'pose you are going to talk about me, aren't you? Is it that you don't want me to hear?"

Acidly Lady Hylton said, "You're much mistaken, young man. We're going to talk about your money, not you. And you may certainly hear, if you wish."

"No, that's all right then," he said with relief, and ran out, almost bowling over Trueman.

When the butler recovered himself and came into the room Lady Hylton said, "Lady Maledon wishes to retire. Please take her upstairs."

Regina was indeed still so weak that she needed help on the stairs. After they left, Lady Hylton said, "I declare, it seems with every passing minute I wish harder that I *would* have strangled that man! I've never heard of a sane man leaving his affairs in such a criminal tangle! And besides, the effrontery of him, to go off gallivanting over the country at such a time, with such a serious illness!"

"It was exceedingly rude of him to go die off in Yorkshire, wasn't it," Valeria commented. "Such a breach of good manners."

"You two ladies are very callous," Alastair said. "I'm having no part in this conversation."

"You needn't be so pious, Alastair," Lady Hylton retorted. "You're the one who suggested that we strap him to the top of the barouche."

Valeria laughed; and she was so pleased, realizing it was the first time she had laughed—or even smiled—in days.

Alastair grumbled, "Mother, that is not how it was, at all, and you know it. I merely asked Kincannon if that's what he thought we would do, when he was stupid enough to suggest we bring Maledon home in one of the carriages."

"I had no idea that you possessed such an acid wit, sir," Valeria said.

"That's because you don't know me very well," Alastair said, "which, of course, it would be my pleasure to remedy."

Valeria stared at him, bemused for a moment, then shook her head. "But it is true. I'm appalled that you all have been obliged to get so deeply involved in all of this. I know you're St. John's and my godmother, ma'am, but I hardly think you envisioned being entangled in this sort of coil."

Lady Hylton and Alastair exchanged quick glances, the import of which Valeria couldn't fathom. Quickly Lady Hylton said, "Yes, well, there are some matters that we need to discuss with you, Valeria, concerning that. But for now, what about that Broadbent person?"

"His name is Broadbill," Alastair corrected her.

"Broadbent, Broadbill, Bent, such stupid names, particularly for solicitors," she said carelessly.

"I don't care to have one more word with him," Valeria said scathingly. "It's useless. I'm convinced he could talk until dawn and we wouldn't know a thing more than we do now."

Trueman returned just then, and Valeria said, "Trueman, go tell Mr. Broadbent—I mean Mr. Broadbill—that we won't be needing his services any longer. Tell him that we will contact him tomorrow."

Trueman hesitated, glancing at Alastair, and then at Lady Hylton. It infuriated Valeria, but just as she was about to reprove him he bowed and left. "Oh! Am I to spend my entire life having men either looking through me as if I'm invisible, or else patting me on the head as if I'm a foolish little kitten?"

"No, you will not," Lady Hylton said decisively.

"I have never, not once, patted you on the head," Alastair said, "and I never shall. Even kittens can scratch."

"I am not a kitten!" Valeria said angrily.

"I believe it was you who referred to yourself as a kitten."

"I did not! At least, I said—what I said was—what I *meant* was—that men often treat women like helpless silly kittens. Just as you are now!"

"That's not at all true," Alastair countered.

"Be silent, children," Lady Hylton said with amusement. "We do have some serious matters to discuss."

Valeria said dryly, "Oh, yes, of course, we have gotten completely distracted from the topic of St. John's money."

"Actually, that's not what we need to discuss with you, Valeria," Lady Hylton said slowly. "At least, that is a part of it, but first I wanted to talk to you about your mother."

"Yes, she is not coping very well at all," Valeria said quietly. "It grieves me to see her so distraught. In all truth, ma'am, I think you are the only person who is really helping her just now."

"She is my closest friend, and I would do anything in my power to help her. And that's why I'm going to make a proposal to her that I believe will relieve her of much of her burden in this intolerable situation."

Valeria glanced at Alastair, who remained impassive, and then asked, "What can you mean, ma'am?"

Lady Hylton seemed to choose her words carefully. "First let me explain to you about the decisions that your mother made when she married Maledon, and that includes facts about your legacy. Did you know that your father, Lord Segrave, left your mother twenty thousand pounds?"

"What?" Valeria breathed. "I had no idea . . ."

"I thought you did not," Lady Hylton said with some regret, "and I've had some second thoughts about telling you all of this, since your mother didn't think it was necessary. But in the last two days, as I've spoken to Regina, I've seen that she's quite incapable of sorting all of this out, and she has, in so many words, asked me to talk to you. Yes, your father was a prudent man. Regina was poor when he married her; and as soon as he did, he made a will that left her twenty thousand pounds. Then, when you were born, he added that you were to have an annuity of two thousand pounds per annum. He always intended that, when you got older, and depending on circumstances, he would increase it so that you would have an extremely favorable dowry when you became of age. Of course, you were only five when he died, so he hadn't made any such arrangements at that time."

"Yes, my mother did explain that to me, when I was—oh, thirteen or fourteen, I suppose," Valeria said thoughtfully. "And she said that when I got a little older, when it was time for me to marry, although that is a small sum, I should have a good amount saved up, as she had never used the moneys and had allowed the funds to accumulate."

"That is what *she* did," Lady Hylton said with disdain, "and that is what she assumed Maledon would do. You see, from the time your father died in November of 1798, until the time Regina married Maledon in 1804, you lived on the interest from her twenty thousand pounds. In the five percents, she received about one thousand pounds a year, and generally your household expenses were only about six hundred pounds a year. When she married Maledon, she had almost twenty-two thousand pounds."

Valeria looked bewildered. "But—so—and my stepfather left her only ten thousand pounds?"

Lady Hylton grimaced, and Alastair's lip curled slightly. Lady Hylton said shortly, "Yes, as we found out just today."

"But—I can't—and so my mother had saved my annuity up until that time, that would be—at least ten thousand pounds..." Valeria murmured.

"Actually, when Regina married, the balance of your annuity was well over eleven thousand pounds," Lady Hylton said evenly. "And so there she was, with a fortune of over thirty thousand pounds. And I tried, oh, I tried so very hard, to convince Regina to have a cunning lawyer draw up marriage articles to secure that thirty thousand pounds, for you and for her. But she would have none of it." Lady Hylton sighed. "Regina believed, and I think still believes, that it would have been a sin to do so. She said, over and over again, 'When you marry, you are one person. If I cannot share everything with him, my heart, my love, and my worldly goods, then how can I think of marrying him?' "

"I know, she's said much the same thing to me when I've questioned her," Valeria said sadly. "But...I hate to say it...I wish that she would have thought more clearly about *my* worldly goods."

"Of course you would feel that way now," Lady Hylton said, "but you must know that Regina was doing what she felt was best for you. You understand, Valeria, that Regina is so—so unworldly, particularly when it comes to money, that she simply cannot make canny decisions. You heard her today; she thought that the three of you were going to have to live on five hundred pounds a year interest."

"I know, and I can hardly bear to see her struggle so," Valeria said passionately. "She's just—just not capable of understanding financial complexities. So now here we are, with my mother utterly at a loss, and I cannot help her, since I have no *legal standing*. After all, I'm only the earl's stepdaughter!"

"No, you are wrong," Alastair said quietly. "You are the Earl of Maledon's sister."

Although of course Valeria knew this in her head, the truth of it had not really sunk in. She stared back and forth between her godmother and Lord Hylton.

Lady Hylton said, "And that, my dear, brings us to the crux of what we wish to propose to your mother. We think that a trusteeship should be formed to manage St. John's estate. We think that it would be in St. John's and your mother's best interest to do this."

"But who would be the trustee?" Valeria asked.

"I think that it should be a joint trusteeship," Lady Hylton said. "You, and my son."

"What! But—but surely—we could never impose—that is—I'm certain I could manage—there's no need for Lord Hylton to assume such a wearisome obligation!" Valeria finally blurted out. She stared at him, appalled, and he, as always, appeared to be entirely neutral. His apparent indifference made her feel even more opposed to asking him for *anything*. In a calmer tone she said, "I know nothing about trusts, but surely, if I am made co-administrator with my mother, there would be no need for you to take on such a thankless task, sir. You couldn't possibly have a vested interest in this, and it seems to me that it would be rather odd for a complete stranger to assume such a responsibility."

Lady Hylton said carefully, "First of all, it would make no sense to appoint your mother as a trustee; she is already St. John's legal guardian. Besides, the point is to relieve your mother of the burden of managing Bellegarde, and any other interests such as the investments that Maledon has made. And I realize that this is hard for you to accept, Valeria, but this is a man's world. No eighteen-year-old girl will ever be accepted, on her own, as the sole administrator of a wealthy estate. You would face innumerable and insurmountable problems. You will need to be cotrustee with a man, and that is the sad and sour truth of it. Alastair is the logical choice, and he has agreed to do it. In fact, he volunteered."

"But—it's such a monstrous imposition! I can't believe that my mother would agree to it," Valeria argued. "She would feel as I do, that Lord Hylton would be vastly inconvenienced to be saddled with such a responsibility."

"No, she won't," Lady Hylton said coolly. "Because she knows, you see, that Alastair does have a certain measure of responsibility for her, and St. John, and even you."

Valeria cried, "What do you mean? I don't understand! He owes me—us—nothing!"

Lady Hylton said dryly, "But he does. You see, Valeria, my sons are the nearest kindred to the earls of Maledon. Their kinship, though distant, is descended through the male line."

Finally Valeria understood. Alastair, Lord Hylton, would have been the heir of Bellegarde if her stepfather had not had a son. If something happened to St. John—*God forbid!* resounded in her turbulent mind—Lord Hylton would inherit.

She was so shocked that for long moments she couldn't breathe. And then all she felt was dismay.

Chapter Twelve

❧

ON THIS NIGHT, AFTER THE CHAOTIC past days, Valeria told Trueman they would have dinner in the dining room instead of the breakfast room. After dinner they went to the drawing room for coffee. Since St. John had dined with them, Lord Hylton and Lord Lydgate had decided not to remain in the dining room for port and cigars. "I miss the ladies' company anyway," Lydgate told St. John. "And to tell you an awful secret, I hate cigars. Not very dashing of me, I know, but there it is."

They went in, and Lady Hylton looked around as she settled on a Jacobean settee, beautifully carved but hard and uncomfortable. "Regina, you really must refurbish this room. It's so gloomy and Gothic. You have such an eye for elegant appointments, you could make it warm and welcoming."

Regina still was wan, with delicate blue shadows under her eyes. But Valeria had seen that she had eaten much better at dinner than she had in the past days. Regina looked around the room and sighed. "Yes, I suppose now...but in truth I'm so worried about the—the condition of the estate that I can hardly think of such things."

Lady Hylton said, "That's precisely what we want to talk to you about, my dear, if you feel quite up to it."

"I am feeling better, thank you. I'm glad that you persuaded me to retire this afternoon, I had a most restful nap."

"Very good," Lady Hylton said with satisfaction. "While you were resting, Alastair, Valeria, and I talked about you behind your back, and about St. John's money." She gave him a wry smile, and he grinned. "Let me tell you—both of you—what we would like to propose." She went on in a businesslike manner to explain about the joint trusteeship. St. John looked puzzled, but Regina's face brightened somewhat.

"You understand, Regina, that this arrangement would be purely for your convenience, and when you are feeling better, you can dissolve it if you wish," Lady Hylton finished.

Regina studied Valeria. "Is this something you really want to do, darling? It is a very great responsibility."

"I've considered it all afternoon, Mamma, and I realize that it is. But I feel certain that I can do it, and so yes, it is what I wish to do," she replied.

Then Regina considered Alastair. "And you, Lord Hylton? It seems to me that this would be a heavy burden to you."

"Yes, ma'am, I know that it seems such to you. But to me it doesn't seem so. This estate is well established, and from what I've seen, your estate agent practically runs it himself. Obviously you're perfectly capable yourself of running the household. The main area in which I think I may be of service is with your solicitor, and with Malcdon's business in the City," Alastair said. "And I would be more than happy to deal with that as long as you feel you need me."

"Thank you, sir," Regina said gratefully. Then she added with some hesitation, "But how is this to be accomplished? Should we apply to Mr. Broadbill to draw up the articles?"

"No, we should not," Lady Hylton said emphatically. "I'm sure his pinfeathers will be ruffled when he realizes that he'll be obliged to deal with Alastair and Valeria instead of you. It would likely take him months and months of *tabulating* to draw up such a document."

"He was singularly unhelpful, wasn't he?" Regina said.

"Bravo, madam!" Lady Lydgate said with her impish smile. "I think that must the most severe sentence you've ever uttered in your life!"

"I can attest to that," Valeria said. "But what is to be done with Broadbill and Bent? Discharge them?"

"Surely that would be too harsh," Regina said with some distress. "They've been Maledon solicitors for three generations."

"I agree with you, madam," Alastair said. "At this time we have no reasonable cause to discharge them, or him. The fact that he spouted legalese without saying anything at all of substance was tiresome, but not really negligent or fraudulent. However, I do have a suggestion. If you will write a letter, Lady Maledon, giving me full powers to act in your name, I'll go to London tomorrow and see my solicitor, Julius Stanhope, and have him draw up the articles of trusteeship. I'll also go to Barclays and get the information on Maledon's account. And if you agree, I'll talk to Stanhope and see if there is some sort of convention by which we can retain him to share the solicitorship. I can assure you that Stanhope won't need much time to give us a full and complete accounting."

"That would be such a relief to me, Lord Hylton," Regina said.

Valeria was feeling utterly useless and cast aside. *There he is, completely in charge of my mother already*, she thought with exasperation. The thought occurred to her that she herself couldn't possibly do what he could do. She knew no other solicitors, and the vision of her sailing into Barclays Bank with a letter from her mummy, demanding to know everything about Maledon's account, was absurd. But the realization only increased her resentment. It truly was a man's world.

Regina, now more alert and lively than she had been since

the moment Alastair had told her of Maledon's death, warmly asked St. John, "Do you understand what we're talking about, St. John?"

He said tentatively, "So Veri and Alastair are going to help us with Bellegarde, and take care of my money and things?"

"That's exactly right," Regina said. "They're going to make sure that everything is in good order until you're old enough to take care of it yourself."

He nodded and sat up straighter. "Do I have much money, really?"

Regina glanced at Alastair; it was odd, but he truly had more idea of her husband's financial condition than did she. Alastair answered, "Yes, you do have quite a bit of money, St. John."

St. John considered this. "Am I rich?"

"Most people would say so."

"Am I richer than you?" St. John asked curiously.

"No, you are not. I have to tell you that I am richer than you, my lord," Alastair replied with amusement. "But I will also tell you that Lord Lydgate is richer than I, and we happen to know several men who are richer than he. There is always someone richer, or more handsome, or more clever, than you are."

"That is so true," Regina agreed. "We've been exceedingly blessed by Our Lord in so many ways, St. John, not just with riches. In particular, I find that having such good friends is a considerable blessing. I appreciate you all so very much. Lord Hylton, if you will assist me, I'll be glad to write that letter."

"As always, I am at your service, madam," he said gallantly.

Lord Lydgate said, "Lady Maledon, Elyse and I too are utterly at your disposal. Is it your wish that we remain here at Bellegarde? The thought has occurred that it might be more comfortable for you if the house weren't full of people."

Regina said, "Sir, I'm grateful for your consideration, but if you and Elyse would stay for a while it would please me very much. I enjoy your company, and I know that Valeria and St. John do too. In fact, I believe that you were so kind as to take St. John out in the phaeton today, is that right?"

St. John's eyes glowed. "Oh, Mamma, it was glorious! Lord Lydgate says that my father's phaeton is a real high flyer!" He realized then what he had said, and his face fell. "I'm sorry, Mamma," he murmured.

Regina said firmly, "St. John, there is no need to apologize. It's going to take all of us some time to adjust. But I tell you now, I'm going to do my utmost to make sure that you, and Valeria, and I get back to our normal lives as soon as possible. We can mourn, St. John, without sitting around in dark gloom and sorrow, afraid to mention your father's name."

He looked up and gave her a blissful smile. "Thank you, Mamma."

With mock sternness Regina said, "So I must remind you that it is now your phaeton, St. John, though the thought of it utterly terrifies me, the way that thing teeters back and forth, and tilts up around corners as if it's about to turn a somersault, horse, carriage, people, and all. It's been my observation that men *will* drive them entirely too fast."

St. John argued, "But Mamma, Niall says that Lord Lydgate is a great whip, and when I grow up I want to be a great whip too! You *must* drive too fast to be a great whip!"

Lord Lydgate was looking very sheepish, and he blurted out, "Er—I didn't say that, ma'am, Niall said it. Apologies, and all that."

"Yes, well, do try not to kill yourself, or anyone else," Regina said. "To tell the honest truth, I'm more worried about my daughter than I am my son. I'm sure that Valeria is going to want to learn to drive that infernal machine herself."

"Of course, Mamma! It's an invaluable opportunity, to have such a great whip for an instructor, so that I too can learn to drive it much too fast," Valeria said mischievously.

Regina said, "Lady Hylton, I appeal to you to try to talk some common sense into your goddaughter."

"I'm sorry, Regina, but I didn't succeed with my own daughter, she runs about in her own phaeton too," Lady Hylton said placidly. "In fact, I must admit that she's as good a whip as Lydgate."

"Coo-eee," St. John breathed.

Elyse said, "Valeria, I'll teach you to drive, it's really such fun, and I know that you will learn so easily."

Valeria said excitedly, "Would you? May I, Mamma?"

"I suppose that if I expect you to manage the estate I must let you do whatever you want," Regina said dryly, "within limits, of course. But at least I do still have charge of one child. St. John, it's getting very late, I think you must go to bed."

In a small voice he said, "But Mamma, must I? I mean, must I get up early and start lessons again?"

Regina considered for a moment. "Today is Wednesday ... no, St. John, I think it will be all right if we forego lessons until Monday. But surely you must be tired, and it would seem that you must be bored with all of this adult talk anyway."

"I'm not tired, at all," he said stoutly. "Mm ... I am a little tired of all this talk about money and things." A sly look came over his face. "P'raps, Mamma, you might let me stay up, just this once, very late. Lord Lydgate said that the billiard room is top-notch, and that he would teach me how to play."

Elyse said, "Lydgate! What have you been saying to this child? First tooling around breakneck in the phaeton, and now billiards? I'm amazed that you and Alastair didn't keep him in the dining room and ply him with brandy and cigars!"

"But I just said I'd teach him billiards sometime," Reggie pleaded.

"Didn't mean to utterly corrupt him in one day, don't you know. Apologies and all that, Lady Maledon."

Regina smiled; and Valeria was so happy to see that her mother's face had regained some of its usual beatific glow. "Somehow I feel that I must be a poor hostess, as one of my guests keeps apologizing to me. Sir, if you want to teach him how to play billiards, please do. After all, it is his billiard room."

"Huzzah!" St. John said.

Alastair said, "I'm loath to tell you this, St. John, but Lydgate isn't nearly as proficient at billiards as he is at driving a phaeton. If he teaches you, you'll learn very ill."

With an injured manner Lydgate said, "All well and good, Hylton, no one can beat you. I'm not that bad really, you know."

"Still, I think I'd do better to teach you, St. John," Alastair said. "In fact, I'll give Lydgate some lessons too, while I'm at it. What do you say?"

"Yes, please, sir!" St. John said, jumping out of his chair. He bowed to the ladies. "If you'll excuse us, ladies," he said, which amused them greatly. Lydgate and Alastair made their exits.

Regina's eyes were alight as she watched them go. "And so, ladies, we have been deserted by the men after all. I am feeling so much better, I'm really not ready to retire. What do you say to a game of whist?"

The next morning Regina insisted that she was well enough to meet with the servants, although she did particularly ask Valeria to stay with her. "I always intended that you should have more of a part in running the house," she said at breakfast. "And now that you've offered to do just that, I shall hold you to it."

Mrs. Banyard, Mrs. Lees, and Trueman dutifully reported to Regina and Valeria in the morning room. Mrs. Banyard turned in her menus for the next week, and Regina glanced at them. "I'm certain they'll be perfectly fine, Mrs. Banyard, as they always are. Also, I'd like to thank you for managing so well for the past few days under such difficult circumstances. It would have been forgivable if all of the meals had been less than perfect, but none of them have been. In fact, I've been proud of my table, as always."

Mrs. Banyard's round red face shone with pleasure. "Thank you, m'lady."

"Mrs. Lees, Trueman, I'm also very pleased with the way the household has run so smoothly; it was impossible to see any upset at all. I thank you."

Valeria was paying strict attention; she could see that her mother knew exactly the right way to show appreciation to the servants while still maintaining her air of authority. Valeria regarded this as a valuable lesson.

Regina continued, "I will advise you all now that our guests will be staying for a while longer. Lord Hylton, as you know, left for London this morning, but he will be returning in a day or so. Lady Hylton has sent for her maid, and she should arrive day after tomorrow. Lord and Lady Lydgate have expressed their satisfaction with Royce and Sophie attending them, so they won't be sending for their servants. Also, Lord Hylton is so happy with Ned, I fear he may try to steal him from us."

"I doubt that will happen," Valeria said lightly. "Ned and Royce are so conceited, they know they're the most handsome and most perfectly matched pair of footmen in England."

Regina looked amused. "Very true, my darling."

Trueman looked disapproving at this bit of levity, but Regina continued lightly, "Is there anything else?"

They discussed ordering more coal, and a few other minor details. Then Trueman said, "My lady, there is one more thing. Mr. Thrale wishes to speak with your ladyship."

Regina looked blank for a moment, but quickly recovered and said, "Very well. If we're finished, you may send him in."

After they left, Regina whispered to Valeria, "I had quite forgotten about him. What am I to do with him?"

Valeria also hadn't thought about Lord Maledon's valet; she hadn't even seen Thrale since he had returned to Bellegarde with Maledon's body. She thought quickly. "Mamma, I beg you will allow me to help you with this; it's just the sort of thing that upsets you, I know. I don't wish to overrule you in any way, particularly in front of the servants, but please let me deal with him."

"Thank you, dearest," Regina said with relief.

Trueman brought Thrale in; naturally, he was not announced. Thrale came to stand in front of Valeria and Regina and gave a courtly bow. He was slender and tall, and handsome in a sort of melodramatic way, with black hair and dark eyes and a full mouth. "My lady, this is the first opportunity I've had to express my great sorrow at the loss of his lordship. I myself feel great shock and grief, as I flatter myself that his lordship and I had a much closer relationship than that of master and servant. I do so regret his lordship's passing, and will miss him extremely for the rest of my days."

Valeria thought that this speech was entirely too emotional—and false. The few times she had met Thrale, she had thought that he was too smooth by half. She had the distinct impression that he was cunning and sly.

"Thank you, Thrale, your sentiment is much appreciated," Regina said gravely.

Valeria said, "Yes it is, Thrale. We do realize that his sudden demise left you in a difficult position. We will extend you a month's wages, and you may remain at Bellegarde until you've found a new position. We're prepared to give you a character, of course, and I'm certain that you'll have no trouble at all."

His eyes shifted back and forth between Valeria and Regina.

When he spoke, he addressed himself to Regina. "I'm sure you understand, my lady, that finding a satisfactory situation is no easy task. I would hope to beg your ladyship's indulgence to give me time to seek out a position that will suit."

Again Valeria firmly answered him. "Lord Lydgate and Lord Hylton have a vast acquaintance, and we will ask them to help find you a position. In the meantime, I suggest that you place an advertisement in the servants' register in the *Times*. As I said, I'm sure you'll have no trouble finding a new place."

His eyes flickered. "Yes, Miss Segrave," he said with the merest hint of insolence. Then he turned back to Regina as if Valeria weren't even there. "My lady, there is another thing I wish to ask of you. His lordship was always very generous with me, in that he always gave me his clothing when he renewed his wardrobe. Indeed, it is customary that a gentleman give his valet his 'castoffs,' as we say, as I'm sure your ladyship gives your dresses to your lady's maid. And so, I thought that it would be perfectly correct for me to have his lordship's clothes. Also, in the course of my employment with him, his lordship indicated on several occasions that there were some items of his personal effects that he would like for me to have. I'm sure your ladyship knows that that is quite customary too."

Regina looked confused. Valeria didn't like to continually talk over her mother, but she realized angrily that it was Thrale who was manipulating the conversation, and she decided that she must take control. Icily she said, "Thrale, what you say about custom and convention may be true under normal circumstances, but such does not apply here. Our family will decide what to do with Lord Maledon's personal property, including his clothing."

At last he addressed her directly. "But Miss Segrave, his lordship did in fact indicate some items that he specifically wished me to have."

"But he didn't do so in his last will and testament," Valeria said bluntly, "which is also customary. That is all, Thrale."

He looked slightly stunned, and then his lip curled slightly. With a bow that was distinctly mocking, he turned and stalked out.

Regina murmured, "Oh, that was distressing... I had no idea..."

"Of course you didn't, Mamma, you simply can't see that people are selfish and will take advantage at every opportunity," Valeria said. "I have no doubt that he would have had everything, including walking sticks and snuffboxes and quizzing glasses and watches, packed up and gone, if he thought he could have got away with it."

Regina sighed. "Sometimes I think I'm so naïve that it's made me quite stupid."

"No, Mamma," Valeria said quietly. "It's because you always think the very best of people. In you that is not stupidity; it is sweetness. And I wouldn't have you any other way."

"You know, Valeria," Regina said with a smile, "St. John and I are very lucky to have you taking care of us. I can't tell you how proud I am of you, my darling."

Suddenly Valeria did not feel useless at all.

꠹

Lord Hylton returned from the City a couple of days later, on Saturday. Regina and Valeria went out to meet him, and were bemused to see that the coach was filled with parcels and bandboxes. "Craigie and Joan gave me very strict instructions about picking up your orders from Madame Tournai," he explained. "In fact, they gave me many instructions, both verbal and written, about fans and shawls and lace and ribbon. Luckily, Madame Tournai was very helpful, for I'm afraid I'm somewhat at a loss when it comes to lace and ribbons."

Valeria observed dryly to herself, *Oh, yes, I'm sure Madame Tournai was extremely helpful. Mamma says she's young and very beautiful, so I would imagine it took you a long time to choose among black lace and black ribbons and black fans!*

They went into the morning room and Lord Hylton asked, "Where is everyone?"

Regina replied, "I finally convinced them that it wasn't at all necessary for them to sit in solemn silence with me all day. I recalled that Lord Lydgate is quite the avid sportsman, so I encouraged him to go shooting. I know that Bellegarde can't compare with Foxden Park, but still, I understand that the shooting is really fine here. And then I found out that Elyse is determined to go out and fire a gun willy-nilly, as Letitia put it, so she's shooting too. And of course nothing would do but what St. John would go with them, so your mother was kind enough to say that she'd like an outing, and she'd make sure no one shot St. John, and that he wouldn't shoot himself, and that he wouldn't shoot anyone else."

"I'm sure that's a great comfort to you, Lady Maledon," Alastair said. "Miss Segrave, I'm surprised that you're not out with your rifle, banging away like my sister."

"I feel sorry for the birds," Valeria admitted. "Well, in the field, anyway. By the time they get to the table I'm not so sensitive. I do love Mrs. Banyard's roast guinea fowl with curry sauce. So, please, Lord Hylton, tell us how it went in London."

"I'm happy to report that I was able to accomplish a very great deal. Right now, Lady Maledon, let me assure you that all is well. The balance of your account at Barclays Bank is about six thousand pounds. Understand that this doesn't include moneys from the harvest, and some debts are still outstanding, but still, you have absolutely nothing to worry about as far as liquidity."

"Oh, thanks be to Almighty God," Regina murmured. "Perhaps it was foolish, but I was so very worried."

"It wasn't foolish at all, Mamma, considering—" Valeria was going to say "considering how insanely Maledon was behaving," but she cut herself off and rather lamely finished, "considering the circumstances."

Alastair gave her a knowing glance, then continued, "My solicitor has returned here with me. I assure you, madam, that he has all the paperwork pertaining to Maledon's estate in perfect order. Anticipating your wishes, I asked if he would come here and meet with me and Miss Segrave first thing in the morning. Is that acceptable to you?"

"Oh, yes, that is perfectly acceptable," Regina said happily. "Already I am so relieved in my mind. From now on, Lord Hylton, it's not necessary for you to worry about my wishes; you have my complete confidence. And I thank God for you too."

Alastair said, "You do me great honor, madam, and I will do my utmost to deserve your trust."

જી

Julius Stanhope, Esquire, was exactly what Valeria, in her rather unschooled mind, thought a solicitor should be. He was a small man, balding, with spectacles, but in spite of his humble appearance he had an air of competence that was in complete contrast to Mr. Broadbill's oily smoothness. They met in the study, and Valeria observed that, rather than holding court with his courtiers, he had exactly the right tone of deference for a professional to show to his clients. "Miss Segrave, if I may make a suggestion, we might go over the articles of trusteeship and sign them at the end of this meeting. They are complete and entire and, I believe, respect all parties' wishes. But first, I'm sure that you would wish to know the details concerning his lordship's estate."

"You are entirely correct, sir," Valeria said.

"Very good. First of all, let me apprise you of the exact nature of my position. Lord Hylton asked me if there was some sort of precedent for retaining multiple solicitors. Legally a person may retain as many solicitors as he wishes, but it is highly unusual; in fact, I don't think I've ever known such, and to be perfectly honest, under normal circumstances it would present a certain difficulty, to me at least, as concerning professional courtesies.

"However, after Lord Hylton related to me the exact situation, I did see the possibility that Broadbill and Bent were not representing their clients' interests to the utmost of their abilities, and in my mind that released me from such delicate considerations of not impinging on another solicitor's account." He removed his spectacles, polished them, and replaced them precisely on his nose. "I say this so that you understand, Miss Segrave, that I have a high regard for exacting professional conduct."

Valeria said, "Mr. Stanhope, you are the first gentleman I've tried to engage in any matter of business who has given a fig for what I thought, and I thank you. I assure you that you have my full and complete confidence."

He gave Valeria a dry little smile. "Now, assuming that you, like Lord Hylton, don't wish a long dreary list of numbers and debitors and creditors, I will give you an overview of the Maledon finances.

"The estate itself generates approximately twelve thousand pounds per annum. The expenses of the earl's holdings, and here I am including the London town house, the stables, maintenance and improvements on the estate, and Bellegarde household and personal expenses, are about ten thousand pounds per annum. So for many years now the earls of Maledon have been growing steadily richer, and this surplus has been used to buy more land from time to time, with other available funds invested in the stock exchange. And, for about the last ten years or so, the earl kept a gold deposit at Barclays, maintaining a balance of about ten thousand pounds."

"Except for the last year," Alastair told Valeria, his lip curling slightly.

"Yes, you said the balance now was about six thousand pounds," she said thoughtfully. "Where did the other four thousand go?"

Alastair and the solicitor exchanged grave glances, which nettled Valeria. "Surely by now, Lord Hylton, you have seen that I'm not subject to womanish vapors. I suspect I already know the answer, anyway. It was Lady Jex-Blake, wasn't it?"

"Some of it, ma'am," the solicitor answered with delicate distaste. "His lordship bought a house in Russell Square for which he maintained all the household expenses, including three servants, two horses, and a carriage. He opened several new trade accounts that were—ahem—related to ladies' clothing and personal items. In addition, it appears that his lordship's own expenses for his wardrobe, last year alone, came to almost one thousand pounds."

"Good heavens, no wonder Thrale wanted his clothes," Valeria muttered darkly. "And so all of these things cost four thousand pounds? That doesn't sound possible."

"No, it is not possible," Mr. Stanhope said. "Those items alone cost about three thousand pounds. No, what I find impossible to believe is where the other thousand went. It seems that Mr. Broadbill found his expenses as executor of Lord Maledon's will of such magnitude that he turned in a bill—to himself, of course—for one thousand pounds, which he then paid to himself!" Mr. Stanhope's indignation was so high that his spectacles almost fell off, and he was obliged to polish them with great vigor. His rather sallow cheeks were tinged bright red.

"What! One thousand pounds! Surely that is nothing but robbery!" Valeria cried.

"Exactly, exactly what I told Lord Hylton, and I said that Mr. Broadbill should be prosecuted," Mr. Stanhope declared. "However, it is not at all clear that such a prosecution would be effective. In most cases the testator makes a separate written agreement with the executor, naming the fee said executor shall receive. Lord Maledon didn't do that. And so it might be construed that in such a case the executor can name his fee, and it is legal, although it is certainly not ethical."

"But surely something can be done," Valeria insisted. "He should face some sort of charges! He stole that money from my six-year-old brother!"

Calmly Alastair said, "We could try to prosecute him in Chancery, but we would have to retain a barrister, and someone would have to appear in court—most likely several times, perhaps for as long as a year—to represent the estate, and that would have to be either you or me, Miss Segrave. The prosecution would be long and expensive. Also, as Stanhope says, there is very little likelihood of a successful conclusion. What he did was reprehensible, but it was not illegal."

"My horrible stepfather!" Valeria exclaimed with heat. "It seems every single day reveals a sordid new situation! I declare, that man was—" She stopped when she saw the looks on the men's faces. Mr. Stanhope seemed upset at her outburst, while Alastair looked coldly disapproving. With an effort she calmed herself down, though she still felt resentment coursing throughout her. "So, Mr. Broadbill has made himself a tidy sum of money from Lord Maledon's will. Well, that is the last of the Maledon money that he will ever see. I want him discharged immediately."

"So Lord Hylton has said, and I heartily agree," Mr. Stanhope said. "I suggest that as soon as you sign the trust agreement the first order of business should be to send an express to Broadbill and Bent, notifying them that you are terminating their services."

"Whoever 'they' may be," Valeria said sarcastically. "I would very much like to see Mr. Broadbill himself, alone, and tell him what I think of his royal we. And, possibly, wring his nose. But—oh, dear. He is the executor of the will, and that cannot be undone, can it?"

"No, but there is little damage he can do there, the will was so straightforward and simple," Mr. Stanhope said. "Her ladyship has ten thousand pounds, and your brother has everything else. All you and Lord Hylton really need to do is decide how you will transfer the money to Lady Maledon, and notify Mr. Broadbill of it."

"And how can that be done?" Valeria asked. "I assume—I hope—from the investments?"

"Certainly that is possible," Mr. Stanhope said. He shuffled some papers, then said, "At present Lord Maledon's investments total about forty thousand pounds. He has investments in several bank stocks, some Exchequer and Navy bills, and some India bonds. The total investment in Exchequer bills is about ten thousand pounds. Perhaps your mother would like to leave her settlement there, for they pay about six percent interest."

It went against every fiber of Valeria's being to admit ignorance to Lord Hylton, but she could not see any way around it. "I don't understand," she said stiffly. "How does investment in the Exchequer work?"

Mr. Stanhope gave no sign at all, but Valeria imagined that she saw disdainful amusement lurking in Alastair's eyes. Mr. Stanhope answered, "It's really very simple, Miss Segrave. You loan the government money to use for government purposes, and the government pays you interest on the loan."

"I see. Mm—no, I don't think my mother would be comfortable with such—such an arrangement. She's very unworldly, you know, Mr. Stanhope, and I know that she would feel much more secure if she had ten thousand pounds invested in the public funds," Valeria said.

"Certainly. I'll be glad to make that transfer," Mr. Stanhope said.

"And so, Miss Segrave," Alastair said, "that brings us to your own trust. I must say you've shown great forbearance in not demanding to know about that first thing."

"No one has ever observed that forbearance is one of my virtues," Valeria said dryly. "I can assure you that I was going to ask. Mr. Stanhope?"

"Yes, ma'am, I have managed to trace the—er—disposition of your trust from the time that Lord Maledon became your trustee, some seven years ago." For the first time he seemed uneasy, and shuffled papers for a few moments. "When your mother married Lord Maledon, she chose not to have marriage articles, defining her property as her own, drawn up. Therefore, all of her money—a sum slightly over twenty thousand pounds—automatically became his. Also, she was, in the strictest legal sense although it was not formalized, trustee of your annuity from your father's estate. Therefore, when her ladyship did not have written documents made to assure that she maintain her own personal property, your stepfather became the *de facto* trustee of your annuity. Soon after their marriage, Lord Maledon invested all of the funds coming from his marriage to your mother, and that was the basis of all of the investments still held now."

"And so he invested my mother's twenty thousand pounds, and my own eleven thousand that had accumulated," Valeria said. "And—theoretically, at least, those funds are still intact, correct?"

"Ye-es, but unfortunately they belong to the Earl of Maledon," Mr. Stanhope said reluctantly.

"But what about the two thousand pounds I've received every year since my mother's marriage?" Valeria demanded. "That would be another fourteen thousand pounds that I should have!"

"Yes, that is correct, and there are two complex legal and bookkeeping procedures that—no, I shall say it plainly. Lord Maledon managed to maneuver so that he had complete control of the funds from your trust, madam. The first step was to become the sole trustee of your annuity. Mr. Broadbill did draw up articles of trusteeship, and there was so much Latin and legal verbiage that

I could hardly decipher it myself," Mr. Stanhope said with righteous indignation. "It was absurdly complicated, so I'm certain your mother—or any other layman, for that matter—could hardly have known what it meant. But what it meant was, to put it crudely, that your money became Lord Maledon's money to do with as he chose; there was not a single clause or even wording in it that obliged him to use the funds, or conserve them in any way, with consideration for your future welfare. And so he took the money each year, and although I have not yet completed my investigation, it seems he spent the two thousand pounds on specific items. One year he bought a neighboring farm; one year he expanded the stables, and bought new brood mares and stallions; one year he bought three carriages."

Valeria stared at him, appalled. "You mean—I don't actually have any money, at all? That I have nothing, nothing left from my father?"

Mr. Stanhope said with some chagrin, "On paper, and in the strictest legal sense, Miss Segrave, but—"

Alastair interrupted him. "But that is pure rubbish, Miss Segrave, and Stanhope agrees with me. Maledon's estate must make reparations to you, and it can be done legally."

Valeria stared at him, then at Mr. Stanhope; and her face was stark white, and her eyes sparked dark fire. Then she leaped out of her chair and stalked to the end of the room, where she circled the refectory desk; then she paced back and forth by the fireplace; then she paced some more, around the desk again.

His face a study in shocked amazement, Mr. Stanhope jumped out of his chair. Rolling his eyes, Alastair stood up slowly. "Miss Segrave is prone to do this, Mr. Stanhope. Don't be alarmed."

"But—is she leaving?" the solicitor asked helplessly.

"I can't tell," Alastair rasped. "I suspect no one can."

After a while Valeria returned and threw herself back into her chair, apparently without noticing the two men standing awkwardly.

With some hesitation Mr. Stanhope and Alastair sat back down. Valeria said, "And so you're telling me that I can just—just—behave like my stepfather, and take whatever I feel I'm entitled to away from my brother's estate? No! No, no, no, I won't."

"But Miss Segrave, your own money has substantially added to this estate. It's not simply a matter of legality, it's a moral issue," Mr. Stanhope said in a pleading voice. "I'm not saying that you should demand the sum of your annuity since the time your father died, which, if it had been properly looked after, would be more than twenty-five thousand pounds. But certainly you could claim ownership of some of the investments. Or an annuity could be set up, whereby a certain sum is paid to you from the estate."

Tightly Valeria asked, "My annuity from my father, when is that paid?"

"Each January fifth, for the previous year."

"And I assume, since my stepfather is dead, and I am of the age of majority, that it will come directly to me this January?"

"Yes, madam, that is correct."

"Then that is what I shall have as my income. I repeat, I will not take money from my brother," Valeria said stubbornly.

Alastair said evenly, "Miss Segrave, I must remind you that I am a trustee of your brother's estate, which means that I represent him, and to the best of my ability, I follow what I believe would be his wishes, until such time as he is able to dictate those for himself. I believe that it would be your brother's wish to make this right with you. In fact, even though he is now just a child, I think he would agree, with full mental capacity, that it be so."

"When he is of an age to understand and comprehend this—this stupid situation himself, then perhaps I will speak to him. Until then, I refuse to contemplate explaining to him what a—what a—what his father was. And I will not subject my mother to what would surely be a crushing sense of guilt if I made these demands.

No, I shall be perfectly content to have a settlement of two thousand pounds a year. That will be more than sufficient for my needs."

Alastair argued, "Miss Segrave, you're quite wrong about that. I know that you're young, and so far have not learned much about society, but you must think of marriage. It would not truly be representative of your wealth, of what should be your wealth, for it to be thought that you have only two thousand pounds a year. It's ridiculous."

Valeria rounded on him with absolute rage. "Ridiculous! How dare you, sir, tell me that if I am only *worth* two thousand pounds a year, I am ridiculous! Here and now let me tell you that I could not possibly care less about ensnaring a husband! Why should I? To me it seems that a woman who marries has three obligations: first, to give her husband all of her money; second, to ornament his drawing room; and third, to dutifully present him with an heir while ignoring his mistresses.

"Well, let me assure you, sir, that I will *never* give any man one ha'pence I own; and I will always attempt to ornament any drawing room I happen to be in, without a husband's assistance; and lastly, if I were such a fool as to marry a man who kept a mistress there would never be the least chance I'd present him with an heir!"

"Oh, dear," Mr. Stanhope mumbled.

But Valeria relentlessly continued, "And so, Lord Hylton, here I am, with my humble two thousand pounds, and I beg that you will make all of your acquaintance aware of it, so that no unsuspecting would-be suitor may fall into my poverty-stricken trap!"

"I'm afraid, Miss Segrave," Alastair said distantly, "that the only person who is falling into a trap here is you."

Chapter Thirteen

❧

Valeria said, "Let me think . . . yes. Today I shall wear the black, Joan."

The maid giggled. "Yes, ma'am. Would that be the black, or the other black?"

"No, I meant the black." In truth, Valeria was depressed by having to wear mourning. The code of mourning for women dictated that their dresses must be made of material with no sheen; only flat matte black was acceptable. The dresses that Valeria and Regina had ordered were of black crape, a dull thick silk, and bombazine, a silk-and-wool blend. Although the black dresses and bonnets might be trimmed, absolutely nothing shiny was to be worn, such as satin ribbons, and particularly not jewelry. The only acceptable ornament was beads of jet, a dull black stone made from coal. Valeria had no jet jewelry, and so her only ornament for her hair was black grosgrain ribbon.

As she dressed, she reflected that always wearing grim black wasn't the only thing that made her despondent. The truth was that she felt like the worst hypocrite. She didn't mourn for the Earl of Maledon; she couldn't. With every passing day since he died, it seemed that she had been faced with more and more evidence of his corruption and betrayals of his family, and herself. Trying to forgive him was no longer even a question. Trying not to hate him took all her spiritual energy.

Anyway, I'm wearing mourning for Mamma and St. John, not for him, she told herself.

The morning was cold and dreary; rain spattered on the windows. Joan said as she worked on Valeria's hair, "It's right cold in here, isn't it, ma'am? I'll have to tell Mr. Trueman we need to bring up more kindling and coal of the mornings."

Valeria had noted that Joan, along with the other servants, even Trueman, had started to address her with the more respectful *ma'am* or *madam*, instead of the juvenile *miss*. She asked, "How are the servants coping, Joan?"

"Oh, we was all shocked, of course. We none of us knew he was so sick, although Mrs. Banyard did allow a long time ago she thought he'd gone lunatic. Mr. Trueman took it hard, he's always been that loyal to his lordship. We all were, as is right for servants, but some of us had come to have hard feelings, you might say. Pertick'ly over the last some years, it was hard for us to see her ladyship . . . well, you know. And then there's that Mr. Thrale, he's been the bane of the servants' hall ever since he came. We're right glad he's going, ma'am, even if we're sorry it's because his lordship died."

"What about Thrale?" Valeria demanded.

Joan's mouth tightened. "He's lazy, he takes advantage, like he made Ned and Royce iron his lordship's neckcloths and wash his smallclothes. He even made Ned shine his lordship's boots, which is meant to be a valet's pride, the sheen of his master's boots, and there! Didn't he always tell his lordship that it was his own secret polish that made his boots look so fine?

"But the worst of it is that he's such a bother to the maids. Won't keep his hands to himself. And poor silly little Callie and Marcia, he's got them so swoggled they're at each other's throats all the time, trying to get his attention. It's sickening." Callie was the fourth housemaid, and Marcia was the second kitchen maid.

In a hard voice Valeria asked, "And Trueman allows this?"

Joan shrugged. "Mr. Thrale just thumbs his nose at Mr. Trueman. You know, ma'am, the valet isn't like the other servants, just as the lady's maid is different. They're really under the lord and lady, not the butler or housekeeper. His lordship wouldn't never listen to anything about Mr. Thrale, I think Mr. Trueman only tried the one time. After that we all knew it was useless."

"Has he ever bothered you?"

"Oh, he tried, once, when he first came, five years ago, and I was the fourth housemaid, just out of the scullery," she replied with a satisfied cat's smile. "But he found that I'm not so foolish as to fall for his guff. And my brothers were that angry with him. They couldn't do much, you know, but Mr. Thrale did find he had wet coal, cold tea, and burnt toast for weeks. Once Royce even greased the bottom of his boots, and he almost slid down the stairs on his—well, you know, ma'am."

"I had no idea, and I know my mother didn't either," Valeria said wrathfully. "Every single day something happens that makes me wonder if I shouldn't take the veil, so I wouldn't ever have to see another man again as long as I live!"

"Now, ma'am," Joan said soothingly, "There are good men, like your father. Miss Platt's told us all about him. And there's your brother, and my brothers, and my father, and my uncles, and my cousins. And there's Lord Hylton, all of us think he's just fine. And us girls think he's maybe the handsomest man that ever was!"

"Lord Hylton, just fine!" Valeria cried. "I think he's proud and cold and arrogant. He looks down his nose at all of us mere mortals, with our foibles and follies!"

"Well, it is such a fine nose. Oh, I'm sorry, ma'am, maybe it's just that we don't know his lordship, of course, we're just the servants and we've barely set eyes on him. Except for Ned," she added carefully, "and he says his lordship's right kind and grateful, and he was careful to ask if valeting him isn't adding too much work on Ned. Unusual, that, if you ask me."

Valeria frowned. Here was proof of Alastair Hylton's character that utterly disputed her own view of him. But then again, she did see that he truly was good to her mother, and he even troubled to take time with St. John. It was his attitude toward her that was confusing. He seemed to continually view her with a critical eye, and she always fell short.

To add to her perturbation, Valeria did wholeheartedly agree with Joan: she thought that Alastair Hylton was an incredibly handsome man. She admired everything about him: his fine physique, his classical features, his aura of physical power. Part of her was strongly physically attracted to him, while another part of her was repelled by his cold detachment. When Valeria was with him her thoughts were always in turmoil.

As Joan finished arranging the ribbon in Valeria's hair she said thoughtfully, "You know, ma'am…maybe if you would ask his lordship—Lord Hylton, I mean—to speak to Mr. Thrale, it might put a stop to his shenanigans."

"Ask Lord Hylton—no, that's impossible! Besides, Thrale is leaving very soon."

"Mm, would you know, exactly, how soon, ma'am? Because it appears to all of us that he's settled in, like, and won't be going anywhere for a while," Joan said disdainfully. "He lays about in his room all morning, then comes down to the servants' hall in the afternoons so's he can torment poor Laurie and Callie. He's said he's set for now, that Lady Maledon—and he calls her ladyship that, too, the toad—said he can stay as long as he wants, until he finds a gentleman that suits him, so he says he's not obliged to be in any hurry, at all."

"What! Why, that lying, sneaking cad," Valeria said with gritted teeth.

"In my mind that's too much of a compliment for him," Joan asserted. "I know some words that a lady like you never heard, ma'am, and I wouldn't never say them out loud, but no one can stop me thinking them."

One sneaky corner of Valeria's mind wondered what those words were, but she made herself concentrate on this thorny problem. What should she do? What could she do? She thought, *I could just send him packing, but should I? It's true that Maledon's death was so sudden that it did leave Thrale in a terrible position. I know it must take time to find a position as a valet . . . but how much time? To be fair, his behavior is atrocious, but he's no different from any other man who abuses his position, and that's because my stepfather allowed it! But how am I to know . . . should I make him leave now? If I don't make him leave, however am I to stop him bothering the maids?*

Valeria was not only confused in trying to understand the fair and just manner to deal with Thrale, she felt pure revulsion in contemplating talking to him about his lecherous behavior. Merely thinking of it disgusted her, and she could see no possible way she could look Thrale straight in the face and speak of it.

With dismay she realized that here, indeed, was a situation that demanded a man's management. She would have to talk to Alastair Hylton after all.

This caused her much consternation as she went down to breakfast. She had such a strong aversion to demonstrating any dependence on Lord Hylton that she considered simply allowing the Thrale situation to play itself out. But she knew she couldn't do that. It wasn't fair to the servants, and in truth, it would be shirking her responsibility to represent the best interests of her mother and brother. Thrale was their employee, and so he was, in effect, their responsibility, but Valeria was now taking on all accountability for

St. John's decisions, and it was impossible to think of her mother's having to confront Thrale. It was even more unthinkable for Regina to be forced to take notice of such sordid behavior than it was for Valeria to do so. And that left...Alastair, Lord Hylton.

Everyone else was already assembled at breakfast. Valeria looked with secret envy at Elyse's pretty cream-colored morning dress and pink shawl, and at Lady Hylton's delicate white lace fichu. Lord and Lady Lydgate, and Lady Hylton, did not dress in mourning garb, for it would have been rather ostentatious since they were such distant relations. Lord Hylton wore a black armband, mainly because, Valeria thought, he had a connection that no one else had, that of nearest male blood kin to Lord Maledon, aside from St. John.

Regina was still a wan shadow of her former glowing beauty, but each day she seemed to be a little better. Valeria saw with satisfaction that she was eating with more appetite, having filled her plate with toast with marmalade and bacon. Lord Lydgate was saying to Alastair, "Can't possibly go shooting in this foul weather. Birds just huddle up and refuse to flush, and I can't say I blame them."

"I'm going for a ride anyway," Alastair said. "I start feeling cramped up when I'm too long indoors."

"I'm going out this morning too," Valeria said. "I've been thinking about Mr. Wheeler's report on the cottages, and I'm going to go see about them."

"But surely there's no need for you to do that, Miss Segrave," Alastair said. "Wheeler's report on the needed repairs was quite thorough."

"Yes, it was. But I feel that I need to get Mr. Wheeler, and the cottagers, accustomed to my attending to these matters," Valeria replied. "Surely you can see my reasoning."

"Not really, no," Alastair said. "I think that Wheeler, along with everyone else concerned, understands our positions as trustees very well. And certainly I don't think it's wise for you to go wandering all over the estate in a dismal cold rain."

"Why is it just fine for you to go riding, but it's foolish for me?" Valeria argued. "You see, that's just the sort of attitude I'm speaking of. You can gallop around and take charge of everyone, while I'm just a girl who's too delicate to get out in the rain."

"You're willfully misunderstanding me," Alastair said sharply. "All I meant was that it's really not necessary for you to tour the cottages right now, this morning."

Lady Hylton said, "You know, Regina, it never occurred to me that St. John's trustees would spend their time continually arguing. Perhaps we should have appointed me as a third trustee to keep the other two in check."

With mild amusement Regina said, "Valeria, surely you must see that what Lord Hylton says is true. It's really not such an emergency that you must go out in the rain for hours and subject yourself to the possibility of getting a cold or fever, or both."

"But I—yes, Mamma," Valeria begrudgingly replied, then added under her breath, "but I can't see why everyone isn't so worried that Lord Hylton will catch a cold or fever."

Elyse said, "Because he's a man, and if he wants to go out riding in a rainstorm, then that's all well and good, and if he comes down with a raging fever, he will still have the satisfaction of knowing that no one can dictate to him; he makes his own decisions, as stupid as they are. I'd like to think that women have more sense."

"I never get raging fevers," Alastair said, "and I am going riding, even if every woman here thinks I'm an imbecile."

"There, you see?" Lady Hylton said with satisfaction. "There's a man for you."

They managed to finish breakfast without Alastair and Valeria getting into another argument. Everyone went into the sitting area, but Valeria stopped Alastair and said, "Lord Hylton, there is a matter I'd like to discuss with you. Would you join me in the study?"

"Of course."

As they left the others and went into the study, Valeria reflected how very odd it was that no one, not even her mother, took any notice of their being alone together. Young ladies were supposed never to be alone with men. It was the peculiarity of the circumstances that made it necessary, for in the past days Valeria and Alastair had spent many hours going over bookkeeping ledgers, tradesmen's accounts, and Mr. Stanhope's reports. It would have been ludicrous for Lady Maledon or Lady Hylton to sit in the study with them. It was still difficult for Valeria, however, even though it was perfectly proper. Of necessity the two of them were required to sit close at the desk, to go over documents together, and Valeria found that physical nearness to him caused her so much confusion she could hardly think. Now Valeria hurried to sit in one of the side chairs drawn up to the refectory table, and Alastair sat across from her.

"How may I be of assistance, Miss Segrave?" he asked with his customary formality.

Valeria hesitated for a long time, then finally said tentatively, "You know Thrale, my stepfather's valet? It's—it concerns him, and I—I have to admit—it's such a—"

"I'm sure I can help," Alastair said coolly. "Please just tell me the facts."

This time his neutral tone made Valeria feel less uncomfortable. She told him everything, relating the conversation with her and her mother, and what Joan had told her, and her own confusion about the most just course to take. "It's maddening, I'm quite at a loss as to what to do," she finished with frustration.

"I'm well aware that you aren't going to appreciate this, but I must be honest," Alastair said ironically. "No lady should be in this predicament, and it's only Maledon's fault that you are."

"Actually, I do agree with you. That's why I've asked your assistance."

Alastair said, "I'm fairly amazed, and flattered, ma'am. I assure you that I can deal with Thrale. Now, you said that the maid told you that Thrale actually didn't attend to Maledon's dress and boots himself?"

Irately Valeria demanded, "Are you telling me that the thing that bothers you most about what I've just told you is that he didn't shine Maledon's boots? That, in your mind, is the most salient point?"

Alastair frigidly replied, "Ma'am, I already said that I'll deal with him, and by that I meant that I will immediately put a stop to Thrale's making a nuisance of himself with the maids. The other problem, as I see it, is his apparent intention of taking a holiday, as it were, instead of immediately seeking a new position. If I am to consider finding him a new position, which I assume is what you wish, then I must know his qualifications as a valet. If he is in fact not qualified for the position, then I won't consider recommending him to a man of my acquaintance."

"But how can you consider recommending such a man?" Valeria said angrily. "When you know that he abuses young girls who have no possible defense, or recourse?"

"I thought I would recommend him to one of my more disreputable friends," Alastair said sarcastically. "But I wouldn't consider it if he can't starch a neckcloth correctly."

"Lord Hylton, you really can be the most exasperating man!" Valeria rasped, jumping up to pace.

With a pained expression Alastair rose from his seat. "Miss Segrave, I must again point out to you that in Polite Society ladies do not bound up out of their seats and fling themselves about the room in a temper. I've observed that you never do such things when you're with your mother, and so I know that she has taught you that ladies must be calm and composed at all times. I can only think that you must make a decision to keep your tempestuous emotions under good regulation."

"I beg you will not speak to me in such a condescending manner!" Valeria stiffly sat back down. "You have no right to dictate to me, sir."

"I'm telling you this because you will only do injury to your reputation, Miss Segrave. Surely you must know that what I say is true. Well-bred ladies don't behave in such a wild, rash manner."

Valeria knew he was perfectly correct. She didn't allow her temper to get the better of her in front of her mother, because she knew it would distress her mother, and it would distress her mother because it was, in truth, very ill-mannered to have temper tantrums, she thought with shame. Even St. John didn't do such things.

Still Valeria was infuriated by Alastair's correction. Stiffly she said, "Very well, I understand and will attempt to behave in a more ladylike fashion. Now, may we return to the subject at hand? So you are inclined to find a position for Thrale?"

"I was considering it, yes, but now I'm not sure, after what you've told me concerning his laziness. I know this is very difficult for you to understand, but the fact that he's a nuisance to the maids is not really pertinent. If he were to be employed by a man who would keep him in check, he couldn't do much damage."

"On the contrary, it's not at all difficult for me to understand. I know that there are men like him everywhere. I just don't want such men here."

"I know I may seem callous, Miss Segrave, but I want to assure you that I personally find such men abhorrent," Alastair said evenly. "In fact, I see no reason why I should exert myself to help Thrale. It was more than fair of you to offer him a month's wages. He has been here...today is the twentieth? He's been here for six days. I will tell him that he can stay at Bellegarde for one more week, and then he must leave."

Valeria sighed and thought, *Regardless of his personal animosity toward me, I am so much relieved . . .*

She said quietly, "Thank you, sir. I truly appreciate your help in this matter."

Alastair's stern face softened a bit. "Ma'am, it is my honor, and my pleasure."

That night after dinner Regina suggested they go to the music room. It was actually one end of a large room; at the other end was the card room, with its comfortable seating area by an enormous fireplace. They all settled down close to it, luxuriating in the hot snapping fire. The night was stormy and cold, but the room was warm and comforting.

"Valeria, dear, won't you play for us?" Regina asked. "It seems so long since we've had music."

"Mamma, Elyse is much more accomplished than I," Valeria said.

"I don't think so," Regina said gently. "I know you don't like to perform, but I really would enjoy that piece by Herr Beethoven, the one you played for me and St. John when he was so ill."

Valeria considered her mother. That afternoon Regina, with Lady Hylton's help, had gone through Lord Maledon's extensive wardrobe. They had decided what clothing and accessories were to be given away, and what was to be kept for St. John. Regina had told Valeria that she had decided to give Thrale three barely worn suits of coat, waistcoat, and breeches, two top hats, an ebony walking stick, and a gold watch and chain. It had galled Valeria, but of course she had said nothing. Tonight her mother seemed saddened and weary.

"All right, Mamma, I will play, but only for you," she said with a smile.

She went to the pianoforte, found the music, and began to play Beethoven's *Silencio*. It was a long piece, and after the first few pages Valeria found that she didn't really need the sheet music; she had in fact memorized the sonata without realizing it. She played, and watched her mother, who stared into the fire with what seemed to be a forlorn, lost expression. But as the quiet, restful music went on, Regina's face gradually took on a look of peace.

When a person plays such tranquil, soft music, in some drawing rooms it becomes background to conversation. But here no one said a word. Valeria was momentarily distracted by the intent expression on Alastair's face. He never took his eyes from her, and Valeria, to her astonishment, thought that he looked utterly absorbed—perhaps even enthralled—by the music.

When the last soft notes faded away, there was only silence in the room for long moments. Then everyone started applauding, and Valeria rose from the bench and returned to her chair next to Alastair. Lady Hylton said, "Valeria, I had no idea you were so gifted! Now that I think of it, I've never once heard you play."

"That's because she refuses to play, except when I beg her to," Regina said. "And even I cannot persuade her to sing."

"That's because I sound like the peacocks wailing," Valeria said. "And I just don't like to play very much. It's not something I particularly enjoy."

"But whyever not?" Elyse asked. "It seems that having such a gift would give you great pleasure."

Carelessly Valeria said, "It's not really such a great gift. Just about anyone can read sheet music and depress the correct keys."

Alastair said, "That's possibly the grossest oversimplification I've ever heard. You played that magnificently, Miss Segrave."

"Thank you, sir," Valeria said uncomfortably.

He looked at her with a penetrating stare. "What is the real reason, Miss Segrave? Why don't you like to play?"

Valeria looked around the room. All of them, even her mother, were watching her with curiosity. "I—it's difficult to explain, I don't think you would understand."

As if she had spoken only to him, Alastair said, "Please at least allow me the opportunity to try."

Valeria frowned and finally answered with some difficulty, "It's just that I can't—lose myself in music, as I do when I'm painting. It doesn't really touch me, it doesn't—touch my heart, or spirit. Even though I suppose I am proficient at the pianoforte, it gives me no real pleasure to play, and particularly I dislike performing for an audience. It makes me feel like a fraud."

Alastair stared at her incredulously, and Valeria said with exasperation, "I knew you would not understand."

"Oh, but I do, perfectly," he said, now with amusement. "It simply astounds me, Miss Segrave, the way you snarl yourself up in so many delicately obscure moral quandaries. You're very hard on yourself."

Valeria said with arid amusement, "Oh, but I have never told myself that I was rash, wild, and tempestuous, and I have never accused myself of flinging myself about the room. That would, indeed, be hard on me."

Alastair rose from his seat next to her and made a mocking bow. "That is true, Miss Segrave. From now on I will allow *you* to punish you for your behavior."

"Thank you, sir."

"At your service, madam."

Lord Lydgate's face was a study in bewilderment. "Do you know what they're talking about, Elyse?"

"I haven't the faintest idea," she answered. "Perhaps we'd best leave them to it."

Regina and Lady Hylton exchanged secret, knowing smiles.

Chapter Fourteen

※

THE FIRST DAY OF OCTOBER was crisp and cool, the turning leaves dazzling, from the deep blood red of the maples to the delicate peach pastels of the hawthorns.

Valeria was walking alone in the Wilderness; and the thought amused her, in a glum sort of way. The Wilderness, or "wild grove," was the oldest garden on the estate, enclosed by a high stone wall with an ancient sagging wooden gate on the west side. The most that the gardeners did to tend the Wilderness was plant shrubbery and trim and prune it to form winding paths, and copses and thickets where stone seats and benches were placed. Valeria was walking down the main path, which was bordered on either side by slender graceful beech trees. She was awed by the silence, and it occurred to her that here was another example of the thoughtful, artistic things that her stepfather had done. Several years ago he had had the gravel walks replaced by turf and moss. There was no hard crunch of gravel underfoot to disturb the tranquility.

But Valeria was far from tranquil. Three days ago Lord Hylton and Lord and Lady Lydgate had left Bellegarde, for they were keen to return to Foxden Park for pheasant season. Valeria had thought she would be relieved, but she was not. She was at first baffled, and then irritated, at how much she missed Alastair Hylton.

Hastily in her mind she amended, *I miss Elyse and Lord Lydgate too. Elyse is near my own age, and she's so lively and entertaining. And Lord Lydgate is so affable, such pleasant company. And Lord Hylton . . . is not. What is it about that man? Most of the time he was here, I was exasperated with him, and now I'm peeved that he's gone?*

As Valeria considered, she came to realize that somehow Lord Hylton had, in her mind, come to represent all the men she had been in some struggle with, in one way or another, for the past month. First there was Trueman, then Mr. Broadbill, and Thrale. Even George Wheeler, the estate agent, had been reluctant at first to teach her about the management of the estate lands; Valeria had had to calculate exactly the right comportment—an air of competence and assurance, combined with dogged persistence—in order to bring him to accept her authority. It had tried her patience, but she finally understood that to take an active part in a man's purview, she must be ready to fight for her place.

It dawned on her that this was exactly what she missed—the battle of wits, and will, that she had continually had with Lord Hylton. They were always sparring, it seemed, and a small smile played on her lips as she thought that their quarrels were fun, even exciting.

But the smile faded as she reflected somberly, *And that just shows how very stupid I am, to think that I'm so clever that matching wits with me is exciting! Why, he must have been bored to distraction! I'm amazed that he was able to stay as long as he did before he felt it was decent to escape . . .*

And there was no escape for Valeria. She knew that her mother was in all ways the perfect example of propriety. Regina would stay in deep mourning, Valeria was sure, for at least one year. In fact, Regina had mourned Valeria's father for two years, and then had been in half mourning for six months, Valeria recalled Craigie's telling her. With a sinking heart Valeria thought that her mother's code regarding mourning her husband might not be determined by the actual level of sorrow she felt. Regina might very well feel that she must pay as strict a respect to Maledon's memory as she had to Lord Segrave's. Valeria reflected that her own future seemed dismal indeed. She might be over twenty years old before she had the opportunity to go to London for a Season. The thought was deeply oppressive. How could she bear to be "buried in the countryside," as the cliché went, for two years? Even now she felt so restless that she could hardly bear to sit still; sometimes she felt she wanted to just run as fast as she could, and maybe shout and yell at the top of her lungs.

Wouldn't Lord Hylton be appalled at that, she thought acidly. *He would lecture me most severely!*

And so she started running.

❦

Bellegarde returned to its normal routine, with the welcome exception that Lady Hylton would stay with them for a while longer. Regina decided, since Lady Hylton was more like family than a guest, that they would return to eating dinner at the early hour of six o'clock so that St. John and Mr. Chalmers could join them. Lady Hylton had said of the tutor, "He's quite a gentleman, he could grace any dinner table. And he's exceptionally good with St. John. You're fortunate to have him, Regina."

"Yes," Regina said softly, "especially now. I believe Mr. Chalmers has been more of a comfort to St. John, in some ways, than either I or Valeria has been."

Regina, Lady Hylton, Mr. Chalmers, and Valeria were gathered in the card room after dinner. St. John had gone to bed at eight o'clock, protesting loudly that he wasn't at all tired, while yawning prodigiously. Regina and Lady Hylton sat close to the fire, talking quietly. Mr. Chalmers and Valeria sat at a card table, but they weren't playing cards. They were conversing—after a fashion—in German.

"*Acht alte Ameisen assen am Abend Ananas*," Valeria said haltingly.

"Again, the *ch* after *a* is a guttural sound, much like Scottish, as in *loch*," Mr. Chalmers said. "Air must be passing over your tongue in order to—oh, Miss Segrave, I do beg your pardon!" His face turned crimson.

To mention the name of any body part to a lady was considered scandalously crass, but Valeria was hardly shocked. She laughed and said, "Mr. Chalmers, please. Instructing me in the most correct method of pronunciation is perfectly acceptable." She repeated the sentence three times, and then started laughing again.

Lady Hylton said imperiously, "Personally, I never found the German language to be so amusing, it sounds quite heavy and humorless."

"That's because you don't know what I'm saying," Valeria said with delight. "I'm learning the pronunciation of 'Eight old ants ate pineapple in the evening.' Quite droll, don't you think?"

"Oh, yes, and it will come in handy when you're next in a conversation with Germans," Lady Hylton said. "You'll be able to tell them exactly how many ants there were, and what they were eating, and when."

"You never know when the topic may come up in a German drawing room," Mr. Chalmers said, his mild blue eyes twinkling. "It's best that a lady be prepared for any eventuality." He started writing down another sentence, and Valeria leaned close and asked him a question.

Lady Hylton said to Regina, "Why on earth would that child wish to learn German?"

Regina replied, "She says it's because she loves the martial sound of it. She maintains that everything you say in German sounds like a colonel of the Hussars commanding his regiment."

"Mm, so it does, even 'Eight old ants ate pineapple in the evening,' if you say it sternly enough," Lady Hylton agreed.

"Actually, I think it's merely something to occupy her mind," Regina continued. "She has such an active intelligence that I think it's hard for her to find something challenging enough to hold her interest. I thought, when she was so eager to take over St. John's trusteeship, that her responsibilities might provide some fulfillment for her. But it seems that your son was right, Mr. Wheeler is so efficient that the estate needs very little hands-on management; Mr. Stanhope has all of the finances well in hand; and it seems that Valeria learned all she needed to know, and more, in a short period of time. She told me that she has very little day-to-day work. She seems restless. I worry about her."

"She is excessively bright, and such people grow bored so easily," Lady Hylton said thoughtfully. "You know, Regina, living on a fine country estate is all well and good for older, settled people. But when you're young and clever and witty and need stimulation, living quietly in the country can be stultifying."

"I know," Regina replied regretfully. "Valeria should have gone to Town last year. This year she's eighteen, she deserves to enter into society and have all the fun and excitement of London in the Season. But what can I do?"

"If you will allow me to again be a meddlesome old lady, Regina, I will tell you exactly what I think should be done . . ."

＊

Three weeks later St. John and Valeria sat in the window seat in the drawing room, looking toward the village of Abbott's Roding, watching the explosions in the night sky. In a conspiratorial voice Valeria intoned, "It was November fifth, 1605. Guy Fawkes, dressed all in black, made his way to Westminster Palace, with dark plans in his heart of assassinating His Majesty King James I. King James was a Protestant—" At the woebegone look on St. John's face, Valeria broke off to ask him, "What's the matter? I thought I was doing a fine job of dramatizing it."

St. John sighed. "This isn't going to be a story all about who said what in Parliament and who was the real king, is it? Like the Wars of the Roses? I never can get all of that straight in my head, except that the Lancasters were the red roses and the Yorks were the white roses."

Valeria smiled. "No, dearest, this was really very simple. Guy Fawkes and his followers—he only had twelve—wanted to replace King James with a Catholic king, and they did a very shabby job of it. The conspirators got caught, the plot was foiled, the assassins were hanged. Ever since then, by Act of Parliament, November fifth is a day of thanksgiving for 'the joyful day of deliverance.' So now we celebrate Guy Fawkes Night with bonfires and fireworks and we burn an effigy of whoever we don't like at the time."

"Coo, that's a much better story than those dumb wars over roses," St. John said. "Lookit, lookit! Green fire!"

The village was two miles distant, but Valeria had seen to it that the best fireworks were supplied for the celebration, and the western sky was lit up with white, green, red, and blue explosions of sparkles. They could not attend, of course, since they were in mourning. Valeria had been proud of St. John, for he had been careful not to show too much disappointment to their mother.

When the spectacular displays were over, Regina said, "Come here, my darlings, I wish to tell you something. St. John, come sit with me."

Mr. Chalmers said, "I'll take my leave now, then, Lady Maledon."

"No, do stay. This concerns you too, Mr. Chalmers."

St. John sat between Regina and Lady Hylton on the sofa, while Valeria and Mr. Chalmers pulled two chairs up close.

Regina smiled at St. John. "You know, St. John, I loved your father. I mourn him."

"Yes, ma'am, I know," St. John said, puzzled. "Me too."

Regina nodded. "I just want to make sure that you understand. You see, St. John, it is right and honorable to mourn for a period of time after one loses a family member. But there is not really a hard and fast rule for mourning. I have prayed long, and thought much, and I've made some decisions as to how we, as a family, will mourn your father."

Kindly she continued to St. John, "You've been a dutiful and faithful son, and it's time you stopped wearing your armband. We all know that you will always revere your father's memory."

In a subdued tone St. John said, "Yes, Mamma. I always will." Slowly he took off his black armband.

Regina said to Valeria. "Dearest, you've been wearing widow's weeds for two months, and that is quite long enough. You can put aside the bombazine, and put pretty ribbons and flowers in your hair again."

"Thank you, Mamma," Valeria said gratefully. "I was definitely regretting my red pelisse."

"You do look stunning in it, and you should wear it tomorrow," Regina said. "As for me, I have decided that I will remain in full mourning for four more months. In the middle of February, I shall go into half mourning, for a very good reason." She smiled, and for the first time since Maledon had died, Regina truly looked happy. "We are going to London for the Season. If we go in February, we will have ample time to order your wardrobe, Valeria, and have it on hand when the Season comes into full swing in April. Also in April, my dear, you will be presented to the Queen."

Valeria was so stunned that she couldn't speak. But St. John wasn't. He wiggled impatiently, then demanded, "And me too, Mamma? Am I going to London with you?"

"Certainly, my dear. Mr. Chalmers is coming too, as you must continue your lessons," Regina said firmly.

"And Niall too?"

"Oh, yes, and Craigie and Platt."

St. John could contain himself no longer. He jumped up and shouted "Huzzah! Did you hear that, Mr. Chalmers? We get to go to London!"

"I did," the tutor answered with pleasure. "Thank you very much, Lady Maledon."

"You're certainly welcome, sir; I cannot fathom how I would manage St. John and Niall without you," Regina said. "Valeria, you look slightly dazed. Don't you have anything to say?"

Valeria laughed, then jumped up out of her seat, joined hands with St. John, and danced with him in a circle. "I certainly do, Mamma," she said merrily. "Huzzah!"

PART III

Chapter Fifteen

❧

Valeria was filled with excitement to finally be going to London for her first Season, but her animation was slight compared to St. John's ceaseless hopping about in the coach. For the fourth time he opened the window and stuck his head out. Regina said, "St. John, I declare I'm going to signal Platt to stop the carriage so that he can nail that window shut. Again, it's entirely too cold, you'll catch your death."

Reluctantly St. John closed the window. "But Mamma, Platt and Ned and Royce and Timothy are out in the cold, and they won't catch their death."

"They're accustomed to it, because it is their job," Regina said. "You, however, are not suited to flapping about in an icy breeze."

"That thin blue blood," Valeria teased.

"Oh, really, Valeria," Regina reproved her. "As if you have anything to say about it."

"Who has blue blood?" St. John asked, puzzled. "That's silly."

"Yes, it is," Regina agreed.

The day, though frightfully cold, was bright and clear. They knew when they were approaching Town because suddenly the light was dimmed. London always had a coal-pall looming over it. They were just coming into the East End; they would go through the City

199

of London and on to the fashionable West End. All of the *haut ton* owned houses in Mayfair. The Maledon town house was located at one of the most prized addresses, Berkeley Square.

Valeria had been to London during the Season three times. The first was when she was ten years old, and Lady Hylton had persuaded Regina to rejoin society. They had stayed at the Hylton town house, just across from the Maledon town house in Berkeley Square. That Season was when Regina had become engaged to the Earl of Maledon.

Then, in 1807, when Valeria was fourteen and St. John was two years old, the family had come to London for April, May, and June, the height of the Season, and they had returned the next year for the same three months. But both of these visits had been rather a bore for Valeria. She was still "in the schoolroom," and her only companion was Miss Howells, her mousy, timid governess. Miss Howells was terrified of London, and wouldn't accompany Valeria anywhere unless Craigie took Niall and St. John for an outing, and Miss Howells would venture to go with them. But this year, Valeria thought, was going to be the most exciting adventure she had ever had!

As they labored through the muddy, narrow, tortuous streets in the East End, Valeria wondered that her mother had decided to travel in such style. It was thirty miles from Bellegarde to London, and although it was only about a three-hour drive with their four magnificent Maledon horses, generally when one traveled that far to another city the footmen didn't ride standing on the back. Ned and Royce, with their blue-and-silver livery, and full-length gray capes with blue satin lining, were stalwartly attending on this trip.

And then there was Timothy, the groom, riding postilion on the near front horse.

Normally this was necessary only when the team had at least six horses. But when Regina had explained to Valeria that she needed to pick a groom to accompany her as she rode in Hyde Park, Valeria had immediately picked Timothy. She had suggested to her mother that he would be thrilled to ride postilion, and somewhat to Valeria's surprise, Regina had agreed, and had personally designed a special livery, a slate-blue skirted riding coat trimmed with silver cord and piping on the sleeves.

Timothy had been almost beside himself with excitement and pride. Valeria had thought that traveling to London, with the footmen and postilion rider, would be what her mother considered ostentatious. Now she reflected that her mother had really been indulging her, in many ways, since Valeria was so excited about London and the Season. She thought, *I just turned nineteen two weeks ago. So many girls have already had two Seasons by the time they're nineteen . . . and after three or four Seasons, if they haven't managed to get themselves married off, they're considered past their prime. Imagine being thought a spinster at twenty-one years old! It's absurd! Oh, well, at least I'll have one or two years of fun!*

They entered into the wider, quieter streets of the West End, and then the carriage stopped in front of Number 23 Berkeley Square. The Maledon town house was one of a long row of gracious four-story houses, built of white stucco with black wrought iron fencing and trim.

Ned and Royce stood on either side of the carriage steps to hand down Regina and Valeria. St. John burst out of the carriage and ran to the iron railing that surrounded what was known as the *area*, the steps and landing leading down to the servants' and tradesmen's entrance. The basement was sunk only partly below street level, so that the kitchens and workrooms could have windows for good lighting. St. John jumped up to rest on his stomach on the railing, looking down the eight feet to the stone entryway.

"Oh, Ned, go fetch him," Regina said faintly. "That boy is going to give me an apoplexy. How happy I'll be to see Mr. Chalmers."

Ned went to St. John, who was hallooing down into the area.

Clasping one muscular arm about his waist, Ned lifted him up bodily. "Begging your pardon, my lord," he said sternly. He carried him back and set him down in front of Regina, brushed him off lightly, and stood back at attention.

"St. John, that entrance is for the servants and tradesmen. You will go into and out of the house by the front entrance," Regina said.

"Yes, ma'am," St. John said unconcernedly. "But you know the servants don't mind me. They don't like grown-ups coming down there, but they don't pay much attention to me."

Amused, Valeria said, "Yes, St. John, we all understand that, thank you. Still, don't go climbing around on the fence like a wild monkey." What he had said was perfectly true. The servants very much regarded the kitchen and servants' hall as their own personal and private spaces. Valeria had learned that Regina made definite appointments on the rare occasions that she wished to tour them. And even though St. John was that august personage, the fifth Earl of Maledon, they were unconcerned when he went into the servants' areas. They tolerated any children invading the servants' hall.

The town house had a full-time housekeeper, Mrs. Durbin. Valeria remembered her well as a bony, severe woman with iron-gray hair. Valeria secretly thought that she made a much better business partner for Trueman than did the motherly, warm Mrs. Lees. The other servants had come ahead so that the house would be fully prepared and ready for the family to simply walk in and be at home. They were all assembled in the entrance hall to greet them: Trueman, Mrs. Durbin, Mrs. Banyard, Craigie, Joan, the two housemaids Sophie and Amelia, and the little scullery maid that Valeria had had such a memorable experience with, Mary Louise. Mr. Chalmers stood a little to the side, smiling. Regina, Valeria, and St. John came in, and while Trueman was taking their pelisses and bonnets, Regina asked, "Trueman, is everything in order?"

"Yes, my lady," he answered.

"We shall tour the house," Regina said, "and then tea in the drawing room, please, Mrs. Durbin. And Mr. Chalmers, would you join us, please?" Turning to Valeria and St. John, she said, "Come with me, we'll go through the house so you'll know just how everyone is situated."

Valeria liked the atmosphere of the town house much better than the cold grandeur of Bellegarde Hall. It was built and furnished in the graceful, airy Palladian style, the rooms painted pastel colors, the furnishings mostly French. Even though the town house was much smaller than Bellegarde, Valeria found it more comfortable. Everywhere were enormous vases of fresh flowers; the sweet scents pervaded the entire house. At Bellegarde during the winter the arrangements were limited to dried flowers, but in London flowers and greenery were available year-round from the hothouses.

The entrance hall was floored with blue and white marble squares, and the walls were painted a light blue. White marble pillars were evenly spaced on either side. On the right was a graceful curved marble staircase with a black wrought iron railing. Down the hall and on the left was the wide arched entrance to the long, elegant dining room with oak flooring that had an intricate parquetry border. The walls were spaced with pilasters with finely carved cornices, painted blue with white trim. Crystal wall sconces were mounted between the pilasters. The long mahogany dining table was surrounded by twelve Louis XIV chairs. Above it, hung from a ceiling medallion, was an elaborate crystal chandelier. Regina told Trueman, "Since we won't be entertaining, I don't want that great chandelier lit every night. The wall sconces will be lit, and the table will be set with the six-candle candelabras."

"Yes, madam."

Regina turned to St. John. "Now let's go to the library, where I think you'll have a great surprise, St. John."

"In the library?" he asked dubiously.

They went down the central passage to the single room that occupied the back of the long narrow house. The library also served as the earl's study and office. The walls were lined with bookcases that displayed Grecian busts, ormolu urns, and other *objets d'art*. On one wall was the desk, a Hepplewhite of satinwood with rosewood inlay. But what astonished Valeria, and instantly enchanted St. John, was the addition of a large rectangular dining table, set somewhat incongruously in the center of the room. The top was covered with an immense map, and on the map were toy soldiers.

Mr. Chalmers was grinning like a young boy. "Now we shall be able to learn all about the Peninsular War in style, my lord." The set was intricately detailed, and comprehensive. There were infantry: foot guards, fusiliers, and grenadiers. The cavalry regiments—dragoons and Hussars—had their distinctive uniforms and were on horseback. There were even artillerymen with cannons. And to add to this magnificence, on the oceans were small models of Royal Navy ships.

"Coo-eee!" St. John breathed. "Is this—was this my father's?"

Mr. Chalmers answered, "The maps are, yes, sir. But the toy soldiers are a gift to you from your cousin, Lord Hylton. He said that his father gave them to him when he was your age."

"Lord Hylton!" Valeria exclaimed. "But surely he should give it—"

Utterly uncharacteristically, Regina interrupted in a soft voice of warning, "Valeria, it was a very thoughtful and generous gift to St. John. I'm sure you wouldn't want to diminish it in any way."

"No, ma'am," Valeria sighed. All she was thinking was that surely the set should go to Alastair's own son, but she did realize that if she said something to that effect it would cause St. John concern. He was sensitive in that way. And then again, Valeria realized ruefully, her instant reaction to anything that Alastair Hylton did or said was to object. *That's so silly and childish, I must stop resenting him . . . at least, when there is no good reason . . .*

Valeria was relieved to see that St. John had paid no attention to her outburst, as he and Mr. Chalmers were already positioning pieces on the map, and Mr. Chalmers was pointing out such famous battle sites as Coruna and Talavera.

Regina said, "I think St. John will be content to see his bed-chamber later. Trueman, go find Niall and tell him he may come to the library."

Stiff with disapproval, Trueman said, "Yes, my lady."

As Regina and Valeria went up the grand staircase, Valeria whispered, "You are in serious breach of etiquette, madam, and Trueman knows it."

Regina sighed and whispered back, "He's very vexed with me, and not just because of Niall. Let's go on up to the bedchamber floors and I'll show you why."

Because the street-level floor was always called the ground floor, the upper stories were somewhat mis-numbered. Through the family bedchambers were located on the third story, it was called the second floor. There were four of them: on one side were the earl's and countess's bedrooms, connected by a dressing room, and the other two rooms on the opposite side were the same size, but un-connected. Regina explained, "I'm keeping my bedroom, because it's in the back of the house and much quieter. Although now, in February, the street isn't busy at night, later in the Season it will be noisy. But I was wondering, Valeria, if you wouldn't like to have this front bedchamber, and we can both use the dressing room."

"That would be wonderful, Mamma," Valeria said with delight. "And I for one want to see everything that goes on out in the street!"

"I thought that you would," Regina said with amusement. "So, St. John will be across from you—and I hope you'll help me make certain that he *will not* be climbing out of the window. Those two birch trees that front the house are beautiful, but I can plainly see that St. John and Niall would think it a great adventure to escape from the house that way. At any rate, I decided, since we have a good-size empty bedroom, to put Craigie and Platt and Niall in the other one."

"Ah, and so Trueman is highly incensed that servants are staying in a family bedchamber," Valeria said gravely. "Scandalous of you, Mamma."

"I suppose so. But also it allows room for all of the servants to stay on the servants' floor. This way the maids don't have to sleep up in that awful garret, and Ned and Royce don't have to sleep down on cots in the basement."

Valeria's eyes lit up as she considered, "So Mrs. Banyard, Trueman, and Mrs. Durbin have their rooms . . . and does that mean that Joan—I mean, Davies—gets her own room, Mamma?" Joan had officially been promoted to Valeria's lady's maid, and she had been so proud that Valeria had determined to refer to her publicly as "Davies" to reflect her newfound prestige, though when it was just the two of them, both preferred she use "Joan."

"Certainly," Regina answered firmly. "As an upper servant, it is her privilege. I had some minor remodeling done to make the schoolroom into two small bedrooms, so Ned and Royce are sharing, and the three maids are sharing. But it's so much better than the attic; I worry so because I know they must absolutely freeze in winter and be stifled in summer."

It was unusual for Valeria to outwardly express affection; but she felt such a surge of warmth for her mother's kindness that she took both her hands and kissed her cheek.

"Oh, Mamma, how I wish I were as dear and sweet as you!"

Regina looked pleased. "Thank you, my darling, that means so much to me. And I'm glad I've taken care of the servants in this manner, no matter how much Trueman glowers at me. At any rate, I don't think it's necessary for us to tour the servants' quarters, and I am more than ready for tea."

"That sounds wonderful," Valeria agreed, and they went back downstairs to the drawing room.

This was the most luxuriously appointed room in the town house. On the street end, instead of casement windows, were two sets of double French doors that opened out onto small balconies. The Adam ceiling, painted a delicate oyster white, was a series of ornately molded circles containing octagons and geometric designs. From the large center medallion hung a gold-and-crystal chandelier. There was a quantity of furniture—sofas, wing chairs, side chairs, settees, cushioned stools—but instead of a clutter, Regina had them arranged into four distinct areas that had a graceful flow. The fireplace had a white marble surround, with fine carvings of vines and grapes. The walls were painted a warm tawny yellow, and paintings by Hogarth and Constable were alternated with large gilt mirrors, to enhance the light. On every side table were elegant double Argand lamps with gold bases and trim and frosted crystal shades.

"I love this room," Valeria said as she settled down on a plump sofa by the fire. "Lady Hylton is exactly right, Mamma, you have a gift for designing a room that is both opulent and inviting."

"Yes, I have decided that I shall make over the drawing room at Bellegarde," Regina said, glancing around the room. "This really is much more welcoming, is it not?"

Trueman came in with the tea tray. "Shall I pour, my lady?"

"No, I will. Did Miss Segrave's stationery arrive yet?"

"Yes, my lady, this morning."

"Then please bring it here."

"Yes, my lady." He returned with a wide flat box. Eagerly Valeria opened it.

Although Regina was in half mourning, her social activities were still limited. According to etiquette, she could make and receive morning calls, but only with close friends; it was not proper that she should seek out new acquaintances. She could attend private dinner parties and private balls, but not large public assemblies or venues such as Astley's Amphitheatre or Vauxhall Gardens. Because of this stricture on Lady Maledon, Lady Hylton and Lady Lydgate intended to sponsor Valeria in society so that she might attend those functions that Regina could not. Accordingly, since Valeria would be making social calls with her godmother and Elyse, she needed her own calling cards, because she would not be following the usual convention of using her mother's cards with her own name written on them. Also, Regina had thoughtfully ordered writing papers that were different from the Maledon stationery. Valeria's were a soft ecru color, and she had her own red sealing wax, and a simple seal with the block letter *S*.

Her calling cards were the same soft beige color, the paper thick and textured. Engraved in plain black block letters was "Miss Valeria Segrave."

"Oh, this is all very fine, Mamma, thank you," Valeria said. "But I was just thinking, shouldn't—couldn't I have my title on my cards?" As the daughter of a baron, Valeria had the courtesy title *the honourable*.

"That would be rather pretentious, dearest," Regina answered firmly.

"But no one is going to know who I am," Valeria said anxiously. "I understand the rule about us honourables being the sons and daughters of lower peers. I've always thought it so odd that although my correspondence is always properly addressed to 'The Honble. Miss Segrave,' yet the title is never spoken aloud when I'm announced or introduced. It's as though it must be kept a deep, dark secret. Anyway, I thought that perhaps since it's proper to include it on correspondence, it might be proper to put it on my calling card."

"It's not that it's improper. It's as I said, I believe it to be pompous. You're mistaken that people won't know who you are. They will."

Valeria looked puzzled, and Regina continued, "Valeria, there are some—many—things that I've never explained fully to you concerning your station in life. One reason is that it was not so vitally important while we were at Bellegarde, for that is the Earl of Maledon's home and domain. But here in London, you are not the late Earl of Maledon's stepdaughter, nor are you simply the Earl of Maledon's sister. You are Valeria Segrave, the daughter of Guy, Lord Segrave. That is how society here will know you."

"Really? I hadn't thought of that," Valeria murmured.

Reluctantly Regina said, "Now I must explain your exact position in London Polite Society. The Segrave barony is one of the oldest in England. Your father was the twenty-first baron, but actually the feudal barony goes all the way back to the eleventh century. Do you understand the import of that?"

Slowly Valeria answered, "I suppose such an ancient lineage is considered more—noble?"

"Yes, it is. Although a barony is the lowest rank of the peerage, such considerations as the length of the line, and the purity of the houses enjoined in that line, are given a certain precedence over the formal rankings. Everyone in society understands this. That's why you are already known in London, I assure you."

Valeria smiled mischievously. "I understand what you're saying, Mamma. I know that everyone reads *Debrett's*, and my father has almost three pages in it. But Lord Maledon's—" She broke off anxiously. *Debrett's Peerage and Baronetage* listed all the peers of Great Britain, and was avidly studied by everyone who was anyone. In cruder terms it was often called *the stud book*.

Regina said softly, "It really is all right, I'm very well able to hear his name. And so your brother is 'only' the fifth Earl of Maledon, with half a page in *Debrett's*, while your lineage takes up a full three pages. And that, I am sorry to say, is meaningful to London society."

Valeria sighed. "Oh, Mamma, no one on this earth could be as saintly as you. I certainly can't. I'm very proud of my father."

"And would you be so proud of him if he hadn't been a baron?" Regina asked.

"Of course! But... I'm still glad that he was," Valeria admitted with a sly smile. "Three pages in *Debrett's* is certainly a plus for me in this town."

"You are incorrigible," Regina said affectionately, "just as your father was. Still, Valeria, there is one more extremely important thing that I must impress upon you. Have you heard the term *noblesse oblige*?"

"'Nobility obliges'?" Valeria automatically translated. "What does it mean?"

"It is a term that means that those who are noble must conduct themselves nobly," Regina explained soberly. "It implies that noble ancestry must evidence itself in honorable behavior, and that with privilege comes responsibility."

"I see. You're saying that because of my status, I must be held to a higher code, I must conform to higher standards," Valeria said. "I find it very ironic that they use a French term. Apparently their own nobility forgot their own code, and they all got their heads chopped off."

"Valeria, really!" Regina said. "If you should say something that outrageous in some drawing rooms, there might be hysterics. Listen to me, child. What was acceptable speech and conversation and behavior at Bellegarde is very different from what is required of you now. I *know* that I've explained this to you."

"Yes, ma'am," Valeria said meekly. "Craigie has scolded me, my godmother has lectured me, and even Lord Hylton on several occasions uttered dire warnings that I must learn to behave acceptably in Polite Society. I will try very hard to be good."

"You must," Regina said sternly. "I know that it's difficult for you to curb your enthusiasms and to tamp down your fiery temperament, Valeria. But the rules are very strict. You must be decorous, calm, composed, and always gracious."

"And dull, and humorless, and only speak of such tedious things as the weather and the state of the roads," Valeria muttered.

"Nonsense," Regina said briskly. "You are bright, and clever, and interesting, and those traits are valued in a drawing room. It's just that you must be discreet, my dear." Then she sighed and added, "And I fear that telling you that is much like telling St. John to behave himself and stop causing trouble. I may be pleading a hopeless cause."

Valeria laughed. "Well, Mamma, as Lord Lydgate says, 'Apologies and all that.'"

That night Valeria was still so energized that she couldn't sleep. The fire had died down and the bedchamber was icy cold, so she pulled on two pairs of woolen stockings and wrapped her plump down comforter around her, then went to sit in the bay window seat. The graceful birch tree in front of her bedroom window was a bare spiky sculpture now, and did not block her view. Three stories below were the fuzzy golden orbs of streetlamps; even the deserted Berkeley Square park was lit up. The scene was such a striking contrast to her bedroom window view at Bellegarde. When she looked out at night there, all she could see was shadows and moonlight and starlight. Here the sky was an impenetrable black.

Already she wished day would come. She and Regina were going shopping, and then in the evening Lady Hylton was giving a dinner party to begin the process of introducing Valeria into society. Valeria was so galvanized that she thought she might never be able to sleep.

She recalled her mother's words that day, that she must be calm and composed and behave with decorum at all times. *How am I ever to do that? It's just not in my nature*...She thought then of Alastair Hylton, and his insistence that she must learn to govern her tempestuous spirit.

So easy for him to dictate, she thought sourly. *He's as stuffy and rigid as an old yew tree.* She thought of the two letters she had received from him after he had left Bellegarde. Again it struck her how peculiar was their relationship. Normally a single man and a single young lady exchanged correspondence only if they were engaged. But Alastair Hylton's two letters had had nothing to do with endearments, or affection; they were strictly business communications.

The first she had received in November, while Alastair was still in Yorkshire at Foxden. Valeria had agreed it would be best to sell some of the Maledon horses, and Reggie Lydgate had decided that his family wanted to buy some. Alastair wished to purchase Achilles, his favorite mount at Bellegarde. Achilles was one of the purebred Maledon "black star'd" horses, a full seventeen hands high, glossy ebony with the distinctive white diamond on his face. Lord Lydgate wanted to buy four matched grays for carriage horses. The prices Alastair and Reggie paid for the horses seemed extremely exorbitant to Valeria, but Alastair assured her that they were fair market prices, for he wished to avoid any question at all of a conflict of interest. Alastair had gone on to say that Lord Maledon had neglected the stables in the past year; there were at least four other horses that could be sold for a good price. Alastair had offered to attend to the Maledon stables. He had recommended that they promote the head groom, Mr. Buckley, Timothy's father, to stable manager. Alastair had said that he would be happy to arrange for the sale of any Maledon horse at Tattersalls Repository, the premier bloodstock auctioneer in England.

When Valeria received the letter, she had told herself that it was high-handed of Lord Hylton, as usual. But then she realized that at least he was courteous enough to inform her. She also admitted that here was another example of a part of managing the estate that she herself couldn't possibly do. She knew nothing of breeding programs or selling horses. And Lord Hylton would probably be coming back to Bellegarde to attend to it...and Valeria severely chided herself for feeling the least bit of anticipation at the prospect of seeing him again. When instead Alastair sent his head groom to see to the Maledon stables, and transport the newly bought horses back to Hylton Hall and Whittington Park, the Lydgate estate, again Valeria scolded herself, this time for feeling such a sharp pang of disappointment.

The other letter that Alastair had sent her had been somber indeed; and this time Valeria had felt no frustration at his cold formality. He had merely informed her that he had arranged for the London house that had been purchased the previous year to be vacated. Mr. Stanhope had said he already had prospective buyers, and he would conduct the sale, and all proceeds would be deposited into Lord Maledon's account at Barclays. Alastair had not mentioned Lady Jex-Blake.

Valeria thought with dread about what she would have done if she hadn't had Alastair Hylton to attend to this. The answer was simple. There would have been nothing at all that she could have done, alone. Again it was pressed upon her how much she needed Alastair Hylton.

No, I don't need him personally! she argued with herself. *In fact, I don't need him at all, it's really St. John who needs his help.*

Why do I brood over him so much? What do I care what he thinks, or what he feels? It's so confusing, one minute I admire him...well, maybe mostly his looks...and the next I'm angry with him. I just—I just have a stupid missish crush on him, I suppose, because he is so very handsome. But obviously it must be a very shallow crush, because I really can't stand the man!

Even as the thought formed in Valeria's mind, she knew that it wasn't true. She didn't truly dislike him. Then with impatience she commanded herself to stop obsessing over Alastair Hylton. She was in London now, she was going to have so many exciting and interesting diversions, and she was going to meet a crowd of new people, including young men who didn't criticize her all the time. Perhaps some of them might even be as handsome as Lord Hylton.

Doubt it, the sneaky little voice in Valeria's head whispered.

"Oh, hang him!" Valeria muttered. "I'm going to bed, and to sleep, and forget all about him!"

She did try. But as she finally began to sink down into slumber, the last vision in her head was of Alastair, Lord Hylton, riding the magnificent steed Achilles to the Barley Mow Fair...searching for her.

Chapter Sixteen

❧

"I FIND IT DIFFICULT TO BELIEVE that you are actually going into a tailor's shop, Mamma," Valeria teased. "It's very bold, for you."

"Not really," Regina said. "Letitia has assured me that ladies always have tailors design and make their riding habits."

"But I told you that, Mamma, after Elyse advised me when I admired her riding costumes so much."

"Yes, but it was Letitia who assured me that it's quite proper. I would hardly have taken your advice on that," Regina said lightly. "My sometimes-too-daring daughter."

"Only sometimes," Valeria said.

Although it was one long street, the only one that ran the entire width of Mayfair, it had been constructed and developed at two different times, and so the north end was called Old Bond Street, while the southern part was called New Bond Street. Old or new, Bond Street was the most fashionable shopping district in London. The storefronts were mostly glassed, well lit and with sumptuous displays: watchmakers, drapers, china and glass merchants, milliners, dressmakers, stationers, confectioners, fruiterers, jewelers, silversmiths.

One of the most attractive features of Bond Street was that stone pavements had been constructed so pedestrians could walk along the street above the mud and muck of the roadway, so promenading along Bond Street had become a popular pastime for the elite Beau Monde. Today, however, the street was not crowded, as it was a cold, dismal, rainy day. Valeria was disappointed, as she had wished to see the Quality in their finery almost as much as she had wished to see the shops.

Platt stopped the carriage at the head of Old Bond Street. Ned and Royce pulled down the steps, and opened large black umbrellas to shield Regina and Valeria from the rain. They walked down the stone pavement, the ladies in front and the footmen slightly behind and to the side. Valeria observed that here again Regina was indulging her in a show of grandeur. Normally ladies were accompanied only by their maids on Bond Street.

The shop of Monsieur Etienne Joubert, Tailor, was indicated only by a small brass sign on the door of what looked like a personal residence, for it had no large storefront windows, only a discreetly draped casement window on either side of the door. Regina and Valeria entered, and immediately Monsieur Joubert came forward to meet them, for Regina had, of course, notified him that they wished an appointment at eleven o'clock. He was a small, neat, precise man with dark hair fashioned in the Titus style, brushed forward with close curls around the face. His manner was courtly and charming.

He bowed low, in the old-world manner with his hand pressed against his breast and one foot slightly forward. "Lady Maledon, Miss Segrave, I'm so gratified to have you ladies as my patrons. I am Joubert, at your service." He spoke with a rich French accent.

Regina said, "Thank you, sir. You came very highly recommended, and I am happy that we can rely on you to design and make my daughter some stunning riding costumes."

His eyes brightened as he looked Valeria up and down. "Ah, yes, sometimes it is hard to please the ladies, but it is my greatest pleasure to see a beautiful lady riding in Hyde Park in one of my creations. You, *mademoiselle*, will show my habits admirably, you're tall and slender and must display very well when riding. The short, plump ladies, pah! They look like the puddings."

Valeria and Regina exchanged amused smiles at this, but Monsieur Joubert was paying them no mind. He walked around and around Valeria, humming and whispering to himself. "Hmm, hmm, *oui, certainement*, the dark blue, hmm, hmm, hmm, the bright green, the olive? Hmm, hmm..."

At first Valeria was slightly uncomfortable with this close-circling head-to-toe scrutiny, but Joubert was so clinical that soon she relaxed.

"Yes, the dark-blue superfine," he announced. "How many costumes, *mademoiselle*?"

"I would like four," Valeria answered. "But I want them to all be very different. It seems that most of the riding habits I've seen are blue and green; that will be acceptable, but I should like differing shades." One reason Valeria was so excited to have new riding habits was that in contrast to frocks, with their prevalence of whites and pale pastel colors, fashionable riding clothes were made in deep rich colors.

"Of course, and I am thinking, yes, I am certain, I have the dark chocolate brown that will do very well for you, *mademoiselle*, with your coloring, and *non*, the other ladies I don't recommend it, they will look too much muddy. Come along, please, this way."

He led them through the shop, and Valeria looked around curiously. On one side, hung on forms, were tailed coats and waistcoats. On the other side was a long glassed case containing precisely folded white shirts, high collars, and cravats. All along the walls, from floor to ceiling, were cubbyhole shelves of folded fabrics stacked neatly, arranged according to color, from snowy white satin for formal breeches to black velvet for court coats.

At the back of the shop were four curtains, and Monsieur Joubert led them through one into a small anteroom that contained a settee, a full-length mirror, and a plain worktable. Four ladies curtsied deeply as Regina and Valeria came in. Joubert said, "These are my most able assistants: my wife, Madame Joubert, and my daughters Sarah, Caroline, and Muriel. They will take the measurements, and show you the different fabrics and trim. Here you see the basic riding habit, and I will explain to you why Joubert's design will assure that you stand apart from and above the other ladies, Mademoiselle Segrave."

The riding habit on the dress form was structured exactly like the only fashionable wear for women for the past five years—in the Empire style. The differences, however, showed what set riding costumes apart from other dresses. They had more of an aura of masculine wear than the gauzy, dainty dresses usually worn. Made of the same fabrics as men's coats, they were tight-fitting at the top, with the "waistline" just under the bosom, and long-sleeved. The skirts were heavily gathered for fullness, with a medium-length train that draped gracefully when the wearer rode sidesaddle. Men's shirts of fine white lawn with ruffled fronts, or even with high collars and cravats, were often worn underneath. The trim that was all the rage at the time was for military touches.

Monsieur Joubert explained how he could make unique designs using frogs, braid, piping, wide lapels. The ladies brought in several fabrics, and Valeria decided on two habits made of superfine broadcloth, one in dark blue, one in bright green; one kerseymere of olive green; and she positively fell in love with the chocolate velvet that Monsieur Joubert assured her would not make her *regarder à la boueuses*, "look the muddy."

After agreeing on different designs for each costume, Valeria went through the most extensive measuring process she had ever imagined. The four ladies were so thorough, and so exacting, that Valeria remarked to Regina, "One would think I were getting fitted for a second skin."

Madame Joubert said, "That would be a great shame, Mademoiselle Segrave, with a complexion such as yours."

Finally the appointment was completed. As they were leaving, Monsieur Joubert said, "Your order will be delivered in five days, *mademoiselle*."

Valeria put out her hand for him to bow over and said pleadingly, "Ah, but Monsieur Joubert, I do so love the chocolate velvet, and I've decided that I shan't ride in Hyde Park until I can wear it. Just that one, perhaps tomorrow or the next day, *s'il vous plaît, monsieur?*"

Monsieur Joubert smiled with a tight, precise little upturning of his lips. "Mademoiselle Segrave, I predict you will break many hearts this Season, for *vous êtes très charmeur*. You will have the brown velvet tomorrow."

⁂

London boasted several clubs where the nobility and gentry enjoyed the pleasures of male exclusivity, luxurious comfortable appointments, outstanding food and fine drink, making and sustaining both social and political connections, and high-stakes gambling in all forms. By far the most prestigious of these clubs was White's. Originally established in 1693 as Mrs. White's Chocolate House, through the years it had gradually achieved preeminence as the most desirable men's club on St. James's and Pall Mall. White's was notoriously the most difficult one at which to gain membership. It was now not only common, but expected, that when an heir of a gentleman of the *ton* was born, the butler was immediately dispatched to White's to place the heir on the waiting list. It had been one of the Earl of Maledon's greatest delights, when St. John was born, to send Trueman for this most solemn of ceremonies.

It was in the famous bow window overlooking St. James's. Alastair Hylton was having a leisurely drink with four of his friends. Alastair watched as young Daniel Everleigh tried to persuade Lord Stephen Tryon to wager with him. Everleigh was a bright-eyed, handsome young man with a puppy-like eagerness that sometimes amused Alastair and sometimes exasperated him. However, Alastair did have to admit to himself that perhaps his impatience with Everleigh's boundless enthusiasms meant that he was getting old and stuffy.

Alastair, Tryon, Charles Ponsonby, and Paul Northbrooke had all been at Eton and Cambridge together and were fast friends. Lord Stephen had taken a fancy to Daniel Everleigh, who at twenty was younger than the others but the kind of lively young dandy who was an amusing companion.

"Tryon, you're always ready for an interesting bet; I'll wager a guinea that Lord Dashalong careens up and down the street at least twice more before the hour is up!" Everleigh said. Lord Sefton had earned the nickname because he was a famous whip, and drove around Town as if all the hounds of hell were at his heels.

Lazily Tryon replied, "Fool's wager, Everleigh. Here he comes again right now. We all know he'll make the rounds he always does and pass by three or four more times."

"Blast, I thought I might be able to snooker you before he flew by again," Everleigh muttered, then brightened. "So, Hylton, speaking of Lord Sefton, he's to be at your mother's dinner party tonight, with Lady Sefton, yes? From what I've heard, it's very wise of your mother to introduce Miss Segrave to Lady Sefton first for her sponsorship of Almack's."

Almack's Assembly Rooms was the most exclusive club for fashionable society. It was governed by a select committee of ladies known as the Lady Patronesses, the "fair arbiters" who in effect decided who would be members of the Beau Monde and who would not. Neither riches nor titles could guarantee admission to Almack's; the strict patronesses made their decisions based upon good breeding, disposition, and deportment.

"Oh? And why should this be such a clever move on the part of my mother?" Alastair asked evenly.

Everleigh shrugged. "Everyone knows that Lady Sefton is the most approachable and lenient of the patronesses. Surely she'll be the most likely to sponsor someone like Miss Segrave."

Alastair repeated, "'Someone like Miss Segrave.' And what, precisely, does that mean?"

"Aw, don't get in a high dudgeon over your ward, old Hylton," Everleigh said, grinning. "We have to get word of the new young ladies from other sources and you're so tight-lipped about her. Lady Jex-Blake says that Miss Segrave is an ill-humored, sour girl and that she has little to recommend her for admission to Almack's. She also mentioned that she's as thin as a stick insect but has fat ankles."

Alastair looked thunderous for a moment, but then his jaw relaxed and he gave Everleigh a wry grin. "If I ever doubted that you're a foolish young pup, that entire little speech just reminded me. First, Miss Segrave is not my ward. We are co-trustees of Lord Maledon's estate, and I've found her to be a surprisingly good businesswoman. And second, if you take Lady Jex-Blake's assessment of Miss Segrave as genuine, and believe that she is an authority on who will be accepted at Almack's and who will not, then you're even sillier than I thought." Obviously a woman like Lady Jex-Blake would never see the inside of the hallowed rooms of Almack's.

Daniel Everleigh's boundless good temper couldn't be dampened by Alastair's harsh words. "Then why don't you tell us the truth about her, Hylton? Is she ill-tempered? What does she look like? And most importantly, are her ankles truly fat?"

Slyly Lord Stephen said, "Lydgate told me she's a stunner, Hylton."

"I think that may be a fair assessment," Alastair said slowly. "But she's poor, Tryon, with only two thousand per annum, so don't flirt with her too outrageously. She's still young and innocent, and she doesn't need a rake like you leading her merrily along." Lord Stephen Tryon was a devilishly handsome man, with jet-black hair and flashing dark eyes. A wealthy, much-sought-after bachelor, he was indeed given to leading women on.

"So she is a beauty?" Everleigh asked with interest.

"Mm, and Lydgate told me that she's tall and slender and graceful, but that she does have a fine figure," Charles Ponsonby said. "He didn't say anything about stick insects." Ponsonby was a rather plain man with brown hair and brown eyes, short and slim, but with an amiable expression that made him appear more attractive than he was.

"I should think not," Alastair grumbled.

"Tall and slender, but with a fine figure?" Everleigh said, his dark eyes shining. "But she's not taller than I am, is she? And is she curvaceous?"

"Everleigh, do be quiet," Alastair rasped.

"Lydgate also said that she had eyes that a man could only dream of," Paul Northbrooke added. He was a more jolly man than his friends, with laughing blue eyes and tow-colored hair, and already had a certain beefy English look about him.

"Reggie never said anything like that," Alastair said sharply, then relaxed as he saw the amused looks that Ponsonby and Northbrooke exchanged. They were his oldest friends, and Alastair knew they could see how uncomfortable he was with the conversation, and were teasing him. But why was he so uncomfortable? Why should he be so reluctant to talk about Valeria?

He was still trying to work it out when Everleigh said insistently, "But what about her disposition? Is she really sour?"

"She is not," Alastair retorted. "She has what may be called a rather fiery temperament, but she is lively and witty and intelligent, and that's why she'll probably be bored with you, Everleigh, since apparently all you ever think about are horses, gambling, women, and their ankles."

"No, she'll find me absolutely absorbing; I can charm a beautiful young lady when I exert myself," Everleigh sniffed. "It's just that most of them are not worth the trouble. I swear, for a solid year now all I've heard from my sister Adele and her friends is talk of frocks, frills, and furbelows, and I'm heartily sick of it. It would be enchanting to converse with a lovely young lady with a brain in her head."

"Enchanting," Alastair murmured under his breath with a distracted air. "Odd that you would...never mind. I'm certain of one thing: if Miss Segrave wishes to take notice of you, Everleigh, then she will, and if she does not wish to, then she will not. She's a lady who knows her own mind."

"She will," Everleigh said confidently. "But you've forgotten the most important thing, Hylton. What of her ankles?"

Alastair rolled his eyes. "I had occasion of observing them a couple of times, and I found them to be quite trim. Tonight, if you're fortunate, you may have the opportunity of judging for yourself."

Chapter Seventeen

❧

VALERIA KNEW THAT SHE LOOKED very well for Lady Hylton's dinner party. Her dress was a thin, crisp silk of the palest golden-yellow shade, her petticoat of the same delicate fabric. The hem of the dress was trimmed with sienna-brown embroidery, and the short puffed sleeves had six tiers of fine lace. Joan had arranged her hair with particular care, entwining in it a brown satin ribbon trimmed with garnets mounted in gold. The only jewelry Valeria wore was square-cut garnet drop earrings. As she and Regina arrived at the Hylton town house Valeria was grateful for her new gown; like all women, she felt more confident if she knew she looked her best.

The Hyltons' butler, who looked fully as supercilious as Trueman, took their wraps and then escorted them up to the drawing room. Lady Hylton's dinner party was scheduled for the fashionably late hour of eight o'clock, but Valeria had insisted that she and her mother arrive ten minutes early. She wanted to be in the drawing room with her godmother and her friends Elyse and Reggie Lydgate when being introduced to the other guests. Although Lady Hylton had fully informed her about all the guests, she felt that receiving them as they arrived would be much more comfortable than walking into a roomful of strangers and being presented to them one by one.

Lady Hylton, Alastair, and Lord and Lady Lydgate all welcomed Regina and Valeria warmly. Elyse took Valeria's hands, then kissed her on both cheeks. "You look stunning, Valeria," she declared. "And I don't just mean your lovely dress. You're positively glowing. Are you nervous at all?"

"Somewhat, but not nearly as much as I thought I should be," she answered. "But then again I may get an abysmal case of jitters when the illustrious personages start arriving."

Alastair said, "I sincerely doubt that. I've never seen anything that makes you nervous, Miss Segrave."

The thought *You do* flitted through Valeria's mind, but she merely said, "Oh, but you've never seen me struggle to impress such a doyenne of society as Lady Sefton. If I don't get accepted into Almack's I shall be ruined before my first Season even begins."

Alastair's lip curled slightly, and Elyse said, "Don't take any notice of him, Valeria, he thinks Almack's is much overrated, and never deigns to attend. Men, of course, can afford to be disdainful of such things, while young ladies cannot."

He said, "When I attended the balls there I felt as if I were a deer being stalked by a crowd of hunters. It was excessively tedious."

With spirit Valeria said, "It is possible for a young lady to simply enjoy attending a ball and forming new acquaintances without being a predator in search of a husband, you know. I, for one, have no intention—" She broke off abruptly.

Alastair's lips twitched. "Yes, I do recall that you have very definite opinions concerning marriage. Your vehemence on the subject almost gave poor Mr. Stanhope the vapors."

Valeria said, "Oh, yes, poor Mr. Stanhope, I'm sure I shocked him terribly. But don't worry, sir, both your mother and mine have lectured me endlessly about maintaining strictly proper comportment, so I shan't be making such scandalous outbursts in public again."

"Oh, really," Alastair said doubtfully.

"Yes, you see, I've no problem at all with *them* lecturing me," Valeria said, her eyes sparkling with mischief. "I'll certainly follow *their* constant instruction upon the improvement of my behavior."

Elyse said with amusement, "You know, Valeria, you're the only girl besides me who has ever dared to stand up to my brother. Most young ladies who try to converse with him get positively frozen into paralysis."

"Most young ladies are babbling idiots," Alastair said succinctly.

"Valeria certainly is not," Elyse retorted.

His cool gray eyes met Valeria's. "No, she is not."

Valeria was trying to work out if this was a high compliment or very faint praise when the other guests started arriving. Lady Sturway and her children Adele and Daniel Everleigh were announced. As Valeria was introduced and made her graceful curtsy, she noted that Lady Sturway was modestly pretty with elegantly dressed dark hair and eyes. Miss Everleigh was plain, and she had a certain pinched look about her mouth that made her appear vaguely dissatisfied. Valeria also observed that Adele's up-and-down appraisal of her from head to toe was extremely sharp and assessing.

In contrast, Daniel Everleigh was a handsome young man, barely twenty, with thick curly light-brown hair, bright brown eyes, and a friendly expression. His appraisal of Valeria was frankly appreciative.

Stephen Tryon, Paul Northbrooke, and Charles Ponsonby arrived then, and Valeria found them exactly as Lady Hylton had described them to her. Lord Stephen, a ruinously handsome man, immediately began exercising his considerable charm on her. Northbrooke and Ponsonby were both mild-mannered, agreeable young men with unremarkable features except that Northbrooke was like a jolly squire and Ponsonby was exceptionally amiable.

When the butler announced Lord and Lady Sefton, for the first time Valeria felt some uneasiness. Lord Sefton was a bluff, barrel-chested man with a pugnacious jaw, a high brandy-drinker's complexion, and a rather loud voice. But his greeting to Valeria was courteous, and his smile welcoming.

But it was Lady Sefton, a rather plain but elegant woman, who amazed Valeria. As she made her curtsy, Lady Sefton smiled serenely and said, "Lady Hylton told me that you would surely be an acknowledged beauty, Miss Segrave, and now I see that it is true. Charming, charming."

Slightly flustered, Valeria murmured, "Thank you, Lady Sefton."

As was traditional for dinner parties, the drawing room where they gathered was something like a holding pen, although when Valeria had observed as much to Lady Hylton, her godmother had rolled her eyes and said, "Don't you dare make such a vulgar remark to anyone in London, Valeria. I swear if you do I'll disown you." Still, Valeria couldn't help but feel that way for the few minutes they waited for dinner to be announced. They all stood; no one sat. No refreshments were served. Conversation was limited to the journeys they'd made—from a trip across the square, as Valeria and Regina had made, to Lord and Lady Sefton's travel from their Park Lane mansion a few blocks away.

At last the butler entered and announced stentoriously, "Dinner is served." Briskly but discreetly Lady Hylton and Alastair arranged the manner in which everyone was to proceed back down to the ground floor and into the dining room.

Regina had explained to Valeria that in contrast to country dinner parties, dinner parties in Town had strict rules for exactly who was to escort whom into the dining room. The precedence, according to each person's ranking in society, was a very serious matter. Regina had told Valeria, "I know of no one, not even Lady Hylton, who has all these rules memorized for every occasion, because generally the guests at each dinner party are different. A hostess is well advised to consult *Debrett's Correct Form* when any guest's particular standing is in question. Still, there are a few general rules you would do well to remember. The host escorts the highest-ranking lady present, and she will be seated by him. The highest-ranking gentleman present will escort the hostess. The seating sometimes may be by rank, but at table it is considered preferable to preserve a lady-gentleman seating arrangement than it is to adhere too strictly only to the order of preference."

Valeria was confused to see that Alastair, as the host, took her mother's arm to escort her in first. She would have thought that Lady Sefton, as one of the patronesses of Almack's, would actually have a much higher standing in society than Regina, Countess of Maledon. After all, Lady Sefton was also a countess. But then Valeria recalled what her mother had told her about the nature of peerages: Regina was the widow of the fourth Earl of Maledon, while Lord Sefton was "only" the second Earl of Sefton. Valeria inwardly sighed; she thought that she would never be able to conduct a formal dinner party in Town without making some silly mistake. Then it occurred to her, as a rather cold comfort, that she likely would never be a wealthy hostess giving fabulous parties.

As the daughter of a baron, Valeria was at the bottom of this exclusive social ladder, and the Honourable Paul Northbrooke was her escort. As he offered her his arm he said, "We may be last in precedence, Miss Segrave, but I must say that I think I have the honor of escorting the prettiest lady."

"Thank you, kind sir," Valeria said as they followed the train of people going downstairs, "but I think that distinction belongs to my own mother."

"She is indeed a beauty, even in widow's weeds," he agreed. Then, with a cautious sidelong glance at Valeria, he added, "Please accept my sincerest condolences upon the death of your stepfather, Miss Segrave."

"Thank you very much, Mr. Northbrooke," Valeria said coolly.

The Hylton town house was larger and more sumptuous than Maledon's. The dining room was long and rectangular, with ravenous roaring fires in the cavernous fireplaces on all four walls. The furniture was heavy and ornate Elizabethan, all red velvet and gold, and the white damask tablecloths were as thick as the heaviest satin. Some slight shuffling around occurred, as the seats were labeled with place cards written in lavish calligraphy. A footman, clad in the dramatic black-and-silver livery of the house of Hylton, stood behind each of the fourteen chairs. Lady Hylton had "borrowed" Ned and Royce, as she had only twelve footmen in Town, and as Valeria surreptitiously observed the grand attendants, she noted with satisfaction that the two Maledon footmen were by far the most handsome. And, she thought with placid satisfaction, their calves were also the most muscular.

Valeria found that she was seated between Lord Sefton and Daniel Everleigh. As the diners all sat down together with rigid formality, with the footmen placing their chairs just so, Valeria determined that she would not keep her conversation fatuous and insipid, as society dictated. A man such as Lord Sefton could hardly be interested in her observations about the weather. The footmen began serving the first course, a choice of three different kinds of soup, braised veal cutlets, assorted sweetbreads, turbot with lobster sauce, and oyster patties with lemon sauce. With an inward sigh she reminded herself of her mother's instructions; dinner was to be five full courses, and although the diners were not expected to partake of every single dish, ladies must appear to appreciatively taste most, and so Valeria knew she shouldn't take more than a bite or two of each dish.

To Valeria's delight the first soup she was offered was her favorite, and she signaled the footman to give her a double portion, utterly disregarding her own advice to herself. "Soup à la cantatrice," she said to Lord Sefton, who was watching her. "My utmost favorite, sir."

He repeated curiously, "*Cantatrice*? Soup of the singer?"

"Yes, sir. The principal ingredients are the yolks of eggs, and the hearts of sago palms, creamed, which have always been deemed very beneficial to the throat and lungs. It is one of Lady Hylton's chef's specialties, and I find it to be perfectly delicious."

"Then I shall have it too," he said decidedly, signaling the footman. Politely he asked Valeria, "I understand that this is your first Season, Miss Segrave. How do you find London so far?"

"Foggy, damp, and cold, sir. But let me assure you that it has not dampened my excitement. Even if it's so thick I can only see as far as my horse's nose I intend to take my first ride in Hyde Park tomorrow," she answered, her eyes shining.

He nodded enthusiastically. "I either ride or take out my carriage every afternoon, regardless of weather. It's one of my favorite pastimes."

"So I hear," Valeria said mischievously. "Your nickname makes your preferences clear."

He looked surprised, for this was a somewhat bold comment for a young lady, but he was clearly amused. "I know you can't have been in Town more than a day or two, and you tell me that you've already heard that foolish sobriquet."

"It doesn't seem silly at all to me, sir; I find it daring, in a good sort of way, of course. 'Lord Dashalong' is so much better than, for example, 'Lord Plodalong' or 'Lord Bustle-along.' Already I've seen some gentlemen riding in Town who could be named such."

He grinned widely. "Isn't it so, and ladies too. Then again, I've seen some ladies who are excellent whips, Lady Lydgate, for example. She rackets around in the Park as fast as do I. Do you drive, Miss Segrave?"

"I can, but I much prefer to ride," Valeria answered enthusiastically. "I have an amazing horse from the Maledon stables, and I can hardly wait to show him off."

"Ah, yes, the famous Maledon horses. I'm positively envious of

Hylton's new Maledon stallion. I've determined to go to Tattersalls on Thursday to see the four that are up for sale. If any of them are up to snuff I might buy one myself."

"Oh, they are all of them up to snuff," Valeria declared. "In fact, you may wish to buy two of them, matched chestnuts that have already shown themselves to be quite showy in pulling a phaeton. They would help to increase your fame as Lord Dashalong."

As they continued an animated conversation about the Maledon stables, Valeria noted that although Alastair Hylton was politely attentive to Lady Sturway, his gaze often rested on her. As always, it made her uneasy, but she managed to direct all her attention to Lord Sefton, who was proving to be a lively and interesting dinner partner.

When the first course was finished and the second, a selection of roasts, assorted sauces and jellies, and vegetables, was served, Lady Hylton "turned the table" and so Valeria turned to Daniel Everleigh. "I'm afraid I've already committed a *faux pas*, Mr. Everleigh," she sighed. "I ate entirely too much of the soup in the first course. I don't know how I shall ever manage to get through four more courses."

"The roasts are always my downfall," he said. "Make quite a glutton of myself sometimes, especially with Lady Hylton's new French chef. Take this roasted leg of lamb with white truffle sauce, one can't get a dish like this anywhere else in London, the man's a genius."

"So Lady Hylton says, and she also tells me that he's an overbearing martinet," Valeria said. "Apparently he has the entire household cowering."

"I doubt Hylton cowers much," Everleigh said, glancing at Alastair. "But for my own part I'd bow and scrape to Monsieur Longet just for the truffle sauce."

"I somehow doubt that," Valeria replied, her eyes dancing. "At least, that is far from the impression Lady Hylton gave me when she acquainted me with all the guests. This is my very first dinner party of my very first Season, you know, so Lady Hylton was kind enough to 'pre-introduce' me to everyone, if you understand."

"Of course I understand. Gossiping in London is one of the chief pastimes. I hope Lady Hylton gave me a favorable recommendation."

"Mm, one might say it was double-edged. She said you've been friends with Lord Hylton for a couple of years, and you make a delightful addition to any dinner party. And then she said sternly that although she knows about all of your youthful indiscretions, she had no intention of recounting them to me. I was quite disappointed."

He grinned. Everleigh really was a most attractive man, with a bright shrewd gaze and a ready smart smile. "Never mind, by the end of the Season you'll know everything about everyone else, as we all do. I understand that since your mother is in half mourning, Lady Hylton will be chaperoning you for public events?"

"Yes; she is my godmother, you see. I'm so excited, for she, and Lord and Lady Lydgate, who have also kindly offered to sponsor me, already have several events planned, although it is so very early in the Season. Lady Lydgate is having a small dinner party on Thursday, and on Friday we're going to Covent Garden. I hear that Angelica Catalani's Susanna in *Le Nozze de Figaro* is simply fabulous."

"She is amazing," Everleigh said enthusiastically. "I've seen her perform several times." Then he paused and made a theatrically downcast face. "I'm devastated that Lady Lydgate didn't include me in her dinner party. It's not fair, for I'm so looking forward to furthering our acquaintance, Miss Segrave. Ah, well, I suppose it's too late now for me to cadge an invitation." Then he brightened. "But I shall hound Hylton to invite me to attend in their box on Friday night. You can't escape me, you see."

"And why should I wish to do such a thing, sir?" Valeria replied brightly.

Daniel Everleigh looked delighted, and continued to flirt outrageously with her throughout the three-hour-long dinner. Valeria thought that she was likely smiling too much, and might have at times committed the sin of laughing softly, and she noted Alastair Hylton's occasional coldly disapproving glances, but by now she hardly cared.

At last the ladies withdrew to the drawing room, leaving the men to their port and cigars. They gathered around a cheery fire, seating themselves on the luxurious sofas and armchairs. Valeria composedly took a seat next to Adele Everleigh. In spite of Miss Everleigh's thinly veiled coldness toward her, Valeria truly did wish to make new friends in London. "Lady Hylton tells me that this is your first Season too, Miss Everleigh. Are you as excited as I am?"

Miss Everleigh answered stiffly, "Of course, every girl is excited in her first Season. It is particularly fortunate that I am to debut this year, as the Queen has resumed her Drawing Rooms. I'm to be presented in her first one for almost two years, since the King fell ill."

Valeria's eyes brightened. "Yes, in April. I too have received my royal summons. In fact, just yesterday I ordered my presentation gown. Do you have yours yet, Miss Everleigh?"

"I have ordered it, yes."

Valeria sighed inwardly; this was hard going. Just then a lull fell in the conversation among the other ladies and Lady Sefton said, "I believe you were speaking of the Presentation Drawing Room in April, Miss Segrave? And so your application has been approved?"

"Yes, ma'am, and I am so sensible of the honor, although I'm exceedingly nervous. I was just telling Miss Everleigh that I ordered my dress, and that in itself was an ordeal," Valeria said with chagrin. "It took hours for me to make up my mind about the fabric, the color, the trim, the accessories. I'm afraid all of my ditherings tried my mother's patience no end."

Regina sighed gently. "It was not I whom you drove to distraction, dearest, it was Madame Tournai. I declare, at one point I thought she was going to suggest that we seek out another *modiste*."

"Really?" Adele Everleigh said icily. "Are you that difficult to please, Miss Segrave?"

"I expect so," Valeria answered. "In most things, anyway. But it wasn't my endless demands to see everything in Madame Tournai's establishment that so horrified her, it was when I tried to convince her that I wanted a different style of dress. To her my suggestions apparently were tantamount to a crime."

Lady Sefton said, "Surely, Miss Segrave, you know that the dress code for presentation is very strict. No dressmaker could countenance one of her creations' being presented to the Queen that was, um, *démodé*."

"Yes, ma'am, so Madame Tournai told me in no uncertain terms, several times," Valeria said. "But it's not as if I wanted to appear in costume, or in a riding habit. All I wanted was for the dress to have a natural waistline, instead of an Empire."

Adele Everleigh frowned. "Whyever should you want such a ridiculous thing, Miss Segrave? You would appear frightfully *à l'ancienne*. Ladies' dresses have not had a natural waist for ages now."

"I know, it's just that the wide hoops we're required to wear look ridiculous, with the dress flaring out from an Empire waist," Valeria replied. "We look like small corks stuck in a big fat bottle."

The reaction to this observation from the other ladies was one of shock, although Lady Hylton didn't appear to be surprised; she rolled her eyes and shook her head slightly. Then Lady Sefton lifted her fan to her face and chuckled. "Miss Segrave, I must admit you are in the right of it, but I wouldn't advise you to advertise that opinion too widely. Some ladies may not see the humor."

"Certainly not," Lady Sturway said under her breath.

"Yes, ma'am," Valeria said to Lady Sefton meekly. "I know that sometimes I express my thoughts too readily. I shall endeavor to correct such inclinations."

Adele and her mother Lady Sturway exchanged disdainful glances. Lady Sturway said, "Yes, Miss Segrave, you must indeed. I am aware that your upbringing has been rather provincial, but there are strict rules of propriety in London that a well-bred young lady must follow. Outrageous pronouncements of any kind are not welcomed in any drawing room."

Lightly Lady Sefton said, "That is true, Lady Sturway, but a bright and clever young woman is always welcomed into society. Enthusiasms must certainly be curbed, but the rules should not be positively stifling."

Lady Sturway looked appropriately chastised, and Lady Sefton turned back to Valeria. "At any rate, Miss Segrave, your dressmaker does appear to be an expert one, if what you are wearing this evening is one of her creations."

"So it is," Valeria said, her spirits rising again. "When we ordered my new wardrobe I was so happy for Madame Tournai to tell me that we are now allowed some more extravagant trimmings for our dresses, such as the new Vandyke edgings and *à la Mameluke* sleeves. Ever since I came out of the schoolroom it has seemed to me that our dresses have been so plainly adorned that in line dances all of us young ladies look like a row of Ionic columns."

This time Lady Sefton immediately laughed softly, while Adele and Lady Sturway managed halfhearted polite smiles.

Just then the men came trooping in, smelling of port fumes and cigar smoke. The men stood around the women, and there was blandly general, polite conversation for a time. Then, with a slightly devilish air, Alastair said, "Miss Segrave, since you are such an accomplished musician, won't you grace us with some music?"

Valeria managed to stop herself from positively making a face at him, though she did shoot him a dagger-ridden glance. Eyeing her with lightly veiled amusement, Lady Sefton said, "Yes, Miss Segrave, I should love to hear you play, I understand that you're very skilled at the pianoforte."

"Yes, ma'am," Valeria said resignedly.

The pianoforte was at one end of the room, with side chairs grouped comfortably around it, and everyone settled themselves as Valeria sat down and filed through the sheet music. Miss Everleigh looked distinctly displeased, and Valeria recalled that Lady Hylton had told her that Adele was a particularly gifted musician. Suddenly feeling reckless, Valeria laid down the sheet music and began to play. She kept her defiant gaze fixed on Alastair Hylton, who looked sardonically amused.

The piece was not particularly relaxing and melodious to the ear, for it was highly technical, fast-paced, with very intricate finger work and a melody that only a skilled musician could truly comprehend. When she finished there was a slight pause, and then the guests applauded politely. Reggie Lydgate, seated next to Alastair, leaned over and murmured, "What was that, Hylton? I've never heard it before, I don't think."

"No, I'm sure you haven't," Alastair said with cool amusement. "It's Scarlatti."

Reggie looked puzzled. "That the fellow that was so jealous of Mozart? And a lot of good it did him, too, no one ever plays him."

"No, Reggie, that was Salieri," Alastair replied. "This was Scarlatti. *Esercizio Numero Uno*, I think." Then he raised his voice and called, "That was magnificent, Miss Segrave. Now, won't you sing? I'm sure we'd all enjoy it immensely."

Valeria rose from the pianoforte bench and reset the sheet music. "I doubt that very seriously," she said acidly. "I know that Admiral Dinkins next door brought some of his hounds to Town. I fear that if I sang it might start the entire pack a-howling."

A startled silence greeted this sally, and then the young gentlemen started laughing. Lord Sefton slapped his knee and chortled, "Admiral Dinkins's dogs! Sharp girl!"

"Oh, really, Valeria," Lady Hylton said with some exasperation, but she too was smiling.

Valeria said composedly, "Now I know we should all like to hear Miss Everleigh both play *and* sing. I think that's a much better idea."

With a superior air Adele took to the instrument. Valeria thought that she was talented, but somehow her air of unpleasantness translated into her voice and even into her playing. On some deep level there was a semblance of discontent in her performance, though it was technically perfect.

After three songs the guests all drifted back toward the seating around the fireplace. This time Valeria took a comfortable wing chair set somewhat back from the group. To her surprise, however, she soon found herself surrounded by men. Daniel Everleigh, Paul Northbrooke, Charles Ponsonby, and Lord Stephen hovered around her. Alastair stood slightly behind them, aloof but still part of the conversational group.

"Admiral Dinkins's dogs!" Everleigh repeated with relish. "Surely you underestimate your talent, Miss Segrave. And I'm told that false modesty evinces just as much pride as vanity."

"I'm afraid you'll never know the truth of the matter, Mr. Everleigh," Valeria replied, "for I have determined never to sing in public. It is one thing to inflict it upon my family, but it's quite another to display it to strangers."

"It seems to me that you display very well," Alastair said mockingly. "For example, I found Scarlatti an interesting choice. It is complex, more for a musician's ear than for a group in a drawing room."

"Yes, and I happen to have all thirty of the *Esercizi* memorized, sir, so I promise you that if you ask me to perform again, you shall have *Esercizio Numero Due*," Valeria retorted.

"All thirty?" Alastair repeated sarcastically. "You were right, Everleigh. I believe that Miss Segrave's reticence is in fact false modesty, and therefore, in truth, vanity."

"I shall defend you, Miss Segrave," Lord Stephen said stoutly. "I thought your playing was marvelous, but if you dislike performing I will take you at your word and believe that you are simply modest."

A very slight murmur was heard from Alastair, but Valeria ignored him. "Thank you, Lord Stephen, you are truly gallant, unlike some gentlemen." She shot a sly glance at Alastair and then, as was the lady's prerogative, changed the subject. "Lord Hylton, Lord Sefton tells me that he is to attend Tattersalls on Thursday, to see the Maledon horses. It seems that Achilles is quite an advertisement for us."

"Superb mount," Paul Northbrooke said enviously. "I wish I could afford that one black stallion from Maledon."

"Yes, that would be Mordaunt," Valeria said eagerly. "He's a magnificent three-year-old, sixteen hands. He could almost be a twin to Achilles, except that Mordaunt has a blaze while Achilles has the true star of the Maledon 'black star'd horse.'"

They pressed her to explain, and with animation Valeria told them the history, and about some of the bloodlines of the Maledon horses. When she finished, Daniel Everleigh said with open admiration, "Fascinating! I must say, Miss Segrave, I've never known a young lady with such expert knowledge of equine matters. I'm amazed that you know so much about the Maledon stables."

"Oh, yes, I know all about all of our horses," she said enthusiastically. "In fact, it's difficult for me to think about Mordaunt's being sold, he's one of my favorites. I'm so worried about his going to a good owner. I've been thinking of attending the sale myself, just so that I can watch over him."

A blank stunned silence greeted this. Finally Alastair said in a funereal voice, "Oh, really, Miss Segrave? You think you'll attend the sale at Tattersalls? Of course. And then we can go to my club, have some fine brandy, smoke some cigars, maybe put a bet or two on the book."

"I beg your pardon?" Valeria said, bewildered.

Through gritted teeth Alastair said, "Gentlemen? Would you excuse us for a moment? I suddenly recall there is an urgent matter of business that I need to discuss with Miss Segrave."

With knowing grins the young men drifted away. Alastair leaned over Valeria's chair to mutter in a rough whisper, "Have you lost your senses, Miss Segrave?"

Valeria retorted in a low grating voice, "I don't know what you're talking about. And—and—how dare you, sir? Embarrass me in such a way?"

"You embarrassed yourself, I'm merely trying to salvage the situation," Alastair said tightly. "Surely your mother has told you that no lady would ever think of attending Tattersalls. It's simply not done, it would be scandalous."

Indignantly Valeria said, "No, I did not know that. Now I do. I assure you I won't mention it again."

Alastair gazed with narrowed eyes at the other four young men who had gathered around a footman bearing a tray of glasses of sherry. "The damage may already be done, but I'll try to tell those young bucks to keep it to themselves. Don't you understand that if you make such grievous errors in deportment you may be labeled a fast woman?"

"Such stuff!" Valeria said crossly. "It was just a silly mistake, said in a private group at a private dinner party."

"No, it was said in London, and you had better learn exactly what that means," Alastair said direly. "I assure you, if Lady Sefton had heard you chattering away about attending Tattersalls, your admission to Almack's might have been threatened."

Now Valeria felt uncertain. "Do you—do you think they will repeat it?" she asked.

"I do," Alastair said grimly, "but not in such a way that it would reach Lady Sefton's ears. Just try to be mindful from now on, Miss Segrave, and make some attempt to behave yourself."

Now Valeria's temper flared. "Stop treating me like a child! You are not my father, nor my brother. It's insufferable that you should keep correcting me like this."

"And if I do not, who will? Obviously neither my mother nor your own can impress upon you how vitally important it is that you stop saying these rash, imprudent things. As I have told you before, it is only for your—"

"Stop," Valeria said imperiously, holding up her hand. "For my own good, yes, I know, it's amazing how concerned you are for my welfare. But I'll thank you to stop chastising me like a cross nanny. It's really quite tiresome."

He blinked, then his face closed down as surely as a heavy door slamming. With icy formality he said, "Please accept my sincerest apologies, Miss Segrave. I would never intentionally impose such a burden of boredom upon a lady." Stiffly he offered her his arm, and with reluctance Valeria rose and the two rejoined the other guests.

And Valeria's heart sank.

Chapter Eighteen

𝕏

Although Monsieur Joubert had been faithful to his word and sent Valeria's chocolate-brown riding habit the very next day, he need not have made the garment in such a headlong rush. For exactly eleven days—Valeria counted them off with frustration—it rained dismally. The fashionable hours for riding in Hyde Park were between five o'clock and seven o'clock in the evening in the height of the Season, but those who were in London in February made an exception for the shortened winter days, and rode between three and four o'clock.

It seemed to Valeria that some vengeful rain gods must be cursing her, for without fail the rain would start every afternoon at about three or four o'clock. Actually, Valeria reflected sourly, it couldn't always be called rain; on four of those long days the infamous London fog was so thick and wet that it was like being in the middle of a sodden sponge. After ten minutes one's hair and clothing were just as soaked as if one had been standing still in a downpour.

Valeria missed riding; at Bellegarde Hall she had ridden, it seemed in golden memories, almost every day. Surely she had never been confined indoors for eleven days in a row, but sensibly she told herself that her memory must be faulty. The County of Essex was just north of London and the weather could not possibly differ that much. It was just that she found London so very dreary, as far as the atmosphere went. The sky was never a bright cheerful blue; the sun, when it managed to filter through the pervasive coal-dimmed skies, was faded and dingy.

However, Valeria admitted to herself that although she did miss the long walks in Bellegarde's gracious grounds, the freshness of the air, the long solitary rides, she was still extravagantly happy to be in London for the Season. Every single night Lady Hylton or Lord and Lady Lydgate had arranged for her to attend the opera, the theatre, a dinner party, a card party. Lady Hylton or Elyse had taken her every day to make morning calls, and on Lady Hylton's at-home days, Valeria received the callers along with her godmother. Even though the Season was not yet in full swing, Valeria had already been introduced to many people, so many that she could hardly keep them all straight in her mind. Somewhat to Valeria's surprise, her mother had been very helpful in reminding her of the wide acquaintance she was making. She had thought her mother so unworldly, and so unmindful of social status, that she could hardly know much about the *haut ton*. Valeria was wrong in this; Regina knew all of Polite Society, and it knew her. Valeria had seen that in the private dinner parties her mother had been able to attend, she was much caressed.

Her mother would dutifully explain who and what everyone was, but for the real tales about people Valeria had to rely on her godmother and Elyse, for Regina flatly refused to repeat gossip, whether idle or plain truth. It had been Lady Hylton who had told Valeria, "My dear, I must warn you that although Daniel Everleigh is a charming young man, he is something of a rake. Also, since he is the heir, he is expected to marry well, and his parents will never countenance his connection with a young woman who is not wealthy. Everyone has already noted his marked attentions to you, and I am obliged to tell you that they will likely come to nothing."

"And again, ma'am, I am obliged to tell you that I care nothing whatsoever about getting married," Valeria said, softening the impertinent remark with a smile. "I find Mr. Everleigh a most entertaining, lively gentleman, and if he wants to waste his time with me then I have no objection whatsoever to wasting my time with him."

Now, on this blessed sunny afternoon, as she was dressing in her brand-new riding habit, she thought of Daniel Everleigh. He had hinted several times that he should like to make an appointment to ride with her in the park on the first fine day, for this was the only socially acceptable liaison between gentlemen and ladies who were not betrothed. But Valeria had been noncommittal about it. Truly she was looking forward to a long, satisfying ride on Tarquin, and she wished to ride alone. Of course she wouldn't really be alone, she would have her groom Timothy chaperoning her, but that was merely a formality that must be observed, and she knew his presence wouldn't affect the invigorating sense of freedom she always felt on a long ride.

Her sense of heady exhilaration—felt at every social event she attended, even on morning calls—heightened when Valeria saw how undeniably attractive she looked in the riding habit. Made of a deep rich earth-brown velvet, heavily napped, it had been trimmed by Monsieur Joubert in a most masculine manner that only heightened Valeria's femininity. The jacket had broad military-style lapels of black velvet, widely notched, with velvet-covered buttons, an upright stiff collar, and upturned wide black velvet cuffs. Underneath Valeria wore a man's shirt (cut down to size, of course), and a starched cravat.

It was the cravat that was giving her and her maid the most trouble. Valeria had no notion whatsoever of how to tie a cravat. Joan had assured her that she had observed her brothers countless times, and she was confident that she could mimic their motions. However, the logistics were proving to be difficult. First Joan tried standing in front of Valeria and tying it, but she said with some con-fusion, "No, no, now it's seeming like I'm backward. Or you are, ma'am."

"Perhaps you might stand behind me? Would that enable you to more closely mirror whatever Ned and Royce do?" Valeria sug-gested.

"You're too tall," Joan said, then suggested, "P'raps if you sit down on your dressing table chair, then I might position myself behind you, and..." Her voice trailed off as she bent over and concentrated on wrapping the stiff neckcloth into a complicated knot with a graceful fall. After long moments of silent effort, Joan frowned.

"Ned and Royce make it look so easy. Here, I'll untie it com-pletely and try again."

Valeria sighed. "And I thought that women had complications in dressing. Perhaps I should just go down to the library and ask Mr. Chalmers to tie it for me."

Joan's eyes widened with horror. "Oh, miss, you can't mean it! Asking a gentleman to dress you—why, Mr. Chalmers would likely be so confounded he might—he might—"

"Faint dead away? Yes, I suppose you're right, he is a very proper gentleman, and perhaps I shouldn't subject him to such an appalling shock. But then what are we to do?"

Sternly Joan said, "You just sit right here and wait, please, ma'am. I'll go get instructions from Ned, and I'm sure I can do this. After all, if my silly brothers can do it I certainly can." She bustled out in-dignantly.

Valeria spent the interval admiring herself in the cheval mirror and trying on her hat. It was a diminished version of a man's top hat, with a brown velvet band; but the ultimate of Monsieur Joubert's genius was the marcasite chelengk, that dashing masculine version of a brooch, anchoring the black-dyed ostrich feather that curled

THE BARON'S HONOURABLE DAUGHTER

fetchingly over Valeria's left shoulder. With complacency Valeria reflected that she looked fine indeed.

Joan came back in with a determined look on her face. "Now, then, ma'am, I have gotten complete instructions from Ned, and I successfully tied his cravat 'round my own neck, which I'm sorry to say was a great source of amusement belowstairs."

Valeria sat back down, and Joan, now with deft fingers, began to tie the long rectangular length of starched silk around Valeria's neck. "This, I'm told, is called the 'Mail Coach' or the 'Waterfall' cravat. I told Ned that I hardly thought you wanted to look like a coachman, but he and Royce assured me that it's very popular with the swells. I mean, with finely dressed gentlemen."

Joan finally finished tying the cravat and said with satisfaction, "Now, you do look—"

"Like a swell?" Valeria giggled. "Good! Now. Help me with this splendid hat, and please do hurry. I'm *so* looking forward to my ride."

Valeria clattered down the stairs in her riding boots—a female version of men's Hessians—and merely stuck her head in the drawing room to say good-bye to her mother. Outside, Timothy, in his splendid livery, held the horses. Valeria, of course, was riding Tarquin, and Timothy was riding his favorite chestnut gelding.

"Good afternoon, Timothy. A ride at last!" she said with animation.

Timothy held the stirrup; Valeria mounted and carefully arranged her skirt so it would fall gracefully. Then, with a beautiful seat, her back erect but not stiff, showing a wonderful grace, she spurred Tarquin on, with Timothy close behind.

It was only five blocks from Berkeley Square to the most famous park in London. Hyde Park was 350 acres of long expanses of perfectly tended lawns, sweet shady glades, wandering pathways and promenades, and the man-made Serpentine River. Now, in winter, the trees were bare and solemn and the lawns and glades soft hues of brown; yet Valeria thought that on this benevolently sunny day she could sense a hint of oncoming spring.

Immediately on entering the park she went directly to Rotten Row, spurning the more sedate Lady's Mile that traced the northern bank of the Serpentine. Rotten Row was *the* place to be seen in Hyde Park, as it was the path that the Quality most loved to ride, drive their fine carriages, or promenade in their best finery. Gigs, curricles, and phaetons, all pulled by fine high-stepping horses, were thick on the bridle path, along with riders mounted on spirited "blood" horses. On each side of the well-beaten riders' drive, crowds of people slowly promenaded along: young ladies with their chaperons, young dandies "doing the strut," nannies with children and baby carriages, doyennes with their ladies' maids in tow, young couples eagerly greeting acquaintances.

Valeria saw several people she knew, including the perpetually peevish Miss Adele Everleigh promenading with her mother Lady Sturway. Valeria thought she detected a hint of envy on Miss Everleigh's face, and her mother looked distinctly displeased, even though they both nodded politely to Valeria as she passed them. Snappily Valeria raised her riding crop and touched the brim of her hat, saluting them. Adele stiffened with disapproval, and Lady Sturway whispered something in her daughter's ear, and she nodded with perhaps more vehemence than was quite called for in a modest young woman. Serenely Valeria cantered past them, her head held high, her eyes sparkling.

She passed Elyse driving her high-perched phaeton with a small-built but magnificently liveried "tiger," a small twelve-year-old boy in full livery, riding on the back, and they exchanged enthusiastic waves. Lord Sefton went by in his high flyer, and as she acknowledged him with a nod, Valeria saw with satisfaction that it was drawn by the pair of Maledon chestnuts she had told him about.

Cordially he turned to her, touching the brim of his hat and grinning his game smile. The gesture made Valeria uneasy, as he was tearing along at a brisk pace, the gold-yellow-and-green phaeton seeming to fly above the ground. Galloping was forbidden in Hyde Park, and Lord Sefton was just barely below it. However, his momentary inattention to the team didn't seem to affect them, as they pranced and danced straight on. Valeria admired his control. She sincerely doubted that she could keep such a team at the brink of a gallop without constant vigilance. *Now I see why they call him Lord Dashalong, he certainly deserves it!* she reflected.

Although this was not the vigorous ride that Valeria longed for, she still relished it thoroughly, and she had no inclination to talk to people she'd met, merely nodding politely to them. Some of the young men—including Mr. Mayhew, that lazy foppish young man who'd been in the disreputable party at Bellegarde—looked distinctly disappointed that she gave them no signal that she wished to speak to them. Contrary to the rules of the drawing room and ballroom, in Hyde Park ladies alone might initiate a conversation, but Valeria did not. She exchanged polite smiles and courteous nods all around but did not deviate from Tarquin's brisk canter.

Just ahead she saw a figure riding toward her that she recognized easily: Daniel Everleigh. He was riding with another gentleman, and between them rode a woman in a daring crimson riding habit. As they neared each other, Valeria recognized Lord Kincannon; he had called on Lady Hylton three times, and had shown Valeria special attention. She found him a charming man, and she liked him, even though her stepfather had met his scandalous end at Lord Kincannon's lodge, and Kincannon had a reputation as one of the most dissipated libertines of "Prinny's set."

But then Valeria's blood froze. She recognized the woman riding with them. It was Lady Jex-Blake.

All thoughts, all speculations about Daniel Everleigh's riding with a woman in the park, about how she should greet Lord Kincannon and the woman, fell away in a red haze. She fixed on Lady Jex-Blake's face, her dark eyes glittering fiercely. When Valeria drew near, she saw the bright smile on Lady Jex-Blake's face fade into a look of momentary uncertainty. But then her eyes narrowed, and she raised her chin with defiance.

As Valeria came abreast of them, she stared without blinking at the woman. Then, slowly, with great deliberation, she shifted her gaze away from Lady Jex-Blake's face and focused straight ahead without so much as glancing at the two men.

To Valeria, even the cut—a rarely used and implacable form of denigrating an acquaintance—was not punishment enough for Lady Jex-Blake. Though it was the highest form of insult one could give, she still found it unsatisfying. She had a momentary vision of slapping the woman's smirking face with her riding crop, and was somewhat shocked at the ferocity of her emotions. But she had not the least regret.

Heedless of the rules, she spurred Tarquin to an all-out gallop. They were at the far southern end of Rotten Row, and without hesitating she rode right out of the park onto Hyde Park Corner, and then onto Piccadilly. Timothy—whom she had forgotten—pulled up alongside her, and glanced at her with anguish on his face. That, and the dense traffic on the street, made Valeria pull Tarquin back to a sedate canter.

Now her thoughts descended into a heated tumult. How could that woman be here, in London, riding with two gentlemen of Quality in broad daylight in Hyde Park? Valeria knew the answer. Although Lady Jex-Blake had a reputation for being fast, because of some preference that the Prince of Wales had shown her, she had not quite fallen into the class known as the *Demi-monde*—the "half-world" of courtesans, women who were kept by wealthy men, none of whom were ever publicly acknowledged. Valeria didn't care if the prince regent worshipped her; in Valeria's eyes the woman was no better than a prostitute haunting the streets, and she had no place even on the fringes of Polite Society.

Which brought up her next flurry of speculation: how could Daniel Everleigh keep company with that woman? Surely he knew of Lady Jex-Blake's connection with her stepfather, and of the rumors of other men who "courted" her for her favors. Then it occurred to Valeria that Everleigh might very well be one of those men, and at that moment she hated him. She thought that she would never speak to him again.

Rousing herself from her black reverie, she looked about. She recognized Hatchards, the bookstore where she had bought a new novel that was all the rage, *Sense and Sensibility*, "by a Lady." Now Valeria knew that she was on Piccadilly. With a sinking heart she realized that she shouldn't be here without a chaperon. Then she wondered about Timothy: if he was considered an adequate chaperon in Hyde Park, surely it would be acceptable for her to shop with him? Vaguely Valeria recalled some special stricture her godmother had taught her about Piccadilly, although she couldn't recall the exact details. In any case, what was she to do? She couldn't possibly return to the town house yet and face her mother, not in the extremely disturbed state of mind she was in at the moment. She must, she *must*, collect herself and calm down.

Then an inspiration came to her; she knew that Piccadilly bisected New Bond Street some blocks north. Valeria had seen a stationer's on the far end of New Bond Street that had displayed some artists' supplies in its window. She was determined to purchase some oil paints and try her hand, but the stationer's had been closed when Valeria and Regina reached it after their long session at Madame Tournai's. Now Valeria thought that if footmen were considered adequate chaperonage for Bond Street, a groom would serve as well. A tiny voice in her head reminded her that when Ned and

Royce had accompanied them, Valeria had been with her mother, but Valeria chose to ignore this. Timothy would do.

She had been obliged to slow Tarquin down to a walk due to the heavy traffic. Timothy pressed close to her, casting anxious questioning glances her way, but she ignored him. She was certain that Bond Street was just ahead.

And there it was; at least, Valeria thought it was, as she tried to picture the streets in her mind. Her notions were cloudy, to say the least, but she thought that if she made the right turn on the next street ahead, she would be on the end of Bond Street—New Bond Street.

She encouraged Tarquin to a confident half-trot, recalling that the stationer's was at the very end of the street. But after passing a couple of buildings she slowed down and looked more closely around her. She was passing buildings that she didn't recognize, great gracious buildings, unmarked by vulgar signs, that fronted directly onto the street, without the wide walking pavement for which Bond Street was so famous. Reining in Tarquin to a slow walk, she stared around, bemused. She saw Timothy, now riding directly beside her. His face was appalled, even horrified. Valeria understood—they were, quite clearly, lost.

Alastair Hylton sat at his regular table at White's, the best one that faced out of the bow window. He was in a deep brooding brown study because he was thinking of Valeria Segrave, for she was the topic of the conversation.

"—and then she said, 'I should set the entire pack a-howling!'" Lord Stephen Tryon was saying with relish. "Admiral Dinkins's dogs!"

Across from him George "Beau" Brummel's dark eyes lit up with amusement. "Do you mean to tell me that such a clever comment came from a well-bred young lady in her first Season? Without fail I have found the creatures to be vapid, banal, and commonplace regardless of their breeding. She doesn't sound like such an insufferable bore."

At this time Beau Brummel was the unquestioned sartorial *arbiter elegantiarum* of the prince regent, and therefore of the whole of male Polite Society. Brummel had banished, single-handedly, the horrid frilly, furbelowed, beribboned, be-ringed, powdered fashions of the previous century. Rather, Brummel had decreed that men should dress exquisitely, yes; but with the elegance of simplicity. Muted colors for a coat, always—black, brown, bottle green, dark blue. Waistcoats in less somber colors were allowed, but Brummel also had strict rules about precisely how bright they might be, and concerning patterns that were not too glaring. Long gone were the violently striped gold and crimson or purple paisley. Above all Brummel insisted on two things: perfect tailoring and scrupulous cleanliness. Any man now seen with a dusting of snuff on his neckcloth or a smudge on his cuff was liable to be strictly censured. Alastair, recalling his father's bright violet coats and puce waistcoats and endless yards of lace and trim, was exceedingly glad that Brummel had made such a sea change in men's attire.

It was a tribute to Brummel's influence that the young men surrounding him were dressed much like him, although of course they differed in the colors of their coats and waistcoats and the styles of their cravats. Alastair, Lord Stephen, Paul Northbrooke, and Charles Ponsonby all wore dark coats, discreet waistcoats, tight-fitting buff trousers, and either top boots or Hessians. Reggie Lydgate was wearing buckskins and riding boots, for he had intended to accompany Elyse on her ride in Hyde Park—only he had forgotten the time, as the men, particularly Brummel, were making such amusing caustic comments on the passersby outside. They had, in fact, seen Admiral Dinkins plod slowly by in his barouche, with a spotted hound hanging out the window, which had brought the anecdote to the gentlemen's minds.

Reggie said, "Elyse told me that while we were having port and walnuts they were talking about their court presentation dresses, and Miss Segrave remarked that with their fripperies—you know, those wide bell things they wear under their dresses—they all looked like corks stuck in big fat bottles!"

This time Brummel laughed out loud, which he rarely did. "How true, and how devilish of her to say so—did you tell me that Lady Sefton was there? She's perhaps the only patroness who would allow a young lady to get away with such a scurrilous pronouncement. And I say, a toast to Admiral Dinkins's dogs, corks in fat bottles, and Miss Valeria Segrave!"

The men all raised their glasses—Alastair reluctantly—and drank. Evenly he said, "You're in the right of it, Brummel, Miss Segrave is definitely not a bore. But she is dancing on a very fine line, and I doubt that Lady Maledon would approve of Miss Segrave's sallies' being bandied about by every rake in all the clubs in London."

"Nonsense," Brummel said briskly. "Every woman—old, young, mother, daughter—craves to be the Toast of St. James's, although they are too coy to admit it. I for one am looking forward to making Miss Segrave's acquaintance. She sounds like excellent company."

Lord Stephen Tryon suddenly straightened in his chair, his eyebrows shot up, and he glanced cautiously at Alastair Hylton. Then a sardonic look came over his handsome face, and he said, "Y'know, Brummel, we've seen that the ladies fall all over themselves to please you. But I've never known one to be so quick and timely."

Alastair followed his gaze, started up out of his chair, and stared. His face darkened ominously. Then he flung away from the table, knocking his heavy chair sprawling, and ran toward the door.

"Ah, so that is the lady, is it?" Brummel said with undisguised delight. "Riding down St. James's with her groom. She keeps a good seat, I must say. Handsome too. Hylton seems quite out of countenance, however."

"That ain't the word for it," Reggie sighed, rising more ceremoniously. "I s'pose I'd better go do my chaperoning duty and help Hylton get her righted, but I've been caught between those two before and I'm not looking forward to it."

Alastair half-ran out of the club onto the street. Every man passing by was staring at Valeria with varying expressions of curiosity, horror, or leers. He noted that Valeria had a most unusual look of bewilderment, and something else—not fear, but extreme uneasiness—on her face. It didn't assuage Alastair's anger, however. With hard quick strides he stepped right in front of Tarquin and grabbed his reins, bringing him to a sudden stop. Valeria looked down at him. For an instant it seemed that some gladness came into her eyes, but then her face hardened.

"What are you doing?" Alastair demanded.

"I'm riding, as I assume you can see. May I ask what business it is of yours, sir?"

"It is my business," Alastair snapped. "Because my mother, my sister, and my brother-in-law are supposed to be responsible for you, and if you are determined to be the scandal of the Season I'm not going to allow you to tarnish their reputations along with your own. Don't you have any idea where you are?"

Her jaw tightened, and her eyes blazed. "No, Lord Hylton, I truly have no idea where I am. But I am assuming that it's somewhere that I'm not supposed to be."

"Your assumption is correct. This is St. James's. No women, not even disreputable women, are allowed on this street. And yet here you are."

"Yes, here I am. But I assure you it's just an honest mistake. I thought I was—that is, I was trying to get to Bond Street."

"Trying to get to Bond Street. In a riding costume. With a groom. That is hardly much better. Weren't you supposed to be riding in the park?"

Valeria cringed slightly at the hard-set, implacable lines of his face. "I was riding in the park. But—I—" She swallowed hard. "I was riding in the park, yes. But I decided to make a quick call on a stationer's in Bond Street, to see if I might purchase some oil paints. Obviously I took a wrong turn somewhere."

"You certainly did, both in direction and in decision. Whatever possessed you to think that you are allowed to go shopping accompanied only by a groom? What made you think that you're allowed to wander the streets of London, guided only by your whim? However did you come to believe that—"

"Sir!" Valeria interrupted, drawing herself up to her full height and looking down at him imperiously. "Really, you are beyond incivility! Just direct me to Bond Street, and I'll be on my way."

"No, I won't do that," Alastair growled. "You must be turned round right now and go back home. And I swear that you don't need a chaperon, you need a jailer."

Valeria sniffed. "Of course you would think that. You would make an excellent turnkey."

More heated words were averted as Reggie Lydgate joined them. "Hullo, Miss Segrave. Riding, are you? Fine outfit, that."

"Here you are, Lydgate," Alastair grunted. "I can't do a thing with her. She thinks she's going to go shopping on Bond Street. Tell her she's wrong about that."

Reggie looked up at Valeria and said in a kindly voice, "Really, Miss Segrave, it really won't do. Why don't we go back home, and Elyse and I will bring you to Bond Street later this afternoon?"

"Very well," Valeria said evenly.

Alastair was still glaring up at her, and she met his gaze with a most rebellious one of her own. Without turning he said in a low voice to Reggie, "If this gets out, she's ruined."

"Mm," Reggie murmured, "none of us would carry the tale to anyone that mattered . . . but what about Brummel? He can be quite catty, you know."

"I'll go talk to him, threaten him with spilling Bordeaux on his breeches at Carlton House," Alastair said. "That should be enough of a deterrent. Good day, Miss Segrave."

"Now, young sir," Reggie said to Timothy, "I'm going to escort Miss Segrave home, so I'll need your horse. Don't worry, we'll take it at a very slow walk so you can follow."

"Yes, sir," Timothy said with vast relief.

꧁

As they made their way home, Valeria's thoughts were in even more of a whirlwind than when she'd recognized Lady Jex-Blake.

How dare he treat me so shabbily, speak to me with such cold cruelty? He's really the most disagreeable man, it was just a mistake, an honest mistake! How can it be that every single time we're close enough to speak, we end up fighting and sparring? Because he's insufferable, that's why!

But Valeria knew that that wasn't really the answer—at least, not the entire answer. She had acted very wrongly, and with apprehension she thought that she might have to pay for it, if the story got around. She glanced at Reggie, riding silently beside her, thoughtful for once. "I—I truly did simply make a mistake, Lord Lydgate," she said in a small voice. "Do you—do you think that I shall be known as a fast, loose woman now?"

"I don't think so," Reggie replied reassuringly. "With your family, your social standing, and of course the support of your friends"—here he gave her one of his sweet smiles—"I doubt very seriously it will be a real stain upon your virtue. At worst, if it does get around, it will simply be seen that you made a foolish mistake."

"So I shall be known as a great ninny," Valeria grumbled. "At least that's not quite as bad."

It didn't occur to her until much, much later that, in spite of Alastair Hylton's harshness toward her, he had indicated that he was going to be one of those "friends" who supported her, for she had fully overheard Alastair's remarks to Reggie. For a moment she again felt resentment; it was so typical of Alastair to speak of her as if she weren't right there.

But then, as she lay in her warm bed, the corners of her mouth turned up as she thought of Lord Hylton fumbling around at Carlton House and spilling wine on Beau Brummel's white satin court breeches. An unlikely picture, she thought; but it gave her a surprising measure of comfort, just the same.

Chapter Nineteen

✣

B Y THE TIME VALERIA ARRIVED back home, it was too late for Lord and Lady Lydgate to take her to Bond Street. The next day, after morning calls (which actually were made in the early afternoon), Elyse and Valeria set out by themselves, Reggie having begged off. Valeria was relieved. She rarely got to talk to Elyse alone these busy days.

In the carriage, after several minutes of silence, Valeria murmured, "It was just a mistake, you know, Elyse."

"Yes, so Reggie says. But I think there's more to it than a mistake," she said quietly. "In fact, I'm sure of it. You saw Lady Jex-Blake, didn't you?"

Valeria's eyes widened. "How did you—but of course, you must have seen her before I did. It quite devastated me. Why didn't you warn me, Elyse?"

Elyse said kindly, "Because, darling, it hadn't occurred to me that you didn't know she was in Town, and I thought that surely you had prepared yourself. I do regret it now."

Valeria waved, a small gesture of negation. "Never mind, you're right. I had managed to forget about her, and all that unpleasantness. I suppose I should have been prepared, but Elyse, what could I do? What would you have done, in my place?"

With sympathy Elyse replied, "Valeria, I've never been so unfortunate as to be in your place, or anything like it. I'm not surprised that you rushed headlong out of the park at first sight of her."

"Actually, that wasn't my first inclination," Valeria said evenly. "My first instinct was to strike her with my riding crop. At least I managed to restrain myself from doing that. I did cut her, though."

Elyse's eyes grew round. "Did you? Oh, dear. Well, I suppose, under the circumstances..."

Impatiently Valeria said, "Please do not tell me that I'm to be censured for that too. Surely that ill-bred, commonplace hoyden can't have so much influence with the prince regent. But even if she does, I'm not sorry, not at all. And I'll never speak to Mr. Everleigh again."

Elyse was silent for long moments, thoughtfully looking out on the crowds thronging Piccadilly, as they always did. "Valeria, although I understand your feelings, or at least as much as I can imagine them, please allow me to give you a bit of advice. Your best course now is to pretend that the entire thing never happened. For instance, are you going to stop riding in the park? Are you going to stop speaking to anyone who speaks to Lady Jex-Blake? Although she doesn't frequent the best circles, she does have a wide acquaintance in London, particularly since the prince has shown some partiality to her."

"Silly Prinny," Valeria grumbled. "Silly, stupid men. No, I suppose I can't stop speaking to every man who cavorts with tawdry women. If I did, my conversations would be strictly limited to ladies."

"Nonsense. There are many men who aren't attracted to that kind of woman at all. Even Reggie, who is hardly the most observant and analytical man, says that Lady Jex-Blake is the perfect example of a flash gimcrack sort of woman, and that she's a downright embarrassment in a drawing room."

Curiously Valeria asked, "What does Lord Hylton say about her?"

Elyse smiled. "Nothing, of course; you know that my brother is so aloof that he rarely comments on anyone at all."

Valeria's eyebrows shot up. "Oh, really? He has commented on me, and to me, many times."

"Mm, yes, so he has," Elyse said noncommitally. "At any rate, I can assure you that he doesn't cavort with tawdry women either."

Valeria giggled. "The mental picture of Lord Hylton cavorting at all—oh dear, it's just too ridiculous." Then she sobered and said, "I do see your point, however. I should have been more, so much more, in control of myself. And from now on I am determined that I shall be. I shall be all that a young lady should be: complacent, composed, calm, and exhibiting only very limited, genteel, ladylike conversation."

"Will you now? I hardly think I will recognize you."

"Oh, very well, you may be as satirical as you like. But I am worried, Elyse. Do you think the story will get out, be widely known and repeated among our acquaintance?"

Elyse sighed. "I'm afraid it must. Too many people saw you, and even if they didn't know you then, they will, and they'll remember. Particularly since we're talking about men."

"I beg your pardon?"

Elyse cocked her head to the side to look at Valeria curiously. "You really don't realize, do you? Amazing. When men see a remarkably beautiful young woman riding on a magnificent stallion down St. James's, they won't forget it."

Valeria grimaced. "Then I shall get a shaggy cob to ride, and I shall make myself plain and drab from here on out."

Elyse rolled her eyes. "Speaking of impossible to picture. Never mind, Valeria, we have already decided upon our strategy to mitigate the damage. As soon as the story starts circulating, we're going to tell everyone that you and your groom were accompanying me in my town coach, and we got separated in the crowds on Piccadilly. As you can see from the traffic outside, that wouldn't be impossible. And here, look. You took this right-hand turn, which is St. James's; and here, just across, is the left-hand turn onto Bond Street. It's understandable, really, for anyone who's not thoroughly acquainted with London. And there you are, a perfectly convincing story of a simple mistake."

"Oh, how can I thank you, dear Elyse?" Valeria said gratefully.

"'Twas Alastair who thought of it, and he persuaded all of his friends who witnessed it, including Mr. Brummel, to go along with it."

"Mm, yes, that is a better plan than Bordeaux on the breeches," Valeria said.

"What?"

"Never mind." Then she sighed deeply and thought, *How is it that Alastair Hylton, of all people, has to be the one who rescues me? How tiresome it is to continually owe him a debt of gratitude, particularly since I'm sure by now he must despise me!*

They arrived at the stationer's, and it was useless. The stationer, though properly obsequious, still had an air of prim disapproval that young ladies should be inquiring about oil paints. As they left the shop Valeria said acidly, "You know, it's as if we were trying to purchase demon opium, or asking for directions to the nearest brothel."

Elyse laughed. "So I see you've been repentant for ten minutes or so, Valeria, and in those ten minutes I must say you behaved admirably."

Mischievously Valeria replied, "The longest ten minutes I've ever spent in my life. I'm so glad that's all behind me now."

༄

In the next few days, Valeria saw Alastair Hylton on several occasions, as he usually was invited to the same parties as Lady Hylton and Lord and Lady Lydgate. She dreaded the first encounter, but Hylton treated her with the same polite detachment with which he treated everyone else. Although she thought that sometimes his gaze, when she caught him observing her, was particularly thoughtful, there seemed to be no rebuke in it. He even smiled at her a few times. Fleetingly she wondered about the exact nature of his opinion of her; but not for long. She was much taken up with Daniel Everleigh, whom she had decided to forgive for his association with Lady Jex-Blake. Neither he nor Valeria mentioned the encounter, of course, and Valeria reflected that so far, she'd had more fun with Everleigh than with any of the other young men who danced attendance on her. He was a lively companion, witty, oftentimes irreverently parodying the more staid and stiff members of Polite Society, which Valeria enjoyed.

The next week, to Valeria's surprise, Lady Hylton called on Valeria and Regina, and Alastair came with her. He greeted them with his customary formality, but Valeria thought—hoped—that she saw a certain warmth in his countenance. They all sat down for small talk, but Valeria was distracted, for Lady Hylton's footmen were bringing in large heavy boxes wrapped in brown paper and setting them in the hall.

Lady Hylton said, "Valeria, you're as transparent as a child on Christmas eve. Yes, the packages are gifts for you."

"They are? May I open them?"

Alastair said, "Perhaps, Miss Segrave, if I could crave your indulgence, and if you can contain your curiosity, I was hoping to speak to you about some estate matters first. Lady Maledon, Mother, if you will excuse us?" He rose and offered Valeria his arm to escort her into the library.

Valeria thought it was typically high-handed of him; but then again he seemed to be in an unusually pleasant mood, so she was determined to make the most of it. As they settled down in two comfortable overstuffed chairs in front of the desk, she said lightly, "So, sir, may I assume that you're not still flaming angry with me?"

"I wasn't angry. And ladies don't say *flaming*," he retorted; then his mouth twitched and he continued, "Mmm. You may have been correct, Miss Segrave, perhaps I do treat you like a cross nanny. I beg your pardon."

"Pardon granted, because to admit the honest truth I was baiting you a little. I wouldn't say *flaming* in polite company—not that you're not polite company—that is, I meant—oh, hang it all. I won't say it again."

"I am relieved, and if you will also exclude *hang it all* from polite conversation I would be *vastly* relieved," he said, but his tone was light. "So, there are some small matters concerning the estate about which I wish to inform you." He went on to talk about the sale of the horses, for which they had received high prices, some events concerning the cottagers, and a problem with the drains in the stable wings.

"I see," Valeria said thoughtfully. "It does seem to me that you and Mr. Wheeler have managed all of these things admirably. Is there anything that I should do? Any instructions you have for me?"

"Instructions for you? Why, yes, there are a few things, perhaps a few dozen things or more." His gray-blue eyes were sparkling.

To her amazement, Valeria could see that Alastair was actually teasing her. She smiled brilliantly and said, "Sir, please stop immediately! If ever a question was worded wrongly, mine was a supreme example. What I meant to say was that it would seem I'm rather superfluous here, it seems that I'm hardly needed at all for help with the estate."

"Of course that's not true, ma'am," he said, returning to his usual formal courtesy. "We are co-trustees, and I simply wish to keep you fully informed. However, if there are matters that you would prefer to deal with yourself, I should be happy to consult you before I make any decisions or take any actions."

"No, no, I'm perfectly happy for you to manage these things, sir," Valeria said hastily. "Indeed, I've been so busy here in Town that I've scarcely had time to think of Bellegarde at all."

He shifted his position slightly and studied her, his expression now sober. "Yes, you are having a particularly successful Season, Miss Segrave, you have many admirers. I have seen that you've shown a marked preference for Daniel Everleigh. You do understand, do you not, that his family would never consent to his marrying you?"

"Great heavens, no one is talking about marrying anyone!" Valeria cried. "I simply enjoy his company, and I think he enjoys mine, and we have fun—you have heard of such a thing, have you not?"

"Yes, I have heard rumors of such," he replied slowly, studying her. "And naturally I want you to have fun. But the problem is that people are already talking about you and Everleigh. I feel I must warn you that he is something of a rake, and at some point in time he's going to move on to another young lady. Surely you wouldn't wish it to appear that you were so foolish as to believe that he was courting you, and that then he carelessly threw you over?"

Valeria's eyes flashed. "Sir, what business of yours is it whom I dance with and whom I sit next to at the theatre and who takes me in to supper? I care nothing for people's perceptions about my relationships with Mr. Everleigh. That is between me and him, and is no one else's concern."

"But surely—"Alastair began, and then his face closed down, and he rose and offered her his arm. "I beg your pardon, ma'am, I didn't mean to intrude on your personal life," he said stiffly. "Since our business is done, perhaps we should return to the drawing room?"

They returned without exchanging another word and Alastair

stood propped at the mantel, gazing darkly down into the fire. Valeria sighed inwardly and thought, *The cross nanny is back. However do I manage to continually irritate him? Just being around me seems to grate on his nerves.*

Letitia and Regina exchanged cautious glances when Alastair and Valeria returned, but Regina said brightly, "Darling, now that I know what your gifts are, I know you're going to be absolutely delighted."

Valeria's eyes lit up. "Oh, yes, my gifts. May I go open them now?"

"You may not, because they contain the biggest litter of oil paints, brushes, palette knives, stretched canvas, and other obscure implements that I've forgotten, and it would make a disgraceful mess in the hall," Lady Hylton replied tartly.

Valeria's eyes widened with delight. "You bought me oil paints? Oh, ma'am, thank you!"

"Don't thank me, child, such an odd thing would never have entered my mind. It was Alastair who told me you were so anxious to have them, and he found out how to procure them," Lady Hylton replied.

Uncertainly Valeria said, "Why, sir, I'm—how did you—and why did you—?"

"Elyse told me of your shopping trip," he said, and once again he seemed to warm a little, "and of the problems you were having trying to purchase oil paints and supplies. I simply asked a friend at the Royal Academy, and he directed me to the warehouses."

Valeria was astounded. "I—I—how can I ever thank you, sir? That's so thoughtful of you, I could never have imagined!"

"No, I'm sure you can't," he said dryly.

Lady Hylton said sternly, "Valeria, I personally made the purchases, for you may never accept a gift from a young man, not even Alastair. You do understand that, do you not?"

Mischievously Valeria replied, "I know I tend to forget some rules, but I do recall that one very clearly. I will never accept a gift from a young man, not even Lord Hylton."

"Thank the heavens," Lady Hylton sighed. "So, Valeria, are you to try your hand at portrait painting? If so, I wish to be your first subject."

Valeria laughed. "Oh, no, ma'am, I think St. John and Niall would do better portraits with finger paints. No, I fully intend to stay with landscapes. And Mamma, I'm so excited, please may I—"

"No, you may not," Regina said calmly. "Letitia warned me about oil paints, and the only place I can think of that I would want to be covered with splotches of unremovable paint is the attic. And it's much too cold for you to work up there just now, Valeria."

"That's to say nothing of the odor," Lady Hylton said severely. "You have to mix the paints with all sorts of noxious substances, I understand."

"That is true, Miss Segrave, you must be particularly careful. We'd hate to have you have the vapors from noxious odors," Alastair said with amusement.

"I have never had the vapors," Valeria said stoutly. "And I never intend to. But please, please, Mamma, may I just run upstairs very quickly, to see about the attic? Perhaps it may not be so cold as you think."

As Lady Hylton and Alastair were closer to family than to guests who must be entertained, Regina relented. "Very well, dear," she said indulgently. "You may go play with your new toys."

Valeria ran out of the room and started calling for the footmen to bring the boxes up to the attic. Regina, Letitia, and Alastair exchanged amused glances. "Sometimes she's still like a child," Letitia said affectionately.

In a low voice, Alastair murmured, "But not childish. Childlike, in innocence. Something to be treasured in a young woman."

Letitia and Regina pretended not to hear.

As it was, Regina was right. Even before Valeria had finished unpacking and marveling at all the paints and supplies, her fingers and toes were icy. Regretfully she thought that perhaps in a week or two the weather would warm up enough for her to be able to work in the attic.

That night Valeria, along with Lord and Lady Lydgate, attended a musicale at Lord and Lady Sturway's, with Adele on the pianoforte, accompanied by two violins, a viola, and a cello. They played baroque music, selections from Corelli and Vivaldi, and they performed exceptionally well. As they were heartily applauding, Valeria said to Mr. Everleigh, who was, as always, seated next to her, "Your sister is very talented, Mr. Everleigh."

"Mm, yes, I suppose she is. What I don't understand is why she takes so little pleasure in it. At least, she doesn't look as if she's taking pleasure in it. Adele was much more fun when we were children, but as soon as she came out of the schoolroom she started doing this." His brown eyes sparkling with merriment, he wrinkled his nose and pursed his mouth, then said in a nasal voice, "This is what I call her 'prim mouth.' I've told her that it makes her look like a malformed fish, but she *will* do it."

Valeria laughed out loud, which earned her some disapproving glances from two elderly dowagers who had risen from their seats just in front of her. Valeria ignored them. "You are wicked, sir," she trilled. "For shame, and your own sister, too."

"I'm unrepentant," he declared. "If she insists upon making a face like the worst prig, then she must pay the price for it. Shall we go help ourselves to some punch? It's my father's own recipe, a delicious concoction of lemon, sugar, nutmeg, cinnamon, and allspice."

"And rum," Valeria added, "and you know very well that I have no head for spirits, only a head*ache*. I would cherish some lemonade, though."

She took his arm and they followed the crowd drifting toward the drawing room, where tables of refreshments had been set up. They made very slow progress, often coming to a standstill so as not to run into the people in front of them. Everleigh said, "Pah, lemonade, such a bland drink for one who is certainly not a bland woman. In fact, you are the most clever, the most fetching, the loveliest—"

"Good evening, Miss Segrave, Everleigh," a deep voice drawled just by Valeria's left shoulder. Valeria looked up to see Alastair Hylton standing by her, holding a glass of champagne. He had a sardonic look on his face, and Valeria thought that he must have overheard Everleigh's raptures. Uncomfortably she replied, "Good evening, Lord Hylton."

Everleigh, unabashed, grinned and said, "Hylton, I must say your timing is wretched, I was just in the middle of telling Miss Segrave something of great import."

"Pray continue, then, don't mind me," Hylton said, deadpan.

"Very well. I was just saying, Miss Segrave, that you are—"

"Oh, do be quiet, Mr. Everleigh, Lord Hylton doesn't want to hear your nonsense," Valeria said, her color high. Turning to Alastair, she said with a trace of stiffness, "Again, sir, please accept my sincerest gratitude. I'm afraid my mamma was right, it was much too cold for me to work at all, but still, it is a gift I shall always treasure."

"You're welcome, Miss Segrave, it was my distinct pleasure," he said with a small bow.

Everleigh frowned. "What's this? Hylton's giving you gifts, and you wouldn't even let me buy you flowers at Covent Garden? That's not at all fair."

"No, he didn't give me a gift, he found out how, exactly, one might purchase oil paints and supplies, which until now I was thinking might be quite as illegal as Napoleon brandy, for the difficulties I've had trying to track them down," Valeria said spiritedly. "There appeared to me to be a vast conspiracy keeping women from purchasing them at any cost. But he managed to find out how Lady Hylton might buy them for me. Again, I am indebted to you, sir."

"Yes, you are, poor Miss Segrave," he said with a strange small smile. "If you'll excuse me, I'm engaged for a game of hazard." He went down the hall toward the card room.

Everleigh sniffed. "If I had known you wanted oil paints, I could have found them for you. What do you want oil paints for, anyhow?"

"To paint with, silly," she replied, but her voice was distant. Her eyes were on Lord Hylton's broad back, as she pondered his last remark.

Poor Miss Segrave, indeed.

Valeria soon forgot all about her new paints, for the next several weeks passed with an extraordinary, dreamlike speed.

The families of Polite Society began to stream "up to Town," as was commonly said regardless of the direction in which one traveled to London. Morning calls, given and received, became much more numerous; riding in Hyde Park reverted to its usual time between five and seven o'clock; balls, parties, and routs became more frequent; and Valeria's social calendar filled up with so many engagements that she saw Joan more than she saw her mother or St. John. In Town, dinner parties were held much later, sometimes as late as eight or nine o'clock, which meant that the party would not break up until midnight—or, if there was dancing or cards, sometimes Valeria wouldn't arrive home until two or three o'clock in the morning. Nights at the theatre sometimes went until the early morning hours, and then there were often late *après-théâtre* suppers given. Valeria's schedule turned into that of a true lady of leisure; most days she didn't rise until eleven o'clock or noon. She regretted that she missed going to St. George's with the family and servants for morning prayers, but soon it slipped her mind.

One blissfully sunny warm noon, as Valeria sleepily ate her toast and drank her morning tea, Joan said, "Oh, ma'am, your presentation dress arrived this morning. It came, you know, not boxed up but on a dress stand, all wrapped in a long, long length of pretty blue muslin, and there's not room for it in the dressing room, so Lady Maledon had them put it in her bedroom, and poor Mrs. Platt has had the devil of a time keeping his lordship and Niall from unwinding it, like a maypole, as they said it was, until Mr. Chalmers grabbed them by the nape o' the neck and led them out to play in the park."

Valeria smiled. Joan's diction had improved since she had become an exalted lady's maid, but she still lapsed into low slang sometimes. Lazily Valeria reflected that so did the Quality, the men at least. In fact, at one of Lady Hylton's dinner parties, whose guests varied but always included Daniel Everleigh because Valeria begged her, for some reason they had gotten into a spirited conversation about low cant, and he had taught her several phrases that were not raunchy, but were definitely not included in a well-bred young lady's vocabulary. Valeria and Daniel were sitting close together in a corner, and Lady Hylton had overheard Valeria repeat, with laughter, "Rum cully, all the crack, boozing-ken!" Later Lady Hylton had told Valeria that if she ever heard her say those words again she would box her ears. Alastair Hylton, who as usual joined in whenever Valeria was being corrected, told his mother that he could supply some strong carbolic horse soap to wash out Valeria's mouth.

At this point Valeria cared nothing for what Alastair Hylton thought of her; in fact, she had grown really reckless about the more stringent of Polite Society's strictures. As the days and weeks had sped by, she had noted no censure, no apparent disdain emanating from the most respectable people. Her hopes were confirmed when she received her voucher from Almack's, and attended the first ball; none of the Lady Patronesses had shown the slightest bit of disapproval toward her.

So she thought that perhaps, against all odds, her St. James's folly might have gone unnoticed. As time went along, and her popularity grew, she became more and more careless.

As she sipped more of her sweet scalding tea, she finally began to wake up and pay attention to Joan's raptures, which, apparently, could only be about the blue muslin covering the dress. "You and Craigie must unwrap it, and place the hoop skirts and petticoats under it so that we may see it in all its glory. And you may have the blue muslin, Joan, we'll cover it up again with some bed linens."

"Oh, thank you, thank you, ma'am!" Joan cried. "It really is ever so beautiful. But surely you'll want to try it on? Before we substitute the bed linens, I mean."

"I certainly do not," Valeria said. "I've tried that thing on for fittings eight times already, and it is the heaviest, most cumbersome, most awkward beast I've ever had the misfortune to wear. I don't know how I shall—" She broke off and pressed her fingertips to her head. "Oh dear, oh dear, what is today?"

"It's Sunday, ma'am," Joan answered, puzzled.

"Sunday? It's already Sunday? And I've missed church again…but what I was groaning about was that next week is the Queen's Drawing Room, and I haven't even practiced my curtsy yet, much less shipping along with that frightful train, and that horrible feather perched on my head."

"Yes, ma'am, Craigie, not to say her ladyship, have been worried about that," Joan said with some reproof. "Her ladyship says that she practiced every night for two weeks before she was presented to the Queen."

"Oh, dear," Valeria moaned again. "Quick, Joan, fetch my calendar." Joan gave her the small black leather-bound journal in which

Valeria wrote her social engagements, various reminders of Who was Who, and infinitely complex notations on Who called When, When Whose at-home days were, and When Whose calls must be returned. "I'm engaged to a card party at Lord and Lady Lydgate's tonight, thank heavens. I can readily beg off from that. I must, I really must practice."

"Yes, ma'am. But may we perhaps see the gown first?" Joan asked with longing.

"Yes, I should like to see it again, my last fitting was a full week ago."

When Valeria had received her summons from the lord chamberlain, included was a thorough description of the rules for dress for those being presented to the Queen. Arms, neck, and shoulders must be bare; a single ostrich feather must be worn in the hair; the train must be at least six feet long; white was the preferred color, but pale pastel hues were acceptable.

Valeria had thought with her customary rebellion that she would choose a pastel shade, but when she saw the white satin, richly gleaming, thick and luxuriant, she decided on it immediately. It was a simple dress, considering how some young ladies adorned their presentation dresses with frills, furbelows, tassels, overskirts, side swags, ruffles, complications of lace and gauze, and spider-netting.

The bodice was plain, off the shoulder and low-cut (but not scandalously so), with tiny cap sleeves. The skirt had only one flounce, a particularly wide one of twenty-four inches, made not of net or lace but of the white satin gathered slightly. It was the embellishment that made the dress spectacular. The sleeves, waist, and flounce were richly embroidered with tiny rose-pink grapes, with entwining pale ivory ivy. The border of the train was trimmed with small ivory satin squares with the bunch of grapes repeated all along it. The delicate, intricate embroidery traced up three feet of the train, diminishing slightly over the rest of the length, until halfway up the train had only sprinklings of the grape-and-ivy motif.

"Oh, oh," Joan breathed as they unwrapped the "maypole," as St. John had named it. "I've never seen such a gorgeous dress in all my life."

With satisfaction Regina said, "It is so much like you, Valeria— unique, a true original. I admit I was uncertain about the ivory on white, but it turned out extremely well. You've shown exquisite taste, dearest."

"Let's go ahead and put it over the hoop skirt and put the necklace around the neck of the form," Valeria suggested. "I haven't tried it on with my jewelry."

Regina had bought Valeria her first parure of precious gemstones. Among all the jewelers' shops in London (and they had searched a dozen or so of the more well known) they had found one, Rundell & Bridge on Ludgate Hill, that had a selection of those rarest of jewels, pink diamonds. Valeria had been staggered when she heard the cost, but Regina had insisted. "I am wealthy, my dear, while you are the poor relation," she had teased Valeria. "We must have them."

A parure—a matched set of pieces—might include as much as a necklace, a comb, a full tiara, a more modest diadem, a studded bandeau, both drop and stud cluster earrings, two bracelets, a ring, a pin, a brooch, and a belt clasp. But Valeria had insisted that she would be positively vulgar with so many trinkets, although of course they were never worn all together. She chose a simple choker necklace, a comb, a diadem, one bracelet, and drop earrings.

Now they put the delicate choker around the neck of the dress form and stepped back to admire it. Craigie sighed a little, no doubt remembering the skinny, awkward little girl who had clung so tenaciously to her after her father's death, and her great sorrowful misty pools of eyes. Now Valeria was tall, slim, elegant, self-possessed— most of the time, at least. She had grown into lovely young woman.

"Mamma, I'll never be able to thank you enough," Valeria said softly. "You truly are an angel."

Regina smiled her sweet smile—the old one, Valeria was glad to note, with no trace of sorrow in it. "You're welcome, darling. But I must correct you, you know. Today I am the Queen."

That evening in the Maledon town house drawing room, a Queen's Drawing Room was held. Regina played the Queen, Craigie played the princesses and the ladies-in-waiting, and Joan played the lord chamberlain and a lord-in-waiting. Regina had required the footmen to move the furniture back so that there was a long open space from the door to the far end of the room, where the French doors were. Here Regina sat on one of the straight-backed dining room chairs, which more nearly approximated a throne. Since the Queen's throne was on a platform, Regina had insisted that the chair's legs be placed on several thick books to give her height so that Valeria would have a truer sense of the scene in the Queen's Drawing Room. When she seated herself, she couldn't help but smile and playfully kick her legs like a child. "I feel like a Lilliputian," she said.

"Don't be silly, my lady, you're the Queen of England," Craigie said, wholly gratified to see Regina looking so happy. It had been a slow, painful process for Regina to recover from her husband's death, and the scandalous circumstances surrounding it. When they had first come to London she had still been pale and wan, and often wept late at night, and many times when she was at prayers. But slowly her youthful bloom had returned; and she had stopped wearing the glum all-black mourning dresses. From Madame Tournai she had ordered several attractive half-mourning gowns of lavender and a becoming pale blue-gray trimmed with white.

"Oh, here she comes, Your Majesty," Craigie said. "Just like a cork in a fat bottle she is, too." She and Regina could hardly stifle their girlish giggles.

From the far end of the room Valeria said with exasperation, "Mamma, it's going to be very hard for me if the Queen is dissolved in laughter when I march in. Joan, we shall begin again."

Valeria did indeed look whimsical. She had no intention of practicing in her real dress, not only because she was loath to put it on again, but also because she was deathly afraid of its getting soiled or stained. She had no gown that allowed for the great bell-like hoop skirt, so she wore it over a plain white gown tucked up under her bosom. To simulate the train Joan had first tried a bed sheet, but Valeria had insisted that it wasn't nearly heavy enough, so Joan had, rather precariously, tied a thick damask tablecloth onto the shoulders of the dress. One towering white ostrich feather was pinned in Valeria's hair.

Joan, as the lord-in-waiting, spread the "train" behind Valeria, then took Valeria's card and went to stand in front of the Queen. Now she was the lord chamberlain; but Joan had absorbed much of Valeria's nervousness, and she stuttered, "Miss–Miss Saleria Segrave—oh, dear." After a confused silence, she, Regina, and Craigie burst into laughter.

"Oh, you're all perfectly hopeless," Valeria grumbled. "Never mind, here I come, Your Majesty."

Joan, Regina, and Craigie all managed to sober up as Valeria majestically made her way down the room. When she reached the "royal throne," she sank into a deep curtsy, much deeper than usual, so that her right knee, behind, almost touched the floor. At the same time she bowed low.

Her feather brushed Her Majesty's face, and Regina abruptly sneezed.

Again there was scandalous laughter, and this time Valeria couldn't keep her countenance either. Still in her curtsy, she began to giggle, which utterly threw her off balance, and she collapsed, her hoop skirt ballooning high over her legs.

"This—this is hardly—what I'd call an auspicious beginning," Valeria gasped as Joan and Craigie helped her struggle to her feet. "Then again, the Queen might never see a more entertaining presentation."

Wiping her eyes, Regina said, "You'll be fine, dearest. In fact, you'll be perfect."

Chapter Twenty

⚜

STANDING IN THE LONG, LONG line of ladies with their sponsors in the chilly endless hall called St. James's Gallery, Valeria said anxiously to Regina, "Oh, Mamma, how shall you bear it? The draft in here is dreadful, and it looks as if we might have to stand in line for hours."

The rigid rules of presentation at court began at the front doors of the palace of St. James's. Ladies were not permitted to wear their shawls or pelisses while waiting on the Queen; outerwear must be left in the carriage. Although the dress code for young ladies making their debut was more strictly defined, the rules of court dress extended to anyone attending royal functions. They were somewhat more relaxed in the case of ladies in mourning or half mourning, but still Regina's arms, neck, and shoulders were bare. She was wearing a lovely lavender dress trimmed with black Brussels point lace, and the obligatory ostrich feather in her hair was much smaller than Valeria's, and dyed black. Her hoop skirt was not nearly as wide, and her train was only three feet long.

They spoke in low whispers, for although the ladies weren't standing too close, for fear of crushing their dresses, the gallery definitely had a hollow echo. "Never mind, dearest, I'm perfectly fine," she replied to Valeria. "And to tell you the truth, I'm rather grateful to see that the line is nowhere near as long as I had feared. Since the Queen hasn't held a Drawing Room in two years, Letitia and I were afraid that there might be five or six hundred girls begging to be presented; and I would imagine that there are, or maybe even more. But it seems to me that this group is closer to the Queen's usual Drawing Rooms, certainly no more than a hundred."

"But we're at the back of the line," Valeria fretted. "I knew that we're presented according to rank, and since barons are the lowest of the peerage, other girls would be presented before me, but I hadn't thought of having to stand in a drafty, chilly hallway for hours."

"Hush," Regina warned her, "You really musn't criticize the royal palace, dearest. And you should understand that just in front of you is Miss Caroline Tree, who is the daughter of Viscount Hering. And behind you are at least a dozen young ladies, so that you are accounted the highest-ranking baron's daughter here."

"Oh, very well, I'll be good. It does cheer me up considerably that my name is not Tree, daughter of a Hering."

"Really, Valeria," Regina scolded, but her blue eyes were lit with amusement.

To their surprise, once the presentations started, the ladies did seem to move along the Gallery fairly quickly. Regina whispered to Valeria that the Queen sometimes, but not always, said a few words to the girl being presented, though to judge by the rapidity with which they heard the lord chamberlain announcing names, Her Majesty must not be too much in the mood for chatting. It was well known that Queen Charlotte had been devastated by her husband's illness and decline into insanity; and little more than a year previously they had lost their beloved youngest daughter, Princess Amelia. It was said that her death had likely worsened the King's decline, and that even the rather shallow, flighty prince regent still burst into tears at the mention of her name. The idea of being presented to the Queen made Valeria nervous enough, but the idea of being presented to a queen who was merely performing a dreary duty and possibly resenting it made it even worse. Regina, sensing her discomfort, patted her arm. "Please don't worry, darling, you'll do very well. I was, myself, pleasantly surprised at the Queen's kindness, and I'm certain you will be too."

This cheered Valeria, for she had never known her mother to exaggerate or tell a half-truth. And in fact, when her turn finally came, she knew that her mother had, as always, spoken the exact truth.

She came to stand at the entrance of the Drawing Room, a long, high-ceilinged room with twenty-foot windows hung with rich red velvet all along one wall, and great paintings of royal personages on the other. At the far end a red velvet canopy embroidered with the royal coat of arms overhung the platform where the Queen sat, surrounded by the princesses royal and the ladies-in-waiting. Various people stood along the walls, all dressed in startling richness. There were no chairs, for of course one never sat in the presence of royalty.

Two lords-in-waiting appeared at Valeria's side; the gentleman on the left gently removed her train from her left arm and began to spread it out. The gentleman on the right took her card and went forward to hand it to the lord chamberlain, the Marquess of Hertford. Valeria didn't recognize the two lords-in-waiting, but she was acquainted with the marquess, as she had met him twice at the theatre and once at Lady Hylton's. Of course he gave no sign, and his voice held the same lack of inflection as for the last eighty or so girls.

"Miss Valeria Segrave."

Valeria began that long, long walk; and she found that she was able to compose herself. She held her head high, and moved with great grace, and her face didn't feel the least bit strained.

Lady Hylton had told her that it was suitable—even expected—that she would keep her eyes on the Queen, and that her gaze not dart around like a cornered doe's. Valeria observed that Queen Charlotte was slightly built, with gleaming silver hair. Though she was not a beauty, her countenance was bright and vivacious, her eyes were sparkling and keen, and her expression was one of good humor. At last Valeria reached the throne, curtsied deeply, and waited. Ladies who were not of noble lineage kissed the queen's hand, but for nobility, as always, the rules were different.

The queen leaned forward and kissed Valeria on the forehead. Valeria held her curtsy for a moment more, then rose. To her surprise, Queen Charlotte said, "Welcome to the court, Miss Segrave. The King and I grieved when we heard of your father's untimely death, at such a young age. Though he did not frequent the court as often as we could wish, he was still a favorite."

To her consternation, tears came to Valeria's eyes, for in spite of her outward composure her emotions were running high. However, they didn't fall; they simply made her dark eyes look even more like great misty luminous pools. The Queen's already genuinely sympathetic face softened perceptibly at the sight.

Valeria's voice was perfectly steady when she replied, "In my father's name, I am deeply honored, Your Majesty. It's a joy to me that he is so kindly remembered."

"So he is; and so he will be from now on, for you certainly inherited his looks and his air, Miss Segrave." Then the Queen nodded gracefully, and Valeria knew that this was her dismissal. She made a curtsy to the other members of the royal family, then a final long deep curtsy to the Queen. Unobtrusively and quickly the lord-in-waiting gathered up her train and draped it over her arm, and Valeria bowed and began to back up, as one must never turn one's back to the Queen. She was conscious that the lord-in-waiting guided her, as it were, by backing up with her; when she was about two-thirds of the way down the room Regina joined her and the lord led them out a side door.

When they reached the privacy of the carriage Valeria said, "Whew! All that kerfuffle for barely a minute! But you were correct, Mamma, she was extremely gracious. I think that I will forgive her for making us wear these dismal hoop skirts after all."

Despite her comment, Valeria was in a tearing hurry to shed the hoop skirt when she arrived home, not only because she despised it but because Lord and Lady Sefton were giving a ball that night. They had invited all the newly presented ingenues and their families, and Valeria had a sumptuous new ball gown to wear.

"Before you do anything, take this horrendous object off my head," she told Joan testily. "I declare I'll never refer to anything as 'light as a feather' again. It feels more like a horsetail than a feather. Now that I think of it, it looks like a horsetail too."

"Yes, ma'am," Joan said automatically, then said eagerly, "Oh, ma'am, aren't you going to tell me all about meeting the Queen? Everyone belowstairs is ever so eager to hear."

As she dressed, Valeria related every detail to Joan, who relished the story, and even committed the grave sin of interrupting Valeria a couple of times to further clarify a point. Finally Valeria was dressed, and Joan said, "Oh, miss, your court dress was that beautiful; but this one is like a dream."

Valeria's first choice for a court presentation dress had been an ivory-pink satin, but Madame Touraint and Regina had convinced her that her white feather and particularly her white gloves would make the shade look somewhat dingy. They had been right; but Madame Tournai had suggested using the fabric for a ball gown, and had designed a unique dress for Valeria.

Indeed, the particular color was unusual; it was a pale, pale ivory but with a pinkish hue like that of a fruity champagne. Madame Tournai had shown Valeria a delicate, airy, gossamer fabric with spider-web-thin gold threads woven through it, called "shot" muslin. Madame Tournai had said that she could perfectly match the unusual hue of the satin, and dye the white muslin, which would not affect the gold threads. Valeria had also persuaded Madame

Tournai to dye her gloves; although white gloves were still most often worn—as were white dresses—some fashionable young ladies had been seen even in full formal dress with gloves dyed to match their gowns. It was considered rather daring, but not necessarily in a loose way, and finally Madame Tournai had consented.

She had been true to her word, for the delicate hue was perfect. The finished dress was a simple Empire-waisted sheath with off-the-shoulder short sleeves made of the satin; it was commonly termed a "petticoat," but of course it was not the same as the undergarment, it was really an underdress. The overdress was made of the shot muslin, and the rich sheen of the satin, combined with the glimmer of the gold thread, had a dazzling effect. The skirt had a small demi-train. The low neckline was square-cut. With her pink diamond necklace, diadem, and earrings, Valeria looked more beautiful than she ever had in her life.

She had heard Lord and Lady Lydgate and Lady Hylton arrive to collect her some time before. She hurried downstairs and gave a flurried kiss to her mother, and the company went to Lord and Lady Sefton's house on Park Lane, which bordered the west side of Hyde Park, and so was only five blocks away. Carriages were lined all up and down the broad street, but finally the Lydgate carriage was at the foot of the steps leading up into the grand mansion. Valeria thought that there must be thousands and thousands of candles, for through the many windows the house glowed like a golden star.

As this was such a grand ball, the host and hostess did not greet the guests at the door. A master of ceremonies took everyone's card, and then announced the guests in a baritone roar that carried throughout the great ballroom.

"The Right Honourable Letitia, Lady Hylton; the Right Honourable the Viscount Lydgate; the Right Honourable the Viscountess Lydgate; Miss Segrave," he boomed, and the four of them walked into the crowd and were instantly separated, for it was already a crush.

"Miss Segrave, I've been waiting for you," she heard, and Daniel Everleigh turned sideways to slide past a rather portly man in full military regalia, and writhed through. He bowed; Valeria curtsied prettily. She reflected that Mr. Everleigh was looking fine this evening in full evening dress. He was wearing a dark blue cutaway coat with gold buttons, a white satin waistcoat, an intricate complex cravat, light-blue satin breeches with gold buckles at the knee, white stockings "clocked" in blue, and the *de rigueur* black pumps with bows. Everleigh was not a muscular man, but he was trim and Valeria observed (not for the first time) that he had good calves. He was distinctly handsome, almost pretty, with his lush curling brown hair, well-shaped heavily lashed dark eyes, small straight nose, and wide mouth.

After their greetings he stared at Valeria, a very bold up-and-down appraisal. In the crowd he stepped very close to her, and said, "You look utterly ravishing. Ravishing. I'm simply ravished."

Valeria smiled, her eyes brilliant. "And repeating yourself, sir, which is very unlike you. However, I choose to take the repetition as a high compliment."

"Please do. Listen—you must come with me," he said, grabbing her hand and leading her, weaving through the crowd. It was unorthodox, first for them to touch at all, much less hold hands for any length of time, and second for him to walk in front of her, clearing a path, as it were. Valeria thought carelessly that in this rout no one could possibly notice, and followed along.

She had time to look around and orient herself, because for the first few minutes she had been dazzled. The crowd was like a riotous rainbow, for older women wore varied colors of bolder shades than the young women, and although most of the men were in Beau Brummel's preferred somber colors, there were quite a few military men in blazing red coats or rich sumptuous blue, with a myriad of gold braids. In the long rectangular room—Valeria reflected that it seemed to be about the same size as the royal Drawing Room that she had just left—four enormous glittering crystal-and-gold chandeliers each held hundreds of candles. Everywhere were lush garlands of laurels, and opulent arrangements of flowers. Only now did Valeria look up and see the minstrels' gallery, which held at least thirty musicians. The music would be resplendent tonight.

Daniel led her to a hallway; at the entrance to the ballroom was set up a long table holding what Valeria at first took to be fans. "Lady Sefton has outdone herself tonight in grandeur; this will surely put one in Mrs. Drummond-Burrell's eye," he said with relish. Mrs. Drummond-Burrell was known as the haughtiest and most icy of the patronesses of Almack's. Heiress to the great Drummond banking fortune, she was the wealthiest of the patronesses, and perhaps because of her lack of title (she had married a minor dandy who appended her name to his), by her lavish display of her enormous wealth, she seemed to try to compete with the other noble ladies who ruled Almack's.

"Oh, how exquisite," Valeria breathed. "I've never seen anything like them."

They were fan-shaped, but they were not fans, they were dance cards. The guardsticks and leaf were of silver, intricately engraved. The sticks—the lower part of the ribs—were of mother-of-pearl, and the dances were listed on them in calligraphy with a royal-blue ink. The slips—the upper part of the ribs—were of very light balsa wood, painted with silver gilt; this was where the gentlemen signed their names for each dance. Attached to each fan were two thick tassels of silver thread, and a blue pencil topped with a silver cap and loop.

The wooden-faced footman standing behind the table wordlessly handed one to Valeria, and grinning mischievously, Everleigh snatched it out of her hand. "I insist on claiming my dances first, ma'am, as I know that as always you will be in much demand."

He turned the fan sideways to peruse the list of dances, then busily started writing.

Lord and Lady Lydgate, followed by Lord Hylton, made their way through the crowd to Valeria's side. "Elyse, just look at these dance cards. Aren't they stunning?"

"Yes, I saw several other ladies with them, and I demanded that Reggie find them," she answered. "My husband will only consent to dance one time with me, but there are plenty of other gentlemen who are glad to please a lady." She dug her elbow into Reggie's side.

"Ow," he mumbled. "Don't care for dancing much, I'm always afraid of forgetting the steps or trodding on someone's foot. I did that one time, you know, "'twas Lady Alvanley, and she didn't take kindly to it, at all."

Impatiently Elyse said, "Oh, come, Reggie, sign for this *contredanse*, it'll be late in the evening and you'll have had enough negus by then that you won't care. Let's go find Ponsonby, he promised me the cotillion."

Alastair stepped up and bowed, and as Valeria made her curtsy she noted that he made Daniel Everleigh look a bit of a flash. Alastair's black coat had cloth-covered buttons, his cravat was simple but perfect, his white waistcoat was of silk, not shiny satin, his breeches were dull black satin, his white stockings without design. Still, with his height, and his breadth of shoulder, and his muscular rider's legs, he was an imposing figure, and the severe but elegant simplicity of his tailoring fit his air of impenetrable reserve.

However, as Valeria regarded him, she was somewhat bemused to find that his expression, normally remote and even cold, was different on this night. A small half-smile, wholly contained, was on his lips, and his eyes, instead of the frigid gray-blue, seemed warmer, even friendly. "Miss Segrave, you are in particular good looks. I assume that confection is one of Madame Tournai's newest?"

Obscurely pleased that Alastair had noticed her frock, Valeria answered, "So it is, sir, and I'm afraid it's to my beautiful gown that I must attribute my looks tonight."

"Not at all," he said, then turned to Daniel. "What's that—oh, so this is the famous dance card. Hand it over, Everleigh. Yes, so I thought, you young dog, you're not going to have three dances with Miss Segrave tonight, it won't do."

To Valeria's astonishment he crossed out Daniel's name and with a flourish wrote "Hylton" with a heavy line upon one of the sticks, then looked at the list of dances. "But—but sir, I've never known you to dance," she said, bewildered. "I was certain you must have sworn it off for life."

"I'm very ill-suited to hopping and skipping and prancing. I'll walk through a cotillion, though I do regret the small bits of fancy footwork; and here I see an allemande, which I will also suffer through." He wrote his name on another one of the slips.

Daniel Everleigh, more than slightly miffed at being called a young dog, muttered, "That's high-handed even for you, Hylton. It's customary to *ask* young ladies for the honor of a dance."

"Yes, I've heard that rumor. Did you ask Miss Segrave for the honor?"

"Well, no, but we have a particular understanding, you know."

"I doubt that Miss Segrave *understood* that she was to dance with you three times," he said sardonically, then, suddenly slightly alarmed, he turned to Valeria and demanded, "Did you?"

In truth Valeria had thought little about it; she was feeling so exultant these days that breaking this silly little rule seemed inconsequential. But she wished to enjoy Lord Hylton's unusual good humor and to avoid another scolding. Languidly she replied, "Oh, certainly, sir. And after that I was going to play the pianoforte and sing at the top of my lungs, and then I was going to dance a ballet."

Alastair relaxed and then actually did smile. "I might worry about the ballet, but I know there is no chance of the musical performance, ma'am. I am content."

"I'm so happy to ease your mind, sir."

The musicians were completing their discordant tuning up, and the crowd thinned as the older dowagers and unfortunate partnerless young ladies began taking their seats on the delicate French side chairs along the walls. Alastair said, "Please accompany me, Miss Segrave, as the cotillion is the opening dance, and we must arrange our partners. I'm glad Ponsonby's dancing with Elyse; the last time Reggie danced the cotillion he ended up not once but twice in the wrong group."

Nodding his head, he indicated to Valeria where Elyse and Charles Ponsonby were standing in the middle of several couples. Unlike Daniel, Alastair courteously walked behind Valeria, and they joined the group. Elyse took Valeria's dance card and said, "Here, Mamma is to hold our fans and cards." She glanced down at it and whispered in Valeria's ear, "Alastair has signed for two dances? I can hardly believe it, he so rarely dances at all, and I can't recall him ever dancing with the same partner twice."

"How fortunate I am for his worshipful lordship to show me such condescension," Valeria whispered back.

Valeria had thought that Alastair would be a stiff and somber dancer but quite the opposite was true. He danced gracefully, with a spare elegance, and on this mysteriously magical night he was inclined to what Valeria thought of as normal polite conversation. He said, "I'm a little surprised that you dance the cotillion so well, Miss Segrave, as it is considered quite ancient by young people, and is so rarely performed."

" 'Young people,' " she repeated mockingly. "You speak as if you were a doddering ancient."

"Sometimes I feel like it. For example, I have never ceased to mourn the minuet, no one ever includes it anymore. I loved the minuet; it was so easy, like taking a leisurely walk. It's the only dance I have ever enjoyed."

"That may be so, but I am sorry to tell you that even if you're perfectly miserable, you're quite a good dancer."

"I'm far from miserable; in fact, I'm in grave danger of enjoying myself. And I never said I was a bad dancer, I believe I said something to the effect that I was not partial to poncing about, making antic gestures."

Valeria laughed, though she kept it to a low, discreet laugh. "I most emphatically agree with you, sir. You never ponce or make antic gestures."

This friendly banter continued throughout the dance, and Valeria felt a strange small thrill as he took her hand and pressed rather close to her, as he escorted her off the floor. Seeing several young men looking eagerly her way, he said in a courtly manner, "Thank you for the honor, ma'am. I look forward to our allemande." Before she could reply, he had slipped away from her side, and she was besieged by Daniel Everleigh and three other young men, all begging to sign her card. She scolded Everleigh very slightly—and said that he had already claimed two dances, and she so feared the wrath of Lord Hylton that she wasn't about to let his taradiddle persuade her into a third dance now. Soon her card was full, though she had prudently insisted on leaving the fifth and ninth dances open, knowing that she would be grateful to sit down and refresh herself with some lemonade.

Valeria's partner for the second dance was Paul Northbrooke, and it was a lively *contredanse* that she was enjoying immensely. Suddenly the musicians faltered, and the music petered out; the dancing hesitated and stopped; a low babble of bewilderment sounded; people looked about in confusion; and in a moment of sheer senseless panic Valeria thought, *Have I done something wrong—again?*

A moment later the master of ceremonies, in a deep reverential tone, announced, "His Royal Highness, the prince regent."

A heavy silence fell on the room like a weight; then all that could be heard was the quiet shuffling as everyone parted to either side of the room, and the soft satiny whispers of the ladies' dresses as they curtsied. After a suitable interval, the master of ceremonies announced, "The Right Honourable the Viscount Kincannon; Lord Stephen Tryon; Mr. Brummel."

Valeria was, of course, in a low royal curtsy, with head bowed, as the prince regent passed by, so she saw nothing at all of Himself, though her curiosity was so avid that she almost risked a glance up from under her lashes. But in spite of her recent forays into risky behavior, she didn't quite have the courage for that amount of audacity. The prince regent said nothing as he passed down the long row of bowed subjects, but when he reached the end of the room, he greeted Lord and Lady Sefton warmly. Raising his rather high-pitched voice he said crisply, "Carry on, carry on." The musicians began again, the couples resumed their positions, and as he had commanded, the dance resumed.

Standing in the line, Valeria despaired somewhat; her back was to the side of the room where the prince had gone, and she knew that the hallway on that side led to the card room, where he likely would hurry, given his penchant for gambling. She grumbled to herself that she would probably never have the chance to set eyes upon Prinny in person.

She was wrong.

As soon as Northbrooke returned Valeria to her group, Lord Stephen went to Valeria's side. "Miss Segrave, the prince regent has expressed his desire to make your acquaintance."

"He has?" Valeria breathed, her eyes glowing. "Of course, I'm honored."

Lord Stephen offered Valeria his arm. Followed by Elyse and Reggie and Lady Hylton they obeyed the royal summons. Stephen said easily, "Your Royal Highness, it is my pleasure to present to you Miss Valeria Segrave, daughter of the late Guy, Lord Segrave. Miss Segrave, His Royal Highness the prince regent."

Reggie made a low bow, and the ladies did their long-lasting royal curtsies. When finally Valeria rose, she quickly studied the prince. He was undeniably handsome, though the fine features of his face were marred because he was so overweight, his cheeks and jowls were pendulous, and he had dissipation bags under his eyes. Still, his expression was very near that of his mother. He looked open, generous, good-humored. "Miss Segrave, I simply had to meet you after I heard of your clever sallies; it seems you might even match wits with Brummel. Oh, of course, you haven't met him. Miss Segrave, Beau Brummel. Brummel, Miss Segrave."

Valeria curtsied to him and he gave a mocking bow, and Valeria turned back to answer the prince, as she had been directly addressed. "Your Royal Highness, I beg you will not repeat my 'sallies,' as you so kindly call them, for I'm afraid that Lady Hylton terms them brash imprudent insolent blatherings, and chastises me cruelly."

"Far be it from me to place such a lovely young lady in danger of being disciplined, for it is indeed tedious and irksome, I find," he said.

"Sir, I am honored to have you as my ally. Perhaps my godmother will temper her ire somewhat, with such a staunch defender at my side," Valeria said, with daring, even outrageous familiarity.

But then Prinny was much given to over-familiarity with his subjects, and therefore took no offense. Far from it; he beamed at Valeria, with obvious admiration. His appreciative gaze held no hint of debauchery in it, however, for his tastes ran to older, more sophisticated, worldly women. "Indeed, you must let me know if Lady Hylton is very severe with you; I'll plead your case. By the by, next month I'm having a fête at Carlton House, and since I understand you were presented to Her Majesty this evening, I shall have your name added to the list, Miss Segrave."

"Thank you, sir, I shall look forward to it," Valeria said.

"Enchanting, quite lovely," the prince murmured by way of dismissal, so they all made their obeisances and he led his entourage down the hall toward the card room.

Lady Hylton had a most severe look on her face as she walked Valeria back across the ballroom; but Valeria could tell that she was amused. "So, you not only excoriated me in front of the prince regent, you bamboozled him into joining in. I congratulate you, Valeria; that was the fastest, neatest bit of royal manipulation I've ever witnessed."

"I assure you it was not intentional, ma'am. I was so jittery that I could barely tell what was coming out of my mouth."

"That seems to happen to you quite often, my dear."

The night went on in a sort of ecstatic haze for Valeria. The Queen had been kind to her, the prince regent had shown her particular favor, even Lord Hylton had been cordial and warm to her during both of their dances. Those were the only times she saw him throughout the evening, for Daniel Everleigh monopolized her attention, as always, on her two dance breaks, and he took it for granted that he would escort her to supper when the dancing was done.

The supper room was just off the ballroom, and was as sumptuously furnished as any dining room. Although there was an abundance of food, equivalent to a five- or six-course dinner, Valeria was not at all hungry, and settled for a small bit of Stilton cheese and an apple tart. After a mere two or three bites she drank an entire glass of cold fresh raspberry water, and Daniel went to fetch her more. When he returned, Valeria turned her chair slightly, and he arranged his to face her, sitting so closely that his knees occasionally touched hers. This had become customary between them.

"I say, Miss Segrave, the word is that you are the darling of the Season. I'm told that the Queen spoke to you this evening; and she only spoke to two other girls, dukes' daughters. Then the prince upsets the whole ballroom by demanding an introduction, and by all accounts he is completely taken by your charms, which I've always said are considerable." He grinned a shark's grin. "All of the young ladies who've never been introduced to Prinny are in quite a taking, they're pea-green with envy. Miss Cranleigh told Miss Mowbray that you're really not at all the thing, she was amazed that the prince had taken note of you, for everyone knows that you're only the daughter of a baron, and not very pretty at that. I took it upon myself to say, 'Everyone knows that, Miss Cranleigh? How very odd, considering that His Royal Highness said that Miss Segrave was handsome, elegant, clever, enchanting, and lovely.' Miss Cranleigh and Miss Mowbray both looked as if they'd taken a bite of a particularly nasty rotten apple."

"Nonsense, he didn't say all of that rubbish," Valeria scoffed.

"He most certainly did, I had it from Kincannon himself. Don't you know that every word said by Prinny is repeated verbatim? It's the highest form of Town gossip."

"He truly did? How marvelous," Valeria said, a fresh wave of jubilation coloring her cheeks and brightening her eyes to an unearthly brilliance.

Everleigh leaned over and motioned her to bend her head so that he could speak in her ear. The two were quite close, and by their body language showed no small intimacy.

Everleigh whispered, "Kincannon told me something else too, and it's going to be great fun. In three weeks he's giving a *bal masque* at the Pantheon, and he wants me to invite you and urge you to come, since he says you're a genuine smasher."

"Why does not Lord Kincannon simply send me an invitation?"

Everleigh said earnestly, "No, it's not that sort of party. It's more like—like the assembly rooms, at home, you see. Certain nights are set for dances, and people just come."

"All right, I see that. Now tell me why we are whispering?"

"Oh, Kincannon's parties aren't to everyone's taste. I'm sure Lady Hylton wouldn't approve, but you have to admit that she is particularly starchy. Lydgate's a sport, and he wouldn't care, but I doubt that Lady Lydgate would want to attend. But a masquerade, Miss Segrave! Tell me, promise me, you'll come with me."

Valeria leaned back slightly and gave him an arch look. Then, again whispering in his ear, she said, "If I'm understanding you correctly, sir, you're asking me to accompany you to a party without a sign of a chaperon."

"You are entirely correct," he said slyly. "Brazen of me, ain't it? But then you're a lady of fire and spirit, Miss Segrave, and it would be such an adventure. I know that you're so keen you'll think of some ingenious costume. That's already half the fun there."

Valeria thought that it would indeed be great fun; she had always longed to go to a masquerade ball, and had never had the opportunity. Still, some semblance of caution existed, even though it was a very dim sense somewhere in the back of her mind. She whispered, "I'll have to think about it, Mr. Everleigh. I may not be quite as adventuresome as you believe."

"Oh, but I know that you are, Miss Segrave, and I believe that when I dance with you at Lady Mowbray's tomorrow night you'll consent to accompany me to Kincannon's party. And as long as we are whispering, may I call you Valeria?"

"I suppose so," Valeria said with a flirtatious smile. "But in that case we must keep on whispering."

Chapter Twenty-one

❦

I N FACT, VALERIA DID NOT consent to go to Lord Kincannon's *bal masque* when she danced with Daniel Everleigh the next night at Lady Mowbray's; nor did she consent when she rode with him in Hyde Park the following day; nor did she consent when he pressed her even more urgently as they sat together in the Hylton box at Covent Garden for a superb production of Mozart's *Così Fan Tutte*.

However, an idea was forming in her mind—a creative, ingenious idea for a costume, so Valeria thought, and the more she thought about it, the more enticing the idea of attending a masquerade in a daring disguise became. She thought that most likely she would never be recognized.

In considering the difficulties of getting her costume, and of attending the ball without her mother or her chaperons knowing it, Valeria solemnly promised herself that she would not tell a single lie, and that omission of the truth was not the same as lying.

The fact that she deliberately acted in a deceptive way, with full intent to deceive, never entered her mind. She was in such a glow from her success, her popularity, and indeed the increasingly adoring attentions from Daniel Everleigh that she felt invincible. She viewed herself as contrasting with the other rather insipid, timid girls; Valeria herself was fiery, audacious, and bold. Men such as

Lord Stephen Tryon, Lord Kincannon, and even the haughty Beau Brummel himself regarded her as such, Daniel had assured her.

Fully aware that it would take some time for her costume to be made, she finally did tell Daniel that she would go to the *bal masque* with him. Delicate arrangements were made, and somehow Daniel (for now he and Valeria addressed each other by their first names, although only in private conversation) made all the secrecy and the dissimulation seem like part of a great exciting mystery, like a scavenger hunt.

Regina and Valeria had stayed late at a card party at Lord and Lady Lydgate's, and the next day Regina was pale and wan.

"Mamma, I just now decided to go to Bond Street, but it's really not necessary for you to accompany me," Valeria assured her. "It's going to be tiresome, for I have to go to Monsieur Joubert's, the milliner, my bootmaker, and the glover's. It will be perfectly acceptable if Joan chaperons me."

Regina considered this for a few moments, then nodded. "Very well, dearest, to tell the truth I am feeling a bit fatigued. I thought I might rest for a while after luncheon. But do, do behave yourself, Valeria, please."

"Oh, Joan will keep me perfectly respectable," she said lightly.

Ewan stopped the carriage at the northern end of the street, and as all of Valeria's stops ranged up and down the street, he agreed to meet them at the southern end. Valeria was relieved. She knew that she could make her stops without being obliged to explain anything to Joan, but Ewan Platt had known her far, far too long and well, and he would likely suspect something immediately. If Ewan and Craigie caught a whiff, she would be doomed, she thought with a wholly unconscious irony.

At Monsieur Joubert's door, Valeria turned to Joan, who was walking meekly slightly behind her, and said, "Stay out here, Joan. I shall only be a moment."

Joan looked taken aback, but of course she said nothing. Valeria went in, and was warmly welcomed by Monsieur Joubert. In spite of the fact that Valeria had tried and tried to think of how to tell the tailor exactly what she wanted, she'd had had very little success in coming up with some brilliant explanation. After his courteous greeting, she said with completely artificial brightness, "Monsieur Joubert, I am considering—that is, we are considering a new servants' livery. Do you tailor that particular fashion, of the old-style coats and long waistcoats?"

He bowed. "*Certainement, mademoiselle.* I would be most heppy to tailor to each servant the livery."

"Yes, yes, of course," Valeria said vaguely. "Do you—would you—perhaps we might do a trial—that is, a sample livery, on what you might call a smaller scale than a—a—full-grown man, to save, that is it would not take so much fabric—" She stopped in utter confusion, her cheeks coloring a bright pink.

Monsieur Joubert's heavy-lidded gaze took on a knowing Gallic look, and then he resumed his customary cordial expression of polite interest. "If I may be so bold, would this perhaps be something that *mademoiselle* herself is interested in? Perhaps it may have to do with the *bal masque, oui?*"

Valeria was vastly relieved. "*Oui, monsieur.* I am attending a masquerade ball, and I have a particular costume in mind. I know that I may rely on your discretion, Monsieur Joubert. Also, my costume is not to be charged to my mother's account; I shall pay for it myself, in cash." She went on to explain exactly what she wanted, and noted that Monsieur Joubert never blinked an eye. Either he was the most self-controlled man she had ever met, or he was so accustomed to the peccadilloes of the *haut ton* that nothing shocked him.

Although Monsieur Joubert had extensive measurements already, some additional ones were required, and Madame Joubert and her daughters were fully as smooth-faced and professionally detached as Monsieur Joubert. They were also professionally thorough, so it took about half an hour. By the time Valeria rejoined Joan out on the boardwalk, her maid looked distinctly worried. Airily Valeria said, "Oh, we had some quibbling about measurements, and some additional ones had to be taken, that's what took so long. Come along, my bootmaker is just up here."

Again Valeria told Joan not to accompany her inside; and the same at the glover's and the milliner's. When they finally reached the carriage, Joan was looking thoroughly mystified, but with satisfaction Valeria observed that she didn't seem suspicious at all. Joan was a sweet-natured, gentle girl, and would never think of questioning her.

As the days wore on at their usual furious pace, Valeria and Daniel spent more and more time together, and the both of them grew more and more excited about the masquerade ball. Valeria refused to tell him about her costume, and he teased and wheedled her unmercifully, but she was adamant. "All I shall say is that I think you'll be surprised. I daresay there won't be another one like it."

"I'm sure there won't," he agreed. "Knowing you, Valeria, you'll out-*masque* us all."

Lord Kincannon's *bal masque* at the Pantheon was set for Wednesday night, beginning at midnight. The weekly balls at Almack's were on Wednesdays, and Valeria, Lady Hylton, and Lord and Lady Lydgate always attended them; and many times, to Valeria's surprise, considering his disdain for the club, Alastair Hylton came with them. On this particular Wednesday night he did not. Valeria asked where he was, and none of them knew, not even Reggie. "He is that tight-lipped, y'know," Reggie said carelessly. "I asked him if he was coming tonight, and he fairly slapped me down and told me to be mindful of my own business and leave his alone."

Usually Lady Hylton tired by about eleven o'clock, and most of the time she went home by herself and sent the carriage back. But on this night Valeria said, "Do you know, ma'am, I'm feeling rather fatigued myself this evening. I believe I'll return home with you."

"Really?" Lady Hylton said with surprise. "You aren't getting ill, are you, child?"

"Oh, no, not at all." Then she added mischievously, "Truth to tell, Mr. Everleigh is also leaving early; he is apparently going to another party."

"Ah, I see," Lady Hylton said knowingly. Valeria and Daniel had been together so much that in spite of Lady Sturway's staunch objections, speculation was that there might indeed be a match in the making.

When Valeria arrived home, she refused Joan's offer of cocoa, hurried her through undressing, then dismissed her. As soon as her footsteps faded away, Valeria began re-dressing. She and Daniel had agreed that he would be waiting for her at the corner of the street at eleven forty-five. It was about five minutes past midnight before Valeria was finished, and she felt a moment's anxiety. But then she realized that of course Daniel would wait for her.

A stealthy figure clothed in solid black, she stole down to the library, then slipped into the drawing room, a mere shadow. She opened the French doors and, as lightly as if she were a gazelle, sprang across a short gap to a thick branch of the elm tree growing just by the house. With her fingertips she was able to close the well-oiled door without a single squeak. Nimbly, for she had mentally rehearsed this, she stepped down onto a lower branch, then another, and then jumped three feet to the ground. Gathering her black cape around her so as to hide the glare of her white shirt, cuffs, and jabot, she furtively hurried to the walk. Down the street she could plainly see, by the streetlamps, Daniel pacing to and fro by his carriage. He wore no costume, for he was exceedingly disdainful of them for gentlemen.

With sudden inspiration, stifling a giggle, Valeria hid behind the hedge and crept toward him. He was pacing directly at the end of a neighbor's walk.

Valeria leaped, abruptly looming up in front of him, drew a pistol, pointed it at his chest, and growled, "Stand and deliver!"

Utter shock, and then a slight frisson of fear, crossed his face. Next he stared incredulously, and then he roared with laughter. "Valeria, you're a genius! It's truly brilliant! A highwayman!"

She wore the clothing that a highwayman of the last century might have worn, although her costume was likely much more finely made and expensive than robbers' ever were. Her black coat was made of superfine broadcloth, and was long, as the last century's fashion had been; and so was her waistcoat. Her shirt had long frilled cuffs, and the collar was flat, with a ruffled jabot. A wide leather belt with a silver buckle encircled her slender waist, and two fine Manton dueling pistols—her stepfather's, stolen from a display of pistols and swords hung on the wall in the library—were stuck butt-out in her belt. She wore her specially made black leather gauntlets with long cuffs, a black tricorn hat with her hair completely tucked up into it, a black mask, and a billowing black silk cape.

Her specially made boots were also from a previous age; they were above-the-knee, with a one-inch heel and a silver buckle. And tucked into these dashing boots were Valeria's trousers.

Daniel was babbling on, his face lit with somewhat libidinous delight: "Trousers, you look simply smashing, Valeria, it's really quite extraordinary how enticing it is—"

"Are we going to stand out here prating all night, or are we going to a *bal masque?*" she demanded, her dark eyes glittering in the mask's embroidered eyeholes. As they climbed into the carriage, Valeria was not really too surprised that instead of sitting across from her, as was customary, Daniel sat beside her and slid his arm around her shoulders.

She looked up at him and said slyly, "You're going to try to kiss me, aren't you?"

"Yes, ma'am, I certainly am."

"But sir, won't you find it most peculiar, to kiss a highwayman?"

"Believe me, Valeria, no matter how much you tuck your hair up and wear trousers, no one would ever mistake you for a man." He bent his head and brushed his lips against hers; it was the first time Valeria had ever been kissed, and she found that it was quite pleasurable. She lifted her face again, and he kissed her, this time with more urgency. At first Valeria enjoyed the embrace, but then she grew disquieted; she was having trouble regulating her breathing, and Daniel was clasping her very closely. She pushed him away, at first gently, but when he resisted her she pushed harder.

Reluctantly he drew away, and he was clearly frustrated. "Why do you push me away, Valeria? You like to be kissed, I can tell, and a woman like you should be kissed, often."

Valeria was nonplussed by this comment; somehow it made her sound . . . well, fast. But surely Daniel had no intention of offending her, she quickly reassured herself. Still, with some asperity, Valeria said, "I'm afraid that I have so little experience that I can hardly judge if you speak truth or not. That is the first time I have ever been kissed, and I did like it, but I prefer to give it some time before I decide whether or not I shall be kissing *often*."

In spite of his ire, Daniel grinned. "You will be sure to let me know when you decide, won't you? Happy to be of service, and all."

The coachman pulled the carriage up to the more discreet side entrance on Poland Street, but even though it wasn't the main entrance, still a rapidly streaming crowd of people hurried inside. Valeria felt no misgivings at all, only a mounting anticipation. When the groom opened the carriage door, with a flourish of her cape she stepped in front of Daniel and jumped down, disdaining the steps. She turned around to laugh up at him, and saw the heated admiration on his face, and knew that though she certainly looked unorthodox, she must be in very good looks indeed.

Daniel tied a mask over his eyes, a white silk one. "Let's go, highwayman."

The Poland Street entrance led directly into the great assembly room, or the rotunda, which was topped by a massive dome that was similar to that of the Pantheon in Rome. Valeria's first impression was of a room of such vast size that she felt dwarfed. Gradually she realized that the square footage of the room itself was not what gave her the impression; it was the soaring ceiling, at least fifty feet high, with friezes all around depicting scenes of ancient Rome. At one end was a stage holding an entire orchestra. On the east and west sides were single tiers of boxes, set twenty feet up, themselves having twenty-foot ceilings and elaborate chandeliers.

But once Valeria had taken in the room, her attention was riveted by the dancers, for to her eyes they were dancing in a bizarre manner. Instead of being arranged in long neat lines with partners facing each other, or in the orderly rectangles of the cotillion and allemande, the couples were closely clasping each other and whirling around and around in dizzying circles. "Good heavens, what are they doing?" she asked, wide-eyed.

"That is the German waltz. Ain't it the utmost? It's all the rage on the Continent, but you just know the bluenoses at Almack's have not and probably never will endorse it, so you don't see it in London."

"No, I can see why," Valeria murmured. However, once one recovered from the shock of seeing such public intimacy, the dance itself could be quite graceful. As always, there were those who danced elegantly and those who danced awkwardly. Valeria particularly admired a couple who turned and glided with an airy grace. The woman was dressed in the eighteenth-century French style, with a towering powdered wig, a whitened and rouged face with a pasted-on beauty mark, and a marvelous golden satin dress with a natural waistline and wide panniers. Her partner was a tall man dressed in simple black formal wear, and wearing a black mask. They glided close by Daniel and Valeria, and with extreme alarm Valeria recognized the woman as Lady Jex-Blake. Their eyes met. Valeria managed to keep her countenance, holding her breath. Lady Jex-Blake's hard gaze swept on without a single sign of recognition. Valeria breathed a sigh of relief.

"Just look at some of these costumes," Daniel said disdainfully. "I told you that even men who generally display good sense make themselves look ridiculous."

Valeria looked. She saw two judges, with long thick curly wool wigs and scarlet robes; an Arabian pasha, with a turban that was coming untied and billowing trousers; no fewer than four Henry VIIIs; a king's jester; a harlequin; and several Romans in togas, sandals, and laurel wreaths. Many other gentlemen were dressed in the style of the French court of the previous century, with satin coats of blazing jewel tones, powdered wigs, and cosmetics. One portly gentleman wearing a bright purple coat evidently was costumed as the lately beheaded King Louis XVI, for at his neck was a lurid dribbling of what Valeria *hoped* was red paint. "Oh, horrors, surely that's—that's not funny," she said in a strangled voice, and then helplessly giggled.

"That's old Colonel Nebbitts, he always did have a bizarre sense of humor," Daniel said, chuckling. "His costume at least shows some imagination."

"But surely you approve of many of the ladies' costumes, at least. They don't look ridiculous."

"Oh no? Did you see that woman in the Marie Antoinette wig with the birdcage and live bird in it? Still, I do like the pretty little shepherdesses, and the ladies wearing the Grecian gowns. Oh, yes, some of those are delicious."

Valeria looked a little closer, and she was stunned to see that several women were wearing the simple tunic gowns of the classical era... and that they were wearing nothing underneath. For the first time it occurred to her that this was not at all like the other parties she had been to, and it caused her some consternation. But then she told herself with great practicality that she hadn't recognized anyone at all so far, except for Lady Jex-Blake, and the woman had clearly not known her. The chances of anyone's recognizing her were slim indeed. Besides, compared to some of the more outrageous costumes she had seen, Valeria's was relatively unobtrusive. She decided that she should just relax and have a good time, and indeed she was looking forward to waltzing.

Tugging on Daniel's arm—he was distracted, watching one particularly curvy woman in one of the diaphanous Grecian gowns—Valeria asked, "Daniel, do you know how to do this waltz?"

"Hm? Oh. Oh, yes, certainly. If you observe, it's really rather simple; it's just ONE-two-three, ONE-two-three, and you keep turning."

"Yes, I see. Can we try it?" Valeria asked eagerly.

"Of course, but I have to warn you. In the waltz, the rule is that the gentleman *leads*, and the lady *follows*. That means that I signal you how and when to turn, and so on."

Valeria raised a sardonic eyebrow and put her right hand on the pistol butt at her left hip. "Oh, really. You're telling me that I'm required to follow a man, and do exactly what he tells me to do? What a bizarre notion."

Daniel grinned, his most devilish. "I know that you have even less experience at that than kissing, but I'm sure you'll be just as good at it, if you try."

Valeria said, "Well, then, stand and deliver."

They were a little tentative at first; and it did go completely against Valeria's grain to surrender herself, as it were, to Daniel's lead. A couple of times she jerked one way when he went the other; and once she stepped square on his right foot. She apologized profusely, but he just said good-naturedly, "Highwayman, I would endure much more than a trodden foot, even by a heavy boot, to be able to hold you close and dance with you like this."

This delighted Valeria so much that she soon found herself easily following his lead, STEP-step-step, and turning, turning, with Daniel's arm warmly encircling her waist, pressing her close to him. Even the strangeness of wearing—dancing in—trousers was peculiarly exhilarating. From sheer excitement Valeria threw her head back and laughed.

But her laugh was choked off abruptly, and she stumbled a bit. She had looked upward toward the boxes, and as if she had directly aimed, she looked straight into Alastair Hylton's face. He sat forward in a jerky, convulsive movement. Even from twenty feet below him, Valeria could see his eyes narrow to slits.

"Oh, no," she muttered.

"What's wrong?" Daniel asked.

"Oh, it's that blasted Lord Hylton. I've just seen him, and I'm sure he recognized me."

Daniel glanced up at the box and shrugged. "Oh, yes, I recall now. Usually Hylton doesn't attend Kincannon's er—larger parties. But it seems that an old friend of Hylton's is on shore leave from the navy, after having been away for a couple of years. Apparently he was grievously wounded in a set-to with a French privateer, a sword-blow to the face, and he is so disfigured that he's shy of going into company. Kincannon and Hylton persuaded him to attend. That's him, with the full-face mask. Anyway, what does it matter? It's none of Hylton's affair what you do."

"I know, but I was rather hoping that no one would know me," she said uncomfortably. "And it never occurred to me that *he* would be here."

Daniel looked up at the box, saw Alastair staring at them, and casually nodded. "I doubt very seriously he will come down here at all, you know he would never waltz. Forget him, my sweet highwayman. I only want you to think about and pay attention to me."

"Surely you can't be jealous of Lord Hylton?" Valeria teased.

"Not jealous," Daniel said carelessly, "just selfish. When I'm with a lady I like her to concentrate on me."

Valeria started to take exception to this curiously impersonal observation, but just then the dance wound down and came to an end. "Let's dance another, if it's a waltz," she said.

"We have all night to dance. I'm dry as a desert, let's go to the supper room first and see if I can get a decent drink," Daniel said. "And I'll try to find you some of your boring lemonade, although I doubt if there's a non-spiritous drink to be had here."

They were moving very slowly, as the crowd was thick, and many people were simply standing still, waiting for the next dance. Valeria threw an ever-so-cautious look upward, and to her dismay she saw Alastair start up from his seat and duck out of the box. A few moments later he was coming down the grand staircase. "Oh, no," she groaned. "He's coming."

Daniel frowned. "Val—Madam, I must insist that you forget him; he probably knows everyone in the place, so it is unlikely that he's coming to talk to you. He's probably going to one of the card rooms."

"Oh, how I hope so," she muttered under her breath.

"Here, the supper room is this—oh, hang it all. There he is, scowling like the god of thunder. I guess we can't duck him," Daniel said with a touch of uncertainty that belied his previous swagger.

Valeria gulped and thought, *Now* I've *got to stand and deliver . . .*

Alastair came to stand in front of them, scowling blackly. Valeria lifted her chin in a clear challenge. "Hullo, Hylton," Daniel said. "As you can see, I have a most charming highwayman for a companion tonight."

"So I see," he said tightly. The first strains of a waltz started, and Alastair said, "This is my dance, Everleigh."

Before Daniel could say a word, Alastair grabbed Valeria's right hand, pinned her around the waist, and whirled her off.

They danced in silence for long moments, staring at each other. Alastair kept his jaw set, his lips a thin line. Valeria looked defiant, her color high. Finally she said, "Why don't you stop glaring at me and let me return to my partner?"

"Oh, but I'm enjoying the dance so very much." His arm around her waist became like a vise, and he pressed her impossibly close to him.

"S-stop it," Valeria said, trying hard but unsuccessfully to pull back.

"Why? You don't think, do you, that this is the worst affront you're going to suffer tonight?"

Valeria lashed out, "No, I think that the endless harangue you're going to give me is the worst I'll have to suffer through tonight."

He tightened his jaw, but loosened his iron grip on her. She looked away, though his arctic gray gaze never left her face. Both maintained stony silence for long moments, and they danced. Alastair was having the mightiest internal struggle he had ever known, trying to find the words to impress upon Valeria what a deadly serious mistake she was making. It devastated him to think that she might be completely shut out of all Polite Society.

Finally he said in a bloodlessly cold tone, "You are correct, madam, I did intend to lecture you, which is ungentlemanly of me considering that you've made it clear that it bores you to distraction.

"I must, however, say two things, and I beg you will bear with me, however noxious you may find it. The first is that I hope that you fully understand that if you are recognized, you will be ruined. Right now I doubt that there are very many, if any, of your acquaintance here; but when Almack's closes, there will certainly be many gentlemen who will attend. When word gets around that you are here, in this costume, the Lady Patronesses will probably void your voucher at their very next meeting, and Polite Society will shun you.

"The second thing I must say is that although I know you are thoughtless, and rash sometimes, I never thought that you were false and cruel. I never thought that you would dream of subjecting your mother to such appalling disgrace. She has suffered much already, having to put the best face on the scandal of Maledon's death; and now this, a betrayal by her own daughter."

Valeria's rage seemed to fade as Alastair's harsh words began to sink in. Slowly, very slowly, her face began to turn pale as she stared up at him. Her brow became furrowed, and her breath began to quicken as if there weren't enough air in the room. Alastair feared she was about to faint as she sagged helplessly against him.

Quickly he half-turned her, anchored his left arm around her waist, and reached across and grabbed her left arm to steady her. His lips close to her ear, he whispered, "Valeria? Oh, no, I—just breathe, take deep breaths." He recalled how he had thought, when he had seen her at the fair, bearing such bad news, that she was made of stronger stuff than her mother. But it seemed now that he had managed successfully to utterly shatter Valeria. Already he felt scalding regret.

Dancers whirled around them, staring curiously; but Alastair ignored them. Finally Valeria straightened up, although her shoulders were stooped. Blindly she plucked at Alastair's hands, pulling them away. Reluctantly he let her go.

"Take me home," she said raggedly, her head bowed.

Very gently Alastair took her hand and threaded it through his arm, then led her out the door. Lord Kincannon's grand barouche box, with a team of six silvery white horses, was parked just at the Poland Street entrance. Alastair barked to the coachman, "I'm Hylton, I'm taking this lady home in Lord Kincannon's carriage. Berkeley Square. You, you, sir," he half-shouted to one of the grooms. "Go inside and find Mr. Everleigh. Tell him that I've escorted the lady home, then go tell Lord Kincannon that I've borrowed the carriage for an errand. I'll be back shortly."

The groom opened the door, and Valeria crept in as if she were an elderly woman, then collapsed onto the plushly padded seat. Alastair sat across from her, then rapped on the ceiling to signal the coachman.

Valeria's head was so deeply bowed that her chin touched her chest. Her tricorn hat fully shielded her face from Alastair. He did see, however, enormous tears falling onto her gauntlets. A small sob escaped her—a pitiful, wounded, helpless sound.

"Valeria," Alastair said softly, unaware that he was using her given name, "listen to me, I—"

Without looking up she said in a muffled weak voice, "Oh, please...please, no...no more."

"But what I want to say is that I'm so very—"

"Please," she whispered brokenly. "Please, my lord, I can bear no more."

The wrenching depth of sorrow in that plea, and, more obscurely, the fact that she had called him by the submissive title that servants used, made Alastair feel wretched.

During what seemed like an endless ride, Valeria cried steadily; it seemed the river of tears had no end. Once, with trembling hands, she reached behind her head, untied her mask, and let it drop to the floor. She never looked up, and that was the only time she moved. Alastair was so desperately unhappy, and felt so guilty for his outrageously harsh words to her, that he couldn't think of a single way to begin to comfort her. He had never felt at such a loss, so utterly helpless.

When they reached the completely darkened Maledon town house, Alastair was uncertain how to proceed. "Do you have a key, Valeria?" he asked.

"No, I—no." The groom appeared at the window, then opened the door and pulled down the steps.

Valeria rose very slowly, as if she were in pain. "No, don't," she said to Alastair, who made a move to follow her. "Just—just please go. Please leave me alone."

This went against every instinct that Alastair possessed. He was loath to leave Valeria in this state. But what was he to do? Escort her in? Impossible; he could plainly see that the house was locked up for the night. He knew that Valeria must have sneaked out somehow.

Valeria stopped and turned, and for the first time, looked up. Her beautiful face was dead white, her eyes big black blotches in the dim light. "Thank you," she said numbly. "Good-bye."

Alastair was so deeply affected by the desolation in her voice that he couldn't bring himself to respond. He signaled the groom to close the door, and knocked once on the ceiling, and the carriage moved off into the night. Slowly he bent and picked up the mask. It was soaked with her tears. Carefully he folded it and put it in his pocket.

And then he released his tightly controlled emotions. He was, in fact, intensely angry at himself, and not at all angry with Valeria. No, he had been completely in the wrong; he had savaged her, accused her of falseness and wanton cruelty. But Alastair knew that Valeria could never be deliberately malicious. In spite of the foolish things she had done, it had always been plain to see that she really was innocent, with an almost childlike naïveté. And he had inflicted such pain on her...

His thoughts continued in this harsh and brutal manner. As they neared the Pantheon, he began to think of Daniel Everleigh with loathing. How could he have treated Valeria so infamously? He knew very well the consequences. How could he be so careless with her reputation? *Stupid, criminally thoughtless young cur...I ought to call him out.*

The idea of fighting a duel with Daniel Everleigh had a particular appeal for Alastair just now. He hadn't fought in years, but when he was younger, and much more hotheaded than he was now, he had been out twice. Unflinchingly he had taken fire—his opponents had both missed—and then he had deliberately shot into the air. Alastair didn't know if he could be so kind with Daniel Everleigh.

Of course, it was impossible; if the two of them fought over Valeria's honor, the story of what she'd done would surely get out.

Abruptly it struck Alastair; he was anxious, even eager, to defend her honor. How...when had that happened?

And then Alastair realized that it didn't matter; really, nothing mattered very much. His confused feelings for Valeria Segrave were of no consequence. Probably the truest, most heartfelt, most honest thing she had said to him on this miserable night was to ask him to leave her alone.

And so he must do as she wished; and so he would.

Chapter Twenty-two

ℰ

ℰVERYTHING THAT ALASTAIR HAD SAID was true, and Valeria was so desolate over those truths that terrible night that she felt ill. In her extremity of distress she managed to really make herself ill. The headache, which had begun when Alastair started talking to her, steadily grew to such an intensity that Valeria could neither speak nor open her eyes, for she couldn't bear even the slightest light or noise. She was violently sick every time she tried to drink even tepid water. On the third day she developed a slight fever, but in her reduced state it weakened her so much that Regina grew afraid, and the next day she called in Maledon's doctor, Sir John Apsley.

After examining her he came down to the drawing room, where Lady Hylton and Lady Lydgate waited with Regina. His features showed appropriate solemnity, but he was not grave. "First of all let me make it clear to you, Lady Maledon, that she is going to be just fine, probably in a few days. There is no call for serious concern at all." He gave them a spare smile. "In fact, she was feeling well enough to tell me, with some impertinence, I might add, that she didn't need me, there was nothing wrong with her except she was indulging in a miserable fit of the blue devils."

He waited a few moments to let the relief overtake the ladies, then continued, "She has what is one of the worst megrims I've ever seen; her sensitivity to light and sound is extraordinarily painful. The fever is really of no consequence, for I can detect no sign of any putrid infection. I attribute it more to her disturbance of mind than to any physical cause. She is exhibiting a worrisome anorexia. Give her light lukewarm barley water, and see if she can keep it down. If so, give her small portions three times a day. I shall call back on Thursday."

Although Sir John was somewhat brusque, Regina felt immeasurably better. As she kissed Letitia and Elyse good-bye, she said, "Perhaps, if she can keep down the barley water, she will be stronger tomorrow and you will be able to see her. I know that it would comfort her a good deal."

As Regina slowly went upstairs, she reflected sadly that she wasn't sure at all whether she had told the truth. It seemed that Valeria didn't wish to see anyone, not even her. On the first day Valeria had said, in a low weak murmur, "Please let Joan take care of me, Mamma. I feel I'm a burden to you just now. Please." Regina had acceded to her wishes, and only sat with her for short periods throughout the day. Valeria rarely opened her eyes or said a word.

It grieved Regina afresh when she came into the darkened room after Sir John's visit. Valeria's face was as pale as death, the shadows under her eyes were like dark blue bruises, and she was noticeably thinner. Without making a sound Regina sat in the chair by her bed, and just as silently Joan left the room. Very gently Regina took Valeria's hand. It was a relief to her that Valeria's skin was cool, even chilled, instead of heat-fevered. Regina adjusted the coverlets more securely around her.

When she sat back down she saw that Valeria's eyes were open, and though her gaze was dull, it was focused. "Hello, my darling," Regina whispered.

"Hello, Mamma. I'm glad you're here."

"Of course I'm here. I'll always be here for you, Valeria."

Valeria swallowed hard and pressed her eyes closed for a moment. Then she looked up again, and to her mother's consternation, Valeria's eyes were filled with tears. "Mamma, I have—I have done something that is very wrong, and I must—"

Lightly Regina laid her finger on Valeria's cold lips. "I forgive you."

"But—you don't know—do you?"

"No, I don't know what you've done, my love. What I do know is that whatever you have done, it was in no way malicious, and that you had no deliberate intention of harming me or anyone else. That kind of sin is not in you, Valeria. The only confession you need make, and the only forgiveness you must ask for, is from our Heavenly Father."

More tears rolled down Valeria's face, and with tenderness Regina dabbed them away. "I can't believe that God could forgive me for—for—"

"Child, if I, a flawed, sinful woman, can freely and completely forgive you, don't you think that the Lord Jesus will forgive you and with infinitely more love?"

Valeria sighed, a shuddering, deep, but cleansing breath, and then nodded. "Yes, Mamma, I know that you speak the truth. I will confess to Him, and I will seek His forgiveness; at least, I will try."

As he had done the past three days, Alastair met his mother and sister in the entrance hall as soon as they came through the front door. "How is she? Is she improved at all?"

Acidly Lady Hylton answered, "She must be, as she was impudent to Sir John, which I'm sure astounds us all."

Alastair was not amused. "What is the prognosis?"

Elyse answered, "What sounds like a vicious megrim, with some slight fever, and a regrettable anorexia. Still, Sir John says that she will be fine in a few days."

Some of the tension went out of Alastair's face. Lady Hylton went into the drawing room, but Alastair laid his hand on his sister's shoulder and said, "I wish to speak to you privately, Elyse. Will you join me in the library?"

"Of course."

They sat down at a splendid mahogany baroque library table. Alastair seemed to have some difficulty in opening up the conversation, for he stayed silent for long moments, staring into space. Elyse thought that he'd had a particularly bleak look these past few days, since Valeria had fallen so ill, and she wondered at it.

At length Alastair said, "It pains me that I must involve you in what is a complex entanglement, most of which I cannot fully explain to you. But it is necessary, it is absolutely imperative, that I make amends, and I cannot think of another way."

This somewhat incoherent speech, wholly foreign to her calm, composed brother, surprised Elyse. With comforting directness she said, "I don't understand, Alastair, but be assured that I will help you in any way that I can."

"Thank you, yes, thank you," he said in a distracted manner. He shifted in his seat, crossed his legs, uncrossed them, and then sat forward, resting his elbows on his knees. "Daniel Everleigh," he bit off, "took advantage of Miss Segrave and placed her in a very compromising situation. I was a witness to—to the situation, and I reacted very badly, perhaps as badly as I have ever done. I blamed Miss Segrave, and I said things that I most bitterly regret."

Elyse started to say something, but with quick harshness Alastair went on, "So I've dealt with that flash little sharp, but I'm not through with him yet. No, don't look so distraught, Elyse, I haven't called him out, though I wish I could. But in that event the—situation would become known, and I've gone to some pains to assure that that will never happen. At any rate, I'm not sure Everleigh would fight me even if I wrung his pert little nose right in the middle of White's," he growled. "You must speak to Miss Segrave, and here is where you—you can—can help me." He jumped up and started pacing back and forth, his head bowed, his hands clasped tightly behind his back. "Are you aware, that is, has Miss Segrave indicated to you the—of the nature of her feelings for Everleigh? Is she—is she in love with him?" he asked, almost pleadingly.

Even in childhood, Alastair had been a self-contained, rather remote little boy, and as he had grown into manhood his dispassionate demeanor had increased. For her brother to openly show such distress, such a lack of control over his emotions, was wholly foreign, and disturbed her. Still, Lady Lydgate was a woman who spoke her mind plainly, and now she rolled her eyes and said, "Alastair, for such an intelligent man you can be a great ninny."

"Yes, so I've learned," he said dryly.

"Of course Valeria is not in love with Daniel Everleigh, she's never shown the least bit of romantic interest in him at all. The highest compliments she's ever paid him are that he's great fun and he has good calves."

"Calves?" Alastair repeated blankly.

"Calves. Of his legs. His legs look fine in stockings."

"Great heavens, is that what refined women talk about—never mind. So if she's not in love with him, then how will she view him now?" he muttered under his breath, still pacing.

"I know Valeria well enough to answer that question, and so should you. When Valeria realizes that Mr. Everleigh has abused their friendship, and treated her with disrespect, she won't wish to have anything further to do with him. And I daresay she won't miss him at all."

"Good," he said brusquely. "Then I'll make it my business to impress on Everleigh that from now on out he will not further presume upon their friendship, or impose upon her. When they meet he must show her deference and courtesy, but keep a proper distance. And I'll tell him that if he snubs her in any way, no matter how slight, I'll horsewhip him." This spate of ferocity seemed, perversely, to calm Alastair, and he resumed his seat.

"I see. And so I am to communicate to Valeria these tender mercies you are exerting on her behalf?"

"No! No, Elyse. You don't understand. When you speak to her, you must not speak of me. I have treated her so—" He bit off his words, set his jaw, and went on with difficulty. "Suffice it to say that I abused her even worse than did Everleigh. In fact, I hold myself wholly responsible for her illness, and am convinced that even the mention of my name would cause her grievous distress."

Elyse was appalled. "Oh, Alastair, surely you exaggerate! I know that you can be rather harsh sometimes, but you are never dishonorable, like Everleigh."

His jaw was clenched, and his voice was ragged. "How I wish that were true. All my life I've told myself that I adhered to the strictest sense of honor, but I've been deceiving myself. My actions, my words, to Miss Segrave were disgraceful. So I intend to take my own advice to Everleigh, and not impose upon her with my presence, which can only cause her further pain. I plan on staying at my flat, so we won't meet here. Furthermore, I'm going to ensure that I don't appear at any events that she attends, as far as possible. For those invitations I've already accepted and for which I cannot make my excuses, I'll assiduously try to avoid her."

Elyse was incredulous. "I see. So you are going to make sure that Everleigh doesn't snub her, but you intend to do so?"

"I beg your pardon?"

"Alastair, never in my life have I seen you so confused of mind. First you tell me that you reprimanded her for an indiscretion, and then you decide you won't see her or speak to her anymore? Don't you think that will be noted, and gossiped about? Has it really not entered in what passes for your mind that everyone will construe that as glaring public censure?"

He sighed deeply. "No...no. I was only thinking of not burdening her with my presence. You're right, of course. But I shall endeavor to intrude on her as little as possible."

Softly she said, "Valeria has a fiery, tumultuous spirit, and she can be obstinate. But she is at heart a loving girl, like her mother, and I know that she will certainly forgive you."

Alastair murmured, "You are wholly right, and you are wholly wrong, Elyse. Valeria does have a loving heart. And she will never be able to forgive me for the way I've spoken to her."

It was two more days before Valeria was strong enough to receive visitors. When Elyse went up to her bedroom, she was shocked at how drawn and thin Valeria looked. But she gave no sign, as she kissed her on both cheeks and said cheerfully, "It's about time you rejoined the land of the living, dearest. Are you feeling better?"

"Yes, much better today, thank you," Valeria answered with a wan smile. "I managed to drink a cup of chicken broth this morning, and a cup of thin tea. Joan tells me the entire kitchen regarded it as a major triumph of expert cookery."

"And I don't blame them, your mother has told us of how difficult it has been to find something that agrees with you. Oh, Valeria, you really must do better than broth and watery tea. You must regain your strength quickly, so that you won't miss any more of the fun. It's already the shame of the world that you're not going to be able to attend the prince's fête."

Valeria looked down and picked at the bedcover. "Honestly, I'm glad that I won't have to go through it, attending a royal function seems to me to be more of a strain than it is enjoyable."

Valeria was, Elyse plainly saw, still very weak and sickly, and she hoped that her apathy was due to that. But she suspected Valeria thought that her indiscretion, whatever it had been, was now publicly known, and she probably thought that she was now a social pariah. Alastair had sworn that no hint of the compromising situation would ever be disclosed, and had insisted that Elyse communicate that to Valeria. But then he had also made her promise not to mention him, and Elyse was sadly puzzled as to how to make these reassurances to Valeria without telling her the careful measures her brother had taken to make sure that no hint of scandal would touch her.

Alastair had suggested that Elyse mention this, and convey to Valeria that, and imply so-and-so, and make clear thus-and-such. For a straightforward, plain-speaking woman like Elyse, such delicate obscurities seemed silly. But she loved her brother, and she had promised.

So now she said lightly, "You only think that because you're ill. When you're better I'm afraid that you will regret it. I'm sure the prince regent will regret it too, and I've no doubt at all that you will be invited to Carlton House again.

"Besides, we are not the only ones who sorely miss you. Everyone is so downcast at your illness, and worried about you. Why, just last night at Almack's Lady Sefton, Lady Jersey, and even Mrs. Drummond-Burrell questioned me closely about your condition, they were so much concerned."

Valeria looked surprised. "Truly? They said—kind things about me? There has been no . . ." Her voice trailed off.

Blithely Elyse went on, "Why should you be surprised, darling, everyone knows you're a favorite. Even the merest acquaintances you've made, such as Miss Tree and Miss Cranleigh and Miss

Mowbray, have all expressed the hope that you'd rejoin us soon. Even Lord Sefton, in his jolly, woolly, horsey way, asked after you..." Elyse prated on for a while, saying everything that she could recall Alastair's telling her to say.

Carefully she watched Valeria's face to see if her reassurances were having the desired effect. She thought so; Valeria did seem to cheer up, though she was sadly lacking her usual brightness and vivacity. Elyse hoped that that was mainly due to her illness.

Elyse had no desire to tire Valeria, so she kept her visit short. On the whole she was encouraged. But as she walked back across the park toward home, she grew thoughtful. Valeria had not mentioned Daniel Everleigh at all, and Elyse wasn't really surprised. She did think that in time Valeria would probably confide in her.

But what worried her was that, as always, Valeria had asked after Lady Hylton; she had asked after Reggie and begged Elyse to tell her his latest conversational gambits and wanderings; and she had questioned Elyse about ball gowns and who had attended Almack's the previous evening and who had danced with whom.

Not once had Valeria mentioned Alastair Hylton.

Chapter Twenty-three

✤

𝒱ALERIA KEPT TO HER BED. The reason was not solely that she had been so ill. She had a natural vigor, and once she began to eat more nourishing food, she started regaining her strength.

It was the turmoil in her mind and heart and spirit that kept her in seclusion.

Over and over, endlessly, she went over that night at the Pantheon, and her appalling behavior, and Alastair Hylton's devastating words. *I never thought that you were false and cruel . . .*

Every fiber of Valeria's being cried out at the injustice of it; she was not a cruel person. Her mother had said, and it had comforted Valeria, that she had no malice in her heart, and that was true. What she had done had not been done with any intention of hurting anyone.

But then, with an insight that made her head pound fiercely, she heard herself, sometimes her voice, sometimes echoes of her own thoughts.

I don't care, I'll never forgive Maledon, or Lady Jex-Blake!

"My first instinct was to strike her with my riding crop. At least I managed to restrain myself from doing that. I did cut her, though."

"Oh, blessed Lord Jesus," she murmured. "Mamma was wrong, I do have malice in my heart. And how can I be forgiven if I won't forgive? 'Forgive us our trespasses, as we forgive those who trespass against us.' Now I want to forgive them, I need to forgive them. I will make up my mind to do so, but only You can make it true in my heart, by Your grace and mercy, amen." The prayer was perfunctory, not really heartfelt, but wearily Valeria thought it was the best she could do just now.

She thought again of Alastair's devastating indictment of her, which had had nothing to do with her internal bitter resentments. Bleakly she realized that though her actions and behavior had not been motivated by the conscious ill will she had harbored toward her stepfather and Lady Jex-Blake, in the end that made no difference. She had been shallow and supremely selfish, and the results could have caused great harm to her mother. Whether from thoughtless cruelty or deliberate malice, the results were the same.

Realizing and facing the truth about herself, confessing to the Lord, asking forgiveness, playing over and over in her mind Alastair's words, weeping, struggling... Valeria could find no peace at all, and felt no comfort. After a second sleepless night, she realized that this internal combat was exhausting her, not only mentally, but physically. Finally at dawn she fell into a restless sleep, and when she awoke she still felt tired and listless, and had little appetite.

But Joan, whom Valeria had found to be just as expert a nurse as Craigie, and even just as comforting in her own way, was having none of it. "Oh, no, ma'am," she said staunchly. "I've spooned gallons of that awful barley water and broth down you the last days, and we're not going back to that. Here is your tea, steaming and sweet and creamy, just as you like; and you will eat at least two slices of this buttered toast, for it's that nice and crisp, and here is a lightly boiled egg." Obediently Valeria ate, and she did feel better. Well enough, in fact, that after she ate, for the first time since she'd fallen ill, she asked Joan to dress her hair, and decided to put on a morning gown.

Still, she didn't want to go downstairs just yet; she wanted to sit at her little table by the window, look down on the busy street, and try again to sort out her thoughts. She had barely gotten seated with a second cup of tea when she saw Elyse and Lady Hylton arrive to make their daily call. "Joan, go ask Lady Lydgate to come right up, I'm so looking forward to visiting with her today."

Soon Elyse came in, her eyes bright, her pretty face wreathed in smiles. "Davies gave me a full report on the way up. I'm so glad you're better."

"So am I. I've realized how very much I despise barley water, and I've recalled how much I love buttered toast. Sit down, please. Tea?"

"Yes, don't bother, I'll pour." Elyse went through the homely little ritual. "Buttered toast, is it, that's put that very little bit of color back in your cheeks? At least now you don't look positively like a waxy corpse."

"Thank you so much, Elyse, I know I can always count on you to tell the exact truth, no matter how painful," Valeria said dryly. Then she sobered and said, "Actually, that is precisely the reason I wanted to talk to you. Because you're honest, and—and because I know that you're a true friend."

"I hope we are more than that, dearest. I've come to love you as a sister."

Valeria swallowed hard. Expressing true, deep affection was difficult for her. "I can't tell you how much that means to me, Elyse, thank you. It makes this a bit easier for me, for I must, I simply must, ask someone. You see, I've done something—I'm afraid I've been terribly indiscreet—oh, bother! I have behaved very badly, and in public, too. Can you tell me, honestly, that there's been no word, no scandal?"

Carefully Elyse said, "I haven't heard the slightest hint of gossip from any of our acquaintances. When did you commit this dastardly deed?"

"It's not funny, Elyse. Um—how long have I been ill? For—for five or six days?"

Sympathetically Elyse answered, "Darling, you took to your bed nine days ago."

"Then ten days ago I made a horrible mistake. No, that's not true; it was no mistake, I'm not stupid, I did it with all my faculties intact and fully functional, and I've no one to blame but myself."

"Really? So you just suddenly made up your mind to go out and be wicked, all by yourself?"

Valeria looked straight at her. "No, I was with Daniel Everleigh, as I'm sure you've already surmised."

Calmly Elyse sipped her tea. "Of course I would know that, Valeria. You two have been practically inseparable for a couple of months now. I've seen that his influence over you has been growing. And whatever happened, I'm sure that he must be mostly responsible—"

"No, no! I cannot allow that, Elyse. I may be young, but I am a grown woman, and I make my own decisions. Nothing happened that I didn't fully participate in, even encourage. And since you tell me that no one has heard of it, then in reality I owe Mr. Everleigh a debt of gratitude for his discretion."

"What? His *discretion*! No, no, Valeria, this is wrong, all wrong!"

Valeria looked puzzled. "What do you mean?"

Elyse almost spluttered with an apparent frustration that Valeria found mystifying. "You are being much too hard on yourself, and much too lenient with Mr. Everleigh."

"Elyse, I am no fool; I can see now that Mr. Everleigh is a not an honorable man, and has treated me with disrespect. Perhaps he did take advantage of me, but that still does not absolve me of guilt. Anyway, I wish to have nothing more to do with him, and I shan't miss him at all," she said.

Elyse sniffed. "Well done. And I still say stop reproaching yourself so harshly. I don't know what you did, and you don't have to tell me if you don't wish to. But I know you, Valeria, and I know that you haven't done anything that is grossly immoral or indecent."

"Perhaps not, but I broke the rules, and the results could have been just as severe on my poor mother. Like you, she didn't demand explanations. I tried to confess to her, but she very gently told me that she had already forgiven me, regardless of what I had done."

Earnestly, with peculiar emphasis, Elyse said, "Darling Valeria, all of your friends, your real friends that know you and love you, feel exactly the same way. We love you, and we forgive you."

"Thank you again, darling Elyse. But oh, I am so weary of thinking of it, and talking of it. Cheer me up, dearest, as you always do. Tell me all about what you wore to the fête, and don't forget your jewelry and your hair."

Elyse stayed for over an hour this time. While she was there, Valeria's spirits were lifted, but after she left they plummeted to the depths again. She felt glum and listless, and Joan clucked reprovingly over her and put her back to bed.

Again Elyse didn't say a word about Alastair . . . she hasn't so much as mentioned his name. Oh, how I wish she would say something, anything at all, that would give me some notion of his attitude toward me now!

As she reviewed the conversation she realized that Elyse was holding something back from her. Elyse was a woman who spoke her mind, and there was no guile in her. Yet Valeria thought that in Elyse's demeanor there had been some stiffness, some discomfort that was uncharacteristic of her.

The cause of this dawned on Valeria, and it made her feel utterly dejected.

Of course she can't say anything about Alastair. He must not have told her about the Pantheon, but I'm sure he completely despises me, is even disgusted with me . . . I know he would never gossip, but surely Lady Hylton and Elyse are aware of his attitude. I suppose if she did talk about him it would only let me know of his contempt . . .

Valeria was not the sort of woman who cried easily. But now she wept, and her headache began all over again.

Another restless night, and Valeria slept very late. When she awoke at eleven o'clock, her eyes were red and irritated from weeping, and the lingering trace of a headache still remained. Overall, however, she was feeling much better and stronger, and determined to go downstairs. With her newfound sensitivity, she realized that by remaining in her room, weeping and brooding, she must be worrying her mother.

She was dressed just in time for luncheon, and was pleased to see that St. John and Mr. Chalmers were joining Regina. Regina kissed her happily, and even St. John came running to her and held up his arms for her to hug him. Valeria managed to plant a big kiss on his cheek, which made him say, "Aw, Veri, I'm not *that* glad to see you."

"So sorry, but I've missed you so much I think I'm going to kiss you two or three times a day now. You'll just have to bear up. Mr. Chalmers, I haven't seen you for an age. I'm glad to see you looking well, I can't imagine the hard life you must lead trying to corral my brother and Niall here in Town. Joan—I mean, Davies told me that they absolutely took off at a dead run in the park and left you standing high and dry."

They settled down at the dining table, which was heavily laden. Regina didn't require the footmen to serve *á la russe* at their informal luncheons, though Ned and Royce stood by to attend to the diners' beverages. The table held platters of cold meats, a tray piled high with sandwiches, pigeon pie and beefsteak pie, an assortment of cheeses, and a pyramid of luscious fruits, including apricots, figs, nectarines, pears, plums, raspberries, and strawberries. Valeria's mouth watered.

Mr. Chalmers replied, "So they did, and I threatened to yoke them around the neck with a three-inch rope if they did it again."

St. John argued, "But, sir, it was Prinny tooling by in his gold carriage. Niall and I just lost our heads, you might say."

Regina said sternly, "St. John, if I ever hear you refer to the prince regent as 'Prinny' again I shall add a gag to Mr. Chalmers's yoke. And that is complete nonsense about you and Niall losing your heads, you know perfectly well that you mustn't go dashing about the park willy-nilly like a couple of mooncalves."

Valeria giggled. "Heavens, Mamma, I couldn't have said it better myself."

Regina sighed. "Yes, I'm afraid you've been a bad influence on me, darling, I find I've gotten rather more forceful and plainspoken than I used to be. Or perhaps it's St. John's influence, as I find it difficult to express my indignation at his outrageous behavior."

Unabashed, St. John repeated, "Willy-nilly mooncalves! I must tell that to Niall. May I have some pigeon pie, and Mamma, please, please look through all the sandwiches to find me a ham, or two."

"I have no intention of fingering every sandwich to find you a ham, you must take whatever is on top. Oh, it is ham, very well, here are two. But St. John, if you don't stop fidgeting, I'm going to send you to your room without luncheon. I probably should do, anyway, for you were squirming and twitching all through morning prayers."

"But Mamma, something happened in the laundry, something about the rinse, or so I heard Mrs. Durbin say when she was dressing down the laundress, and my smalls are itchy, and so are Niall's."

Valeria giggled, and though Regina managed to look disapproving, she did have trouble hiding a smile. Mr. Chalmers had much more experience in controlling his amusement at the boys' antics, so he said, "My lord, a gentleman should never discuss his smallclothes with ladies, not even his mother or sister. You must tell me of such discomforts, and I will address it with Mrs. Durbin."

In a small voice St. John said, "But you weren't asking me why I am fidgeting, Mamma was."

"And you should have simply apologized, and said that you would do better."

He sighed deeply. "Yes, sir. Next time that turnip-headed feeble-brained fumble-fingered laundress turns out my smalls feeling like they're bloomin' salt-crusted canvas, I won't mention it to anyone but you."

Valeria laughed out loud, and even Regina giggled. Mr. Chalmers began, "My lord, you must never..." But his voice was strained, and finally he collapsed into mirth.

Valeria said, "Oh, St. John, how happy I am to see that you and I are so similar. Our mother is horrified, I know, and I do feel so sorry for poor Mr. Chalmers, but there it is."

"There it is," he said, grinning and taking an enormous bite of ham sandwich.

"Mamma, you must not reproach him too harshly, we know very well that St. John would never say such outrageous things except to us, he really is a good boy. At least he did go to morning prayers. I'm so ashamed, I can't recall the last time I went to church, even."

"You have been extremely busy, darling," Regina said. "With such late nights it is difficult to get up in time for morning prayers or church."

Thoughtfully Valeria said, "True, but now that I think of it, I have missed them. Mamma, would you like to go to Evensong with me this evening?"

"I'd be delighted, it's been an age since I've attended Evensong. I believe it's at five o'clock, so that will give you time to rest. Although you're obviously better, dearest, your eyes do look tired, and you are still a little pale."

Valeria said slyly, "At least I don't look like a waxy corpse."

"Coo-ee," St. John said in admiration. "A dead bloodless waxy corpse."

"Now look what you've done, Valeria," Regina said.

"I didn't say it, Elyse did," Valeria protested.

To Mr. Chalmers Regina said, "We shall never get them raised."

※

St. George's, Hanover Square, was a majestic, lofty, luxuriously appointed church. Its magnificence, however, was not overwhelming; it still evoked a reverential, prayerful air. As soon as Valeria entered and took her seat, she felt some of the tension and worry in her mind subside. She wasn't at all surprised that the congregation was sparse in fashionable London. She herself was usually riding in Hyde Park at this time, along with just about everyone else who lived in the West End. She was glad to see, however, that the choir stall was full. The Evensong service was called so because the service was primarily sung, and St. George's was renowned for the excellence of its music.

Although Valeria had prayed much in the last days, somehow she had never felt fully reconciled to God, and still didn't. The guilt and shame, she knew, must somehow be overcome, but she felt helpless, as if she had no rule at all over her own spirit.

The service began, the so-familiar words were spoken, and Valeria tried very hard to hear them anew. At first they made little impression on her. Although she knew the order by heart, and for years now had had no need to follow along in her prayer book, now she started reading as the minister spoke. Slowly the Scriptures being read, and the minister's injunctions to the congregation, began to take on meaning. As with new eyes she read the instruction, "A general Confession to be said of the whole Congregation after the Minister, all kneeling."

They knelt, and instead of repeating words by rote, Valeria closed her eyes and truly prayed, perhaps for the first time in months.

Almighty and most merciful Father; We have erred, and strayed from thy ways like lost sheep. We have followed too much the devices and desires of our own hearts. We have offended against thy holy laws. We have left undone those things which we ought to have done; And we have done those things which we ought not to have done; And there is no health in us. But thou, O Lord, have mercy upon us miserable sinners. Spare thou them, O God, who confess their faults. Restore thou them that are penitent; According to thy promises declared unto mankind in Christ Jesus our Lord. And grant, O most merciful Father, for his sake; That we may hereafter live a godly, righteous, and sober life, To the glory of thy holy name. Amen.

Valeria meant every word of it. And she knew that she had received absolution and remission of her sins even before the minister pronounced it.

After that Valeria's mind was wholly engaged by, and absorbed in, the service. In particular she felt her spirit lift when the choir, accompanied by the magnificent organ that Handel himself had loved, sang "Magnificat," "Nunc dimittis," and "Deus misereatur." Everything was fresh, everything was new, and everything had a special meaning to her; God was her own Almighty and most merciful Father, Christ Jesus was her Lord, and the Holy Ghost was her Comforter.

After the collects she was struck by the odd but solemn instruction in the prayer book: "In Quires and Places where they sing here followeth the Anthem."

It was Handel's "As pants the hart." The poetry of the words moved Valeria deeply. Then, in the sixth movement, a phrase suddenly struck her as particularly apt to her own mind and spirit: "Why so full of grief, O my soul: why so disquieted within me?"

It came to Valeria then that much grief and disquiet had been impossible for her to overcome not solely because she had been mired in guilt, although that had certainly been a part of it.

But the rest of it was that she grieved deeply at the loss of Alastair Hylton's esteem. For a few moments she wondered at this; often she had told herself that he probably despised her. But she had known that this wasn't at all true; in truth she knew that he enjoyed their sparring, their battles of wits, as much as did she. Even in his disapproval over her previous gaffes she had sensed that he was more concerned for her than he was angry, or judgmental.

Until that horrible night at the Pantheon. She recalled his arm around her waist and his hand gripping hers, like vises; his thin nostrils flared, his eyes narrowed to flint-gray slits, his strong jaw clenched tightly. Everything about him displayed his disgust. Nothing in her life had wounded Valeria so deeply, nothing, not even her stepfather's ill treatment and abuse.

Why? Why is it that the idea of Lord Hylton thinking ill of me pains me so grievously?

And then it came to her, not as a shock, or with trepidation, or with a sense of dread. The revelation was bittersweet, and poignant.

She was in love with Alastair Hylton. She didn't know exactly when or how it had happened; she would have to think, to consider, much more to understand that. It had no bearing on the simple fact, however.

She prayed: "Oh, merciful Father, Lord Jesus, what am I to do? What can I do?"

The answer, simple and clear, came to her instantly, directly from the fervent prayer she had just prayed.

We have left undone those things which we ought to have done; And we have done those things which we ought not to have done.

Certainly Valeria knew she had done things she ought not to have done. She wanted to be certain, now, not to leave undone those things she ought to do.

She must conduct herself with dignity, and grace, and decorum from now on, and never again flout and abuse the rules of the society to which she belonged. She must do this, not only because it was right, but because she must show Alastair that she had truly repented, and was changed. She knew very well that he could never love her, but for her own sake—and for his—she must prove that she was worthy of his esteem.

Valeria was surprised that she felt so calm and untroubled, but then she realized that Almighty God had forgiven her, and would help her on the right course. She longed for Alastair, with a deep, passionate yearning; but she knew that whatever happened, as long as she remained faithful and true, she would know peace in her soul, if not in her heart.

The service ended, and Valeria and Regina rose to leave. When they turned, Valeria was shocked to see Alastair at the back of the church, coming out of a pew. He looked up, and their eyes met, and Valeria felt a true, physical wave of uncomfortable warmth assail her. She felt the heat rise in her cheeks.

He looked wholly impassive, wholly devoid of emotion, as was customary for him. He gave her and Regina a small bow of recognition, then left.

After long frozen moments, Valeria took a deep sighing breath.

At least he didn't look at me the way he did at the Pantheon. At least he showed no outward disgust.

It was comfort, but cold comfort indeed.

Chapter Twenty-four

❧

Bᴜᴛ ᴛʜᴇ ᴘᴇᴀᴄʜ, ꜱᴏ Mᴀᴍᴍᴀ ꜱᴀʏꜱ, does compliment my complexion, and I'm still a little pale, don't you think, Joan? Perhaps it should be the peach. But I don't have any jewelry to go with it, except the carnelian, and it's simply not grand enough for a ball...what about the white? Would it wash me out too much? Or the green, I do love the color, like fresh grapes, but the only slippers I have to wear with it are white, and it's trimmed with gold tassels, no, no, that wouldn't do..." Her voice trailed off uncertainly.

Valeria had been dithering all day about what she was to wear to Lord and Lady Sturway's ball, the first event she had attended since that fateful night at the Pantheon. She was anxious because it would also be the first time she'd seen Lord Hylton (except at Evensong) since that night. She had barely considered that it was Daniel Everleigh's family giving the ball. Valeria cared nothing for Daniel Everleigh's opinion. All she really cared about was Alastair Hylton's attitude toward her now.

With practicality Joan said, "Yes, ma'am, so the peach won't do, the white won't do, and the green won't do. That leaves the blue. It's really a lovely dress, and if I may say so the shade compliments your coloring just as well as the peach. Such a soft pretty blue, it reminds me so much of her ladyship's Wedgwood cameo."

"Oh! Oh, Joan, you're a genius!" Valeria cried so forcefully that it startled her maid. "Quick, quick, go ask Mamma if I may borrow her Wedgwood and pearls, and the pearl hairpins."

Joan ran downstairs to ask Trueman if she might have an audience with Lady Maledon, he went in to secure Lady Maledon's permission, and Joan had a breathless short interview with her ladyship, who readily gave her permission for Valeria to use any of her jewelry that she wished. Joan then rushed downstairs to find Craigie, who had the key to her ladyship's jewelry trunk, then chivvied Craigie to hurry, hurry, Miss Segrave was waiting for her.

"Oh, fie on her," Craigie said with no ill will at all. "She's always in a tearing hurry for one thing and another, and there's no sense in you running about like a lunatic in Bedlam trying to keep up with her, Miss Davies. It's only half past three, and that ball doesn't even start until ten."

"I know, Miss Platt, but Miss Segrave is in a rare taking today, I've never seen her so distraught just from choosing a dress," Joan said. "I think her nerves are still all ahoo from being so ill. And still I don't know what distressed her so that she cried so pitiful for days on end," she hinted to Craigie.

The rumor belowstairs had been that Valeria and Mr. Everleigh had had a break, but Joan had scorned that to one and all. "Her heart didn't break over him, that's nonsense. She liked him, and enjoyed his company, but she was never ever starry-eyed over him. No, Miss isn't crying her poor eyes out over Mr. Daniel Everleigh."

Uncharacteristically, Regina had not confided in Craigie about Valeria at all, so now Craigie ignored Joan's hints and merely looked thoughtful. However, she did take the stairs up to Regina's bedroom a little more quickly. The jewelry chest was in the connecting dressing room between Valeria's room and her mother's. Valeria was in there, holding the blue dress up on her shoulders and anxiously peering at her reflection in the full-length cheval mirror. "Oh, good,

good, Craigie, if the Wedgwood doesn't work with this I swear I'll be in utter despair, I won't have a thing to wear."

"Christian ladies don't swear, missie," Craigie said sternly. "And there's no call for you to be talking of despair when you have so many pretty gowns, for shame. Here, let me see. You couldn't have matched it better if you'd tried."

The choker was three strands of pearls, with a Wedgwood cameo clasp that was designed to be worn in front. The blue cameo was exactly the same color as Valeria's dress. "It's perfect, just perfect," she murmured.

Joan breathed out a sigh of relief, and Craigie winked at her, then said, "Here are the hairpins, and you might as well take the earrings too. I'm not going to run up and down these stairs like a house afire again. Such a pother and bother over a dress, for all love."

Valeria continued her pothering and bothering all afternoon and evening, until Joan was almost at the point of distraction herself. Finally, however, Valeria was dressed.

Her gown consisted of an underdress of gossamer white silk and the "Wedgwood blue" overdress of delicate gauze. The hem, neckline, and short sleeves were trimmed with a finespun white Alençon lace. The sash of white satin had a sheen that mirrored the pearls. The choker, which was small and not in the least ostentatious, was particularly graceful on Valeria's long slender neck, and the pearls in her dark hair looked like stars.

In the carriage with Elyse and Reggie and Lady Hylton, Valeria could scarcely pay attention to the conversation. She was struggling, as she had been struggling all day, to reconcile herself to seeing Alastair again. It seemed that she was split into halves. On the one hand she was looking forward to talking to him with the highest anticipation; and on the other she felt a heavy sense of foreboding. No matter how hard she tried, she simply couldn't make herself stop racketing wildly between the two.

Lord and Lady Sturway, Adele, and Daniel greeted the guests at the door. Valeria had met Lord Sturway several times, and she always marveled at how very different he was from his wife. He was a short, rotund, bluff, hearty gentleman with red cheeks, bright blue eyes, and a bush of gray hair. He greeted her heartily. "Miss Segrave, we're so glad that you recovered from your illness in time to come to our little party," he said, beaming at her. "Aren't we, m'dear?"

"Yes, indeed," Lady Sturway agreed. "Your absence was much regretted, Miss Segrave."

Valeria found, to her surprise, that Lady Sturway was looking pleased, and not at all like the grim harridan that she had seemed to be before. In fact, even Adele greeted Valeria with a measure of warmth, and Valeria observed that when Adele's face wasn't set, as Daniel had once said, like a prune-prude's, she was actually pretty.

Daniel seemed to be the only one who felt some constraint. He swallowed hard when Valeria curtsied to him, and his bow was more like a spasm than a courtly gesture. "Good evening, Miss Segrave. And so you have recovered from your illness; we were all mightily concerned."

"Yes, sir, I'm fully restored. Thank you for your consideration, both now and in the past days," Valeria said with composure.

He seemed nonplussed at her *sangfroid.* "Er—I don't suppose you'd care to dance the cotillion with me, would you?" he asked uncertainly.

Matching his undertone, Valeria answered, "No, I wouldn't care to at all, Mr. Everleigh. But I will always be grateful to you for your discretion."

Elyse, who was just behind Valeria, locked arms with her as they entered the ballroom, with Reggie trailing them. "Bravo, dearest, you handled that with great grace, even though I still say that you don't owe that scoundrel one scintilla of gratitude. At any rate, that's over, I have some news that Reggie just told me. I declare, he is lamentably lacking in his comprehension of the truly important things in life. Did you remark that Lady Sturway and Miss Everleigh are looking particularly pleased with themselves tonight?"

"I did, like two cats coming out of the creamery."

"Apparently Miss Everleigh and Charles Ponsonby are a match. Now, it's true that Charles is a third son, and I know that Lady Sturway had her heart set on a title, but in fact Ponsonby is relatively warm, his estate in Suffolk is worth about eight thousand a year, perfectly respectable. And since Adele's portion is twelve thousand pounds, they will be comfortable, I daresay."

"Ah, I see. Miss Everleigh looks happy; is Mr. Ponsonby genuinely attached to her, or is this another example of a younger son managing to latch onto a wealthy heiress?"

"Nonsense, Valeria, you know Ponsonby better than that. He would never engage himself to a woman without affection on both sides. He's like Reggie in that way, warm and fuzzy and perplexed and obliging, but really quite adamant about marrying for love."

Valeria giggled at Elyse's description of her husband. She had been paying close attention to Elyse, bending her head somewhat to hear her half-whispered comments. Now she looked up to see Alastair Hylton standing just in front of them. As her gaze met Alastair's, the smile died on her lips; and though she was completely unaware of it, her face showed dismay. Valeria had never been very good at controlling her emotions, nor at hiding them. If she had known the pain her change in countenance caused Alastair, she would have been horrified. She recovered quickly, however, and curtsied with great grace.

"Good evening, Miss Segrave," he said quietly. "I'm happy you've recovered enough to rejoin us."

He spoke with his customary gravity, his face betraying no emotion whatsoever. Nervously Valeria said, "Thank you, Lord Hylton,

I too am glad that I've rejoined the land of the living, as Elyse has said."

"Yes, just so. I'm sure you'll have a pleasant evening, ma'am." He bowed and slipped away.

Valeria looked after him helplessly. He had not been curt, and no hostility was evident in his countenance. But he had been so impersonal and remote, he might have been speaking to a servant.

"He has been much concerned for you," Elyse said quietly.

"Oh, yes, I'm sure, he seems distraught indeed," Valeria said caustically. Then she realized that this attitude was not going to help her at all in her determination to win back Alastair's respect, so she smiled at Elyse and said, "Never mind. Tell me, who *is* that gorgeous woman with Lord Stephen? This is the third time I've seen her, and yet I've never been introduced."

"That is Mrs. Lorimer, and she is a wealthy widow, and I will tell you why we don't like her at all, aside from the fact that she's a raving beauty..."

Valeria listened with all appearance of mild amusement to Elyse's story of how Mrs. Lorimer had been a *particular* favorite of Prinny's before her husband died, and how complacent Mr. Lorimer had been before he keeled over in the saddle on a fox hunt, apparently from a massive heart attack.

In fact Valeria felt downcast and despondent. But slowly she realized that by brooding at parties and in drawing rooms, feeling sorry for herself and moping, she would completely fail to impress Alastair with her newfound mature and decorous persona. She determined that she would be cheerful, and, she hoped, bright and vivacious—in short, she would simply be herself, without her previous arrogance and near-impropriety. He would surely see that she was not a weak, miserable, defeated person; she was determined to do better, and would do so.

But she didn't see Alastair again at all that night. And to her chagrin, she soon discovered that his behavior at Lord and Lady Sturway's had been the beginning of a pattern. Everywhere she went, whenever she saw him, he immediately came up to greet her, said two or three sparse sentences, bowed, and left her, not to be seen again. Gradually it dawned on Valeria that he was publicly acknowledging her so as not to cause speculation, as it surely would if he did not. Painfully Valeria thought it must be a heavy burden on him indeed, to be courteous to her; and doubtless he was doing it only for Lady Hylton's and Elyse's sakes. This comprehension depressed Valeria extremely, but she maintained her outward composure, and even Elyse didn't see how dejected she was. As if they had an unspoken pact, neither Elyse nor Valeria spoke of Alastair at all.

Valeria resumed her regular rides in Hyde Park, and as she'd known she would, she again saw Lady Jex-Blake coming toward her, accompanied only by a groom. Valeria took a deep breath, set her face to a pleasant expression, and rode directly toward her. As Valeria neared, Lady Jex-Blake's eyes narrowed darkly, her mouth drew into a thin hard line, and she lifted her chin. Valeria stopped Tarquin just by Lady Jex-Blake's mount.

Saluting her by tapping her hat with her riding crop, Valeria smiled sweetly and said, "Lady Jex-Blake, how glad I am to see you. I must apologize to you for my behavior before; it was inexcusable, and very wrong. I sincerely beg your pardon, ma'am."

Lady Jex-Blake's eyes widened with shock, and her mouth even dropped open a bit. For a long moment she was speechless. Then she swallowed hard and nodded to Valeria. "That's very gracious of you, Miss Segrave. I—I—thank you. Thank you so much."

"You have nothing to thank me for, ma'am. I hope you have a pleasant ride, and I'm sure we'll meet again." Politely nodding, Valeria rode on. It amazed her how much she had utterly dreaded this chore that she had known she had to do for her own salvation—

and how very much better she felt now. The last remnants of bitterness she'd felt toward Lady Jex-Blake and her stepfather faded completely away.

Valeria was still determined to try to speak to Alastair in private. She grew so desperate she considered sending him a note, requesting that he meet with her concerning some estate matters of Bellegarde. But what could she say? Anything she thought of to discuss would be blatantly contrived. Mr. Wheeler had begun writing to her every week and no matters had come up that required any urgent attention. Now it dawned upon Valeria that likely Alastair had requested Mr. Wheeler to report to her so that he wouldn't have to. The realization made Valeria feel hopelessly desolate.

A wonderfully warm, green, and pleasant June melted into a stifling, steaming July. The heat made the tons of horse manure deposited daily in the streets and the open sewers of London stink, and families began their exodus to the benevolent climes of their country estates.

Valeria had grown desperate. Alastair's avoidance of her had been a complete success. She thought that altogether she might have seen him for ten minutes in the last month. Her only hope now was that Lady Hylton was having a last dinner party, a private one, inviting only Valeria and Regina. "Alastair and I will be leaving the next morning for Hylton Hall, and Elyse and Reggie for Whittington Park. So it's the last time we'll all be together for a while."

At public events Valeria hadn't been able to simply walk up to Alastair and start talking; young ladies did not accost gentlemen, they had to wait until the gentlemen approached them. But at this last family dinner, as it were, she would find a way to engage him, and somehow she would express to him that she had truly changed.

Valeria and Regina arrived at eight o'clock, and in such an intimate setting there was no nonsense about standing about discussing the weather. They arranged themselves comfortably in the drawing room. Alastair had greeted Valeria, maintaining his usual distance. Valeria seated herself on a sofa next to Elyse, and Alastair took his stance leaning against the mantelpiece, talking quietly to Regina. The butler duly announced that dinner was served, and Valeria thought she would sit by Alastair even if she had to chase him around the table.

He took his seat at the head, and Valeria sat at his right, across from Elyse. Regina sat by Elyse, with Lady Hylton at the foot and Reggie seated by Valeria. Valeria was so happy to see that they were using a small dining table that just seated six comfortably, so that the diners weren't stranded four feet away from their neighbors.

But also, as this was an informal gathering, the rules of polite discourse didn't apply, so one was not obliged to spend a certain amount of time alternating between dinner partners. As soon as they were seated and had started on the first course, Lady Hylton announced to the table, "We have made a decision, and I'm sorry, Regina, but we're determined you will have to go along with us whether you like it or no. We would very much like for you, Valeria, and St. John to come to Foxden Park for the grouse at the beginning of August."

Regina's eyes lit up. "And you're apologizing to me for this? I love Foxden, and St. John is of an age now when I think he'll truly enjoy learning to shoot. And it would be a good time for me to give poor Mr. Chalmers a holiday, although I'm sure I don't know how I'll ever handle St. John and Niall by myself. Oh, Letitia, would you possibly include Niall in the invitation? He and St. John are inseparable . . ."

Reggie then began talking to Regina and Lady Hylton, rhapsodizing about the good shooting at Foxden, and promising to take St. John and Niall in hand.

Valeria turned to Alastair and asked politely, "So will you be at Foxden too, sir?"

He seemed to search her face with some caution, and his answer was vague. "I haven't yet decided, ma'am. Much depends on what needs to be done at Hylton Hall."

"I see," Valeria said, her heart sinking. "I suppose I may have many things to attend to at Bellegarde too, after being away for five months."

"Perhaps not. I have been in contact with Mr. Wheeler, and it seems to me that he is so capable that the estate needs very little attention. Are you inclined to wish to go to Foxden? Or perhaps you may think it would be a tedious bore after the diversions of London."

Valeria tried hard to discern if he spoke with sarcasm, but his countenance was impassive. Even if he meant no reproof, obviously he was trying to find out if Valeria would go ... and in that case, she thought sadly, he likely would not. Still, Valeria knew that it would upset her mother if she refused to go, especially as she could give no reason. Finally Valeria answered in a low voice, "As a matter of fact the excitements of London have worn on me. I'm looking forward to going home. I'm sure that in a month my mother will be anxious to see Lady Hylton again, and my brother will surely be wild for going to Foxden."

He nodded noncommitally, and they sat in stony silence until finally Elyse started talking to Valeria about how very cool it was in the north even in August, and how much she liked having fires every night, and how even the storms on the moors had a wild romance of their own. During the rest of the dinner Alastair's conversation with Valeria consisted of two comments, regarding the roast veal and the excellence of the pear and blackcurrant cream ices.

Alastair and Reggie had no desire to stay and drink port while the ladies retired, so they all went back to the drawing room together. By now Valeria was feeling almost a feverish desperation; she thought that this might be the very last chance she would ever have of communicating to Alastair her burning wish that they might go back to their old familiarity. But what could she do?

After they had sat in the drawing room for half an hour, with Alastair again remote and silent at the fireplace, Valeria had an inspiration. It was somewhat melodramatic; but now she didn't care if she showed her heartache to the entire world. She had nothing at all left to lose.

In a lull in the conversation she said brightly, "You know, Godmother, that I began my first Season by entertaining you all with my musical accomplishment; and I certainly achieved my goal of never being obliged to perform again, for since then no one has evinced a passionate desire to hear more of Scarlatti's *Esercizi*." She smiled at Alastair but he remained impassive. With determination she continued, "However, just between us here, I should like to have a chance to redeem myself. May I play for you tonight, to end my Season?"

Lady Hylton said, "Good heavens, child, I would have asked you all the time if you hadn't been so outspoken dead set against it. Please, please do grace us."

Valeria went to the pianoforte, bent her head and closed her eyes for a brief moment to compose herself, then began to play. The tune was simple, and she played it very softly, a haunting strain in a minor key. Then, to the astonishment of all, Valeria sang.

My young love said to me,
My mother won't mind
And my father won't slight you
For your lack of kine.
And she laid her hand on me,
And this she did say:
It will not be long, love,
Till our wedding day.

As she stepped away from me
And she moved through the fair
And fondly I watched her
Move here and move there.
And then she made her way homeward,
With one star awake,
As the swan in the evening
Moved over the lake.

The people were saying,
No two e'er were wed
But one had a sorrow
That never was said.
And I smiled as she passed
With her goods and her gear,
And that was the last
That I saw of my dear.

Last night she came to me,
My dead love came in.
So softly she came
That her feet made no din.
As she laid her hand on me,
And this she did say:
It will not be long, love,
Till our wedding day.

Valeria's midnight-dark eyes shimmered with unshed tears, and she kept her gaze fixed on Alastair's face as she sang. He watched her, his expression one of slight confusion. But did Valeria see his eyes flicker, perhaps with comprehension, understanding, and acknowledgment? She didn't know. He remained an enigma to her even until now . . . at the end.

A profound silence pervaded the room as the last sweet true notes died away. Regina, watching Valeria and Alastair, brushed her own tears away from her eyes, and she and Letitia shared a very quick worried expression. Elyse's eyes darted from her brother to her friend, and perturbed incomprehension marred her face.

Lord Lydgate was the only person who didn't sense the heated undercurrents in the room, and with distinct pleasure on his friendly features he began clapping loudly, and naturally everyone then joined in. "Miss Segrave, you've really been hiding your candle under a bush, haven't you?"

"Under a bushel, Reggie," Elyse corrected him.

"Never could understand that, makes no sense if you ask me," he muttered. "A bushel of what?"

"Valeria, I had no idea you could sing like the very angels," Elyse said. "Shame on you for deluding us in this infamous manner."

Slowly Valeria rose and sat back down by Elyse. Only now did she take her eyes off Alastair. "I have been deluding all of you," she said in a low voice, "but I can assure you that I never meant to do so in an infamous way."

"Course not," Reggie said cheerfully. "But still, really, Miss Segrave. 'Set the pack a-howling,' indeed!"

Valeria and Regina stayed until eleven o'clock, and not another word passed between Valeria and Alastair. Studiously they avoided each other's gaze. As they went home, Valeria thought, *I see now that it is hopeless, I have lost him forever. I'm so glad that we're going home . . . I don't want to see him anymore, it hurts too much. Surely after some time and space between us this sorrow and bitterness will fade.*

And so she prayed earnestly for the Lord to heal her and to console her, and she knew that He would be faithful in doing so. But in that endless sleepless night, and for many nights to come, healing and consolation seemed infinitely far away.

Chapter Twenty-five

✧

RETURNING TO BELLEGARDE DID RELIEVE Valeria. It lifted the heavy burden of tension she had felt at the end of the Season. The sorrow and pain remained, but as the days went by, she found that the keen knife edge of them was lessened. Now she found much comfort in morning prayers, and at church, and she reflected that although she had determined that she would change her behavior and attitudes, her newfound relationship with her Heavenly Father and Savior had changed her soul, and the rest had followed as sweetly and as easily as the sun coming out after a long gentle rain.

Carrying her luncheon basket, she lifted her head and smelled the ambrosial scents of the flowers in the cottage garden: sweet peas, snapdragons, alyssum, forget-me-nots, nasturtiums. The flowers grew in rich profusion right up to the walls of the summerhouse, a small cottage with large casement windows on all four walls, long ago painted blue but now faded to a gentle blue-gray. Actually *summerhouse* was a misnomer, for it had never been used as a house. Until this summer it had been a small, out-of-the-way shed that the gardeners used to store their tools. But now Valeria had taken it over, and here she had found another solace: painting. When she was working with her oils seemed to be the only time she was fully absorbed, and experiencing a keen pleasure. She unlocked the door, propped it open, and then opened the windows. The cheery August sunlight was perfect for an artist's studio.

As she worked she reflected that it was going to be extremely hard for her to leave her oil paints behind for a month. What Lady Hylton had said was true. Oils had to be mixed with either linseed oil or turpentine, and there was a constant pervasive smell of the strong chemicals. It was especially true of Valeria's studio, for she had found that she spent much more time learning how to mix the paints than she did actually painting. Some colors worked better with linseed oil, others with turpentine, and there were thousands of variations of each, requiring hours of experimentation. Valeria had resigned herself to the fact that she must go to Foxden Park; she would likely be no more listless and apathetic there than she was here. The Hyltons' hunting lodge, though not really a small house, still had no adequate place for an odorous artist's studio. Valeria consoled herself, only slightly, by reminding herself that she could take her watercolors at least.

She forgot all about luncheon, and was surprised when she finally noticed that the slanting bright sunbeams had grown dim. "Oh, dear, by the time I get all of this blasted blue paint off I'll be late for dinner," she mumbled to herself.

When she joined Regina, St. John, and Mr. Chalmers in the cozy morning room, the first thing St. John did was lift his head and sniff. "You smell like a sputtering lamp, Veri. Why do you always smell like that at dinner?"

"Oh, do be quiet, St. John, you're not supposed to talk about how people smell," she said crossly. At Regina's mildly reproving glance, she smiled at her little brother and went on, "It's my new eau de cologne, *Arôme de la Lanterne*."

St. John's downcast countenance instantly transformed into a bright grin. "Aroma of the Lantern!" Casting a sly glance at his tutor, he said, "You see, Mr. Chalmers, I really was attending to the French lesson."

"I find that remarkable, my lord, since it seemed all you were doing was blowing bits of paper through a tube at Niall," Mr. Chalmers said with equanimity.

"Actually, it was spit-wads, and it was Niall's own fault, as he showed me how to make them," St. John said in an aside to Valeria.

Appalled, Regina said, "Really, St. John, how can you think that it's acceptable to talk about smells and—and—" The ever-genteel Regina couldn't bring herself to repeat the word. Helplessly she went on, "Oh, I give up. I simply can't think how I shall manage without your civilizing influence, Mr. Chalmers. No, no, please don't offer again to accompany us; you fully deserve a month's holiday. Indeed I can't imagine how you've kept your sanity this long. Anyway, I've had a letter from Lady Hylton today that relieves my mind considerably."

She cast an apprehensive glance at Valeria, but when she went on she sounded cheerful. "Lord Hylton has decided to join us at Foxden; in fact, he has gone ahead to make arrangements for us at the coaching inns." To St. John she said sternly, "Lord Hylton is a firm man, and he would likely box your ears if you say such things as—as—what you said in the company of ladies."

"Maybe, but he's a right sport anyway. Does Foxden have a billiard room?" St. John asked eagerly. "Remember, we never finished my lessons."

"I'm afraid it's hopeless, Mamma," Valeria said, but with a distracted air. "St. John is destined to become a rake. So—so Lord Hylton suddenly decided to go to Foxden? Does Lady Hylton—is there—any indication of why he changed his plans?"

"I'm not so sure it was really a change of plans, dear," Regina answered cautiously. "He usually does go every year for the opening of grouse season."

"Yes, yes, of course," Valeria said listlessly, and she lapsed into thoughtful silence for the rest of the meal.

After St. John and Mr. Chalmers had left them in the drawing room, Valeria said, "Mamma, I must tell you something. I—I can't go to Foxden. It's difficult to explain, but I beg you will not make me go."

Regina did not seem shocked, but she was openly distressed. "Oh, dearest, I'm so very sorry. Are you completely sure? Won't you reconsider?"

Valeria swallowed hard. "I won't change my mind, Mamma."

Regina searched her face. Valeria was looking down, staring blankly into the mass of flowers on the cold hearth. Regina saw no trace of tears; but Valeria's face was as desolate as if she had been weeping for hours. "Very well, my dear. If you are unable to go, then of course I won't go without you, and leave you alone here."

Sighing deeply, Valeria said, "I anticipated that you would say that, Mamma. But surely you know that it would be unfair to St. John, and even to you, for I know how much you enjoy being with Lady Hylton. So if you won't go without me, I will go.

"But please understand this. I love you and St. John, of course, and would never wish to be without you. But in these days I've found that solitude has offered me a chance to reflect, to think, and to come to terms with—with—the future. So I would not be un-happy to be alone for a while, at all. In fact, I would welcome it."

Regina reflected that for someone who was supposedly in a wel-coming frame of mind, her daughter seemed to be very sad. Of course Regina knew the cause. Though Valeria had not been openly ecstatic about going to Foxden, she had been willing to go—until she had found out that Lord Hylton would be there. Regina and Letitia had often spoken about the estrangement between Valeria and Alastair. But neither of them had any idea whatsoever about the reason for it. Just as Valeria had not confided in Regina, Alastair had not mentioned a word to his mother about her. Regina sighed deeply. "Very well, as I said, I won't force you to go against your will. But dearest, I know that you are distressed and upset; can't you confide in me at all? I might be able to help, you know."

Valeria shook her head. "Talking about it would do no good. There is no help for it in heaven or on earth."

Alastair said to Fleming, "No, no, the blue won't do, it's too formal. The green, I think, with the brown waistcoat." Finally the bottle-green coat, simple brown waistcoat patterned in black, buff breeches, and top boots satisfied him. "That will do, Fleming. Tell my mother I shall be down shortly."

He went to look out the old mullioned casement window, which faced out across the long moors, and the straight road leading to Foxden. It was too early to expect them, he thought, but still he had been searching all day. In his solitary afternoon ride, he had even ridden a couple of miles up the road, with some halfhearted notion that he might meet them. "Fool," he muttered blackly to himself.

He went back to his chest and opened the top drawer. Inside, neatly folded and arranged, were collars and neckcloths. He reached into the very back of the drawer and pulled out a small black mask. Slowly he went to sit on the bed, letting the soft silk run through his fingers, remembering.

He had not intended to come to Foxden, for he was a strong-willed man, and he'd fully meant to fulfill his vow not to burden Valeria with his presence. But as the past weeks had gone by, and he had gone over and over in his mind every meeting he'd had with her since that night at the Pantheon, he had begun to feel a very slight glimmer of hope. She might have lost any fondness she might have had for him, and even believe him to be dishonorable; but at no time in her countenance or air had he detected any anger or disgust. Gradually he had come to think that away from the rarified hothouse atmosphere of London, in the warm and familial air of Foxden, he might be able to finally show her how bitterly he regretted his unforgivable words and actions of that night. He might be able to win back her respect.

Sighing, he carefully folded the mask and slipped it into his coat pocket. He had been carrying it ever since that night that Valeria had let it fall to the floor of the coach, awash with her tears. Angrily he told himself—again—that he was like some sort of lovesick sentimental languishing fool, a fully grown man carrying around a meaningless piece of cloth like that putridly virtuous Sir Galahad wearing a lady's favor into a joust. But still he left it in his pocket as he went downstairs to the drawing room.

His mother, Elyse, and Reggie were having tea. Elyse was sitting on the floor at the hearth, toasting crumpets over the small bright fire. "Reggie, that is the fifth crumpet you've eaten, your appetite for dinner will be ruined," Letitia warned.

"Can't help it, ma'am," he said, his voice rather muffled. "Toasted crumpets are like walnuts, you can't eat only one, don't you know."

Elyse asked, "Alastair, do you want a crumpet?"

"No, thank you. I will take a cup of tea, though, Mother, if you'd pour for me." Letitia fixed his tea and handed him the cup. He sat for a few moments in the wing chair by the fire, then restlessly took the cup to stare out the front window, sipping in an abstracted manner. Elyse and Letitia exchanged knowing looks, while Reggie furtively took a sixth crumpet.

Pointedly Elyse said, "With the rain yesterday, the road from Cawton Bridge might be mired; it's such a dismal rutted track at the best of times. I hope they won't be much delayed."

Reggie mumbled something unintelligible, for again he was talking with his mouth half-full. Letitia started to say something, but just then Alastair stiffened like a dog pointing a bird, and his teacup clattered on the saucer. "I see them, they're here," he said in a strained voice. Elyse rose and dusted herself, straightened Reggie's neckcloth, and brushed crumbs from his chin, Letitia set aside her embroidery, and they all went outside to greet their guests.

The splendid Maledon coach came dashing up the drive, Ewan driving with his usual flourish. As soon as it came to a stop Alastair opened the door, and stepped back as they all came out. Regina came first, then St. John, then Craigie, and then Niall. Letitia and Elyse greeted Regina and St. John with kisses, all of them talking at once. Alastair stood mute by the carriage, his face stunned.

Regina came to him and extended her hand, which Alastair took and bent over. "I'm afraid Valeria was unable to join us," she said softly.

"Is she ill?" he demanded, half with concern and half with hope.

Regina had rehearsed many times what she would say to him, so smoothly she answered, "No, not ill. But it seems that she is still very tired from the rigors of London. She explained to me that she was really treasuring the peace and solitude of Bellegarde just now. She might, perhaps, join us in a week or two."

Alastair's eyes narrowed, and his jaw worked. He seemed not to be able to make any answer. After a few uncomfortable moments, Lady Hylton said calmly, "I am so sorry that Valeria felt unable to come. I shall write to her immediately and admonish her severely for her neglect of us. Come, let's go into the house and get out of this wind."

They all went into the house, but Alastair hesitated in the entrance hall. "I—I have just thought of something I need to attend to, if you'll excuse me," he said in a distracted manner, and hurried up the stairs.

"Oh, dear," Regina said in a low voice. "Letitia, I couldn't do a thing with her, all she would say is that there was no hope for it."

Reggie looked astonished, staring up the stairs as Alastair disappeared. "What's happened? No hope for what?" he asked plaintively.

"Well, she's wrong," Elyse rasped, and then with hard steps went up the stairs.

Bewildered, Reggie asked, "Who's wrong? Wrong about what?"

Letitia smiled indulgently and said, "Come along, St. John, if Reggie has left any, you shall have some crumpets. And you too, Niall, we've already decided that we must keep the two of you together, to minimize the number of incidents."

Upstairs Elyse went straight to Alastair's room and banged on the door.

"Who is it?" he asked in a hard voice.

Elyse opened the door, stepped in, and shut it behind her. Alastair was darkly pacing back and forth in front of the window. Without preliminaries, Elyse said, "It's high time to put a stop to all of this nonsense. You have acted, and are acting, stupidly, and Valeria is acting stupidly. Just stop it."

Icily he snapped, "I may be stupid, but Valeria is not. How can you say that it's not patently obvious that she wants nothing to do with me?"

"Because that's stupid," Elyse said with heat. "If anyone has made anything patently obvious, it's that you want nothing to do with her. All I've seen from Valeria is that she wishes to make it up to you."

"What do you mean? Has she said that?" Alastair demanded.

"Of course she has not said anything of the sort. I was constrained by my promise never to mention your name, and what do you think she made of that? Of course she would think that you were angry with her, and that I couldn't speak of you without offending her!"

He frowned darkly. "But that was not the impression I wished to give, as you well know. I spoke to her every time I saw her, and I believe I was particularly cordial, and yet she never gave me any encouragement at all."

"Never gave you—Alastair, have your wits gone completely astray? What about when she sang that heart-wrenching song?"

Alastair frowned. "I've thought much about that, but I finally realized that she was merely—she was just pleasing us—all of you, for I know that Lady Maledon dearly loves to hear her sing. It had nothing to do with me personally."

Elyse bowed her head and pressed her fingertips to her temples. "Stupid, stupid, I must think of another word. I really can't right now, however, for it suits so well." She looked back up at her brother, and with a visible effort made herself speak calmly. "Alastair, listen to me. She was singing for you. She was singing to you, and you only. Honestly I don't know the exact nature of her feelings toward you, but I am certain that she wishes to end this coldness between you."

"You're—you're certain," he repeated cautiously.

"Yes."

He nodded, and then lifted his head. Light flickered in his eyes, which made them look midnight blue. "Then I must go to her, and explain, and beg her to forgive me. A part of me still thinks that she'll never look kindly on me again, but I have nothing at all left to lose."

Alastair took Achilles, and his hunter, Imperius, riding them in eight-hour shifts. He stopped to sleep only twice. By the time he reached Bellegarde the horses were utterly exhausted. Alastair was travel-stained and weary, but he was so looking forward to resolving things with Valeria, for good or ill, that he felt buoyed up.

He rode up to the Hall at a dead gallop, threw himself out of the saddle, and was banging on the door even before the grooms appeared to take care of the lathered horses.

Trueman finally opened the door, his normal imperturbable manner disturbed by Alastair's sudden disheveled appearance. "Lord Hylton!" he blurted out in alarm, then recovered and bowed deeply. "Lord Hylton, please come in."

Alastair stepped inside and asked bluntly, "Where is Miss Segrave?"

"I believe Miss Segrave is down in the summerhouse. If you'd like to come into the drawing room, my lord, I'll send a footman to—"

"The summerhouse? Is that the little blue cottage down by the water garden?"

"Er—yes, my lord, but—" He was speaking only to empty air, for Alastair had wheeled and hurried off.

As he almost ran toward the southwest end of the park, he said to himself over and over, *I'll just tell her, as simply as I can, that it was I who behaved so badly that night, that I was horribly wrong, and ask her to forgive me. I won't make any demands of her, I'll just tell her that I hope one day we can be friends again . . .*

Valeria daubed at the canvas, at first tentatively, and then eagerly. She was actually getting the backlighting correct, for the first time, after countless attempts. It was a soft amber glow, with just the perfect orange tint of a sunset in summer. Now she worked fast, perfecting it. As she finished she realized that she was humming happily to herself.

And then she realized the tune she was absently humming: *And then she made her way homeward . . . with one star awake . . . as the swan in the evening . . . moved over the lake . . .*

She stepped back, and her head drooped. Tears started in her eyes. After long moments she straightened her shoulders with determination and dashed the tears away. "There now, it's official. I am a perfect mess," she said with distress. Glancing down at her bib apron, she added, now with wry humor, "And that would be both internally and externally." Her bib apron was covered with colorful blotches; her fingers were stained; a huge dollop of orange paint had plopped down and landed on her right big toe, for her feet were bare. Thick strands of hair had escaped from the neat braided bun Joan had done for her that morning, and hung wantonly down around her face and wandered over her shoulders. Valeria spied a streak of blue paint in one long wavy dark strand.

Shrugging, she returned to her painting. Under her breath she murmured, "Yes, sometimes I am a complete wreck; but I'm better. I really am getting better. This is helping me, I know. This is how I can make an end to it. Even sad endings are better than thinking of eternal hopeless longings."

A shadow fell across her canvas from the doorway, and Valeria turned to admonish the trespassing servant or gardener, for they had all been strictly forbidden to come to the summerhouse when she was painting.

Alastair Hylton stood there.

Valeria gasped, and dropped her paintbrush and palette. "Oh, no, not you!" she blurted out.

At her first glimpse of his face she had seen a sort of confusion of hope, determination, and uncertainty that sat strangely on Alastair's smooth marble features. At her words he abruptly looked utterly desolated. And then she saw his quick, darting glances around the room. His eyes widened with astonishment.

All over the summerhouse were sketches, drawings, watercolor studies, and paintings in various stages, from barely begun to half-finished to finished but discarded. All of them were of Alastair. Pinned on one wall was a charcoal sketch, done with a very light touch, of him with his head slightly bent and a smile on his face. A complex oil painting of him riding Achilles was stood up in one corner; though the depiction of Achilles was excellent, the rider had no face. But in the painting that Valeria had just completed, she had finally captured Alastair to perfection. He was wearing his blue coat, and his eyes, she could now see, were the exactly right shade of gray-blue. He looked remote, yet there was a warmth in his gaze, and his mouth was relaxed into a half-smile. The painting depicted Alastair Hylton at his warmest, kindest, most approachable moments.

But finding the real Alastair suddenly before her, Valeria was so astounded that she couldn't think at all; her mind was in a maelstrom of confusion. He took in the room, and as quick as lightning, his countenance changed again. His eyes blazed into a fiery blue, and fierce joy came over his face.

He took three quick strides to her, and helplessly she looked up at him. "You love me, Valeria!" he said in a guttural voice. "You truly do, I can see, you must, because of—" He waved his hand to encompass the room.

"Love you?" she repeated. "But of course I do! But you hate me! Don't you?"

"Wha—hate—no! No! I love you, I just thought you could never forgive me," he said, moving ever closer to her and searching her face hungrily.

"Forgive you? For what? No, you have to forgive me, I—stop. Stop. What did you say?" she asked helplessly.

Alastair closed his eyes for a brief moment, took a deep breath, then looked down at her and laid his hands on her shoulders. "We can talk about all of that later. Right now all I want to talk about is how much I love you, Valeria. I do. I have fallen hopelessly, irretrievably, helplessly in love with you."

Valeria felt her heart light up like the brightest fireworks on Guy Fawkes Night. She threw her arms around his neck and jumped, and he grabbed her waist and lifted her up high, whirling her around.

"He loves me! He truly does! Oh, thank you, thank you, my most blessed Lord!"

Valeria was dizzy when he set her down, but she kept her arms around him and said, "Oh, Alastair, I do love you so, I don't know how it happened or when it happened, and then I was so awful, and I thought you despised me, and I loved you so desperately I didn't know what to do, and then—"

He laid his finger on her lips, and he smiled with a delight that she had never seen on his face before. "You're blithering, my darling. Strange how now I find that perfectly adorable. But just now I wish to ask you—"

"Of course you'd ask," Valeria said in a hoarse voice. Then she pulled his face down to hers and kissed him, a long deep passionate kiss full of promise.

When they finally drew apart, while still holding each other closely, Valeria said breathlessly, "Lord Hylton, you now have my permission to kiss me whenever you'd like, without asking first."

"I'm very glad to hear that, ma'am. But there is another question I'd very much like to ask you," he said in a deep voice.

"What is that?" Valeria whispered.

He dropped to one knee, looked up at her imploringly, took her hand and kissed it. His lips were warm. "Dear Valeria, my beautiful starlight, will you do me the greatest honor, and consent to marry me?"

She pulled him up and blurted out, "I will! Oh, yes! When? Soon? Please?"

"As soon as ever I can, dearest one," he said, then kissed her again.

❦

And it was soon, for Alastair, Lord Hylton, easily obtained a special license from the bishop. He offered to give Valeria a magnificently grand wedding at St. George's, but Valeria much preferred to be married at the humble little parish church at Bellegarde, Our Lady of Grace.

It was filled to overflowing, not only with thousands upon thousands of flowers, but with friends and family.

With a cloud of fragrant orange blossoms in her hair, virginal and pure in her white satin dress, Valeria looked up at her betrothed and repeated the solemn vow.

"I, Valeria Segrave, take thee, Alastair Edmund James Hylton, to be my wedded husband, for better, for worse, for richer, for poorer, in sickness and in health, to love, cherish, and to obey, till death us do part, according to God's holy ordinance; and thereto I give thee my troth."

Alastair took her left hand in his, held up the plain gold band, and spoke in a deep, rich voice filled with gladness: "With this ring I thee wed, with my body I thee worship, with all my worldly goods I thee endow."

Then, touching the ring to the tips of her thumb and first two fingers, he said, "In the name of the Father, and of the Son, and of the Holy Ghost."

The ring slid onto her finger.

With open thankfulness Alastair said, "Amen."

Reading Group Guide

1. Valeria's inability to forgive her stepfather and Lady Jex-Blake was the beginning of her gradual falling away from the Lord. When you have such problems with others, are you able to overcome your resentment and bitterness and honestly ask the Lord to give you a loving, forgiving heart even toward your enemies?

2. At Evensong, a passage from the Confession particularly touched Valeria's heart: *We have left undone those things which we ought to have done, And we have done those things which we ought not to have done, And there is no health in us.* Many times we're more conscious of committing sins than we are of simply neglecting to do the things we should do to maintain the "health" of our relationship with the Lord Jesus Christ. Can you think of such things in your spiritual life that would enrich your walk with the Lord?

3. In a novel, *textures* are very important. This is writing with a clarity that not only gives the reader a mental vision of the scene, but that evokes a deeper immersion in the book. In *The Baron's Honourable Daughter*, were there any textures that you particularly responded to? For instance, did you imagine the feel of a heavy satin dress, think of what turtle soup smells like, or try to sense the heavy coal-dirtied air of London?

4. Minor characters in a novel often play almost as important a part as the major characters. Did you find the minor characters to be vivid? Did they hold your interest? Did you have a favorite, one that you might have liked to know more about?

5. Valeria finds that painting offers her not only an outlet for her creativity, but that it gives her solace and emotional comfort. God has given us all sundry gifts to help sustain us. Have you found your God-given talent?

6. Regina teaches Valeria about *noblesse oblige*, or "nobility obliges." Nowadays this may be considered archaic, but the concept is actually a spiritual law. Do you understand the parallel of "with privilege comes responsibility" and the teachings of the Lord Jesus? See Luke 12:48.

7. When Valeria is wearing mourning for her stepfather, she feels like a hypocrite. Do you sometimes feel that when you "go through the motions" you are being hypocritical? Do you think that even when we don't "feel spiritual" we should still maintain our outward appearance of being a Christian? Are you able to seek the Lord's help, even with persistence if the heavens seem to be made of brass?

8. The early 19th century was in all respects foreign to our times. Did you find that you were able to relate to the characters and their problems? Did you enjoy some of the more obscure references (such outmoded things as *chelengk, sarcenet, parterre*) or would you have preferred fuller descriptions?

9. When Valeria finally realizes the depth of her sins, she is completely unable to find comfort either from her mother or her best friend. Only when she understands that she must first seek forgiveness from the Lord is she able to finally find comfort. When you are unhappy, do you sometimes depend upon others to comfort you, or do you first seek cleansing and solace from the Holy Spirit?

10. What might be called the height of Valeria's sin was wearing trousers in public. Although this is laughable today, in 1812 it was indeed shameful behavior. Still, simply wearing breeches wasn't really the sin; like all of us, she experienced a gradual

falling away from God. What was the first indication of her estrangement from the Lord? What very small steps along the way led toward her "fall"? In your life have you experienced apparently harmless thoughts or feelings that eventually separated you from God?

Look for Lynn Morris's next Regency-era romance, coming from FaithWords in 2015.